DA
HONOU
HUSBAND
BY
DAY LECLAIRE

AND

A CLANDESTINE
CORPORATE AFFAIR
BY
MICHELLE CELMER

MILLS &
BOON

Gianna must have realized he had no intention of leaving.

With a sigh of irritation, she walked to her closet, flinging open the door and disappearing inside. Curious, he followed.

"Madre di Dio," Constantine murmured faintly.

"I don't want to hear a word about it," she retorted, her back to him.

He caught the defensive edge in her voice. "Just out of curiosity, how many pairs of shoes do you own?"

Gianna turned, clutching a pair of heels. "Not enough. They're not all mine. Some of them are Francesca's. We discovered a while back that we both wear identical sizes."

Constantine folded his arms across his chest. "Should I assume that if some of these are hers, she has some of yours?"

"That's none of your business," she muttered.

"It will be when we marry."

She held up a hand. "Okay, stop right there. There is no 'when.' There is only a very shaky 'maybe.'"

Dear Reader,

It has been such a pleasure to write about the Dante family romances, to see each member succumb to The Inferno, that all consuming blaze of heat and electricity that a Dante experiences when he or she first touches their soulmate. Now it's Gianna's turn and she has an even more difficult path to happily-ever-after than any of her brothers or cousins.

You may remember meeting the hero, Constantine Romano, in *Dante's Contract Marriage* where Lazz Dante and Ariana Romano met for the first time while exchanging their wedding vows. Constantine is Ariana's brother and apparently that infamous wedding day saw more than one Romano Infernoed!

But Constantine Romano isn't a man easily manipulated, not even by The Inferno. He is a man who makes his own decisions in life and controls his own destiny. And he isn't happy to discover that control taken away from him by either The Inferno or the woman on the other side of that first, electric touch—Gianna Dante.

I hope you enjoy discovering how Gianna's love story plays out. But stay tuned. Although this is the final book in the current quartet, it may not be the final tale in THE DANTE LEGACY.

Warmly,

Day Leclaire

DANTE'S HONOUR-BOUND HUSBAND

BY
DAY LECLAIRE

Published in Great Britain 2012
by Mills & Boon, an imprint of Harlequin (UK) Limited,
Eton House, 18-24 Paradise Road, Richmond, Surrey TW9 1SR

© Day Totton Smith 2011

ISBN: 978 0 263 89144 7

51-0312

Harlequin (UK) policy is to use papers that are natural, renewable and recyclable products and made from wood grown in sustainable forests. The logging and manufacturing processes conform to the legal environmental regulations of the country of origin.

Printed and bound in Spain
by Blackprint CPI, Barcelona

USA TODAY bestselling author **Day Leclaire** is a three-time winner of both a Colorado Award of Excellence and a Golden Quill Award. She's won *RT Book Reviews* Career Achievement and Love and Laughter Awards, a Holt Medallion and a Booksellers' Best Award. She has also received an impressive ten nominations for the prestigious Romance Writers of America's RITA® Award.

Day's romances touch the heart and make you care about her characters as much as she does. In Day's own words, "I adore writing romances, and can't think of a better way to spend each day." For more information, visit Day on her website, www.dayleclaire.com.

To Mary-Theresa Hussey.
An absolutely brilliant editor.
A kind and generous person.
As always, it's been such a delight working with you.
Thank you for making my books more.

Prologue

"Don't go."

Constantine Romano closed his eyes and fought for control. "I have no choice." His integrity, his honor as a Romano, everything that made him a man demanded he leave.

"Then let me go with you." Gianna Dante lifted her gaze to his, her striking jade-green eyes bright with tears, her hair a glorious tumble of autumn-gold and brown. "I can help you."

Her plea pushed him to the limit of his self-control, where he teetered between honor and caving to the intensity of his need to make her his. He fought to resist and couldn't, not entirely. He cupped her face and snatched a kiss. Took another, then sank in. God, she was amazing. Stunning. Intelligent. Graceful. Possessing a femininity that left him desperate with longing.

They'd met when his sister, Ariana, had married Gianna's

cousin, Lazz. The moment he'd taken her hand in his, he'd been hit by an overwhelming flame of desire. A physical flash and burn that had shocked him to the core with its all-encompassing depth and strength and power. In that instant, every other thought and emotion had ceased to exist except for a cascade of urgent directives....

Take her.

Make her his.

Put his stamp on her in every and any way possible.

"I want you to come with me, even though I don't understand any of this," he admitted. Didn't understand how he could want so fast and so deeply. How a single weekend with her could make him so certain that she was the only one for him. "How is it possible that in just a few short days I know that you're the woman I want to spend the rest of my life with?"

Her gaze dropped and for a split second she looked almost guilty. Though what she had to feel guilty about, he couldn't imagine. It wasn't her fault that he'd been overwhelmed with this desperate need to possess her. More than anything he wanted to take her to his bed, but he knew, even without her telling him, that she'd never been with a man before. And if he couldn't put his ring on her finger, he refused to dishonor either of them—or their families—by making love to her. Not until he could afford to offer marriage.

"I didn't expect to feel such intense desire, either," she confessed. Her gaze flitted upward, filled with heartbreak. "Please, Constantine. I don't want you to leave."

He tugged her closer and allowed their bodies to collide and meld once again. "I don't want to leave, either, *piccola*. But until I have something more to offer than my name, I must return home to Italy."

"For how long?"

A good question. Too bad it was one he couldn't answer.

"Until I get my restoration business up and running. Until I can afford a wife and have the means to support her." He stopped her when she would have argued, stopped her in the most delicious way possible. "Don't, Gianna. Don't ask me to compromise my values. I'll return as soon as I can. And when I do, I'll be in the position to offer you marriage. To put my ring on your finger. This I swear on my family name."

He could see endless arguments building, arguments she controlled and suppressed, impressing the hell out of him. "I'll wait. You know I'll wait. And in the meantime, we can talk on the phone." Her chin quivered, but she used a considerable amount of will to steady it. "And there's always email. I'll fly over as often as I can. Maybe you can visit during holidays."

Every word she uttered made it more and more difficult. Nearly impossible. He gathered her hands in his. "Listen to me, Gianna... In order to get back to you as soon as possible, I must focus on work. Every minute of every day. It's the only way to make it happen quickly."

A frown formed between her brows. "What are you saying?"

"I'm saying that you're a distraction. I'm saying if you're with me or come to visit or if we are constantly calling one another or emailing, I won't be able to give my full attention to my business. It's at a critical point right now. The only way I can return to you in the least amount of time is if I give one hundred percent of my time and attention to Romano Restoration."

Her breath hitched. "Oh, no. Constantine, you can't mean it. No phone calls? Not even emails?"

She was killing him by inches. He closed his eyes so he wouldn't cave while everything within him insisted he do just that. "Please understand, *amore*. Please trust me."

A tear escaped, but she swept it away. Determination filled her expression. "Okay, Constantine, we'll do this your way. For now." Her eyes glittered with emotion. "But you come back. Soon," she ordered fiercely.

"As soon as I can," he promised.

And then he left her. He forced himself not to look back, even though it was one of the most difficult things he'd ever done. With every step he took, he felt that odd connection that joined them. Felt it compelling him to return to her arms, urging him to take what was his. He'd never experienced anything like it. Oh, he'd return to her. He had no choice. But it would be on his terms.

Soon. Dear God, just let it be soon.

Gianna watched Constantine walk away until the tears blurring her eyes made it impossible to see any longer. Should she have told him? Had she made a mistake not explaining about The Inferno—the family "blessing" that sparked between a man and a woman whenever a Dante first touched his or her soul mate? Perhaps. As for keeping it a secret… Well, she had her reasons, not that he'd appreciate them once he discovered the truth behind their odd connection.

She closed her eyes, accepting the hand fate had dealt her. The Inferno had struck almost all of her other Dante relatives…all of her *male* Dante relatives the first time they met the women who were their soul mates. As the lone female Dante, no one knew whether it was even possible for her to experience The Inferno. She'd learned the answer to that question when she and Constantine first touched. She could and she did. Unfortunately the secret she'd learned about The Inferno hadn't altered that basic fact.

But she'd been afraid to explain the Dantes' odd…condition…to Constantine. In the short time she'd known him, she'd realized he was a man who preferred to govern his own destiny, to control his world and those in it. Once he discovered that The Inferno drove the desire and passion he felt, would he be compelled to fight it? They'd had too little time together to know for certain. Until she could be sure, it would remain her little secret.

Now all she could do was wait for Constantine's return. Wait and see if The Inferno was real…or an illusion. If her family had been correct in their beliefs about it…or if the secret she'd uncovered all those years ago was the real truth. Only time would tell.

Soon. Dear God, just let it be soon.

One

He'd returned.

Constantine Romano entered the room as though he owned the place. But then, he possessed the sort of presence bred into the very essence of the man. The sort of presence that went with his aristocratic name and stunning bone structure and taut, muscular body. He wore his hair longer than before, the ebony curls and fierce black eyes summoning images of dangerous pirates and ferocious duels of honor. Beneath that elegant exterior smoldered a man of action, who would risk everything, dare all and take whatever he wanted.

And he wanted her.

Gianna Dante shuddered, struggling to gather up her self-control. She'd have to face him and soon. Since their first meeting, over a year and a half ago, a lot had changed. Though she now doubted Constantine had experienced The Inferno during that unforgettable weekend they'd shared,

The Inferno had given him an uncanny knack for sensing her presence. That much she remembered. Any second he'd hone in on her and she'd darn well better be prepared.

"Gianna? Would you care to check the display?"

It took her a moment to switch gears and focus on work. Tomorrow marked Dantes' Midsummer Night's gala and a million details remained, each requiring her immediate attention. As Dantes' event coordinator, she took care of everything from the catering to the decorations to the displays to the invitations. Fortunately she had an excellent assistant who was every bit as detail-oriented as she was herself.

"Thank you, Tara. I'll be right there."

Considering that Constantine stood between her and the display in question, she might as well get the coming confrontation over with. She took a deep breath. No big deal, she tried to tell herself. The feelings she'd experienced that long-ago weekend had faded over the ensuing months, months which had ticked by with excruciating slowness. The legendary Dante Inferno, that amazing sensation of volcanic fire that erupted when he'd taken her hand in his had quieted, drifting into dormancy. She could handle this.

She'd simply make it clear to him that she'd moved on.

Gianna started across Dantes' ballroom toward him, thankful that by some blessing of fate she'd chosen to wear one of her "killer" outfits. The vibrant red jacket and tight, short skirt showed off her figure to its best advantage, and the mile-high open-toe heels were the perfect showcase for the gorgeous legs she'd inherited from her equally gorgeous mother. Her hair was longer than the last time she'd seen him, flowing in heavy, layered curls to the middle of her back.

Let him look. Let him want. And let him regret.

She hadn't traversed more than a half dozen steps before Constantine stilled with abrupt predatory awareness. His head turned in her direction and his ink-dark eyes glittered with unmistakable intent. He came for her, moving with a focused grace that almost sent her fleeing in the opposite direction. To her shock, he didn't stop when he reached her, but kept coming. He invaded her space and swept her into his arms. Then, with her name on his lips and a smothered protest on hers, he kissed her.

He devoured her, the kiss one of blatant possession, branding her with a mark of ownership that in any other situation she'd have fought with every ounce of her strength. Instead all thought of resistance melted beneath the blazing heat and she sank inward, opening herself to him. He tasted like ambrosia combined with a hint of spice and topped with a hard, masculine kick. It utterly devastated her senses, along with every scrap of practicality.

It had been so incredibly long since they last touched—nineteen months, five days, eight hours and a handful of minutes. Desire in the form of The Inferno had exploded between them at that first touch. Then after a single weekend of bliss, he'd left her.

Despair vied with an incandescent joy. His coming now, after all this time was too little, too late. Why now? Why, when she'd finally come to terms with the impossibility of knowing the sort of Inferno love affair that everyone else in her family possessed, had Constantine chosen this moment to return?

It wasn't fair.

"Stop," she managed to protest. "This is wrong."

How could she tell him? How could she say the words that threatened to break her heart? She'd moved on. She'd found someone else.

He finally picked up on her signals and pulled back a

few precious inches. "Stop?" He captivated her with a single smile. "What are you talking about, *piccola?* After all this time, we're together again. How could something so incredibly right possibly be wrong?"

She slipped free of his embrace and tugged at the bottom of her jacket to straighten it. Somehow the first two buttons had come undone revealing a tantalizing flash of black lace. She did her best to neaten all the various bits and pieces he'd rumpled. She moistened her lips, aware he'd kissed every bit of lipstick from them.

"It's good to see you, Constantine," she said with polite formality.

He froze. "Good to see me?" he repeated softly.

She flinched at the dangerous tone, one infused with the warmth of his Tuscan home, yet chilled with the ice of his displeasure. This was going to be far more difficult than she'd anticipated. "Are you here on business? I hope you'll take a few minutes to drop by my grandparents before you return to Italy." She offered a friendly smile to cover up her nervous chatter. "They were asking after you the other day."

"Don't you understand? I've relocated to San Francisco."

No. No, no, *no!* It wasn't fair. Not now, after all this time. Praying that none of her thoughts were echoed in her expression, she kept her smile pinned in place, a careless, nonchalant one that made it clear that his news didn't make the least difference to her. "Congratulations."

He caught her chin in the palm of his hand and tipped her face up to his. "Is that all you have to say to me? Congratulations?"

Her smile faded along with all attempts at concealing her emotions. Pain and anger ripped through her and she jerked back from his touch, her impetuous nature decimating her common sense. "What do you want from me, Constantine?" she demanded, the question escaping in a low, fierce undertone. "It's been nearly two years. I've moved on. I suggest you do the same."

His head jerked back as though she'd slapped him. "Moved on?" His accent thickened, deepened. "What does this mean…moved on?"

She dismissed the question with a sweep of her hand. "Don't give me that. You understand idiomatic English just fine. It means precisely what you think it means."

"There is someone else?"

"Yes, Constantine. There *is* someone else." For the first time, Gianna realized they were the center of all eyes and warmth swept across her cheekbones. "Now, if you'll excuse me, I have work to do if I'm going to get this place ready for tomorrow's gala."

She'd never seen him look so hard or distant. He inclined his head in a regal manner. "Please. Do not let me get in your way."

Gathering up her emotions and stuffing them behind an equally regal manner, she spun on her heel and crossed to the nearest display case. She stared blindly at the contents. She wasn't the one who cut ties or ended their relationship prematurely, she reminded herself. He'd given her a handful of amazing days when they first met and then walked away from what might have been. The fact that he'd been able to do that solidified her suspicions about The Inferno. Her family didn't know the entire truth about the family "blessing." But she did. She'd been thirteen years old when she'd overheard how it really worked.

As for Constantine… If he'd experienced the depth of desire she had, he managed to control it well all this time. To dismiss it while he took care of more important business. Until they'd met she'd thought it impossible to fall in love so completely. She thought Constantine had fallen in love with her, as well. Foolish of her, Gianna now realized. She'd spent all these endless months overwhelmed by a cascade of passionate emotions. Emotions that—had he shared them—should have made him incapable of leaving her. Clearly he didn't share a damn thing.

She'd suffered while he'd walked away.

That left her with a single, logical and thoroughly devastating conclusion. He didn't love her. Not really. And that forced her to face an agonizing realization. If she surrendered to him now, he'd own her body and soul. But what would she possess? A man capable of picking her up and setting her aside whenever he wished. She couldn't live like that. She *refused* to live like that.

For her, for whatever reason, the burn of The Inferno only went one way. Otherwise, Constantine wouldn't have left her. Otherwise, he couldn't have stayed away for so long or curtailed all communication. Well, if he could turn off The Inferno, so could she, though she'd never learned that portion of the secret. Somehow. Someway. Even if it killed her, she'd put an end to it. She closed her eyes against the tears pressing for release.

God, she loved him.

Figlio di puttana! Constantine watched Gianna walk away. Bitter frustration ate at him. Nineteen damn months. For nineteen months, five days, eight hours and a handful of minutes he'd fought and clawed to get his fledgling business, Romano Restoration, off the ground and soaring so that he could emigrate to the United States and establish a stronghold in San Francisco. All to provide Gianna with more than a name when he asked her to marry him. And now that his company had taken off and he was in a position to support a wife, the only woman he wanted was walking away with a hip-swinging stride that knocked every last brain cell off-line.

Another man! His hands collapsed into fists. *How could she?* He'd promised he'd return the instant he could provide for her, and she'd agreed to wait. For nearly two years he'd worked endless days and nights to make that happen. How could she turn her back on what they had? What they could have? Didn't she feel it, that ferocious wildfire that exploded into flames whenever they were in the same room together?

He stared down at his balled hands and it took every ounce of resolve to ignore the relentless itch centered in the palm of his right hand. It was an itch that had flared to life the first moment Gianna Dante had slipped her fine-boned hand into his, and it had continued over the course of the ensuing months, no matter how much distance separated them.

Constantine knew what it was. Though Gianna had neglected to explain what she'd done to him—a lengthy and pointed discussion for another time—his sister, Ariana, had described it in graphic detail after her husband, Lazz, had Infernoed her when they'd first joined hands at the altar on their wedding day. Those damned Dantes and their damnable Inferno. It wasn't enough that they'd used it to overpower his sister. That wasn't good enough for them. Hell, no. For some reason, the sole Dante female had chosen him for her mate, had used The Inferno to steal every last crumb of his own self-control. Ever since that day he'd been trapped with no hope of escape other than to surrender to its demands.

And now, he couldn't even do that because Gianna had "moved on." He wanted to roar in outrage. Not a chance in hell would he let her get away with it. She'd soon discover that she couldn't move on, up, down, or sideways without his being right there waiting for her. Whoever she'd chosen to infect with The Inferno this time around was out of luck.

No matter what it took, no matter whether she faced her fate willingly or otherwise, he intended to claim Gianna Dante for his own. The Inferno might have caused him to lose his legendary control, but marriage to her would allow him to regain it. Once he had his ring on her finger and her delightful curves in his bed, this hideous need would ease and he'd be able to wield it as *he* saw fit. Until then… He stared at her broodingly.

God, he wanted her.

"Did you hear the news?" Elia Dante asked. She lounged in a chair outside the dressing rooms of a snazzy little boutique called Sinfully Delicious. "No, Gianna. Not the salmon. Go with the bronze halter gown. It complements your eyes better than the other one."

Gianna held up one gown, then the other, before nodding in agreement. Though why she bothered to compare the two, she didn't know. When it came to fashion, her mother was infallible. "What news?"

Elia took a delicate sip from a tiny cup of espresso before announcing, "Constantine Romano has moved to San Francisco. He opens the doors to Romano Restoration any day now. Apparently he organized the transition all the way from Italy."

Gianna stiffened, grateful she had her back turned to her mother. She should have anticipated this. Foolish of her not to, all things considered. "That's rather unexpected, isn't it?"

"Do you think so?" Elia asked softly. "Somehow he's gotten his entire operation up and running without any of us being the wiser." She lifted a delicate eyebrow. "I'm guessing as a surprise for a certain someone?"

Gianna sighed. Her mother was the only person who knew what she'd experienced when she and Constantine first met. She'd been very careful to keep it from everyone else, knowing her family would interfere if they knew. "Yes, Mamma, it is. What we had, or rather, what I thought we had ended a long time ago."

"The Inferno doesn't end, *chiacchierona*."

"Maybe it does."

Gianna swung around to face her mother. What would Elia say if she knew the whole truth about The Inferno? If she'd heard what Gianna had when Uncle Dominic explained the facts to Aunt Laura? Or watched what he'd done to rid them both of The Inferno? She'd never dared tell anyone, terrified that she'd see other relationships ruined as a result of her revelation. If the rest of her family believed in The Inferno with all their hearts, maybe they'd never discover what her aunt and uncle had…

That The Inferno *wasn't* forever.

Gianna hesitated, still unwilling to tell her mother the entire truth. She chose her words with care. "Maybe it's different because I'm a woman instead of a man," she suggested. "Maybe it only went one way and he doesn't feel what I do."

"If that were so, Constantine wouldn't be here."

"Maybe I can take The Inferno back," she dared to suggest.

Elia simply laughed. "That's not possible. The Inferno is forever."

Oh, but it wasn't. Gianna set her chin. "It doesn't matter if Constantine is here now. It's too late."

A mother's wisdom gleamed in Elia's dark eyes. "That's your pride speaking, not your heart."

"I've moved on," Gianna insisted, wincing at the defensive edge underscoring her words. "I'm dating David d'Angelo now."

"Well, he is Italian…like Constantine," her mother conceded. "And comes from a good Fiorentini family, though not one anywhere near as noble as the Romanos."

"Maybe not, but they're respected bankers."

The family was even receiving some sort of banking award in another few months. As for David, he possessed stunning good looks. Granted, they were more classical than swashbuckling. More attractive even than her brother, Rafe, whom the family called the "pretty Dante." Not that David could help his looks.

As for his personality, he couldn't be nicer. Even if Primo had muttered *untuoso* under his breath, which had bothered Gianna no end since she didn't consider David the least unctuous. Nonna adored him, which counted for a lot. David was intelligent, respectful and amusing, despite possessing the faintest air of entitlement.

And if he hadn't told her he was Italian by birth, she'd never have guessed it by his accent, perhaps as a result of his studying abroad for so many years. Now that she thought about it, other than his intelligence he was as different from Constantine as a bird of paradise from a panther.

"David's not like Constantine," Elia murmured, the comment an uncomfortable echo of Gianna's own thoughts.

"He is in some ways," she argued. "But the important point here is that I like him very much. That's all that matters, right?"

Elia made a face and set her cup and saucer aside. "*Like*. What an insipid word. Would you really trade an earth-shattering passion for a tepid 'like'?"

"It's safer," Gianna whispered.

Safer not to surrender to the dangerous emotions flaring back to life. Safer not to allow the more impetuous side of her nature free rein. Safer to like a nice guy than to love someone as dangerous to her emotional stability as Constantine Romano.

"I spoke to Ariana about the situation."

Uh-oh. "She and Lazz are still in Italy?" Gianna asked, hoping to turn the conversation in a new direction. No doubt a wasted effort.

"Yes. For another two months." Sure enough, her mother lasered back to her point. "According to her, Constantine's come back for you."

"His sister is a romantic. The Inferno has a way of doing that to you. I guarantee that before she met Lazz she was the most pragmatic of people." Gianna made a face in the mirror. "That's what The Inferno does to people. It messes with them."

"Mmm." The sound was one of delighted agreement. "With luck you will soon discover yourself in the middle of your own Inferno mess."

The comment contained a reminiscent tone and Gianna suspected her mother was recalling when she'd first fallen in love with Gianna's father, Alessandro. Though her parents' relationship could be tumultuous on occasion, there'd never been a doubt in her mind that they shared a white-hot passion, as well as being utterly devoted to each other.

"No, thanks, Mamma. I think I'll stick with David."

"I'm sure Constantine will try to change your mind about that." Elia paused for a beat, before adding, "And I suspect, you hope he'll succeed."

Since Gianna couldn't think of a response to that painful bit of homespun truth, she set the salmon gown aside and carried the bronze confection to the front desk. If only… came the wistful thought. If only The Inferno had worked as well between her and Constantine instead of backfiring so badly. Maybe she'd be sitting in a chair with that delicious

smile on her face, lost in memories of endless days and
nights filled with an eternal love.

If only.

As always, David arrived right on time. He looked spectacular in his tux, the light brown hair and turquoise eyes
he'd inherited from the northern branch of the d'Angelo
family giving him a movie-star sheen. It wasn't a coincidence
that his coloring was the complete opposite of Constantine's.
If he'd possessed hair as dark as night and eyes like jet, she'd
never have agreed to go out with him the first time he'd
asked. In fact, she hadn't. It had taken a full three months
of patient persistence before she'd caved to his barrage of
invitations.

He greeted her with a slow, easy kiss that didn't come
close to impacting the way Constantine's had. If she were
perfectly honest with herself, his kisses left her cold. No
doubt she could thank The Inferno for that unfortunate
wrinkle. She'd hoped—heaven help her but she'd hoped—
that she'd been mistaken about what she'd felt when she and
Constantine first touched. That at some point she'd begin
to feel a modicum of that sort of desire for David. It was
possible, regardless of what her relatives thought.

If their embraces lacked a certain spark, David never
seemed to notice. And sure enough, he didn't this time,
either. Perhaps he wasn't in the position to make the sort
of comparison she could. He pulled back and studied her,
his gaze warming in appreciation. He gestured toward her
hair and gown. "You look stunning, Gia."

"Thanks," she said.

Aware of the tepidness of her response, she gave him
an impulsive hug. What was wrong with her? David was
drop-dead gorgeous. He'd made it clear that he wanted her,
that his intentions were both honorable and serious—his

words, which she found quite endearing. Regardless of how endearing, she just couldn't bring herself to take their relationship to the next level. And now that Constantine had returned…

No! She wouldn't go there. Couldn't. Constantine had made his feelings all too clear months ago when he'd left her. When he'd proved beyond a shadow of a doubt that The Inferno hadn't taken root with him the way it had with her. She'd moved on, and the man she'd chosen stood in front of her. David was everything she could ask for. A dedicated banker in international finance with a bright future ahead of him. A physique that left women drooling. And a calm, practical nature that balanced her more passionate, impulsive one. Maybe The Inferno would strike later in their relationship.

"Ready?" David asked.

"All set."

"Will the entire family be there?" The question held a certain edginess that had her wincing. David often found her family a bit overwhelming. "Will I finally get to meet Lazz and Ariana, or are they still in Italy?"

The question caught her by surprise. But then, he'd acknowledged a distant, passing acquaintance with the Romanos, so maybe it wasn't all that odd. "They're still on a working holiday for another couple months."

"A shame," he murmured, though she suspected a certain insincerity in the comment.

After locking the door of her elegant row house with its pretty gingerbread trim, they crossed to his Jaguar. As always, he opened the door for her, his courtesy an innate part of his personality. They drove to Dantes' corporate office building, chatting about inconsequential matters along the way. They'd almost reached their destination when David steered the conversation into more turbulent waters.

"I have to fly out to New York next week for a meeting," he announced after a momentary silence. He flashed her a quick grin. "A very boring meeting."

He'd mentioned the trip the previous week. "I understand." She spared him a sympathetic glance. "How long will you be gone this time?"

"Four days. Friday through Monday."

"Well, that's not too bad. And at least it isn't overseas."

"No, it's not." He pulled up to a red light and spared her a brief, meaningful glance that didn't sink in until he added, "I'd like you to come with me. My business won't take long. This particular meeting is more of a formality than anything else."

"Oh, I don't know, David," she began.

The light turned green and he continued through the intersection. "I'm not finished." A single glance at the determined set of his jaw and she fell silent. "I was thinking we'd get a suite at the Ritz."

The offer came so out of the blue that it took her a moment to switch gears. "The Ritz?" Wow. Then the rest of his comment filtered through. "Wait a minute. Do you mean… share a suite?"

"I mean a romantic weekend." His mouth compressed. "As in, no family breathing down our necks."

Gianna stiffened and she swiveled in her seat. "You feel as though my family is breathing down our necks?" she asked, excruciatingly polite.

He didn't take notice of the warning in her voice. "In a word, yes. You're twenty-five, Gianna. We've known each other for six months, been dating for three, but you're still holding me at arm's length."

"And you think my family's to blame for that?"

He still didn't seem to realize that he'd wandered onto extremely thin ice. How could he have dated her for even a week and not picked up on the fact that family meant everything to her? With the Dantes, family came first and foremost, just as she thought it must with the d'Angelos, despite David's more cosmopolitan lifestyle. *La famiglia,* right?

That also extended beyond blood ties. There was nothing the Dantes loved better than finding someone new to add to the fold. If David weren't so suspicious of their intent, right down to insisting that they keep their relationship on the down low until the past month when he'd finally agreed to be introduced to everyone, he'd have discovered that for himself. But for some reason, David's attitude caused her family to hold him at a cool, polite distance, except for her Nonna.

She saw the Dantes' corporate headquarters come in to sight. "I don't blame your family for the way you've held me at arm's length. Not exactly. I understand that some of it is probably the old-fashioned way you were raised."

Oh, this just kept getting better and better. "Is that right?" she murmured. "Let me take a wild guess here. You consider me old-fashioned because I haven't jumped in the sack with you like every other woman you've dated."

"Again, being blunt here. Yes. The rest of the world has moved forward, Gia, but the Dantes are still living in a different century, with all the rules, social mores and restrictions that entails. As you know, I was educated at Oxford and enjoy a very sophisticated lifestyle. My entire family actually lives in the twenty-first century."

"Unlike mine." She didn't give him time to respond, instead smiling sweetly. "And for some reason you think a trip to New York will leapfrog me into the current century?"

He countered her smile with a warm, sensuous one of his own. "Hoping, sweetheart. Seriously hoping. Your family is protective. I get that. But still… You're a grown woman, Gia, with emphasis on the *woman*. Why shouldn't you live your life the way you see fit instead of by a set of antiquated rules?"

"Did it ever occur to you that I'm fully aware that I'm a grown woman and that, rather than caving to the old-fashioned dictates of my family, I've deliberately chosen to live by some of those antiquated rules you regard with such disdain?"

He released a sigh. "You're forcing me to spoil the surprise I have planned." He shot her a swift, smoldering look before lifting her left hand and kissing it, his thumb stroking across her bare ring finger. "A surprise that will give everyone cause for celebration and allow your family to turn a blind eye to our little romantic escapade. What do you say to that, sweetheart?"

Gianna's breath caught. Okay, it didn't take a mental genius to add up those clues. He planned to propose. She chose her response with care. "There's nothing I can say, is there? I mean, it's still a future surprise, not an actual proposition." She hesitated. "Is it?"

"Not yet. But I'm hoping to hear a loud, excited 'Yes, David, I will' in the very near future."

Gianna bit down on her lower lip. Gently disengaging their hands, she glanced out the passenger window at Dantes' corporate offices while she fought for control. Why now? Why tonight of all nights? She strongly suspected Constantine would be at the gala. In fact, knowing her family, she could pretty much guarantee it. How could she possibly consider starting an affair, let alone an engagement, with another man while he stood in the wings watching with that fierce, predatory hunger?

Gianna shivered at the thought. She could pretty much guarantee that if she and Constantine had been dating for three months their relationship would have been consummated long ago, whether they'd planned to wait or not. They wouldn't have been able to help themselves. No doubt, he'd have hustled her to the altar at the earliest moment, considering his family was as "old-fashioned," not to mention "antiquated," as hers.

She spared David a brief glance. She always knew this moment would come, when David would force her to make a choice between settling for second best or being alone. She hoped she'd have more time. That her feelings for him would change. But they hadn't and she'd have to make a decision about him—and soon.

He pulled into the parking garage beneath Dantes and slipped into the space reserved for VIP guests. Unbuckling both their seat belts, he surprised her by pulling her into his arms. Then he leaned across the console and kissed her, his warm lips wandering across hers. She allowed the embrace, attempted to lose herself in it.

More than anything, she wanted to fall for David. Wanted The Inferno to strike with someone who wanted her as much as he did. Who would put her first in his life instead of picking her up when he found time—an afterthought that he could discard whenever he tired of her. And why, when David kissed her with such hunger were her thoughts consumed by Constantine? She pulled back, pasting a smile on her face.

"Well?" David prompted softly.

She avoided his gaze. "I need some time," she replied.

He stilled, his expression cooling. "Time. Time to decide about New York? Or time to respond to my surprise?"

"I'm a little distracted by the gala," she explained, avoiding a direct answer. "I also need to check my calendar."

He lifted a light brown eyebrow. "Does that mean you're interested in a romantic weekend and all that entails?"

"I'm interested in discussing it," she temporized. She checked her watch and winced when she saw the time. "I'm sorry, David. I need to get inside. Could we table our discussion until later?"

"Table our discussion," he repeated.

Gianna sighed. "Sorry. I didn't mean to sound so businesslike."

"That's fine. I get it."

Without another word he exited the car. Circling the Jag, he opened her door and helped her out. They walked in silence to the elevators, the silence deepening as they shot upward to the appropriate floor.

The instant she stepped into the hallway, she sensed Constantine. He was nearby. Her reaction, primal and fierce, made her think of jungle animals responding to the pheromones of their mates. Part of her wanted to leave David's side and search through the warren of corridors until she found Constantine.

She closed her eyes and took a deep, steadying breath. This had to stop. Now. She couldn't remain on this emotional roller coaster. Pushing emotion aside she focused on logic and practicality. If she caved to desire she'd be lost. She needed to focus on David d'Angelo. But with every step she took, all her senses remained tuned to one man. Consumed by him.

Constantine Romano. The man who'd stolen her heart and soul.

Two

Gianna stepped into the ballroom to discover that most of her family had already arrived. The instant they caught sight of her they descended and swept her off with David following reluctantly in their wake.

She remembered his comment about her family breathing down their necks and couldn't help wondering if he felt like a Dantes' afterthought the same way she felt like Constantine's afterthought. What a mess.

After checking to ensure that all the various details for the gala had been finalized, Gianna joined her family in the reception line while David helped himself to a flute of champagne and wandered among the various displays, attempting with only limited success to conceal his boredom.

"He is the only man I know who can look at the most beautiful jewelry in the world with all the excitement of someone tasting sour milk," Gianna's brother Rafe growled in her ear. "Make him stop before he sends all of our guests fleeing into the night."

"How do you suggest I do that?"

"Your date. Your problem. But you'd better hurry up or I'll have to go over there and give him an attitude adjustment."

"Are all of you this polite to David when I'm not around?" she asked suspiciously.

Her eldest brother, Luc, joined them, followed by Draco. They started in as though they'd rehearsed their remarks, which possibly they had. "We don't like him," Draco announced, folding his arms across his chest. "And he doesn't like any of us."

"He's preoccupied with money. Granted, he *is* a banker."

"But it's all about the bottom line with him."

"He has no poetry in his soul. He's cold-blooded. We don't want our baby sister married to someone so passionless."

Gianna held up her hands. "Wait a minute. Just wait a minute. You've all been doing the big-brother thing with him, haven't you?" She eyed one after the other of her older siblings, none of whom had the grace to look the least shamefaced. She groaned. "Oh, Lord. You have."

"He didn't pass the test," Rafe explained helpfully. "He refused to attend a Giants game with me. *Box* seats."

Luc nodded in agreement. "Failed miserably. He doesn't even *play* basketball. I don't think he likes to sweat."

"He's a jerk," Draco offered with a toothy grin that would have done a dragon proud. "He turned down a case of Primo's homemade beer. Sneered at it. I've never seen our grandfather so ticked off."

"I would kill for a case of Primo's beer." A new voice dropped into the conversation. A painfully familiar voice. One which had haunted her thoughts and memories for nineteen impossible months. "What a foolish man to turn it down. Who are we talking about? Is this fool a friend of yours, Gianna?"

She spun around to face Constantine, her eyes widening at the sight of him. He was absolutely devastating in his tux, filling it out even better than David. Everything feminine within her responded to him. "What are you doing here, Constantine?" she demanded in a ragged undertone.

"What do you think?" His black gaze fastened on her as though she were the only one present. "I've come to claim what's mine."

From the corner of her eye, she saw David approach. Not that it mattered to Constantine, if he even noticed. Instead, with her date and relatives looking on, he captured her chin in his hand and tilted her face up to his.

And then he consumed her.

Gianna didn't attempt to evade Constantine's kiss, regardless of who was watching. His lips took possession of hers and ignited a flame she'd never experienced with any other man. Definitely not with David. For a brief moment she forgot all those witnessing the potent embrace. Forgot the time, the day, even her own name. All that remained was the strength of Constantine's hold, the heat of his body and that incredible mouth that moved on hers with such possessiveness.

He said so much with that single kiss. He spoke of longing, of their endless parting. Of hunger and intense pleasure. But most of all he spoke of the simple, yet undeniable fact that the two of them belonged together. There was a certainty to his kiss, a confidence in the way he took her mouth. A rightness. He knew her and what she wanted. And he gave it to her.

Any thought of resistance faded. Why would she resist when she wanted this more than she wanted air to breathe? Everything about him drew an elemental response from her.

His crisp, unique scent. The hard, undeniable maleness of his body locked against hers. The molten burn of his touch. Just a single touch and The Inferno went wild, shaking her to the very depths of her being. Even the beat of his heart resonated with her own.

And all the while, the explosive desire that heated their embrace sizzled with an intoxicating joy that they were together once again. She could practically feel his certainty grow with every second that passed, a fierce determination that formed the foundation of his character. It told her that he would have her for his own regardless of what obstacles he faced—including David.

It didn't matter that Constantine came from Italian aristocracy or that he'd been educated in the finest schools or that the Romanos were renowned for their civility and propriety. When stripped of all his social refinement, the man who held her remained a pirate at heart, intent on taking what he considered his. Intent on taking her.

She shivered within his hold, teetering on the brink of surrender. It wasn't until David dropped a hand on her shoulder and literally ripped her from Constantine's arms that she realized where she was—and in whose arms.

Heat burned in Gianna's cheeks and she took another hasty step backward, struggling to regain her composure. How could she have kissed Constantine like that in public, with her entire family looking on, not to mention the A-list roster of clients she'd personally invited to the gala? What must they all be thinking? She spared David a brief glance and cringed at the blatant outrage darkening his expression. No question what *he* thought.

Snatching a deep breath, she fell back on the sort of courtesy she had been taught since the moment she could first form coherent sentences. "David, this is Constantine Romano. He's…well…he's a member of the family. Sort of."

She spared Constantine a swift glance, startled by the flash of recognition when he first looked at David, fury following swiftly. That's right. They had a passing acquaintance. By the looks of things, maybe a passing enmity would better describe it. Tension thickened the air between the two men. "Constantine?" she asked hesitantly.

"I am not a member of the family," he contradicted in a hard voice, adding, "Yet. And David and I have met."

David smiled with a cold, cutting amusement that stole every ounce of charm from his expression. "Romano." He flicked a speck of lint from the cuff of his snowy dress shirt, making her wonder if he'd like to flick Constantine out of his way with a similar disdain. "As usual your timing leaves something to be desired."

Constantine took a step in his direction and to her alarm, her brothers packed in behind him. "What you mean is…as usual, I've arrived just in time." He spoke to Gianna without taking his gaze off David. "Is this him?" he demanded. "Is d'Angelo the bastard you told me about?"

How in the world did she answer that? She couldn't remember ever feeling so uncomfortable before. "He's the man I mentioned to you, yes," she confessed. "We've been dating for the past couple of months."

"You don't owe Romano an explanation," David said. "He's not a factor in your life, any more than he's a member of your family."

"To the contrary. Gianna and I are discussing ways we might change that. In the very near future I intend to be a permanent fixture in her life."

David froze and his intense blue eyes narrowed. Sharpened. "What the hell do you mean by that?"

Constantine smiled, a dangerous, predatory baring of his teeth. "I mean just what you think I mean. I've moved to

San Francisco with the express intention of asking Gianna
to do me the honor of becoming my wife."

Conversation exploded around them. "Oh, God," Gianna
murmured, swaying in place.

As though from a great distance she could hear the
excitement and approval of her family, the congratulations
that made it clear that the Dantes were firmly aligned in
Constantine's corner of this hideous triangle. She spun to
face an infuriated David.

He gathered up his self-control and forced out a smile.
She couldn't begin to imagine how much effort it took.
"You're delusional, Romano. Gia and I already have an
understanding, one that will be cemented on our upcoming
trip to New York City. A private suite at the Ritz. Candlelight
and roses." He gestured carelessly toward one of the display
cases. "Is Sev the one I should see in order to purchase a
Dantes' engagement ring? I'm assuming Tiffany's or Cartier
is out of the question. A shame really."

Dead silence followed David's comment. She could feel
the waves of fury pouring off Constantine, which was no
doubt the point. And after the crack about Tiffany's and
Cartier, her family didn't appear any calmer. How could
David be so foolish? It was so unlike him. Granted, he
hadn't formed the sort of tight relationship with her brothers
she'd hoped he would, but he'd never been deliberately rude.
In fact, he'd always been polite, intent on making a good
impression, even if it lacked a certain warmth.

Time to act, Gianna realized, and fast. The first item on
her agenda was to remove David from the line of fire before
someone decked him. Then they'd have a talk. A *long* talk.
She needed to decide once and for all whether there was
any possibility of a future for her with David. If not, the
only honorable option was to end things between them.

"If you'll excuse us, my date and I have a few important matters to discuss," Gianna announced.

David grinned in triumph and dropped an arm around her shoulders, tugging her into his arms. For a split second she thought matters might turn physical. Maybe they would have if David's impromptu embrace hadn't placed her squarely between the warring factions. An accident, she was certain. Her oldest brother, Luc, grabbed Constantine's shoulder in one hand and Rafe's in the other, actively restraining the two men.

"Later," she heard him murmur. "This isn't the proper time or place."

Clearly David had no intention of waiting for the proper time or place. "Yes, boys, heel" came his parting shot before he swept her away.

"What is going on?" she demanded in an undertone.

His congenial mask faded. "I planned to ask you the precise same questions."

"Answer mine, first. What's between you and Constantine?"

"Old history. Nothing to do with us. Come." He gestured toward the terrace off the ballroom. "Let's find somewhere private to talk."

Though it was midsummer, a cool haze embraced their surroundings, creating a pale, misty curtain. The sprawl of the city glittered softly through the veil, muffling sight, sound and light. It was almost as though they were cut off from the rest of the world, trapped within an oasis of fog. Tables dotted the terrace, situated in cozy, shadow-draped alcoves. David selected the most private.

"Why don't you sit here for a moment while I get us both a drink."

She wasn't going to let him off the hook. "Then you'll explain?"

"Absolutely. Just as you will."

She heard the clipped warning in his voice and winced. She didn't look forward to that part of the conversation at all. She used her time alone to consider how to describe her relationship to Constantine, not to mention that kiss. It would be lovely if she could get away with a short: "It's none of your business." But she knew David better than that.

Before she could come up with a firm plan, he returned with a flute of champagne for her and a Campari for himself. He even offered a congenial smile. After his earlier anger, his sudden equanimity surprised her. She took a sip of champagne and wrinkled her nose at the aftertaste. What in the world...? She'd had this wine before and never experienced the faintly bitter finish she did on this occasion.

He raised his highball glass. "To us."

Aware that David was waiting for a response, she quickly switched gears and tipped her flute in his direction. "To us," she hastened to repeat, gently tapping her glass against his and took another tongue-curdling sip of her wine. As much as she preferred to avoid the coming confrontation, she knew she couldn't. But maybe she could delay her own explanation by taking the offensive. "What's going on, David?"

"You tell me." He eyed her over the rim of his glass. Though he'd banked his anger, she could sense it smoldering just beneath the surface. "That wasn't exactly a familial kiss you exchanged with Romano."

"We're old friends."

"*Intimate* old friends?"

She couldn't discern his expression in the darkness of the terrace, but his tone didn't require the bright light of day to decipher. He was flat-out furious. She took her time responding, sipping her champagne, then wished she hadn't bothered. She chose her words with care. "We dated," she admitted. "Very, very briefly."

"You slept with him."

Anger rippled through her and she set her flute on the table, the crystal singing against the wrought iron. "That's none of your business."

She thought he'd argue the point. He must have reconsidered, because he shrugged. "You're right. It isn't," he conceded. He lifted her glass and handed it to her again, in what was clearly meant to be a peace offering. "I was jealous. Considering that kiss you and Romano exchanged, is it surprising?"

"I guess not."

She accepted the glass. This time when she sipped, she attempted to analyze what was off about the wine. It wasn't flat or sour. The carbonation remained strong and crisp, the flavor light and fruity with a hint of yeast. And yet, the bitterness persisted. She made a mental note to check with the caterer. For now, she'd let the problem go and give her full attention to David.

"So, is it over between you and Romano?" David pressed.

"I'm not sure," she admitted honestly.

It certainly hadn't felt over, not after that kiss. Her palm itched and she curled her fingers inward, wishing she could ignore the sensation. How many Dantes had described that exact same reaction and attributed it to the connection formed when they'd first touched their soul mate? Every last one of them. She closed her eyes. Since Constantine's return, the itching had grown progressively more noticeable. She could sit here with David and deny it until dawn broke across the horizon, but it wouldn't change the facts.

She and Constantine were connected in a way she and David weren't...and quite possibly never would be, no matter how hard she'd tried to ignite that connection.

"Finish your drink, Gia, and then let's go."

The clipped order caught her off guard. Had he seen the regret on her face? "Go? Go, where?"

"For a drive. We need to talk and I'd rather not do it here where Dantes or Romano could burst in on us at any moment." She caught the gleam of his smile in the darkness. "Besides, it will give everyone time to cool off. Don't you think that's the smartest choice?"

Gianna weighed her options. If they stayed, chances were excellent that her family would appear within the next ten minutes with some excuse or another, no doubt one related to business. She toyed with her wineglass and grimaced. Particularly if they tasted the champagne. She didn't have a single doubt that Constantine would head the parade of invaders. He wouldn't be able to help himself. She closed her eyes, an unexpected wave of exhaustion settling over her. She couldn't deal with any of that tonight, she really couldn't.

"Finish your champagne and let's go," David prompted again.

"Okay." But instead of drinking, she set it aside. She could tell her actions didn't please him and wasn't quite certain if he objected to her contrariness or the fact that he'd gone to the trouble of bringing her a drink she hadn't bothered to finish. She touched his hand to distract him. "But then you'll explain about you and Constantine and whatever this old history is between you, right? His sister, Ariana, is married to my cousin Lazz, remember? And I flat-out adore her. I don't want your disagreement with Constantine to interfere with my relationship with her."

"Of course not." He stood and held out his hand. "Why don't we slip out the back way?"

"If it'll avoid a confrontation, I'm all for it," Gianna agreed.

* * *

"Why didn't you tell me they were dating?" Constantine demanded of Gianna's brothers.

Luc shrugged. "Didn't know it had anything to do with you."

Draco frowned. "And just out of curiosity, why does it have anything to do with you?"

Time to make one thing crystal clear to all the Dantes. Constantine folded his arms across his chest and eyed them one by one. "From now on everything about Gianna has to do with me," he stated.

"Wait a minute, wait a minute." Rafe held up his hands. "I know you two met at Lazz's wedding. But when the hell did it go from how-do-you-do to she's-mine-let's-kill-the-competition? Not that I mind, you understand. I'd just like you to fill in a few of the blanks."

How could they even ask that question? They knew how The Inferno worked. They must know what Gianna had chosen to do to him. "It went from one to the other as soon as we shook hands."

Luc's brows shot upward. "The Inferno?"

"She Infernoed you?" Rafe burst out laughing. "Way to go, little sister."

"This is not a laughing matter." Constantine could hear his accent deepening and fought for control. "It might have been polite to ask before she…Infernoed me."

Draco gave him a sympathetic slap on the back. "Yeah, sorry about that. Doesn't really work that way, I'm afraid."

Constantine's eyes narrowed. "When we have more time, perhaps you would be so kind as to explain exactly how it does work."

"Hell, if any of us knew that we wouldn't all be standing here with a ball and chain manacled to our ankles," Rafe said cheerfully. He shot out his hand and captured his wife's wrist, reeling her in. "Isn't that right, my sweet little chain?"

"You just said that because you knew I was standing there, didn't you?" Larkin demanded crossly.

"If you can't handle the truth, don't eavesdrop." Her mouth opened to give him a piece of her mind and he took immediate advantage. They both reemerged a moment later, a bit bewitched and bewildered. He cupped his wife's face and gazed down at her with unmistakable adoration. "Just so you know, I've never been more grateful for that chain or the fact that it goes both ways…and I always will."

A short time later, Gianna found herself in David's car, pulling out of the Dantes' garage. He gave the Jaguar its head, the powerful car eating up the hills of the city a little faster than she'd have liked. He was so different from Constantine. It was almost as though David had something to prove. As though he were trying to show her that he was the better man. Instead of being impressed, she found his actions vaguely sad.

She yawned. "Where are we going?"

"Nowhere in particular. I just thought we'd take a drive out of the city, then park and talk."

He sped through a yellow light and she touched his arm. For some reason it took serious effort, almost as though her limbs had turned to lead. Preparing for the gala must have worn her out more than she realized. "Pull over for just a minute."

"Wait until we're out of the city."

"No, seriously. Pull over. I want you to do something for me."

He spared her a brief, impatient look, then braked a little harder than necessary and rolled to a stop in a red zone beside a fire hydrant. "Okay, I've pulled over. Now what?"

"Would you kiss me?"

A streetlight cut across his face, giving the illusion that his pale eyes were translucent. She could still read his reaction—a mixed one. Part of him wanted her with a deep, primal hunger that he didn't bother to disguise. Another part, one she suspected he would have hidden from her if he could, hesitated. She knew why. He'd guessed she wanted to compare his kiss to the one Constantine had given her. And he'd be right.

The time for pretense was over. She needed to know the truth, once and for all. Either she had serious feelings for David or she didn't. For the past three months she'd thrown herself into the relationship, hoping against hope that desire would flare to life. That The Inferno would strike with him, the way it had with Constantine. She knew for a fact that could happen. Even so, she couldn't create a fire without combustible materials. At the very least she should feel as if she'd struck a match when they kissed. Generated a hint of smoke. Created a flicker or two of flame. Something. If not, the only honorable course was to end things between them.

David took his time. Reaching for her, he drew her as close as possible given the console between them. He cupped her face and leaned in, taking her mouth slowly, then more passionately. His breathing grew ragged as the moments slipped by and his fingers thrust into her hair so he could control and deepen the kiss.

It took every ounce of self-possession to keep from jerking free of his hold. His touch felt wrong. Wrong on every conceivable level. No matter how hard she attempted to fight it, there was only one man for her. And he wasn't the one kissing her.

Even so, she didn't fight him or pull back, despite the muffled instinct urging her to do just that. For some reason it felt as though she'd left her brain on the terrace at Dantes, trapped within that dense summer fog. More than anything she wished she could curl up and go to sleep. Maybe a drive wasn't the best option.

It wasn't until he groped for the fastening of the halter top of her gown that she stirred. "No, David." He pulled back, a protest blazing across his face. Before he could say anything, her cell phone rang, loud and strident within the confines of the car. It cut through the drag of exhaustion, giving her a moment of clarity. "I need to get that."

"No, you don't," he argued. "For once in your life, ignore your family."

"I'm a Dante, David," she explained gently. "You know it doesn't work that way. They'll worry if I don't answer."

She took the call, but instead of one of her brothers as she expected, it was Constantine who spoke. "Where are you, *piccola?*" he asked.

"With David. We're going for a drive."

A brief silence, then, "Tell him to take you straight home."

"Is that an order?"

"There's something you should know about David, Gianna. It's important. I wouldn't ask if it weren't."

She might have argued, but with David sitting there listening to every word, she decided to choose prudence for once in her life. "I'll call you later when it's more convenient."

"I'm leaving Dantes in another few minutes. I'll wait outside your place until I hear from you."

She sighed. "It might be a bit. David and I…" She spared her date a brief glance, not the least surprised by the anger sparking in his gaze. Could he hear Constantine's voice, tell it wasn't one of her brothers who'd called? Or had he guessed what was happening based on her responses? "We need to talk."

"Going to dump him?"

"That's none of your business."

"Everything about you is my business," he responded with devastating simplicity.

She flipped the phone closed and dropped it in her purse. "David—"

"Don't."

She fought through her exhaustion, attempting to find the kindest, gentlest words possible. "David, let's be honest with each other. We've been dating for three months. If we shared something that could have become permanent, we'd have felt it by now."

"We have felt it," he argued. "You can't deny you feel something for me. You've just allowed Romano to confuse you. Give me a chance, Gia. Give *us* a chance."

It was truth time. She would never want this man. Not the way a woman should want the man who hoped to share her bed. No matter how hard she tried, no matter how she attempted to lose herself in David's embrace, some part of her remained remote and untouched. That secret part of herself flinched from allowing any other man to hold her. Touch her. Kiss her. Only one man had that right. She closed her eyes, caving to the inevitable. There wouldn't be a private weekend in New York. Or a romantic suite at the Ritz, not to mention an engagement.

Nor would she ever share David's bed.

"I have given us a chance," she told him as compassionately as she could manage. She fought back another yawn. The fog returned, relentless, rolling toward her at breakneck speed. "It's not working."

"I'll make it work." He turned a knob on the console

which put the Jag in gear and fishtailed away from the curb. "Lean back and close your eyes, Gia. We'll be there before you know it."

She shook her head, but it didn't help. The fog descended, consuming her, and she tumbled into its cold gray embrace. "What's wrong with me?" she murmured.

"Put your seat back and go to sleep. When you wake it'll all be over."

What would be over? But it took too much effort to ask the question. And she slept.

Three

"She's not at her house and she's not answering her cell." Constantine paced up and down the sidewalk for the umpteenth time. After twenty endless minutes, he knew every crack and stain by heart. "That can only mean one thing. D'Angelo has her. There's no other possibility."

Luc sighed. "He doesn't *have* her. They're simply out together. I hate to say this, Constantine, but they've been dating for a couple of months. She's a grown woman. If she isn't answering her cell it's because she doesn't want to talk to you. I'm sure she'll be in touch in the morning."

"No," Constantine snarled into his cell phone. Every instinct he possessed screamed in protest. He had to find her. *Now.* "If we wait until morning, it will be too late. He knows I am on to him. He'll have to move tonight if he has any hope of keeping her from me."

"What the bloody hell are you talking about?" Luc snapped.

Constantine forced himself to explain in a calm, crisp manner that didn't sound like *he* was the deranged one, rather than d'Angelo. "D'Angelo has drugged at least one other woman in the past in order to take advantage of her. *Attempted* to take advantage of her. I stopped him in time."

"Dear God. *That's* what he meant about your timing leaving something to be desired?"

"Yes." Constantine checked his watch, also for the umpteenth time. "If d'Angelo wishes to do this to Gianna...if he wishes to drug her and take advantage of her, where would he take her?"

There was a brief silence and Constantine could practically hear Luc mentally sorting through the possibilities. "He's renting a suite at one of the hotels here in the city while he waits for escrow to close on the mansion he's purchased. I don't remember which hotel, though I could probably find out. One of the pricier ones, I'm sure."

Constantine considered for a moment, then shook his head. "No, he wouldn't take her to his hotel. Too many witnesses. It would be someplace private."

"Let me check around." Sick tension bled across the airwaves. "I'll get back to you."

"Make it fast," Constantine advised. "The clock is ticking."

"Romano—" Fear ripped apart Luc's voice.

"Remain calm. I'll find her. And I'll be in time."

For the sake of his sanity, he didn't have any choice.

Gianna stirred, slowly surfacing, vaguely aware that the Jaguar was slowing. The wipers were on, swishing softly while rain pelted against the windshield. Were they home? She must have fallen asleep during the brief drive, she realized groggily. How strange. Her head lolled toward the window and she squinted at the darkness that consumed the car. No, not home, she realized. They weren't even in the city.

"David?" she murmured sleepily.

"Almost there. I hadn't planned to make this trip tonight, so I need to stop for gas. Then it's not much farther."

"Where are we?"

"A little north of Calistoga."

The information filtered through with sludgelike speed. When it did, the confusion clouding her mind began to clear. *Calistoga?* It took her a moment to place it. When she did, her breath caught. That was a solid hour outside of the city at the north end of the Napa Valley. Why in the world would he have driven so far? It didn't make sense. "I don't understand. What are we doing in Calistoga?"

He spared her a brief, impatient look. "You should have finished your champagne. You were supposed to sleep until we reached the lodge."

Once again it took time to sort through his comment, but little by little she could feel the sluggishness fading away. She didn't understand the wine comment and focused instead on his second statement. Lodge? What lodge? "I'm not going to any lodge with you. I want you to take me home."

"I'll be happy to." He paused a beat. "Tomorrow."

She shook her head in protest, shocked by the weight of it. Why was it so heavy? She could barely hold it up. "Something's wrong with me," she said. "I feel so odd."

"You're just tired. Put your seat back and go to sleep."

He'd said that to her before. This time it wasn't a request, but an order, so firmly delivered, she almost didn't resist. More than anything she wanted to obey him and surrender to the darkness just waiting to consume her once again. The champagne. He'd said something about the champagne.

"You drugged me." She didn't pose it as a question.

Instead of protesting, he grinned like a schoolboy caught with his hand in the cookie jar. "Maybe just a little."

Fear, sudden and abrupt, coursed through her system burning through the remaining mists blanketing her thoughts. He'd drugged her. Dear God, he'd actually drugged her. She attempted to moisten her lips but found it impossible. Her mouth and throat had gone bone-dry.

"Why?" she managed to ask. "Why would you do that to me?"

He shrugged, taut muscles rippling beneath the impressive expanse of his dress shirt. He must have removed his tux jacket at some point while she slept. She shuddered. What else had happened while she'd been unconscious?

"Because I want you," he admitted, as though that were explanation enough.

And maybe it was, for him. She'd always been aware that he possessed an overdeveloped sense of entitlement. More than once she'd heard him excuse the occasional excessive indulgence with the excuse, "But I deserve..." Whether a suite at the Ritz-Carlton or a third Rolex or a fully loaded Jaguar, David always felt entitled to the best. Apparently he'd now decided that he "deserved" her. Anger ripped through her, combating the drugs, as well as her fear. Well, not if she could help it.

"It doesn't bother you that drugging and kidnapping me was the only way you could achieve your ends?" she asked. Maybe if she kept him talking, it would give her time to think...and plan a way out of this.

"Drugging you wasn't the only way, just the most expeditious."

He took his eyes off the road long enough to frown in her direction. It occurred to her that if she had any hope of escaping her present predicament, she'd be wise to pretend the drugs had a stronger hold on her than they did. Otherwise, he might decide to administer a little more and she'd never get away. She closed her eyes with a soft sigh and allowed her head to roll to one side.

"So sleepy," she murmured.

He trailed the back of his hand along the curve of her cheek and it took every ounce of self-control to keep from flinching. "Trust me. By morning you'll wonder why you held me off for so long. And by tomorrow afternoon…"

"By tomorrow afternoon…?" She deliberately yawned out the question.

"We'll be engaged."

She lifted a hand to her forehead. "I…I don't understand."

"Once I explain what happened to your grandfather, abashed and contrite that we allowed passion to overcome Dante propriety, your family will demand I do the honorable thing and marry you. In fact, I'll insist it's the only reasonable solution."

She stiffened in outrage. What the hell did he know about honor? She almost asked the question, keeping her mouth shut at the last instant. Being a *chiacchierona* as her family affectionately called her—a chatterbox—wouldn't help in her current situation. Restraint and discretion would.

"I seem to remember hearing that Luc and Téa found themselves in a similar predicament—caught in the act— and Primo insisted they marry immediately," David continued with a pensive air. "I'm sure he'll be even more insistent with his only granddaughter, if only to uphold the family honor."

"And if I tell my grandfather you drugged me?" She fought to keep the sharpness from her voice and ask the question in a vague, confused manner.

He chuckled. "You won't remember that, any more than you'll remember this conversation."

He pulled into a gas station, the only spot of brightness along the remote stretch of road. Darkness poured from the interior of the cement block storefront. No help there. Nor from the closed and padlocked service bay doors. But the pumps were lit and available for credit card purchases. Maybe someone else would stop for gas. Someone who could help her.

He turned in the leather seat to face her. "Before you fall back asleep, I have one final question for you."

"Can't. Too tired."

"Ah, ah, ah," he scolded, giving her a little shake. "You can sleep after you answer my question."

She made a feeble gesture for him to continue before allowing her hand to flop back onto her lap. "What?" She deliberately slurred the word.

"Where's Brimstone?"

She blinked, staring at him blankly, unable to make sense of the words. And not because of the drugs. "What?"

"The Dante fire diamond, Brimstone. Where is it?" he asked urgently. "My sources tell me it disappeared. What happened to it?"

"I don't know what you're talking about."

He swore in Italian. "Don't give me that. It's practically a Dante legend. My father told me all about it and he got it straight from Vittorio Romano."

Vittorio. Constantine's father. "I...I don't know anything about it."

"It was supposed to go to the Romanos after your cousin and Ariana married. But it never did." He paused, speaking more to himself than to her. "Unless that bastard, Constantine, financed Romano Restoration with it. I can't imagine any other way he could have done it in so short a time. Not with my father blocking his every attempt to get a loan."

She forced out a yawn. "I'm so tired...I don't understand a word you're saying."

He took a moment to think it through. "If Romano has the diamond, he wouldn't be here, sniffing after you. And despite what my sources say, you don't just lose a fire diamond as valuable as Brimstone. Which means..." His focus returned to her. "Does your family still have the diamond? Is that why Romano's here? That's it, isn't it? He's hoping to romance it out from under you by marrying into the family."

"Never heard of Brimstone," she mumbled.

And she hadn't. But she sure as hell intended to ask about it the minute she got herself out of her current predicament. She shuddered. Assuming she could. Please, God, let someone come.

His gaze pinned her in place, sharp and ruthless. "Fine. Pretend you don't know. It won't change a thing. Once I've married into the family, it won't matter, anyway."

"'Kay." She closed her eyes and slumped in her seat.

"Gia?"

She didn't so much as twitch.

"Gianna!"

She kept her breathing slow and deep. She never realized how much effort it took to feign sleep when her heart galloped like a racehorse and panic threatened to consume her. She must have convinced David, though. She heard him push a button near the steering wheel which she gathered released the gas tank cover, then he opened the car door and exited. Peeking from beneath her lashes, she held her breath while he circled to stand at the rear of the car with his back to her and removed his wallet from his pocket, extracting a credit card.

She wouldn't get a better opportunity. She'd watched him start the Jag any number of times. It didn't require a key. She simply had to apply the brakes, then push the "start" button on the console between the two seats. Once the engine fired, a knob popped up which controlled the gear settings. After that, matters might get a bit more dicey.

The instant David inserted his credit card in the gas pump, she moved, slinging her legs over the center console and sliding into the driver's seat. She jammed the door release lever with her elbow, locking all the doors. Next she hit the brake with both feet and slapped the start/stop button on the console. The Jag purred to life. Just as she'd seen countless times before, the gear knob released.

Behind her, she heard David shout. Not that she listened. She turned the button from P for Park to D for Drive. Now for the tricky part. To drive a car for the second time in her entire life. Taking a deep breath, she hit the gas.

The Jag responded with a throaty roar of enthusiasm and leaped forward, careening across the cement lot toward the road. She fought to contain the power, jerking the wheel one way and then the other. The Jag responded to every movement—and then some. She attempted to compensate for her oversteer, overcorrected instead, and the back of the vehicle fishtailed, the tires screaming at her mistreatment.

Slow down, slow down!

But for some reason she couldn't peel her foot off the accelerator. She was too desperate to escape to let up. Just before she reached the road the right side of the car hit a curb, sending it spinning. It made a half dozen 360s across the two-lane road before clipping a tree with its rear end. Metal shrieked, airbags exploded around her. Then silence descended.

The Jag had come to rest facing the gas station. She'd

made her escape, all right. She'd gotten a solid two hundred yards down the road. For a split second, she and David stared at each other. Then with a shout of fury, he charged in her direction.

Gianna fought for breath. This was not going to end well.

"Calistoga?" Constantine punched the name into his GPS. "Where the hell is Calistoga?"

"This I do not know," Vittorio Romano responded. The connection faded for a brief moment then kicked in again. "The business associate mentioned a fancy lodge that the d'Angelo boy owns near this Calistoga. He uses it to entertain clients."

For once, the nine-hour time difference between Italy and California had worked to Constantine's advantage. It might be after midnight for him, but it was bright and early in the morning at the Romano palazzo. "A suite at the Ritz. A mansion. A Jag. Now a lodge. I have to tell you, Babbo. All these years we've been doing something wrong."

"Something right," his father corrected. "I have been hearing rumors about the d'Angelos and their banking practices. Creative accounting is the term being thrown about. Soon, all of Firenze will be talking. It won't be long before they are talking in San Francisco, too."

"Too bad the rumors couldn't have hit the States a couple of months ago," Constantine muttered. He checked the GPS. "Okay, I've found Calistoga. Do you have an address?"

"No. But I am still waiting for information from another source."

"Call me as soon as you hear anything."

Constantine didn't waste any more time. Once more the late hour worked to his advantage and he drove onto the Golden Gate Bridge in record time. If he broke every speed record out there, he could make it to Calistoga in under an hour. That would still put him a solid thirty minutes behind d'Angelo. Maybe longer.

His hands tightened on the steering wheel. If he thought about what was happening to her, what d'Angelo might be doing right now, he'd go insane. *Focus.* First, he'd focus on getting to Calistoga as quickly as possible. Then he'd focus on finding Gianna. But the instant he found her and ensured her safety... David d'Angelo would regret ever touching his woman. Or any other woman, for that matter. He planned to see to that.

Personally.

Move, move, *move!*

Gianna thrust open the door and erupted from the Jag. At the last instant she remembered her cell phone. Flinging herself across the driver's seat, she batted the deflated airbags out of her way and snagged her beaded handbag from the passenger side floor. Sparing a swift glance in David's direction—heaven protect her, he was close—she darted into the forest along the side of the road.

Rain pelted her. It soaked her dress, causing it to cling to her legs, making running awkward. Worse, bushes grabbed at her ankles, threatening to trip her up. But it was her mile-high heels sinking into the boggy earth that ultimately did her in. She went down, the wet, needle-strewn ground absorbing the impact of her fall and cushioning her rolling descent into a shallow depression. A small, shocked cry escaped before she could suppress it. She could only hope the rain muffled the sound.

As it turned out the fall saved her from discovery. David crashed through the underbrush practically on her heels. She heard him standing directly above her, his breathing harsh and ragged from the exertion of chasing after her. He would have seen her if she weren't enveloped by the heavy, protective darkness of the depression.

"Gia! Don't be an idiot," he shouted. For the first time since she'd known him, his Italian accent came through loud and clear. It was nowhere near as smooth and lyrical as Constantine's, but coarse and discordant. "Come out. This is all some hideous mistake."

Gianna didn't so much as breathe. Sure thing. She'd come on out and he could explain the mistake while he…how had he put it? The words came back to her through the lingering effect of the drug he'd poisoned her with. While he allowed passion to overcome Dante propriety. Yeah, right. Not a chance in hell. She closed her eyes like a child hiding from the boogeyman. If she couldn't see him, he couldn't see her.

He thrashed back toward the Jag and swore. "Look what you did to my car." He called her a name in Italian, one she hadn't heard before. Probably best she didn't know what it meant. "Do you have any idea how much it'll cost me to have this fixed?"

Slowly she stood and kicked off her heels, deciding that going barefoot, no matter how difficult, made more sense than risking a twisted ankle or broken leg. If that happened, she'd be at David's mercy. She squinted through the rain. In the darkness, the woods appeared impenetrable.

She was wet and cold, with bracken clinging to her skin, hair and clothes. She could only hope that the dirt helped camouflage her. She held her arms out in front of her so she wouldn't run blindly into a tree and stepped gingerly across the forest carpet. Rocks and sticks littered the area and she winced at the scrape and poke. Little by little, she slipped deeper into the woods.

She didn't want to stray so far from the road that she couldn't find her way back. But she also didn't dare stay close enough that David might find her. In the distance, she heard the Jag start and hoped she hadn't damaged it so badly he couldn't leave.

Please, leave!

Lights flickered across the trees and then stopped, shining directly toward her. She instantly dropped to a crouch behind a huge, thick evergreen, possibly a redwood. The car door popped opened and slammed closed, and David's shadow flashed across the path of the headlights. He hurried into the woods once again, using the high beams to guide him.

Gianna hugged the tree, shivering, its rough bark cutting into her exposed skin. Until that moment she hadn't realized how cold she was. Maybe fear or adrenaline had kept her from feeling anything else. No doubt reaction was setting in. She didn't dare move, knowing he'd find her instantly if she did. All the while he came closer, making a beeline in her direction. Could he see her? Sense her? Had he found the trail she'd left through the brush? Unable to help herself, she rocked back and forth, a whimper of terror building in her throat. *Please let him give up and drive away,* she prayed. *Please.*

Her prayers were answered a moment later. In the distance she heard the sound of an approaching vehicle, something large and heavy. A truck? With the damaged Jag skewed across the road so it could face the woods, chances were excellent the driver would stop to help.

David froze at the sound, not more than a dozen feet away. He must have come to the same conclusion she had about the approaching vehicle because he swore violently. "Fine. Freeze to death for all I care, you crazy bitch," he shouted. She heard him retreat at a swift clip as the truck lumbered closer. "But you're paying for the damage you did to my car, you hear me?"

He really was insane. She couldn't think of any other explanation for such irrational behavior. She heard the car door slam and he gunned the engine repeatedly before taking off. Something metallic banged and rattled along behind the Jag. Maybe the rear bumper or the muffler. It must have come loose because she heard it bounce along the road before clattering onto the shoulder as David roared away. An instant later, the truck flashed by and disappeared. No help from that direction.

She waited for endless moments, straining for any hint that David might have changed his mind and returned. Then she remembered her cell phone. She leaned her forehead against the tree trunk and fought back a hot rush of tears. She'd dropped her purse at some point during her escape, probably when she'd fallen down the incline. Gathering herself up, she dropped to the ground on hands and knees and began to search.

Inch by agonizing inch, minute by bone-freezing minute, she worked her way toward the depression, fanning her hands through the bracken littering the forest floor. More than anything, she wanted to curl into a ball and weep hysterically. She didn't dare. She didn't think she'd last through the night if she lost control now. But she was close, so close to giving up and giving in. Then her hand glanced off the slick beads of her purse.

Shock was setting in, along with a numbing cold. Her fingers shook so hard it took three attempts to open the stubborn clasp of her handbag. Even when she managed that, she could barely hold on to the phone. She didn't have a hope in hell of punching out a number. It took her an instant to realize David must have switched her phone off while she'd been unconscious. It took her full concentration just to get it powered back on. The instant it flared to life, her cell phone gave a soft beep warning that her battery was running low.

No. Oh, no, no, *no!* This was not happening. She literally would not be able to handle it if her phone died now. How many times had she drained the battery because she'd forgotten to plug it in? She suspected that wouldn't happen again—ever. And how ironic that David's turning it off, no doubt to keep any incoming calls from waking her, had preserved the last of the cell's battery power.

She managed to punch Redial with a trembling finger. An instant later Constantine answered.

"Gianna?"

She burst into tears. "Help."

Four

Constantine raced into the service station at full speed and braked the Porsche to a screaming halt beneath one of the lighted gas pump overhangs.

He scanned the area. Nothing. No one.

Gianna's cell had died midway through the call and he could only hope that he'd found the right gas station on the right road. The rain had subsided in the past fifteen minutes, easing off to a fitful mist. But that didn't change the fact that she was out there somewhere in the wet and cold.

He tore open the car door and burst from the vehicle. "Gianna?" he shouted. His voice bounced and echoed off the concrete lot and buildings, an eerie sound in the stillness of the night. "Where are you, *piccola?*"

A movement across the street caught his eye and Gianna exploded from the undergrowth. She took one look at him, and his name escaped in a low, choked whimper. In the next instant, she lifted the drenched skirts of her gown to halfway up her thighs and raced barefoot across the street toward him, splashing haphazardly through the puddles in her path, the back of her dress making wet slapping noises against her bare legs. He froze for a split second, gut-wrenching relief fading in the face of horrified concern.

He barely recognized her. Gone was the elegant woman he'd seen earlier in the evening, replaced by a filthy, bedraggled waif. Debris covered her from head to toe, dirt ground into what little he could see of the torn sweep of her skirt. Scratches gouged the pale skin of her arms and legs. And her feet... He swore silently. Her poor, bare feet. He didn't know how she could walk, let alone run. Maybe the shock kept her from feeling the pain.

He charged toward her, meeting her halfway. She flung herself into his arms and he wrapped her in an unbreakable hold, relieved beyond measure at finding her alive and safe. She burrowed against him, weeping and talking and shuddering so hard he couldn't make out a word she said. Damn it to hell, she was freezing.

He lifted her into his arms and carried her rapidly to the car. "I need to get you warm," he warned. "We have to get you out of these wet clothes."

She was too far gone to process his words. He set her down again and she winced the instant her feet hit the pavement. He silently swore again. D'Angelo would pay for every last scratch on Gianna...and pay dearly. Reaching behind her, he fumbled for the closure of her halter gown. Unable to figure it out, he dealt with it in the simplest, most expeditious way. He ripped it off her.

"Easy, *piccola,* easy," he soothed. "I'm just trying to get you dry and warm."

He stripped her in one swift move, steeling himself against her distress and confusion and weeping protests. Then he yanked off his own shirt and tux jacket and helped her into them before urging her to the passenger side of the car. The instant he had her buckled in, he cranked up the heat.

It took her three tries to speak. "You scared me for a minute there, but I get it now," she murmured in a low, shaky voice. She waved a hand to indicate his shirt and jacket. "The undressing and dressing to warm me up thing, I mean. Thanks."

"Are you okay?" He shook his head at his own stupidity. "Foolish question. I should say, did d'Angelo... Did he hurt you?"

He couldn't use the real word for it. But he could tell from her expression she understood what he meant. She folded her legs against her chest and wrapped her arms around them, hugging herself for warmth no doubt. She splayed blue-tipped fingers in front of the air vent and released a blissful sigh, before answering his question.

"I got away before he could."

He probably shouldn't push. Not now. But he couldn't help himself. "How did you manage it? To escape, I mean? I'm surprised you weren't out cold the entire time." Her head jerked around and unspoken questions filled her gaze in response to his observation. He shrugged. "I know d'Angelo drugged you. He's done it before."

Her eyes widened, went black with shock as she assimilated the information. "I would have been out cold," she confessed after a long moment. Her wet hair curled wildly around a face gone bone-white. "At least, that's what David said. But I didn't finish the champagne. It tasted...off. So, I didn't get a full dose of whatever he'd given me."

Madre di Dio. Luck. It all boiled down to sheer, unadulterated luck. "When did you wake?"

"Right before he stopped for gas. He...he was going to compromise me so that Primo would insist we marry."

Apparently she couldn't use the actual words for what d'Angelo had almost done, any more than Constantine could. It was too soon. The words too vile. The events still so new and raw that they defied full comprehension. "It probably would have worked if I hadn't escaped while he was running his credit card through the gas pump."

It had been close. Unbelievably close. If she'd finished her drink, she wouldn't have woken until far too late. If David hadn't needed gas, he wouldn't have stopped the car until they reached his lodge. If Gianna had been too frightened to keep her wits about her, to think and plan and act on the spur of the moment, she'd never have run when the opportunity had presented itself. Providence had smiled. On both of them.

"What do you say we get out of here?" he asked gently.

She managed a shaky smile. "Yes, please."

He put the car in gear and headed south toward the city at a far more circumspect speed than the trip north. "We should call Luc and let him know you're safe. I'm sure he's going out of his mind with worry."

"My cell is dead."

He fished his out of his pocket and handed it to her. She placed the call and spoke at length to her brother, making light of the experience, describing it as an unfortunate "mis-understanding." When she disconnected the call, Constantine shot her a sharp look, one she avoided.

"Why did you lie to him?"

She released an exhausted sigh. "You know why. If I told Luc what really happened, my brothers would take David apart limb by limb."

"That's going to happen, anyway."

"But—"

"Why the hell are you defending him?" Constantine nearly growled.

Tears threatened. "I'm not defending him. I am *not* defending him," she repeated. It took her a moment to gather herself. "Do you really think that if I went to the police it would help? I have no proof. It'll be my word against his. And the publicity—" Her voice broke and she swiveled to stare out the window. After a moment, she said, "I did wreck his Jag. You have no idea how much pleasure that gives me, knowing I did that much."

Well, hell. "How did you do that?"

"I crashed it into a tree."

"I thought you didn't drive."

"After my first driving experience, which consisted of smashing Luc's precious Ferrari, I don't. I haven't had the nerve." A tiny smile played at the corners of her mouth. "Thus, the tree with David's Jag."

"So, the two times you've ever driven a car—expensive cars, no less—you wrecked them both?"

"Two for two," she confirmed.

Huh. He made a mental note to check his insurance coverage…and up it. "How did you even manage to get behind the wheel?"

"I waited until he got out to pump the gas, then locked the doors, climbed behind the wheel and took off. Granted, it was a short trip. But I got far enough away that I could escape into the woods before he caught up with me."

Constantine couldn't help himself. He laughed. "You never cease to amaze me."

"To be honest, I'd have preferred a much less amazing night" was her heartfelt reply.

"That makes two of us." To his relief, she'd stopped shivering. "Put your seat back and go to sleep. You'll feel better."

For some reason, his suggestion made her flinch. "If you don't mind, I think I'd like to stay awake."

"Of course I don't mind."

"I just..." She shuddered. "I can't go to sleep. Not after..."

He caught an undercurrent of emotion ripping through her voice—fear—and his hands clenched around the steering wheel. No matter what it took or how long the wait, he would see to it that d'Angelo suffered for his actions. That he never had the opportunity to take advantage of another woman. Constantine hadn't been in a position to ensure it last time. This time he had all the resources he needed. Plus, he had the Dante family behind him. Or he would once they heard his version of what transpired this evening.

She spoke again after a brief silence. "There's something that keeps nagging me about this whole thing."

"Really? There's quite a bit about it that's nagging me," Constantine retorted.

"Why would David want to force me to the altar?"

That stopped him and Constantine turned her question over in his mind, frowning. "What do you mean?"

"He said that he was..." Again the hesitation. "He was compromising me in order to force me into marriage. But I can't figure out why he'd want to do that. What's in it for him?"

Constantine's frown cleared. "That's easy enough. I suspect it has to do with money."

Gianna shook her head. "That can't be it. David has money coming out of his ears."

"Don't be so sure. According to my father, there have been rumors circulating about the source of all that money."

"You're kidding. What sort of rumors?"

"I don't have all the details. But I intend to find out."

"Funny."

Constantine shot her a swift look. "You find something amusing in all this?"

She yawned. "Just that if you're right, David only wanted to marry me because I have money." Her eyes fluttered closed. "And that's the only reason you wouldn't."

"Not the only reason, *piccola*," he said softly.

But despite her decision to remain awake, she'd fallen asleep, fully relaxing for the first time. She remained curled in a ball, snuggled deep into the leather seat. Even with the shallow cuts marring her long legs, they were sleek and shapely beneath the trailing tails of his tux jacket. She'd slicked her damp hair behind her ears, but the humidity caused it to escape in a riot of soft brown and gold curls, framing her scratched face. She looked pale, drawn and exhausted.

And Constantine had never seen a more beautiful sight.

Another few miles down the road she jerked awake with a whimpered cry, bolting upright in her seat. "You're fine," he soothed. "You're safe."

"Sorry, sorry." She shot a hand through her tousled hair. "Did I fall asleep?"

"Do *not* apologize." He struggled to temper the grittiness in his voice with only limited success. Just what she needed. Another male scaring the hell out of her. "Yes, you fell asleep."

"I didn't mean to do that."

"You probably needed it." And she did, despite her residual fear. "We're just coming into the city. I'll have you home in a few more minutes."

She didn't reply, but intense relief speared across her face.

A short time later, Constantine pulled up outside of her row house. Gianna started to open the car door and he stopped her. "Will my Porsche fit in your garage or do you use the space for storage?"

She stared at him blankly. "My garage?"

"I'm staying the night and I don't want to spend the next several hours searching for a legal place to park," he explained patiently. "Will my car fit in your garage?"

He could see the progression of her thoughts written in her expression. Confusion. Dawning comprehension. Stubborn refusal. "That's not necessary."

"D'Angelo is still out there. I'm assuming he was seriously ticked off when he left you. I'm not going to take the chance that he may come by while you're sleeping off the last of whatever he gave you. Your choices are…" He held up a finger. "One. We go to the emergency room and get you checked out. At the very least, they should look at the cuts on your feet."

She instantly shook her head. "There's no need. I'm fine. Like I told you, I didn't get a full dose of the drug."

He refused to let her get away with the lie. "What you mean is… If you tell the doctors what happened, they'll call the police and you want to avoid that particular complication."

She sighed. "Something like that."

"Exactly like that. Fair warning, if those cuts are bad you're going to the emergency room whether you want to or not." He held up a second finger. "Two. I take you to the relative of your choice and you spend the night there."

She immediately shook her head. "You know what will happen if I do."

Yes, he did. "All hell will break loose and—surprise, surprise—they'll insist on calling the police."

"Or, more likely they'll want to take matters into their own hands. I can't risk that happening."

That was going to happen anyway. She just didn't realize it. Yet. He held up another finger. "Three. I come in and spend the night. Someone needs to be available in case you suddenly get sick and need to go to the emergency room.

Or if d'Angelo follows you here, you need someone who can take him down. That would be me, in case you were wondering."

She blew out a sigh. "I sort of figured out that part."

"I'm glad to hear it. So." He lifted an eyebrow. "Which option do you choose?"

"Three," she conceded grudgingly. She fished through her purse and pulled out a key. "There's an automatic garage door opener, but I don't have the controller since I never use it."

Constantine took the key she'd given him and opened the door manually. A short minute later, he had the car parked in the miniscule garage. After locking up, he led the way, making a swift search of her neat-as-a-pin home, one she'd thoroughly stamped with her unique personality.

The colors she'd chosen were as vivid as she was. Strong, bright blues and greens with splashes of lavender, all accented with crisp white trim. She'd blended antiques with contemporary furniture and pulled it off brilliantly. She definitely had an eye for color and balance. If she ever tired of working for Dantes, he could use her in his restoration firm.

He checked each and every room, including closets and beneath furniture. Anyplace a man might hide. He didn't expect to find anyone. The house had an undeniable air of emptiness, but he refused to take any chances with Gianna's safety.

"Do you really think David is hiding under the bed in my guest room waiting to attack me?" she asked near the end of his search, exasperation clear in her voice.

Even after the events of that evening, she still didn't get it. "When it comes to d'Angelo, anything is possible." He could hear the Italian in his voice deepening, thickening.

"Since your safety is paramount, I search the house. The entire house."

She instantly caved. "You're right. Of course you're right."

She trailed behind him, a distracting sight in his shirt and tails. The outfit hung on her slender frame, giving her a vulnerable, disheveled appearance that stirred his most primal protective instincts. She didn't look well, her face even paler than before. Without a word, he headed for her bedroom.

"Do you want a shower before bed?" he asked. "You'd probably feel better. Then I want to take a look at your feet and make sure you don't need stitches."

She pulled a leaf from her hair and wrinkled her nose at it. "My feet are fine. If any of the cuts were bad enough to require stitches I wouldn't be able to walk. That said, I definitely want a shower. I'm filthy and I think I brought half the forest home with me." She folded her arms across her chest, the ends of his tux dribbling off her fingertips. "But I don't want to go to bed."

He fought back a smile. She sounded like a recalcitrant five-year-old. "You're afraid to go to sleep. I understand. But I swear to you, Gianna, I'll keep you safe."

Tears filled her eyes and she stepped into his waiting arms. "It was so close, Constantine."

"Not as close as you might think," he lied, holding her tight against him. She was safe, he reminded himself. And relatively unharmed. "I'd tracked you as far as Calistoga and wasn't too far behind you. I knew d'Angelo owned a lodge near there, and my father was working to get the exact address."

She stilled. "You called Vittorio? He knows what happened?"

"I would have called His Holiness, himself, if I thought

he could have given me d'Angelo's address. Fortunately my father has excellent connections. One way or the other, I would have reached you in time."

Her chin quivered, her jade-green eyes overflowing as emotion set in. "Thank you."

"You're welcome." He released her, nudging her in the direction of the bathroom. "Try not to fall asleep in there, okay?"

She didn't linger. Ten minutes later she emerged, pink-cheeked and smelling subtly of herbs and flowers. She'd wrapped herself in a thick, velour robe. After checking her feet and finding only minor cuts and bruises, he turned down the bed while she stripped off the robe and climbed between the sheets. He lifted an eyebrow at the thigh-length cotton shift she wore beneath. With the light behind her, it was practically transparent. He kept his eyes off the press of feminine curves thrusting against the thin cotton, all the while fighting to maintain an ironclad hold on his libido.

"I think I'd like to leave the light on," she said, pulling the covers up to her chin.

"That's fine." He indicated a heavily cushioned chaise lounge chair covered in antique-rose velvet. "I'll be right here if you need me."

She frowned. "Don't be ridiculous, Constantine. You'll never get to sleep on that. It's way too small. Use the guest room."

"I'm staying right here." His voice brooked no opposition. He held up his hand when she would have argued. "You'll sleep better, *piccola,* having someone close by. And I'll sleep better having you where I can keep watch over you."

She examined the chair again, then him. "Are you sure?"

"Positive. Knowing that all I have to do is open my eyes and see you, safe and sound, will put me right out."

Tears filled her eyes again. "Thank you, Constantine," she said in a husky voice. "You have no idea—" She broke off and shook her head.

"I think I do." He approached and, using the utmost restraint, kissed her forehead. "Try to sleep."

She did, which came as a huge relief to Constantine. He waited until she was deeply unconscious, then slipped from the room and placed a call. When he finished, he returned to the bedroom. He paused at the foot of the bed, gazing at Gianna, and made a silent vow.

No matter what it took, he'd keep this woman safe from harm. He knew that part of the drive to protect came from this peculiar Inferno which connected them, the link so strong it didn't give him any other option. But it went much deeper than that. When she hurt, he hurt. When she hungered, he felt the need to feed her. What gave her joy, he was driven to provide for her. Her wants and his were so tightly bound that they were almost indistinguishable.

Even as he acknowledged those binds, they chafed, stealing his independence. He hadn't asked for this connection. And though he wanted Gianna, he didn't want to be controlled by her. It felt unnatural.

Well, that would change soon enough.

What David d'Angelo had set out to accomplish would happen, just with a different man. Instead of d'Angelo being honor-bound to take Gianna as his bride, Constantine would be the one. Oh, his bride-to-be wouldn't be pleased with his ruthlessness. But she hadn't given him any other choice. She'd inflicted him with The Inferno, infecting him with its fever and desperation. Then she'd had the unmitigated gall to change her mind and allow d'Angelo to come within inches of harming her.

Now she'd deal with the consequences. Her family would take care of the problem from this point forward, sweep them up in an unbreakable net of demand and propriety and cart them to the altar—willingly or not.

And then he would be in charge of The Inferno. He would find a way to douse the fire. At the very least, he'd wield the flames instead of suffering from the constant burn of its touch.

Gianna woke a few hours later with a panicked gasp, swimming to the surface from a terrifying nightmare landscape filled with monsters and screaming tires and bogs of quicksand that sucked at her legs and prevented her from fleeing from some unseen threat. Before she'd shuddered out a single breath, Constantine joined her on the bed, pulling her into the warm protection of his embrace.

"Easy now," came his steadying voice. "You're safe. He can't get to you."

His mouth drifted across the top of her head in the lightest of caresses. Reassuring. Passionless. Compassionate. Although she appreciated the reassurance and compassion, she didn't want passionless. She wanted to feel something other than fear. She curled tight against his bare chest. His warmth surrounded her, easing her bone-deep chill, while the calm, steady beat of his heart soothed her.

"Nightmare," she explained through chattering teeth. "Bad."

"I gathered." She thought he might have feathered another kiss across the top of her head, though she couldn't be certain. But it gave her hope. "It's not real," he soothed.

"I know. At least, part of me knows. The other part—"

She broke off with a shrug. Unable to help herself she pressed closer, sliding her arms around his waist and clinging. To her relief, he didn't push her away, though she sensed a serious internal debate raging. Not that she cared. She was scared and alone, and tired of being both. It wasn't a case of "any port in a storm." She needed Constantine. Only Constantine.

"Stay with me," she whispered.

He swore in Italian, a soft, intently masculine comment that under other circumstances would have made her laugh. "Gianna, this is dangerous."

"I'm not asking you to make love to me."

"I may not be able to help myself."

"You're not David."

He stiffened. "No, I'm definitely not d'Angelo. But I'm still a man. You're vulnerable right now. It's late and I'm tired. And you're not wearing many clothes. For that matter, neither am I." He adopted a reasonable tone. "Admit it, Gianna. Given our reaction to each other, it's a volatile combination."

True. That didn't change anything. "I swear I won't take advantage of you." To her relief, he released a snort of laughter. "But right now I need someone to hold me."

He sighed. "I should have taken you to your parents."

"Probably," she conceded. "Since you didn't, you're stuck with me."

He hesitated, then nodded. "Fine. Lie down."

She did as he requested. To her surprise, he jerked the covers up to her chin so she was completely cocooned, then slid an arm around her while he remained on top of the sheet and blanket.

"Seriously?" she asked.

"Seriously." The metaphorical—or maybe not so metaphorical—immovable object. "Now go to sleep. It'll be daylight in another few hours."

"Would you do one more thing for me?"

"Are you hungry? Thirsty?"

"No." She leaned into him, doing her best to be an

irresistible force. In her case, definitely not a metaphorical one. "Would you kiss me good-night?"

"You are determined to test the limits of my self-control." He spoke in Italian, a dead giveaway.

"Would you rather David was the last man to have kissed me?"

It was the wrong thing to say. Absolutely. Totally. The. Wrong. Thing.

The soft light from the bedside table cut across the rigid lines of his face, striking off the hard planes and sinking into the harsh angles. He gazed down at her, his eyes black crystals of barely suppressed emotion, anger in the foreground, hot desire glittering behind. He said something else in Italian, the words fighting each other. Biting words that came too fast for her to catch. Not that she needed to understand each and every word. The underlying message came through loud and clear.

Constantine wasn't a man to taunt.

He moved so fast she never saw it coming, stripping away the covers and baring her to his gaze. He took his time, looking his fill. The cotton shift she wore provided next to no protection, the fabric so sheer it revealed more than it concealed, hugging her feminine curves and misting his view just enough to make it all the more enticing.

He took his time, studying the generous curve of her breasts, the nipples tight coral peaks thrusting against the cotton and betraying the extent of her hunger. He noticed. Of course he noticed. How could he not? His gaze wandered lower, across her belly which quivered in reaction. Lower still. To the soft brown shadow at the apex of her thighs.

He lifted his hand and for a split second she thought he'd touch her. That he'd rip off her nightshift the way he'd ripped off her gown in the gas station parking lot. Her breath caught and held, waiting for that touch. It never came. Instead his hand hovered a scant inch above her, before following the same path as his gaze. He splayed his fingers, heat pouring from his palm and burning through her shift. Not once did he touch her, though her body reacted as though he had.

She waited for the acrid wash of fear to sweep over her. But it never did. Hunger and want—those existed without question. So did a keen edge of pleasure. Her breasts felt painfully full, lush and acutely sensitive. A heaviness invaded the very core of her, loosening and softening and ripening. A woman preparing for the possession of her mate.

One emotion was lacking.

"No fear," she murmured in relief. "None at all."

He froze. "This is a mistake."

She smiled. Hell, she beamed. She was just so thankful that Constantine could look at her with such intense desire without it sparking flashes of David. "A lovely mistake." She caught his hand in hers, guiding it to her body. "Touch me," she whispered. "Touch me the way a man is meant to touch a woman."

And then he did. As though unable to help himself, he trailed a finger from the juncture between neck and shoulder downward over the slope of her breast. Her nipples pressed against the cotton, so tight she almost couldn't bear it. He hooked a finger in the neckline of her shift and nudged it down just enough to expose them. Gently, sweetly, he took the first into his mouth and caressed it with tongue and teeth. A cry caught in the back of her throat, a keening sound of intense pleasure. Then he turned his attention to the other.

Her head tipped back and the breath shuddered from her lungs, his name escaping on a moan of delight. She slid her fingers deep into the heavy waves of his hair and held him close. "How can this be a mistake?"

He lifted away from her, ignoring her attempts to pull him back into her embrace. Then he waited, allowing the tension to build. Stillness settled over them both, their breath harsh in the silence of the night. Then, slowly, oh, so slowly, he cupped her head. Little by little he leaned in until their lips were no more than a breath apart.

Then he erased even that bit of space. He kissed her, eradicating all memory of everything and everyone who'd gone before. He took his time, the kiss slow and potent and deliciously thorough. She responded, helpless to resist. And why should she? She wanted this as much as he did. Maybe even more. She'd waited for months. Nearly two full years. She refused to wait another minute.

"Make love to me," she urged.

To her distress, he shook his head. "That's not going to happen, Gianna."

"But—"

He stopped her with another kiss that had every thought seeping from her head except what he was doing to her and how he did it. "D'Angelo drugged you tonight," he murmured between leisurely, sampling tastes. "It's likely that you're still feeling the effects."

"I'm not. I swear I'm not."

"You were drugged, attacked. Terrorized. Still in shock." She wished she could deny his catalog of events, but she couldn't. "And you just woke from a nasty nightmare. That makes you vulnerable, and I don't take advantage of vulnerable women."

"Even if the vulnerable woman in question says it's okay? Because that's what I'm saying. Okay. Go right ahead. I'm all yours." He was killing her. "Please, Constantine."

"Would you have me compromise my sense of honor?" he countered.

She closed her eyes. "Considering how I feel right now? Yes, yes I would." An inner debate raged, one that filled her with frustration. Damn it, she'd been a Dante for too long, knew all too well the importance of honor. She continued to debate for another full minute while he waited her out. Then she caved. "When you put it like that…"

"There's no other way *to* put it."

She couldn't argue, not about an issue as serious as a man's honor. It wasn't something the Dantes took lightly, any more than the Romanos. "Will you still hold me?"

"That I can do." He covered her again and settled in beside her. Pulling her into his arms, he just held her. "Better?"

"Frustrating."

He chuckled. "That makes two of us." He kissed her with unmistakable finality. She could still feel the edge of desire, banked, but white-hot around the edges. "Go back to sleep. And this time, try not to press my buttons."

She yawned. "Push your buttons. And I wasn't."

"No? I seem to remember you throwing David in my face. You didn't just press my button. Or even push it. You kicked it with those spiked heels you love to wear."

"Maybe." Honesty forced her to concede, "Okay, definitely."

"Don't do it again. Not with d'Angelo."

She looked at him curiously. "David said the two of you had a history."

Tension speared across the muscles in Constantine's jaw. "Is that what he called it?"

"What would you call it?"

"Funny. I'd have said you were in a better position to answer that question."

She stiffened. "I don't understand. What do you mean?"

"How would you describe what he attempted to do tonight?"

She didn't want to say the word. Couldn't. It would make it too real. She moistened her lips. "After you rescued me… You said he'd done this before. I'd forgotten until just now."

"The drug will do that to you."

"Who else did he drug? Who did he do this to before me?"

"Ariana."

Five

Gianna bolted upright in bed. "Oh, no. Oh, Constantine, no. Not Ariana."

"It's all right. I found her—"

She burst into tears. "How could it be all right? He… he…" She fought to get the words out. "She would have been terrified when she returned from Italy and saw me with him. I'd never have gone out with him if I'd known. And I'd have made him pay for hurting her. I swear I would have. Somehow. Someway."

"Calm down, Gianna." Constantine lifted onto his elbow and smoothed her hair back from her face. "She wouldn't have been terrified when she saw the two of you together for one simple reason. Unlike you, she consumed all of the drug d'Angelo gave her. She has no memory of the events of that night. Not being drugged. Not of how close she came to disaster. Not of my arriving in time to save her. I saw no reason to tell her the sordid details then, or mention it since. She was barely seventeen."

"Seventeen?" Tears slipped down Gianna's cheeks. "So, he didn't…?" She couldn't say the word.

"No. I got there in time. She barely even remembers d'Angelo."

Something else clicked. David's opening salvo at the Midsummer Night's gala when he'd first spoken to Constantine. "That's what he meant about your timing."

Constantine nodded. "I wasn't in a position to make him pay with Ariana. But I swear to you, he won't get away with it again."

"What happened? To Ariana, I mean?"

"Come." He eased her back into his arms and she surrendered to the embrace, using his warmth to comfort her distress. "I'll tell you the story if you promise to go to sleep afterward."

"I promise." Honesty forced her to add, "If I can."

"You have to understand something that is very uncomfortable for me to speak of."

He'd switched to Italian again, his voice stiff with pride and something else. Pain? "Something from your past?" she hazarded a guess.

"It has to do with the manner in which I was raised."

"Old Italian aristocracy?"

"That's at the root of it, yes. The Romanos have the name, but not the money to go with it. We own the land and the palazzo, but have no way to maintain it. Because it has been in our family for so many generations, it would be sacrilege to sell. So we struggle over money."

"Why not get a job?"

Constantine laughed without humor. "You and I think alike. Unfortunately my father considered this beneath him. We are only recently poor. My grandfather made some unfortunate investments and my father finished the job with other bad choices. More than anything, I wished to start up my own business. But there was no capital. No seed money. I attended Oxford. My grandmother—she wrote the Mrs. Pennywinkle children's books before Ariana took over. You are familiar with Mrs. Pennywinkle?"

"Sure. I loved her stories as a child." They were beautifully illustrated tales, all about a china doll named Nancy who passed from needy child to needy child. With each subsequent owner came exciting adventures and heartrending problems for whichever youngster came into possession of the doll. By the end of the book, Nancy had helped resolve the child's problems and magically moved on to the next boy or girl in need. "I even owned a Nancy doll. It was one of my favorite toys growing up."

"My grandmother, Penelope, paid for my education with the royalty money she earned from them. But I could not take her money to start up my business. It would have been—"

"Dishonorable?"

He slanted her a swift, hard look. "Are you making fun of me?"

"Not even a little," she instantly denied. "I'm in total sympathy with you. Our family also went through a period of financial difficulty."

"I vaguely remember Babbo telling me about that. It involved your uncle Dominic, didn't it?"

"Yes. He made some unwise investments, expanded into other areas of the business too fast, and nearly put Dantes out of business. Since my father never handled any of the financial aspects of the business, he had no idea how to turn things around. Like Luc, he dealt with the security end of things. So, after Uncle Dominic's death, Sev stepped in and salvaged the business. It was a point of honor that he make up for his father's mismanagement. But it was touch and go there for a while and we had to sell off almost all of Dantes except for the main jewelry business. It took Sev years to buy back all we'd lost."

"Then you do understand." He hesitated. "This brings me to the d'Angelos."

She made the connection. "They're bankers. They were in a position to loan you money for Romano Restoration."

Darkness descended. "Yes. D'Angelo and I met at Oxford. I had the name. He had the money. I didn't think anything of it. We were…" He shrugged. "Friends. Or I thought we were. I didn't realize at the time that he deliberately set out to cultivate a friendship. He liked bragging about his close relationship with a Romano."

"I assume at some point he met Ariana."

"It happened on a vacation we took with the d'Angelos when Ariana was in her early teens." There was something in his voice when he said that, something unbearably painful and forbidding. Something he wasn't telling her. "At first, I didn't think anything of it. When I looked at my sister, I saw a child. D'Angelo saw a toy that he didn't yet own. And he needed to own all the toys."

She thought about David's Jag and Rolex and suite at the Ritz. "He still does."

"I'm not surprised." Constantine scrubbed a weary hand across his face. "At some point, d'Angelo made a comment about dating Ariana and I came on like the typical big brother. She was too young, the differences in their ages too great."

"I gather that didn't stop David."

"Not at all. If anything, it made him want her all the more."

"Because she was forbidden fruit."

"Yes. It caused a rift between us. I began to really look

at him, listen to him. When I did, I heard rumors about d'Angelo and women. Ugly rumors that perhaps not all the women were willing. I learned afterward that d'Angelo's father kept it all hushed up with huge payoffs."

Constantine trailed a finger along her arm. He did it in an absentminded manner, not really paying attention to his actions. The featherlight caress sent desire cascading through her and she shut her eyes, fighting to focus on the story instead of his touch.

"What happened then?" Gianna managed to ask.

"By this time we'd become somewhat estranged. But one day he came to me unexpectedly and offered to arrange an interview with his father. He said Aldo was extremely interested in financing my start-up restoration business. It surprised me. But hell, I'd talked about it for years. I thought perhaps d'Angelo extended the offer as an olive branch." He hesitated. His mouth compressed and he shook his head. "I'm deluding myself. I went along because I wanted the opportunity so badly—"

"Stop it, Constantine." She wouldn't allow him to shoulder so much of the blame. "David is responsible for his own choices, not you."

He didn't argue the point, but she didn't think she'd convinced him that he didn't bear some fault in what happened. "A time was set," he continued the narrative, "and I showed up in my best suit, prospectus in hand, my sales pitch polished. David should have been there, but I wasn't too surprised when he wasn't."

"Why not?"

"His family is—or maybe was—ridiculously wealthy. He didn't need to work and invented as many excuses as possible to avoid it. Still, as my former friend and considering he'd set up the interview—"

"You expected David to be there."

"Yes." Constantine closed his eyes, all emotion draining from his voice. For some reason the very lack of emotion made the telling that much worse. "At some point I asked where he was and Aldo gave this laugh."

"Oh, no."

"I knew then. Aldo realized he'd given the game away and told me to let it go. That he'd make it worth my while. That it was only a little fun between consenting adults."

"How many teeth did you knock out?"

A cold smile slashed across Constantine's mouth. "Only one. It took me forever to track down my former friend. I arrived just in time."

"Ariana doesn't remember any of this?"

"Nothing of that night, no. Despite my attempts to hush it up, she later found out that David and some of his friends took bets to see who'd be the first to have her. Fortunately, whoever told her the tale prettied up the details somewhat. She assumed that d'Angelo and his friends were trying to make her fall in love with one of them in order to relieve her of her virginity. She thinks it was because of her name and status."

"That's bad enough."

"True. But the actuality would have been far worse. He wanted her. But more than that, he wanted to hurt me. I could never have lived with myself if Ariana had found out that d'Angelo attempted to get back at me for ending our friendship by using her to make his point."

Gianna rested her hand on his arm, feeling his muscles clench beneath her fingers. "I think it was more than making a point. He may have money, but you have something he could never hope to possess. Honor. Ethics. And a name that stood for just that. I suspect David couldn't stand the idea of your possessing something he didn't. Something he could never possess." Constantine didn't respond and she sensed she'd missed something. It only took a moment's thought to key in on it. "It's not your fault. You must realize that by now. You couldn't have known David had an ulterior motive."

She'd guessed right. Fury tore through him. "That's just it, Gianna. I knew him. I should have known, or at least suspected what he might do. I'll never forgive myself for putting my own selfish interests ahead of my duty and responsibility to Ariana. If I hadn't been so desperate to gain financing for my business, I'd have guessed what d'Angelo was up to."

"You did figure out what David was up to. And you rescued Ariana, just like you rescued me." She pressed her fingertips to his mouth. "Before you say it, you're also not to blame for tonight. You had no way of knowing that he would act so fast. If it's anyone's fault, it's mine. I should have listened to my instincts…and to you."

He kissed her fingertips. Then he leaned in and kissed her. She surrendered to the embrace, helpless to resist. How could she have ever thought she'd someday feel this sort of desire for David? It either existed or it didn't.

It was like The Inferno. Some people melded, driven together by forces beyond their control. Others didn't. And even though she knew that Constantine wasn't the only man capable of sparking The Inferno, she'd never felt it with anyone else. Did it really matter that he didn't experience it the way she did? That for him, there'd been a glitch in the connection, enabling him to walk away from her? Couldn't she be happy with what he was willing to give her?

He deepened the kiss and she moaned in longing. Why couldn't he want her as much as she wanted him? As though to prove the point, he pulled back and brushed her hair behind her ear.

"Sleep now," he said.

"Yeah, right. I'm sure your bedtime story will put me right off."

"Try." A slow smile played at the corner of his mouth. "For the sake of my sanity, please try."

"Well, when you put it like that..."

She closed her eyes, if only to shut out the sight of him. And though she didn't think she'd sleep, the instant she snuggled against him, she went under.

A loud pounding woke Gianna the next morning. She bolted upright in bed, disoriented. Confusion battled with a sudden, overwhelming alarm, made worse by the empty indentation beside her.

"Constantine?" His name escaped, edged with panic.

"Right here."

At some point he'd left the bed and returned to the chaise. At the commotion emanating from below he stood, looking strong and rested despite all they'd been through the night before. His air of calm immediately relaxed her. He still wore the trousers from his tux, but hadn't bothered to don the shirt or jacket he'd loaned her the night before, possibly because she'd left them in a heap in the corner of the bathroom.

She vaguely recalled hearing him in the shower at some point in the early hours of the morning, though a dark shadow clung to his jaw indicating he hadn't borrowed a razor, and his hair fell across his brow in heavy, unruly waves. Despite that, his "morning after" look made him almost unbearably appealing.

He checked his watch. "Don't get up. I'll see who it is."

"What if it's David?"

He didn't hesitate. "Then he'll soon regret ever coming near you."

She despised the wave of fear that swept through her when she thought about David. She'd never experienced that before. Nor had she ever considered herself weak or vulnerable. He'd stolen her innate feeling of security and, for that alone, she'd never forgive him. As for the rest, she'd find some way to make him pay for drugging her, for attempting to assault her. Because there wasn't a doubt in her mind he would have done precisely that if she hadn't gotten away.

Determined not to surrender to cowardice, she tossed aside the covers and swept up her robe. She tied the sash around her waist in a quick, angry motion, then followed Constantine from the bedroom. He opened the front door just as she reached the foyer. To her horror, Primo stood there, his gaze moving from a half-dressed Constantine to Gianna in her bathrobe, bare feet and bed-head hair.

Uh-oh. This couldn't be good.

"May I come in?" Primo asked, excruciatingly polite.

Gianna thrust her hands through her hair in an effort to smooth the unruly curls. Not that it helped. It simply drew attention to the horror of it all. "Of course. We…I wasn't expecting you."

"This I can see."

"I'll start a pot of coffee," Constantine said, and disappeared in the direction of the kitchen.

She didn't know which was worse. The fact that he'd deserted her. Or the fact that—from her grandfather's perspective—he was familiar enough with her home to fix the coffee. Not that he was. But it certainly must seem that way to Primo. Warmth burned her cheeks and she avoided his gaze.

She trailed after Constantine like a caboose on a runaway train, helpless to prevent it from careening onward to its predetermined destination. She didn't have a hope in hell of preventing the coming disaster. Still, she was driven to try. "Just so you know, this isn't what it looks like," she said, in an attempt to divert the impending train wreck.

"It looks like Constantine has spent the night."

Gianna reddened. Sharp curve ahead! "Well, yes, he did. But not the way you mean."

"And which way is that, *chiacchierona?*" he asked gently.

"He…we…I—"

"Cream? Sugar?" Constantine interrupted.

Primo waved aside the offer. "Black. And strong enough to grow hair on my chest. At my age I could use some."

Gianna decided to give up on trying to explain the situation to her grandfather. There was no excuse Primo would find acceptable to explain Constantine spending the night with her. "Please don't take this the wrong way," she said to him. "But what are you doing here?"

"Constantine called me."

Shock froze her in place for an instant as her train jumped the track and completely derailed. She stood amidst the carnage and swung an outraged look in Constantine's direction. "You. Called. *Primo?*" Didn't he understand the ramifications of that?

Apparently he didn't because he appeared neither concerned, nor the least apologetic. "Yes. I explained about d'Angelo. It was my duty."

"Now that Constantine is your fiancé, it is only proper that he discuss such matters with me," her grandfather informed her. He turned his attention to Constantine. "I have made some phone calls. My understanding is that d'Angelo has left the country. The claim is urgent business."

"I'm not surprised."

Primo nodded in agreement. "Nor am I."

Gianna held up her hands. "Wait a minute. Wait just one

darn minute here. Could we forget about David? If he's left the country, he's not of immediate concern."

"He's of concern to me," Constantine retorted.

"I am also concerned," Primo added with a nod.

She refused to allow them to sidetrack her. Her gaze narrowed on her grandfather. "First, Constantine is *not* my fiancé. And second, it was my place to tell you about last night, not his. I'm not some delicate piece of china to be placed on a shelf while the men take care of business. I'm a woman in charge of her own destiny."

Primo gestured toward Gianna's mug. "More sugar," he instructed Constantine. "And for the sake of your marriage, I warn you to avoid conversation with our Gianna until after she has had a full cup of sweet coffee. Better if it is two."

She gritted her teeth to keep from saying something she'd regret. "Primo—"

"*Ascoltare me,* Gianna Marie Fiorella."

"Little flower?" Constantine murmured, his eyes filled with laughter. "Somehow I never thought of you that way."

She shot him a smoldering look before returning her attention to Primo. "I'm listening."

Her grandfather's index finger thumped against the table. "In the eyes of your family, you are engaged to this man. He proposed to you last night in front of us all. And he has now spent the night with you."

"But we didn't—"

"He was in your bed?"

Color burned across her cheekbones. "Primo," she muttered.

"I'll take that as a yes." He nodded as though that sealed the deal and drank a long swallow of coffee. "I will speak to the priest and discuss dates while you and your mother attend to such matters as the dress and flowers. Your babbo will have a conversation with Constantine about his duties as a husband. Are we clear on this matter?"

She waited a split second to see if Constantine planned to say something helpful. Anything. Apparently he didn't, since he simply stretched out his long legs and buried his smile in the steam rising from his coffee mug. Gianna shot to her feet, tightening the belt of her robe with a swift jerk that nearly cut off her circulation.

Fine. She'd just claimed she was a woman in charge of her own destiny. Time to prove it. "I understand why you think we should marry, Primo. But you can't force me to the altar." She glared at Constantine. "None of you can. I'm not Luc and Téa to be threatened into a marriage I don't want."

"Who says you don't want it?" Constantine spoke up for the first time. "You know perfectly well this is where our relationship has been heading. There was never any doubt about that."

"*What* relationship?" she shot back. "We felt a few sparks. Exchanged a few kisses. But we don't know anything about each other. Certainly not enough for marriage."

"You have felt The Inferno with this man?" Primo broke into the conversation.

She'd never been able to lie to her grandfather. She doubted she'd be able to this time, either. She came as close as she could manage. "Maybe."

Constantine held out his right hand, palm up. "Definitely. We felt it the first time we touched." At Primo's lifted brow, he added, "Ariana's wedding."

"So many months ago?" her grandfather marveled. "And you have not acted in all this time? How is this possible?"

Gianna stabbed a finger in Constantine's direction. "My point exactly. How can it be The Inferno? If it were, he never could have stayed away. Certainly not this long."

A hint of anger sparked in Constantine's gaze and he slowly climbed to his feet, towering over her. "You know damn well why I stayed away." It was a darn good thing she could speak Italian considering he used it every time he got angry. Which, it would seem, was often. "I had no choice."

"You did have a choice. You *chose* to stay away," she retorted, folding her arms across her chest. She didn't care if it made her look defensive. She felt defensive.

"Chose?" Anger flashed, caught fire. "I had nothing to offer but my name."

"That would have been more than enough for me," she retorted.

"It would have dishonored me to live off my wife's money and provide nothing in return," he shot back. "For the past nineteen months I have worked day and night to build a business. And I succeeded. I succeeded well enough to move here. Did I ask you to come to me in Italy? No. Because I know how much your family means to you. Instead I opened my business in San Francisco so we would have each other *and* your family. And what do you tell me when I arrive?" Fury ripped through his voice. "You tell me you've moved on. *Moved on!*"

"It had been nearly two years," she protested. "Was I supposed to wait forever?"

He kept going as though she'd never interrupted. "You had moved on to that bastard d'Angelo. A man without scruples, without honor. A man who tried to drug you in order to force you into marriage."

"If he'd succeeded—" and just the thought had her breaking out in a cold sweat "—I would have told him the same thing I'm telling you. I won't be forced into marriage. Not by anyone, for any reason."

"I don't understand. If you don't want marriage, then

what the hell *do* you want from me, Gianna?" Constantine demanded. "Why am I here? Or have these past nineteen months been a waste of my time?"

Good question. She planted her hands on her hips and spared her grandfather a swift glance. He continued to drink his coffee, watching the drama unfolding with an expression of utter delight. Honestly. There were times her family drove her crazy. She looked at Constantine uncertainly. "Are you interested in marriage?"

He swore. "Why do you think I returned? Why do you think I'm listening to this craziness instead of carting you off to bed and spending the next week compromising you so thoroughly you'll have no choice but to marry me?"

Color darkened her cheeks. This time she didn't dare look at her grandfather, though she heard his soft, choked laughter. She held up her hands. "Enough, already. If you're serious about a relationship, then you'll have to go about it the normal way. The old-fashioned way."

That stopped him. "What are you talking about?"

Exasperated, she said, "I'm talking about dating, Constantine. I'm talking about going out to dinner and getting to know each other. Learning each other's likes and dislikes. Figuring out whether or not we're actually compatible." She shoved her palm in his direction and shook it at him. "This isn't any guarantee of happiness. I happen to know that for a fact."

Silence reigned at the end of her tirade.

"Exactly how do you know this for a fact, *chiacchierona?*" Primo asked, the question dropping into the abrupt silence.

Oh, no. She refused to go there. Refused to share the secret she'd kept since her thirteenth birthday. Her entire family believed implicitly in The Inferno, believed that it was permanent and everlasting. No way would she be the one to disabuse them of a legacy they celebrated and cherished.

She folded her arms across her chest and—for once in her life—closed her mouth and kept it closed.

To her profound relief, Constantine inadvertently came to her rescue. "Gianna has a point," he offered, albeit reluctantly. "Even though we've known each other for more than a year and a half, we've only been together for a handful of days."

"What do you suggest?" Primo asked.

"Time," Gianna immediately replied. "Time for the two of us to become better acquainted. To look before we leap."

Primo didn't want to agree, she could see it in the brilliant gold of his eyes. After a moment's reflection, he nodded, also reluctantly. "Very well. I will say nothing of what I have learned here this morning while I give you this time." He fixed Gianna with a cool, pointed stare. "One month, *chiacchierona*. After that you marry, willing or not, even if I have to carry you down the aisle, myself."

Six

The instant Primo left, Gianna retreated upstairs, no doubt to change. Constantine followed. He wasn't about to give her the opportunity to fortify her barricades or find a loophole buried within Primo's ultimatum.

"I need to change," she informed him the instant he entered her bedroom.

He made himself comfortable on her chaise lounge. "I'm not stopping you."

She turned on him, planting her hands on her hips. "What is it with you? Last night I practically threw myself at you and you wanted nothing to do with me. This morning you won't give me an inch to breathe."

"You have an inch." He eyeballed the distance between them. "By my calculation, you have quite a few inches."

"You know what I mean."

She must have realized he had no intention of leaving. With a sigh of irritation, she spun on her heel and crossed to her closet, flinging open the door and disappearing inside. Curious, he followed.

"Madre di Dio," he murmured faintly.

"I don't want to hear a word about it," she retorted, her back to him.

He thought he caught a defensive edge in her voice. "Just out of curiosity, how many pairs of shoes do you own?" he asked.

She turned, clutching a pair of heels. "Not enough." She glanced at the huge rack of tidily shelved shoes which covered every spectrum of the rainbow. "Besides, they're not all mine. Some of them are Francesca's. We discovered a while back that we wear identical sizes."

He folded his arms across his chest. "Should I assume that if some of these are hers, she has some of yours?"

She waffled for a second, before conceding, "Maybe."

Oh, yeah. Definitely defensive. He examined the closet and shook his head. "What did you do, convert an adjoining bedroom into a closet?"

The blush sweeping across her elegant cheekbones gave him the answer. "Not that it's any of your business," she muttered.

"It will be when we marry."

She held up a hand. "Okay, stop right there. There is no 'when.' There is only a very shaky 'maybe.'"

He crowded her against a row of silk business suits. "You heard Primo. You have one month of 'maybe' and then it's a lifetime of 'when.'"

A deeply feminine confusion crept across her face. "Why are you going along with this? It's ridiculous."

He fisted his hands around the lapels of her robe and drew her to him. "You started this, Gianna, when you decided to infect me with The Inferno. You can't blame me if I finish it. What choice did you leave me?"

Her eyebrows shot up. "Infect?"

He gave it to her straight. "Sometimes it feels like that, particularly since I had no choice in the matter."

"It wasn't deliberate," she insisted. "It's not like I can control it. It just happens."

Well, at least all the Dantes were telling identical stories. "Your brothers said the same thing. I'm not sure I believe them." He watched her closely. "Did you Inferno d'Angelo?"

She shook her head. "Absolutely not."

"And yet, you continued to go out with him."

Her chin shot to a combative angle. "Maybe The Inferno is smarter than I am."

"Maybe it's smarter than both of us."

He reeled her in by the lapel of her robe. They stood shoe-to-bare-toe for an endless moment. Unable to resist, he slanted his mouth over hers and slammed them both into a whirlwind of desire. He still wanted her with a desperation every bit as fierce as when they'd first met. It hadn't diminished. Not over time. Not over distance. And definitely not with her winding her arms around his neck and surrendering herself unconditionally to the embrace. He heard the high heels she held hit the carpeted floor one after the other.

Want exploded between them, hot and heavy. More than anything he wished he could sweep her into his arms, carry her back to bed and make love to her for the rest of the weekend. If he did, it would force her to commit. Her family wouldn't give her any other option.

But then, he'd be no better than David.

Her lips parted beneath his and she made a low, hungry sound that threatened to steal every last vestige of his self-control. He yanked at the knot holding her robe together. Stripping away the binding, he slid his hands beneath the

heavy velour and over her shoulders. The robe dropped at
their feet, leaving her standing there in nothing but the thin
cotton shift she'd worn to bed.

"I want you," he said between fierce, biting kisses. "It
eats at me, never going away. Never easing."

"I know, I know. I'm sorry." Her arms tightened around
his neck and her head fell back, giving him greater access
to the long sweep of throat and shoulder. "It's the same for
me. I thought I could push it away or ignore it. But it's too
strong."

He hooked his fingers in the bodice of her shift in order
to slip it downward at the same instant she pulled back. The
thin cotton split, the sound of rending cloth harsh in the
confines of the closet. For a split second, they both froze.
The tattered remains of her nightie hung from her arms,
exposing her breasts and belly. He'd never seen anything
more beautiful in his life. He started to reach for her, to
touch her.

Then an image of David flashed through his mind. Dear
God, what had he been thinking? Swearing, he released
her and drew back. Without another word, he turned and
stepped from the confines of the closet.

"Get dressed." His voice escaped, low and guttural. "I'll
wait for you downstairs."

"Constantine—"

He refused to look back. That way led to disaster. "I'm
not David. I swear to you I'm not."

"I know that. Of course I know that." Concern mingled
with the frustrated hunger underscoring her words. "You
never could be. This was an accident."

He fought for control, fought with every ounce of strength
he possessed. "Which is why I'm going downstairs. Before
I do something I can't live with afterward."

"But—"

He spun around, pushed to the limit of his endurance. "What are you saying, Gianna? That it's acceptable to sleep with me, but I'm not someone you'll marry?"

She drew back in alarm, clutching the remnants of the shift around herself. "No! Of course I'm not saying that."

"Then what are you saying?"

She closed her eyes. "I want you," she confessed.

"And I want you. But I won't use you like some sort of one-night stand. How could I face Primo if I did that? How could I face your brothers?" He softened his tone. "Let's slow down and do what you suggested. Let's get to know each other better."

She nodded. "Okay."

His mouth curved upward in a dry smile. "As soon as you're dressed we'll leave, since clearly, Primo was right."

"As much as I hate to admit it, he usually is." She glanced at him hesitantly. "And after we leave? What then?"

"We'll get to know each other better."

Her brows shot up. "We're going out on a date?"

"Nothing so formal. I thought I'd show you around Romano Restoration. It took a lot of work to put everything in place without you being any the wiser. But I wished to surprise you by having it fully operational when I arrived. It helped that Ariana was in Italy so she didn't accidentally let it slip." He glanced down at himself and grimaced. "Going to Romano's will also give me the opportunity to change since my apartment is above the office complex."

He didn't dare remain in her bedroom a moment longer. He retreated to the kitchen where he leaned against the counter and drank a second cup of coffee. Maybe it would help him regain his self-control. Because if he planned on spending any time around Gianna, he'd need every bit of it. To his relief, she didn't keep him waiting for more than ten minutes.

She appeared downstairs wearing a casual pair of camel-colored slacks and a cream silk blouse. Not as attractive as the shift, but definitely safer. She'd secured her long, gold-streaked brown hair with a simple clip, the curls rioting down her back in joyous abandon. Her makeup was minimal, a touch of mascara and lipstick. She'd used a heavier hand with the blush, no doubt to hide the lingering paleness resulting from the events of the night before.

"I'm set," she announced brightly. Her gaze swept over him and a broad grin spread across her mouth. "My, aren't you looking...dissolute."

He glanced down at the dress shirt and tux jacket he'd rescued from her bathroom floor. He suspected the wrinkles might be permanent. "It's the new me. I call it my morning-after look. What do you think?"

"Very sexy." She actually sounded like she meant it.

He dumped the dregs of his coffee in the sink and rinsed the mug. Turning, he held out his hand. She didn't hesitate, but laced her fingers through his. Their palms melded and the burn from The Inferno flared to life, creating an undeniable heat, tightening the bond that had been created when they first met. Together they headed for the garage.

A few minutes later they were moving easily through the Sunday morning traffic toward Romano Restoration. He found a parking spot on the street, though he could have used the underground lot that serviced the building. This was just more convenient. They entered through the front door of the office complex and took the private elevator to the floors housing his company.

The doors parted and he gestured for her to take the lead. "Romano Restoration occupies the top four floors plus the building's penthouse suite," he explained. "The lower floors handle the business side of the company—accounting, contracts, that sort of thing. The upper two levels deal with customer relations, and the more creative aspects. like architectural and interior design."

A handful of lights sent a soft glow across the pearl-gray carpet, the cloudy morning leaving the remainder of the floor in silky shadow. Even in the dim light Constantine could see the questions building in Gianna's expression. He kept his distance, careful not to touch her. If he made that mistake again, he wouldn't be able to keep his hands off her. And from there it would be a short, sweet step to making her his in every sense of the word.

"It's very elegant," she offered without hesitation. "I love the openness and the understated elegance. It really showcases your business."

"Thanks." He gestured toward the corner office. "That one's mine."

She immediately crossed to look. "Mmm. Nice." She took a deep breath and swung to face him. He could see her steeling herself to say something, something he wouldn't like. "Just one question…"

He tempted fate by taking a step in her direction and cut straight through to the heart of the matter—the issue that had hovered between them like an angry, black cloud ever since his return. The issue that had driven her into d'Angelo's arms and come so close to ending in disaster.

"Why did I wait so long to return to you?" he asked. "Is that what you want to know?"

The question provoked an immediate reaction. The anguish filling her eyes threatened to snap his control. "You said you'd come back."

"And I did."

She shook her head, her mouth tightening. "It took too long. Far too long."

"I came as soon as I could," he argued.

"You never responded to my emails or phone calls. You actively discouraged our communicating and you flat-out refused to let me visit you in Italy." She stepped closer. "Couldn't we have done that much, at least?"

"I warned you about that. You agreed to it." Didn't she get it? "I didn't dare communicate or visit. I sure as hell couldn't have you with me in Italy. It would have distracted me and I'd never have gotten my business off the ground."

Gianna swept a hand through the air to indicate the plush area around them. "You had time for this, though. You had time to build Romano Restoration into a going concern."

"And why do you suppose I did that?" His accent thickened, just as his voice lowered. Darkened. "Why do you suppose I left you?"

"You said…" Her chin wobbled precariously for a brief instant before she clamped down on the helpless betrayal. "You claimed you weren't in a position to support a wife, but that would change. I understand that you wanted to bring more to our relationship than just a name. I really do get that."

"If you get it, then—"

She cut him off with a swift, chopping sweep of her hand. "You said soon." Anger warred with her tears. "Damn it, Constantine, it's been more than a year and a half. That isn't soon."

He couldn't argue her point. Each month he'd been away from her had felt like a year. "I know, sweetheart. I really do. It couldn't be helped. If there had been any other way—" he stopped her before she could speak "—any other way that I could have lived with, I'd have taken it. Please believe that."

"I just wanted to be with you. We could have found a way, either in Italy or here."

Gianna took another step in his direction, and Constantine clamped down on the clawing need to settle this once and for all in the most basic way possible. "As much as I wanted to be with you, I am not the sort of man who can live off the generosity of others. I watched my—" He broke off, switched gears more roughly than he'd have liked. "I've seen others live that way. But I won't. Ever. You do understand that, don't you?"

Her chin shot upward. "Do I understand that your pride is more important than anything else? You made that abundantly clear."

His anger broke free. "How do you think I spent the past year and a half? When Lazz and Ariana married, I'd just scraped together enough money to launch my company in Firenze. I worked day and night to build a small, modest business into something prosperous enough that I could afford to relocate here. Do you think such a thing happens overnight? Do you think it easy to acquire the contracts necessary to give me the start I needed over here? Do you think I could have accomplished such a thing in nineteen short months if I hadn't funneled every ounce of drive into my business?"

She moved closer still, everything about her impacting like a physical blow. Her sweet scent. Her generous curves. Her staggering beauty. "I could have worked with you," she whispered. "Helped you."

"Distracted me," he corrected. "If I'd had you waiting in my bed I never could have accomplished a tenth of what I've been able to, because I never would have been willing to leave your arms."

She smiled while tears of pain glistened in her green eyes. "Then we would have been poor. But at least we would have been together."

He shook his head. "You must allow me to be a man,

Gianna. You cannot control all things in this relationship."

She stiffened. "What do you mean by that?"

He stared broodingly at his open hand. It never ceased to amaze him that there wasn't a physical brand to mark the presence of this Inferno the Dantes generated. He ran his thumb across his palm in a habitual gesture. It didn't matter how hard he rubbed, he could never erase what had been done to him.

"You started this the first time you touched me," he informed her, holding out the hand she'd infected. "But I intend to finish it."

She stilled, the prey sensing the predator for the first time. "How?"

Daring fate, he closed the remaining distance between them and laced their fingers together, used the pull of The Inferno to draw her in. "You made me yours. You caught me. It doesn't matter whether you still want me or not. You initiated something that can't be stopped with a simple, 'I've changed my mind.' It's too late for that. You will be mine."

Her mouth firmed. "You're right. It is too late. I'm not someone you can simply pick up or set aside when the mood strikes you."

"Did it sound like I was setting you aside when I proposed marriage?"

"You mean at the gala? You consider *that* a proposal of marriage?" she dared to scoff. "That was simply your clever way of removing the competition."

"You mean David?"

"Of course I mean David."

Constantine shook his head. "You know damn well he's not my competitor and never could be."

"We know that *now,*" she corrected.

"It still would have been a simple matter to get rid of him without proposing in front of your entire family."

That gave her pause. "How?" she asked, genuinely curious.

He smiled tenderly. "Simply by being with you. David would have seen what everyone else sees whenever you and I are together. The very air around us is on the verge of bursting into flames whenever we touch. It isn't something either of us can hide."

"Try."

"Damn it, Gianna!" He shot a hand through his hair. "What the hell do you want from me?"

"Nothing. I don't want a thing from you."

"And you call me proud." Unable to help himself he swept her into his arms, praying his restraint wouldn't snap. She might end up a bit ruffled and undone, but if he could rein in his self-control, it wouldn't go any further than that. "I have spent endless months working night and day doing everything within my power to get back to you as quickly as possible."

Tears welled in her eyes again. Tears of regret. "It's been so long."

"I know, I know. I'm sorry." He feathered a kiss across her mouth. Unable to resist, he deepened it. "I came back as soon as I could, I swear."

She wound her arms around his neck. "I missed you so much. You have no idea how hurt I was by your silence. There were nights I'd lie in bed and ache for you."

He closed his eyes, her brutally frank words impacting like a blow. "I am so sorry. It was never my intention to hurt you. I have missed you beyond measure. But I am here now. Don't let pride keep us apart any longer."

Finally they had the privacy he needed to allow his hunger loose and he couldn't take advantage of it, not after the promise he'd made to Primo. Or at least, not until Gianna had fully committed to him by allowing him to put his ring on her finger. He settled for another lingering kiss, one filled with promise. Filled with longing. A kiss that teetered on the edge of losing control. Her lips parted and her hands slid from his neck to fork deep into his hair, anchoring him in place. Her moan spoke of endless hunger, urging him to take that next, irrevocable step.

"We can't," he murmured against her mouth. "We need to take our time and do this the right way."

To his relief, humor gleamed in her eyes in place of anger. "Do you think either of us is capable of that?"

"We better be or I'll have a tribe of Dantes willing and able to take me apart."

"I won't tell if you won't."

"Are you saying you're ready to wear my ring? To commit to marriage?" He didn't need to hear her response. "No, I can see from your expression that you're not." He snatched a swift kiss, then set her firmly from him. "Come on. Let's go upstairs. I need to change."

He escorted her to his apartment and left her in the great room with its expansive view of the city while he disappeared in the direction of his bedroom to shave and change. He joined her a short time later and found her studying the 3D replica he'd made of the Diamondt building for his presentation to the family, along with a thick book of drawings and samples that detailed the various aspects of the renovation.

"This is gorgeous," she marveled. "I love how you've melded their name with the updates to the building. Are these beveled diamond panes going to be made from leaded glass?"

"Good eye. There are a lot of leaded glass windows in the older homes in the Seattle area. Since this is an older building, it seemed to suit. We're also planning an immense stained-glass window for the foyer."

"I wish I could see it. I'll bet it's gorgeous."

"We're still negotiating the contract, so unless there's a problem, I won't be going up there until it's ready to be signed. But next time I do, you're welcome to accompany me." Maybe it would even be as his wife, though he was careful not to say as much.

"Thanks. I just might take you up on that."

She studied the building a final few minutes, a frown growing between her brows. That couldn't be good.

"What's wrong?" he asked.

"I'd almost forgotten. It wasn't until I saw this model and the Diamondt name that I remembered," she murmured. She shook her head in annoyance. "It would seem you were right. That drug David gave me affected me more than I realized."

Constantine studied her in growing concern. "What have you remembered?"

"Something David said about a diamond. I was going to ask you about it the minute I saw you." She shuddered. "I hadn't expected my escape to be quite so dramatic or frightening, or I would have thought of it sooner." Her gaze shifted from the model to him. "Have you ever heard of a diamond named Brimstone?"

Figlio di puttana! He fought to keep his voice even. "You might say that. Are you telling me David knows about Brimstone?"

She nodded. "He seemed to think I should, too. In fact, he seemed certain that you either had it in your possession and used it to finance Romano Restoration…or you were marrying me in order to get your hands on it." She tilted her head to one side, pinning him with her jade-green eyes.

"What is Brimstone, other than a fire diamond? And why is David d'Angelo trying so desperately to find it?"

"I suspect he's desperate to find it because it's worth somewhere in the neighborhood of ten million dollars." Constantine shrugged. "Perhaps more. And to answer your other question, Brimstone is the reason your cousin, Lazz, and my sister, Ariana, married, sight unseen. To be honest, it's a long story, and it occurs to me that we missed breakfast." He gestured in the direction of the kitchen. "Why don't we throw something together while I tell you about it."

"Now that you mention it, I'm starving." She followed him into the kitchen and took a moment to explore the generous area. Then she made herself at home, raiding the refrigerator. "Looks like you have ingredients for omelets. And maybe… Yup. Fruit salad?"

"Sounds disgustingly healthy."

She held up a package of bacon and a small wheel of cheese. "Better?"

"Much."

He pitched in to help cut and chop right alongside of her while bacon sizzled in the background. She gestured with her paring knife. "So, go on. You were going to explain about Brimstone. What is it? Where did it come from? David seemed to think it disappeared."

"He's right about that much. It did disappear." Constantine sliced into a peach bursting with juice. "As for the rest of the story… Let's see. Where should I start?"

She spared him a swift grin. "Where all good fairy tales start. Once upon a time…"

"Once upon a time," he repeated obediently. "There was an adorable Italian princess named Ariana, who was the apple of her father's eye. One day, when Princess Ariana was just six years old, a prince from a faraway land came to visit. His name was Lazzaro Dante."

"Seriously?"

"Seriously," Constantine confirmed. "Like all good fairy tales, the instant Ariana and Lazzaro touched, something odd happened between them."

Gianna dropped her knife on the counter and spun to face him, openmouthed. "Are you *kidding* me? They felt The Inferno? At such a young age? I didn't even realize that was possible."

"According to my father it was an incipient form of The Inferno. But, yes. Something sparked between them. For some reason, Dominic went insane when he realized what was happening and demanded that he and my father create a marriage contract. He wanted to ensure that my sister and your cousin were strongly encouraged to marry once they were older."

"No way."

He lifted an eyebrow. "No one ever told you any of this?"

Her eyes narrowed in displeasure. "Uh, no. And trust me, someone will pay for that oversight. All I heard was that they felt The Inferno when they met in Italy and decided to marry."

"Ah, but they never actually met in Italy. That was merely the story they put out to explain their whirlwind wedding so that your grandparents and my grandmother wouldn't find out about the contract and the true reason for their marriage. They needed to wed quickly in order to fulfill the terms of the contract."

Gianna picked up her knife again. "Okay, now you've lost me."

"There was a stipulation in the contract that the two must marry by Ariana's twenty-fifth birthday. When the contract came to light they negotiated the marriage by phone and email. They never even met until the actual wedding ceremony."

"But, that's...that's barbaric," she sputtered. "You're telling me they *had* to get married because of some contract your father and Uncle Dominic signed? Why didn't they just tear it up?"

He hesitated. "There may have been a small incentive that made it worthwhile for all parties involved."

Comprehension dawned, turning her eyes a brilliant shade of green. "Brimstone."

Constantine nodded. "Dominic knew about my family's financial issues. So, he offered to give my family half of Brimstone when Lazz and Ariana married."

"And if they didn't marry?"

"Brimstone would be thrown into the ocean and neither family would profit."

"Dear God," Gianna said faintly. "From barbaric to insane."

"You and I think alike, *piccola*. My father, who might be barbaric about some things, is not the least insane when it comes to financial opportunities. He jumped at the offer." Constantine couldn't prevent a hint of bitterness from crawling into his voice. "After all, what did he have to lose?"

"Oh, Constantine," she murmured.

He focused on decapitating strawberries, using a shade more force than strictly necessary. "Not to worry. As it turned out, we never did succeed in selling Ariana off. Though the two married, when the time came to turn over Brimstone, we discovered the diamond had gone missing."

Gianna smothered a laugh. "You'd have thought Lazz

and Ariana would make sure they knew where the diamond was before going to all the trouble of marrying."

Constantine's mouth tightened. "My father didn't inform Ariana of the disappearance until moments before she walked down the aisle. None of the Dantes realized it was missing. You see, Dominic made the mistake of leaving the diamond in my father's safekeeping. I gather it was part of the contract negotiations. As it turned out, Gran... My Grandmother Penelope—"

"The author of the Mrs. Pennywinkle books?"

"That's the one," he confirmed. "She overheard Babbo and Dominic talking about the contract. She was outraged by what they planned."

"As any normal person would be."

"Agreed."

Finished with the fruit salad, he started a pot of coffee, then leaned against the counter and watched Gianna sauté onions, spinach and mushrooms in olive oil. She poured the egg mixture she'd prepared into a pan and added the sautéed vegetables, topping them with a sprinkling of bacon.

"Anyway," he continued, "she stole Brimstone from my father and sewed it into a Nancy doll."

"I used to own a Mrs. Pennywinkle Nancy doll." Gianna snapped her fingers. "Maybe it's in my doll."

"Doubtful. She placed it into the original Nancy doll. The prototype. Ariana gave the doll away to a needy child shortly after she married Lazz."

Gianna's eyes widened. "Oh, dear. I gather she didn't know Brimstone was inside?"

"She didn't have a clue," Constantine confirmed. "By then, she and Lazz had fallen in love and decided to let fate determine where it ended up."

She smiled softly. "How romantic."

"Foolish," he corrected.

She shrugged. "A matter of opinion. Though I can understand your family's disappointment at the loss." A sudden thought occurred. "Just out of curiosity, would you have taken the money from the diamond to start up Romano Restoration?"

He hesitated. "I would have been seriously tempted. But in the end…" He shook his head. "It still would have been money I'd neither earned, nor deserved to profit from. So, no. If the Romanos had taken our share of Brimstone, it wouldn't have changed the past nineteen months, if that's what you're asking. We'd still have been apart."

"Damn it," she whispered.

"What?"

She frowned at him in open displeasure. "I'm beginning to see your point of view in all this. It's really annoying, too."

Amusement combined with a deep tenderness and affection. He loved her honesty and frankness. Loved that she didn't pull her punches, even on those occasions when they stood on opposite sides of the proverbial fence. It also pleased him that she considered the Brimstone contract as much an outrage as he did. He found it encouraging that they were so closely aligned on certain issues. Which reminded him…

"Let's not forget the original problem."

It only took her a moment to follow his line of thought and she winced. "David."

"Yes. Unfortunately d'Angelo has excellent inside information. He knows that Brimstone is missing."

"Not really. He only suspects."

"But once he decides neither family has it—"

"He's going to try to find it," Gianna finished his sentence for him. She expertly folded the omelets, then plated them, grating cheese over the top for the finishing touch. "I wonder if David knows Brimstone is sewn into one of the dolls. I'd hate to think he's running around gutting every poor Nancy doll he can find in a frantic search for the diamond."

Constantine grimaced, gathering the necessary items to set the table. "Hell, I hadn't considered that possibility."

"Maybe we should. And maybe we should find out where the diamond went before he does." She busied herself filling two bowls with fruit salad while she considered. "One final question."

"Just one?"

She chuckled. "For now." She helped him carry food from the kitchen into the dining room. "Why do you suppose Uncle Dominic went to such extremes to ensure Lazz and Ariana married? I mean, creating a marriage contract seems a bit out there. He couldn't be certain they were experiencing an early form of The Inferno. After all, they were only children."

Constantine shrugged. "Apparently Dominic decided that marrying someone who wasn't his Inferno bride guaranteed a disastrous marriage and he didn't want Lazz and Ariana to experience what he did with his wife, Laura."

Gianna stiffened. "No, that's not right. You or your father must have misunderstood."

He shook his head. "I don't think so. Weren't your aunt and uncle planning to divorce shortly before their deaths?"

"Yes, but the two definitely felt The Inferno for each other. Even though they were Inferno soul mates, it didn't work out for them." She set the plates on the table, avoiding his gaze. "That's what I've been trying to explain to you. Experiencing The Inferno isn't a guarantee of a happy marriage. That's why I want to make sure we're compatible before we take our relationship any further."

"Che cavolo!" He snagged her chin, forcing her to look at him, practically vibrating with fury. "Are you telling me

you've inflicted me with The Inferno, *but we may never know true happiness together?*"

Misery invaded her gaze. "Yes. That's exactly what I'm saying."

Seven

Gianna winced at the combination of outrage and anger that burned in Constantine's expression.

"Why would you do this to us?" he demanded in Italian.

She allowed a hint of her own temper to show. "You keep saying that like I had a choice. I didn't and I don't. It just happens, okay? The Inferno chooses, not me."

"That is a very convenient gift," he accused. "All you have to say to escape blame is it's not your fault. It's The Inferno."

"It *isn't* my fault. And it *was* The Inferno." She confronted him, hands on her hips. "Do you really think I took one look at you in all your magnificence and decided… Yeah, let's zap him for the rest of our lives?"

"I don't know." He stuck his truly magnificent nose in her face, speaking between gritted teeth. "Did you?"

She wanted to scream in frustration. "We were meeting

for the first time when it happened! Until then, we'd never spoken one word to each other. Why would I want to saddle myself with a man I don't even know?" She held up her hand before he could offer another sarcastic comment. "Don't you get it? The Inferno works the way it works. I'm as much a victim of it as you are. Do you think I like having decisions made for me? That I like having some weird flash of heat and electricity decide that you're the one?"

"Considering you would have chosen d'Angelo over me, maybe you're better off trusting The Inferno," he shot back.

"Oh! That is beyond low—"

He cut her off without hesitation, all the while struggling to rein in his temper. "Let me see if I have this straight. You and I have felt The Inferno."

She folded her arms across her chest and glared. "Yes."

"But someday you may shake another man's hand and feel The Inferno for him." Constantine had keyed in on the one part of this entire situation that she hated the most. "I will only want you and no other woman for the rest of my days. You may Inferno any number of men. Is that correct?"

Her cheeks warmed and she nodded. "I think so, yes."

Until this moment she hadn't realized how much he resented The Inferno or what had happened between them. Of course, she'd grown up with The Inferno, he hadn't. She'd heard Primo and Nonna relate the "fairy tale" of their first meeting from the time she was a toddler, had seen the joy and happiness between her own parents, just as she'd witnessed the misery Uncle Dominic and Aunt Laura had been unable to conceal. It made for a confusing picture.

Her cousins and brothers had never believed in the family "blessing" or "curse" as they'd jokingly called it. They'd held tight to their lack of faith right up until it had happened to them. Throughout it all, Gianna had stood on the sidelines watching while, one by one, cousin and brother had fallen and fallen hard. And she'd kept her mouth firmly shut about what she'd learned on her thirteenth birthday, not wanting to put a damper on all that delirious "forever after" Inferno love.

If they only knew.

The years had passed and she'd waited to see whether a female Dante was capable of feeling The Inferno, of sharing it with her chosen mate, not quite sure whether or not she wanted the experience. Then it happened. What she hadn't foreseen was Constantine's adverse reaction. Her indignation faded.

"You hate The Inferno, don't you?" she asked miserably.

"I hate that it's taken away my choice," Constantine admitted. He corralled the intensity of his anger. "That it eats into my self-control and ability to determine my own destiny. That I am unable to decide yes, no or maybe, and am simply swept along like a helpless minnow plummeting over the rapids of a raging river."

Gianna struggled to conceal her pain. All this time she'd thought he'd wanted her. And all this time he'd resented that want. The knowledge forced her to offer a way out. It was the only honorable course available to her. She took a step back so her closeness wouldn't influence him. Ridiculous, really. If they'd felt the unrelenting pull when they'd been separated by six thousand miles of land and ocean, a few feet wasn't going to change anything.

"Would you rather not feel The Inferno?" she forced herself to ask. "If I could undo it, take it away, would you want me to?"

Instead of jumping at the offer, to her surprise and relief he hesitated. "You can do this?"

"I don't know," she admitted. "I've never tried."

"If you did, I would feel nothing for you?"

She shook her head, unable to give him an honest answer. "I have no idea. It's possible."

He stared down at his palm for several long minutes, digging his thumb into the center while he considered. "It's hard for me to imagine not wanting you." He focused on her once again. "What about you? If you took back The Inferno would you still feel it toward me?"

She bit down on her lip to keep it from trembling. "I think I'll no longer feel it for you when I feel it for someone else. *If* I feel it for someone else." Tears flooded her eyes and she blinked them away. She flat-out dreaded the day that would happen. She couldn't even imagine loving someone more than Constantine. "All I know for certain is that I've never wanted anyone but you or felt The Inferno with any other man than you. Even so, I can't make any promises for the future."

He softened ever so slightly. "But then, that's life, isn't it? People fall in love and marry. For some it lasts a lifetime. For others…" He shrugged. "Not so long."

Now for the tough question. "Do we keep going and see if it'll work for us?" Her throat thickened and she had to force the words out. "Or do we put a stop to it while we still can?"

The question hung between them for a timeless moment. Then, "I can't," Constantine said. Just those two harsh words, sounding as though they'd been ripped from the deepest part of him. For an instant, her world ended until he added, "I can't let you go."

She moved without conscious thought, hurling herself into his arms. "Oh, Constantine."

He lifted her face to his and kissed her. Deep. Urgent. Desperate kisses. Taking her under until nothing existed but him. His mouth. His touch. The relentless burn of The Inferno. She suspected they'd have taken that final, irrevocable step if her stomach hadn't chosen that moment to growl. She broke away with a laugh, one he shared.

He tucked a lock of hair he'd loosened during their embrace behind her ear. "Okay, *piccola*. Here's what we'll do. We'll spend the next month keeping our promise to Primo. We'll get to know each other. Then we'll decide about The Inferno."

She could scarcely contain her relief. She'd been so afraid he'd want to be released from the hold of The Inferno, despite the intense desire they shared. It said a lot that neither of them questioned the level of passion they felt for the other. At least that aspect of their relationship had never been in doubt.

If they managed to put an end to The Inferno, the fragile bud of trust developing between them would be nipped off. The slow growth of passion into something deeper and more permanent would be cut down before it had a chance to bloom. By moving forward that tiny bud would have the opportunity to flourish and she realized just how badly she wanted to see what sort of flower blossomed as a result. She had a feeling it would be spectacular beyond belief.

A smile exploded from her, wide and radiant. "Well, okay. That's what we'll do. We'll get to know each other better." She gestured toward the table with trembling hands and scolded, "What are you waiting for? Sit and eat. Breakfast is getting cold."

The next two weeks flew by. Gianna and Constantine approached the whole "getting to know each other" agreement a trifle self-consciously. At least, that was how she felt about their initial dates, dates to dinner or the movies or a quiet evening at home.

Granted, once they were together for a short time, the awkwardness vanished. In its place passion exploded, a passion they struggled to contain. She wished she could say nothing more than sheer lust existed between them, but that would be a lie, Gianna conceded. The truth was, she *liked* Constantine.

She enjoyed his intellect, and his observations about life. She found his work fascinating, particularly the interior design branch of Romano Restoration since she utilized similar skills and abilities when planning an event or staging one of Dantes' high-end receptions. Constantine also possessed a calmness she appreciated and a way of taking control of a situation by smoothing over any rough edges. And as much as she'd like to fault him for holding her at a firm distance, she couldn't fault his sense of honor, not when it went to the very core of who he was as a man.

Sitting behind her desk, Gianna tapped a pen against the catering contract spread across the glass tabletop while she analyzed her relationship with Constantine. She didn't even mind that he tended to be a bit of a control freak. Even there, they meshed well. She might be a bit scattered at times and possess a strong tendency to act on impulse, particularly in her personal life—David being a prime example. But when it came to her job, she was detail-oriented and on top of things. Her work at Dantes demanded it.

The phone at her elbow rang and she answered it absently, perking up when Constantine's sexy accent sounded in her ear. "How is your day going, *piccola?*" he asked.

Mmm. Just hearing his voice made her want to melt right into her chair. "Better now that you've called," she admitted.

"Then I'm sorry to say that I'm about to make your day worse."

"Tonight?" she guessed with a disappointed sigh.

A light tap sounded at her door and Juice, a longtime family friend, stuck his gleaming bald head into her office. He'd first been adopted by the Dantes when he'd worked for her brother's private security firm, before Luc had taken over Dantes Courier Service. Juice specialized in background checks, finding what others didn't want found, and all things stored in cyberspace. Occasionally he helped the Dantes with his expertise. Gianna was hoping this would be one of those times. She waved him in and toward a seat near her desk.

"Do you need to change our plans?" she asked Constantine.

"I have to cancel them, I'm afraid. Some last minute alterations to a proposal."

"Oh, no," she said sympathetically. "Not the Diamondt account, I hope."

"I'm afraid so."

"But, you've worked so hard on that one. And the plans you've designed for the restoration are gorgeous. What's the problem?"

"A family disagreement. Apparently there's a son-in-law who owns enough of his late wife's share of the family business that they need his approval on my restoration project before going to contract."

"It would have helped if they'd told you about him beforehand."

"My thoughts, exactly. Now I am forced to make a number of alterations that I hope will satisfy all the various parties. I may even have to fly up there to meet with Moretti in order to resolve the problem."

"Moretti? Is that the son-in-law's name?" For some reason it rang a distant, rather muffled, bell. "Sounds like the Diamondts and the Dantes have something in common. We both have our little family squabbles that require a firm hand to resolve. In our case, Primo's hand."

"Not even close," he assured her. "The Dantes adore each other and squabble accordingly. The Diamondts put me more in mind of the Borgias. Unfortunately they don't have a Primo to straighten them out, which means they're all jockeying for control."

She chuckled. "That bad, huh? Okay, I'll let you get back to it. How about tomorrow? Do you have to work over the weekend?"

"I'm free both days," he assured her. "Think about how you'd like to spend them."

"I'll do that." She spared Juice a quick glance and kept her voice light and casual. "I'll talk to you later."

A brief pause, then, "You're not alone, are you?"

"Good guess."

"Family?"

She winked at Juice to include him in the conversation. "An old family friend."

"You tempt me to say something that will make you blush."

"Do that and it will be the topic of conversation for quite some time to come," she warned.

"Ah." It took every ounce of self-possession to keep from shuddering at the deep, sexy way he drew out the sound. "That sort of old family friend. I assume that means you're not the only *chiacchierona*."

"He'd resent that. He'd also resemble it—but only on occasion. In his line of work he has to know when to talk... and when not to."

That elicited a laugh. "Then I'll spare your blushes and call later when we can talk dirty in private."

He'd succeeded in making her blush, anyway, a fact Juice noted with an uplifted eyebrow. "I'll definitely make it worth your while," she shot back.

"Now I'm blushing."

And with that the line went dead, leaving her grinning like an idiot.

"I see the rumors aren't rumors, after all," Juice observed in a deep, rumbling bass. "Would I be correct in assuming Constantine Romano caused you to turn that interesting shade of red?"

Her smile broadened. "You would."

"Serious?"

She hesitated, then nodded. "I think so."

"I'm happy for you." He leaned forward and rested his massive arms on his knees. "So what's up, G? You said you had a job for me."

"I do." She glanced toward the open door. Better if they weren't overheard, she decided, and crossed her office to close it. "Would it be possible to keep this between the two of us?" she asked, resuming her seat.

"I'd have to know the particulars before I answered that question."

She blew out a sigh. "Fair enough. I'd like you to find a diamond for me. It went missing about a year and a half ago."

"I don't suppose you're talking about Brimstone?"

Her mouth dropped open. "You *know* about Brimstone?"

"I know lots of stuff." His dark eyes gleamed with laughter. "Most of which you don't."

"That doesn't seem fair," she complained. "I don't suppose you can tell me the whereabouts of Brimstone?"

"I can't."

Hmm. "Can't...or won't?"

"Can't," he repeated gently. "I don't know where it is."

"Could you find out?"

His gaze intensified. No wonder Luc had hired Juice. Brilliant. Able to find anything or anyone. And, when he chose to be, one of the most intimidating men she'd ever met. "Why do you want to find it?"

"Someone else is after the stone and I think the Dantes should find it first."

"Makes sense."

"One more thing... In addition to finding Brimstone, there's a person I want you to track down. Don't approach him or do anything once you locate him," she hastened to add. "Just keep tabs on him."

"If you're talking about David d'Angelo, that's already covered."

She should have known. "Luc?" she guessed.

He ticked off on his fingers. "Luc. Rafe. Draco. Your father. Primo. Various cousins. Pretty much the whole Dante clan."

Alarm filled her. "What are they going to do when you find him?"

"Make him disappear." He paused a beat. Then a slow grin split his dark face. "God, you're easy. I'm kidding, G. They want the same thing you do. To keep tabs on the guy. Dig up any dirt on him. Make sure he doesn't take advantage of some other poor woman. They want to see him pay...legally. After what he did to you, would you expect any less?"

"Oh." For a minute there, she'd actually believed him about making David disappear. Scary thought. She cleared her throat. "Well, okay, then."

"I'll see what I can do about Brimstone. Anything else?"

"That's it." She eyed him in open curiosity. "What do you think the chances are you'll find it?"

"Fair-to-middlin'. What do you think the chances are that you and Constantine will hook up?"

"We're only dating, Juice."

He tipped his head to one side. "I heard engaged."

"Nope. Just dating."

"Okay." He stood and headed for the door, turning at the last moment. "Just so you know, I have a hundred on this weekend."

She stared in confusion. "Excuse me?"

"The pool for when you and Constantine will make it official. I have this weekend. Winning might upgrade the chances of my finding Brimstone from fair-to-middling to who's-your-daddy." And with that, he exited her office.

It took Gianna a full thirty seconds to catch her breath sufficiently to respond. When she did, she bellowed, *"Rafe!"*

Taking pity on Constantine and his business woes, Gianna decided to pick up dinner and drop it off at Romano Restoration. She wouldn't stay, she promised herself. If he could spare a half hour she'd let him talk her into hanging around long enough to share a meal with him. But otherwise she'd make herself scarce so he could put the finishing touches on his proposal.

She caught a cab to his office building. The receptionist was no longer on duty, but the security guard tipped his cap when he saw her, recognizing her from her frequent visits. He even called the elevator for her, holding the door with a friendly smile. She stepped inside and used the key Constantine had given her to access his apartment. All the while, the delicious scent of the dinner she'd picked up at the Oriental Pearl filled the small space.

He wasn't in the apartment, which meant she'd find him in his office. She'd assumed as much, but she had a few things she wanted to nab before she joined him. Snagging a throw off the back of his couch, she gathered up napkins, a bottle of wine and wineglasses. At the last minute she remembered to add a bottle opener to her stash and headed downstairs. Sure enough, he sat behind his desk, hard at work.

She paused unnoticed in the doorway and took the opportunity to study him. Usually he sensed her. But she suspected he was so focused on the job at hand that it would take more than even The Inferno to pry him loose.

His ink-black hair fell across his forehead in thick, unruly waves. She'd have called them curls, but suspected he'd take immediate exception to the term, a fact that made her smile. He jotted a note in the margin of the paper he held, the desk lamp casting sharp light across his features.

Dear heaven, but he was a gorgeous man. Elegant, and yet intensely male. His features were also intensely male—a firm, straight nose, a wide sensuous mouth, strong chin and jaw, high, aristocratic cheekbones. But the most devastating feature of all were his eyes. So dark. So sharp. So direct and honest.

Something deep inside of her gave a quick tug. A little lurch. She closed her eyes, unable to hide from the truth. She suspected that if she didn't actually love this man, she was teetering on the brink. Dante pride had kept her from admitting it, but she couldn't lie to herself. Not now. She'd fallen in lust the moment they'd touched. Her family called it The Inferno, but she knew lust when she felt it.

At some point in the dozen plus days they'd been together,

her feelings for him had grown. Deepened. Matured. It would only take a tiny nudge to send her tumbling. She almost laughed at the thought. If left to Constantine, it wouldn't be a nudge, but a full-body tackle from "maybe" to "happily ever after."

She knew the instant he sensed her. A predatory stillness consumed him. He didn't move. Didn't speak. He simply lifted his eyes and stared at her. She returned the look, not moving or speaking, either. She let him eat her alive with his gaze while she returned the favor.

"Are you real?" he asked with a slow smile. "Or just a delicious dream?"

"Definitely real." She held up the bag of food. "And extra delicious. Can you spare a few minutes for dinner?"

His smile grew. "Maybe you can feed me while I work."

"Now you are dreaming."

He chuckled. "It was worth a try." He eyed the blanket she carried. "Cold?"

"Nope. I thought we'd have a picnic." She slipped out of her heels. "Kick off your shoes and relax for a few minutes."

He hesitated, shook his head. "I don't kick off my shoes."

That gave her pause. "Seriously? Never?"

"Seriously. Never." His expression darkened. "You can't be ready to go at a moment's notice if you're not wearing your shoes."

She blinked. That never would have occurred to her. "I'm not sure what might happen in the next half hour that you'll need to be ready to go at a moment's notice, but I'll take your word for it."

"Thanks."

Now she knew something was off. Thinking back she realized that even when she and Constantine had been their most relaxed during evenings at her row house, he'd never taken off his shoes. He'd also kept his possessions neatly gathered so all he had to do was pick them up on his way out the door.

Not the least like her. Half her possessions were scattered across every Dante home in the Bay Area. The Italian version of *mi casa es su casa*. She'd have dismissed Constantine's obsessiveness as a personality quirk if she hadn't caught that telltale darkness flitting across the hard contours of his face. Something was up there and she made a mental note to explore it at a future date. Until then, no point in making a big deal about it or attempting to involve him in a heavy discussion. Not when he was in the middle of a work crisis.

Keeping the mood light and easy, Gianna offered a cheerful smile and shrugged. "Oh. Okay. Keep your shoes on if it makes you more comfortable." She held up the bag of goodies. "Hungry?"

"What did you bring for us?" he asked, only too happy to go along with the change of subject.

She grinned. "Everything."

The next half hour turned out to be a brief moment of enchantment. They spent the time together eating and laughing, using the chopsticks that came with their meal to feed each other tidbits from the selection of cartons. The office setting faded into the background while they sat on the butter-soft blanket she'd liberated from his apartment. The light from his desk barely reached them, illuminating their impromptu picnic with a muted, distant glow.

"Will it always be like this?" she asked at one point while she refilled their wineglasses.

He paused, chopsticks lifted halfway to her mouth. "Like what?"

"Fun. Romantic." She shrugged. "Wonderful."

Raw pleasure shot through his gaze. "Considering who I have to be fun, romantic and wonderful with, it shouldn't be too difficult," he replied, much to her delight. "Have you thought about what you'd like to do this weekend?"

She hesitated. "There's one thing…"

"Name it."

"My family owns a place about three hours north of here. It's on a good-size lake. Great fishing and sailing. Over the years we've acquired all the property around it, so it's pretty private. Maybe Ariana mentioned it to you?" she asked uncertainly. "The entire family goes each summer for a huge Dante blowout."

"Sounds like fun. Is this weekend the family blow-out?"

"No, not for another few weeks." She hesitated. "I thought we could go ahead of time, just for the weekend."

"I'm not sure this is what Primo had in mind when he gave us a month to get to know each other better."

"True." She caught her lip between her teeth. "Even so, I'd like to go."

He studied her for a moment and she wondered if he could read the truth in her face, if he could tell she had an ulterior motive. "If that's what you'd like, of course we can go to the lake. Do we need permission from Primo?"

She shook her head. "My brothers and cousins and I all have carte blanche to visit anytime we want. We can either stay at the main house or in one of the cabins by the lake. You can decide which you prefer when we get there."

"What's going on, Gianna?" he asked bluntly.

She drew her legs close to her chest and wrapped her arms around them, resting her chin on her knees. All the while she avoided his gaze. "I'd just like to take you to the lake without my entire family watching our every move."

"And…?"

She blew out a sigh, deciding to come clean. "And, I'd like you to help me get over my fear of the water without my relatives catching on."

He sat up straight. "*Accidenti!* Of course I'll help you if I can. But I'm not qualified to handle something so serious." He reached for her, unwrapping her arms and legs, and tucked her tight against him. The firm beat of his heart steadied her as nothing else could have. "What has caused this fear, do you remember?"

She leaned into him. "It started when Uncle Dominic and Aunt Laura drowned. I was terrified to go in the water after that."

He considered that for a moment. "They drowned while sailing, yes? It didn't occur at the lake?"

She shook her head. "I'd never have been able to return to the lake if it had happened there."

His frown deepened. "Why hasn't your family helped you get over this fear?"

"They don't know," she confessed. "I've kept it hidden all these years. I sunbathe and splash a bit in the shallows. But I spend my time there hiking or reading or any activity that doesn't involve swimming." She searched his face. "Would you be willing to try to help me?"

"For you? Anything."

She made a sound, half laugh, half sigh. "I'm not sure whether to be grateful or sorry."

He lifted her face to his. "I vote for grateful." He feathered a kiss across her mouth. "Very grateful."

As it turned out, Constantine didn't return to work until a long time later.

* * *

Constantine picked up Gianna early the next morning. One look at her face warned she hadn't slept well. He took her overnight bag and tucked it away in the trunk of his Porsche.

"We don't need to do this, you know," he informed her as they headed out of the city. "You're allowed to change your mind."

She hid her exhaustion behind a pair of sunglasses, but the set of her chin told its own story. She'd go through with her plan no matter how difficult. "You can thank David for this," she told him.

He spared her a brief, hard look. "Explain."

"He scared me. Terrified me. As a result, I discovered something about myself." She looked at him then, glaring over the top of her sunglasses. "I don't like being afraid."

"I'll protect you from d'Angelo. I swear it."

To his intense pleasure, she nodded in complete agreement. "Of course you will. Because that's who you are. But here's the thing…" She angled her body in his direction and stabbed her finger to emphasize her point. "Even though I was terrified, I still found a way to escape."

He allowed his admiration to show. "Yes, you did."

"If I can overcome my fear of David, I can overcome my fear of the water. And that's what I'm going to do." She nudged her sunglasses higher on the bridge of her nose in a decisive movement. "With your help, that is."

He shot her a swift grin. "I've thought of a possible solution."

"Oh, yeah? What's that?"

"I'll distract you."

"Hmm. Not sure that'll work. I don't think there's anything you can do that'll distract me to that extent."

"Sure it will."

"What?"

"Two words… Skinny. Dipping."

She chuckled, relaxing for the first time that morning. "Okay, that just might work."

He could tell she thought he was kidding. In just a little over two hours she'd find out he was serious. He smiled in anticipation.

Very, very serious.

Eight

They arrived at the Dantes' summer property right at noon. Constantine parked in a gravel section between a large workshop and equally generous-size storage shed. He took a moment to stretch, then looked around in appreciation.

"Impressive," he said to Gianna. "And quite beautiful. Peaceful."

She smiled, clearly pleased with his reaction. "We like it."

The main residence, a rambling rough-hewn log building, complete with a pair of stone chimneys, perched on the lake's edge. Two more modern wings bookended the main section and cantilevered over the water. On the lakefront, a pier and boathouse occupied one end of the curved shoreline and the Dantes had trucked in soft white sand to form a sweeping beach. Tucked into the nearby woods he spotted individual cabins.

Gianna noticed the direction of his gaze and gestured

toward the closest one. "For the married couples who prefer a bit more privacy than being under one roof with everyone else."

"And if the couple in question isn't married?"

She shot him an impish grin and jerked her head toward the main house. "Opposite wings."

"And of those two options, where would you prefer to spend the night?"

Her eyes narrowed in consideration and she caught her lower lip between her teeth. For some reason she was having trouble making a decision. "The first cabin," she finally decided. "That way we don't have to open up the main house. Plus the closest cabin has two bedrooms."

"Are we going to use both?"

She fussed with her sunglasses for a moment. "What happens if we only use one?" she asked. She tried to make the question sound casual and failed miserably.

"You and I announce our engagement the moment we return," he answered, not the least casual about his response.

"Okay," she said. Reaching inside the car, she snagged the groceries they'd picked up and started across the driveway toward the cabin.

Okay? What did she mean by that? "Okay, we can announce our engagement?" he called after her. "Or, okay we'll use separate bedrooms?"

"Yes," she tossed over her shoulder.

He snatched up their bags with a broad grin and followed after her, appreciating the view. Her endless legs ate up the distance with ease, the feminine sway of her pert backside drawing his gaze. Her hair tumbled down her back in loose curls, the sunlight losing itself in the glorious streaks of brown and gold. What would she say if she knew he'd purchased a Dantes' Eternity engagement ring…just in case? Panic, or set the fastest wedding date on record?

Maybe he'd find out.

After grabbing a quick lunch, Gianna took Constantine on a tour of the complex, followed by a hike partway around the huge lake. He knew she was avoiding the true purpose for their visit. But he didn't push, instead allowing her to set the pace. She'd tell him when she was ready to act.

They returned to the cabin late that afternoon to enjoy a cup of coffee on the deck and Constantine leaned back in his chair, stacking his feet on the top railing. The cabin rested within the protective embrace of a stand of cedar trees, about fifty feet from the water. A solid two hundred yards from shore a raft teetered back and forth against the slap and drag of gentle wind-driven waves. From his current position he could look out across the shimmering blue lake to the dense forest beyond, with the Sierra Nevada mountains rising majestically in the background. It was an amazing sight, one he'd be all too happy to view on a regular basis. No wonder the Dantes loved this place. And how fortunate to have been able to acquire all the surrounding property. He couldn't help but wonder how many years that had taken.

"It's getting late," Gianna commented.

Constantine kept his voice calm and nonchalant. "The sun doesn't set for hours yet."

"Still…" She took a final swallow of coffee and set her mug onto the glass-topped table beside her with a decisive click. "Let's get this over with."

Without another word, she stood and disappeared inside the cabin. He followed in time to see her vanish into the bedroom she'd staked out, and continued on to his own. Stripping off his clothes, he changed into trunks and returned to the deck.

Gianna joined him a few minutes later, wearing a pale

lime-green one-piece, the color somehow intensifying the unusual shade of her eyes. The squared bodice was modest, just hinting at her generous cleavage. And she'd tied a misty drape at her waist that fell to her calves in a swirl of blues and greens. All he could think about was how quickly he could strip away that drape, followed by her swimsuit.

She shot him a questioning glance over her shoulder. "What?"

He gave her a slow, hungry smile. "Skinny. Dipping."

She darted across the deck with a laugh, her curls bouncing against her back. "You have to catch me first."

A short stack of steps ended at a narrow pathway leading to the stretch of beach closest to the dock and boathouse. She hurdled over the stairs in a practiced maneuver and hit the path at a dead run. The predator in him roared to life and he gave chase. He would have caught her, too, if she hadn't frozen at the water's edge. Her stillness had him pulling up beside her, careful not to do anything that might spook her.

"You don't have to go in," he reassured.

"I know, but I've delayed long enough," she said grimly. She untied the drape and tossed it onto the sand in a resolute manner. "Let's give it a try and see what happens."

It didn't take long. Constantine stuck right by Gianna's side. She waded in until the water lapped around her waist. One minute she seemed perfectly normal and the next minute her breath hitched and she spun awkwardly around. Before he could sweep her from the water to safety, she tripped, plummeting beneath the surface.

He was on her within seconds, snatching her up and lifting her high in his arms. But the damage had been done. She lost it. Curling into him, she choked on the water she'd swallowed, weeping in terror. He carried her straight to the cabin and into the bathroom. He turned on the shower, the spray hard and hot. With her still in his arms, he walked into the huge mosaic tiled stall.

"I'm okay, I'm okay," she wept.

"I know you are. We'll just stand here, anyway, until you're more okay."

He lowered her onto her feet and pushed the wet hair from her eyes and simply held her tight against his chest until her shuddering sobs faded and her heartbeat calmed to a slower rate. The heat helped loosen her tight muscles and ease her trembling. Finally she tilted her head back and looked at him.

"Damn," she whispered.

His mouth twitched. "Didn't go the way you planned?" he asked tenderly.

She slicked the moisture from her face. "You could say that."

"Did you really expect your phobia would disappear the minute you stepped in the water?"

"Yes," she grumbled. "I did. It's an irrational knee-jerk reaction. I'm not the one who drowned."

"Clearly."

"I've never even had a close call," she continued. "There's no logical reason for me to fear the water."

He hated to suggest it, but given the circumstances... "Have you considered therapy?"

"No. It wasn't until David that I was even willing to accept that I had a problem." She reached around him to turn off the water and squeezed the water from her hair. "I want you to know this is unacceptable."

"The shower?"

"No." A brief smile flirted with her mouth. "That was sort of nice."

"I can turn the water back on and we can have some more nice," he offered generously.

Her smile grew. "Thanks, but no." She exited the stall and grabbed a towel for herself and tossed him the spare. She dried herself in short, angry movements. "I'm telling you, Constantine, before we leave here I *will* get over this fear. When David had me trapped in his car, I refused to allow him to scare me so badly I couldn't act. I'm not going to let some ridiculous phobia keep me from enjoying the lake now."

Constantine dried himself at a more leisurely pace. "I don't doubt it. Not if you've made up your mind to do it."

She nodded decisively. "Darned right. I used to love to swim. I used to spend all day out on the raft and do flips and dives off of it." She tossed her towel onto the floor. "I was good, damn it."

"Ready to go again or do you want to wait until morning?"

Gianna vacillated for a split second. He saw the instant she came to a decision, her mouth assuming a stubborn slant. "No. Now. Right this second while I'm still mad. Before I remember to be scared again."

She practically ran from the bathroom. He went after her, determined to keep pace with her every step of the way. This time he'd be ready. This time she wouldn't go under.

The instant they hit sand, he took her hand in his. Farther out in the lake the wooden raft rocked, creaking and jangling against its metal chain and anchor. Together they walked to the water's edge where he tugged her to a standstill. "Not so deep this time," he instructed. "And not so fast."

She nodded in agreement. Taking a deep breath, she waded in until the water hit her knees. Then she slowly stooped, allowing the water to wash upward over her body. He followed her down. Her fingers tightened in his and her breathing kicked up a notch.

Screwing her eyes closed, she muttered, "Just like a

bath." She settled onto the lake bottom, the water lapping around her chest. "That's all I'm doing. Soaking in a nice deep bathtub."

Constantine plastered himself behind her and wrapped his arms around her waist. He drew her back between his legs and pressed her rigid spine tight against his chest. "I'm thinking either Hawaii or Alaska."

Gianna jerked in surprise at the non sequitur. "What?"

"For our honeymoon. Follow my reasoning here... Alaska requires a lot of clothes because even in the summer it can be chilly. But you have that unbelievable scenery and a lot of nakedness in front of a roaring fire."

"Have you lost your mind?" She splashed water in his direction. "We're not even engaged."

"The benefits of Hawaii are the lack of clothes...so, more nakedness."

"I'm beginning to sense a theme here," she said drily.

"Well, it is our honeymoon. Nakedness will be involved."

She held up her left hand and shook it in his face. "Please note. Bare finger. Bare finger equals no engagement. No engagement equals no honeymoon."

Hmm. True. But had she noticed she wasn't panicking? Might be too soon to point out that minor detail. He allowed his hand to drift upward from her waist to settle just beneath her breasts. Maybe it was the buoyancy of the water that caused his thumb to drift upward, as well. Or maybe he'd lost control over it and it went crazy all on its own. Somehow it swept across her breast. Repeatedly.

"We could always start with the honeymoon," he suggested. "Get that out of the way first. Work on the engagement and wedding afterward."

She shivered. "Honor and all that, remember?"

She sounded a bit desperate, as though she were reminding herself as well as him. The possibility made him grin. "Parts of me remember. Other parts…" he shook his head "I am forced to admit, not so much."

"Maybe you should send a memo to those other parts."

Taking a chance, he scooped her up and spun her around to face him. Her legs closed automatically around his waist. At the same time, her arms wrapped tight around his neck. She gazed into his eyes, a funny little smile catching at the corners of her mouth.

"You don't think I know what you're doing, but I do," she informed him.

"And what am I doing?"

"Distracting me." She tilted her head to one side. "What do you say I distract you instead?"

He didn't have an opportunity to respond. She took his mouth in a deep, hungry kiss. Her lips parted, beckoning him inward. He didn't need a second invitation. He sank into honeyed warmth, their tongues dueling briefly, mating slowly, pleasuring thoroughly.

Using extreme care, he eased them into deeper water, keeping her tight within his control. Then he slid one hand downward over her abdomen to the top of her leg where silky bathing suit met satiny skin. He drew a finger along the elastic edge, then slipped under.

Gianna buried her face against Constantine's shoulder and released a sound that threatened his sanity. A helpless feminine plea. A soft siren's call that spoke of blatant need. He had no choice but to respond, to try to give her what she desired. He found the hot core of her and stroked. She came apart in his arms, her sweet cry drifting across the lake.

It took her a long moment to recover her voice enough to speak. "I can't stand it any longer, Constantine," she managed to say.

"Neither can I."

More than anything he wanted to keep his promise and not touch her until his ring was on her finger or they were married. But he'd reached the end of his rope. He couldn't keep his hands off her a minute longer. Cradling her close, he waded toward shore.

Before the sun set, Constantine intended to make Gianna his in every sense of the word.

Constantine carried Gianna to the cabin with a strength and ease that impacted on the most feminine level. He kicked open the door to her bedroom and entered. The tantalizing scent of forest cedar gently spiced the air. It was dusky and cool, lit only by the late-afternoon sunlight filtering through the gauzy drapes covering the windows. The fading light slid into the room, bathing the bed in a benevolent rosy glow.

He set her on her feet and took a step back. She understood why. He wanted her to be certain, to commit without his touch influencing her. What he didn't understand was that he was the only man with whom she could commit. For the next few hours she intended to forget everything but the two of them. With the rays of a setting sun cloaking them and the privacy of their mountain retreat to hide them away from prying eyes, this moment would be theirs. Just one special day to come together without worrying about right or wrong, or The Inferno, or family expectations.

Constantine continued to keep his distance. "Are you sure, Gianna?"

"Oh, yes. Definitely, yes."

Even though she knew they both wanted this more than anything else, she caught something in his expression, just a brief flash that hinted at regret. It didn't take any guesswork to figure out the cause. She closed the distance between them, leaned into him and sighed in relief the instant his arms closed tight around her. It was time. Time to let go of her pride and follow her heart.

Long past time.

"As much as I'd like to make love to you, Constantine, we can't take this any further," she informed him. She pulled back and smoothed the furrow lining his brow with a tender hand. "Not quite yet. I believe there's something you have to do first so that tonight is the way it should be. The way we'll always want to remember it. A night without regrets or blemish."

A slow smile built across his face, the most beautiful smile she'd ever seen. Ever so gently, he swept the back of his hand across her cheek. "Thank you for this," he whispered.

"Anytime," she whispered back.

He took her hands in his and dropped to one knee. If anyone else had done such a thing, it would have been beyond corny. In this special moment, it was beyond romantic. "Gianna Marie Fiorella Dante, will you do me the honor of becoming my wife?"

She opened her heart, allowing it to show in every bit of her expression. "Yes, Constantine. I'll marry you."

He stood, cupping her face. "No second thoughts?"

Her tearful smile felt shaky, but from happiness not nervousness. "Not a single one. I couldn't have chosen a more perfect man to share a more perfect moment."

The contours of his face softened, hunger kicking in. "I don't know if I can make this perfect for you, but I swear I'll do my best."

Constantine kissed her with unmistakable passion, stamping her with his possession in the most delicious way. It went beyond mere exploration, and became a thorough taking. Not rushed. But slow and deep and giving.

Gianna's breathing quickened, desire rising like a storm-driven tide, building inexorably, need an immense tidal wave flinging itself toward shore. It broke, spilling over her in a great rush and she clung to him, hanging on tight, then tighter. His tongue dueled with hers, lips and mouth teasing, mating, and he thrust his hands deep into her hair, using the tangle of thick heavy curls to anchor her to him.

"Finally," he muttered. "Your hair has been driving me crazy all day. Flirting. Taunting. But not anymore." He wrapped the weighty mass around his hand and drew her up. "Now you can't get away."

Her mouth curved into a slow smile. "Why would I want to get away? There's only one place I want to be and that's in bed with you."

He said something in Italian. Something thick and dark and demanding. For some reason, she couldn't make sense of it. "Take off your swimsuit," he repeated in English.

She lifted her chin in open challenge. "Take it off me."

His gaze flared darkly. "My pleasure."

His fingers slid from her hair to the narrow straps banding her shoulders. He lowered them, sweeping them down her arms inch by excruciating inch. A light breeze drifted in through the open window and tripped along her spine. Her suit slipped downward, settling around her hips. A swift, gentle tug and it slid to her ankles.

She stepped free of her suit and stood nude before him in acres of skin turned blush-pink beneath the benevolent kiss of a ruby sun. She thought she'd feel nervous or apprehensive or self-conscious. Instead she just felt the rightness of being with him.

"Your turn," she informed him.

He couldn't take his eyes off her. "I'm a little busy." He cupped her breast and stroked the tip with the rough pad of his thumb. "I've never seen anything so beautiful."

Her nipple tightened in response and she shuddered, the

intense pleasure arrowing straight to her core, making her painfully aware of her femininity. She burned with it, a melting heat that made her want to dissolve into his arms.

She shook her head to clear the sensual fog. "There's this interesting rumor going around that what you have in mind can't be accomplished unless you're naked, too." She shot him a teasing smile. "Besides, it's only fair."

"Normally I'd say you shouldn't listen to rumors." His voice deepened. "Though in this case, there may be some truth to them."

His fingers dragged across the peak of her breast again, the sensation a delicious agony, and she lost it. With a muffled cry of demand, she yanked him to her, kissing every inch of him she could reach. Touching every bit of him. The endless width of his chest. The ripple of hard, curving muscle and toned sinew. The rumble strips down his abdomen. An endless, beautiful display of burning hot skin. And it was all hers.

God, he was in incredible shape, especially for a man who spent his life in an office. Or maybe he didn't. Maybe he helped out with the actual restoration process. Something had put all those delicious ridges of muscle on his chest and shoulders.

Unable to help herself, she pressed a kiss just above his heart. He groaned softly and caught her close. "You undo me, *piccola*," he whispered. She reached for his swim trunks and he stopped her. "Considering my current state, I think I'd better take care of this part myself."

In one swift move, he stripped off the trunks. He was painfully heavy with desire and she shivered before the intense maleness of him. As though sensing her skittishness, he corralled her in the direction of the bed, tossing aside the covers. She tumbled backward onto the thick, soft mattress, the cotton sheet like velvet against her back. He braced himself above her, hovering for an endless moment. Inch by inch, he lowered himself onto her, pressing her into softness while covering her with delicious heat.

"Constantine!" His name escaped in a pleading sigh, asking for something she couldn't quite bring herself to express in any other way. She couldn't get enough. Not close enough, not fast enough…just not enough. "More. I want more."

"I'll give it to you, I swear." He touched her, a soothing stroke, while determination filled his expression. "But for your first time, slowly. With care. And I need to make sure you're protected."

She wanted to argue, but couldn't. She was too swept up in the moment. He disappeared briefly. When he returned, she realized he must have brought a condom with him…just in case. He returned to the bed and his mouth came down on hers, the gentle joining of lips and tongue at odds with the fierce hunger that underscored it. There was a familiarity to their kiss, as though they instinctively understood each other's needs and wants and were intent on supplying it. It took them to a new, unexpected level of intimacy. Passionate, yet generous. Arousing, yet open and vulnerable.

He cupped her breasts, teasing them into hard peaks with tongue and teeth. All the while he whispered the most exquisite words of love, the soft Italian making them all the more beautiful. He pressed kisses slowly downward, over her quivering belly and lower still. She gripped his shoulders to stop him.

"Don't." He interlaced her fingers with his. "Let me know you. All of you."

He reared back, so dying sunlight spilled across her, exposing her. She gazed into his black eyes and her heart rate kicked up, a fierce pounding in her ears as she waited for his reaction, waited to see what he'd do next. A slow smile curved his mouth, one of love and intense pleasure. Without taking his eyes off her, he lowered his head to her abdomen again and kissed her, sliding steadily lower.

She shuddered beneath the intimate touch feathering across her belly. With each lingering kiss, liquid heat splashed across her skin, the warmth of his breath fanned flames outward in ever-growing waves.

"I can't get enough of you," he murmured. "I don't think I ever will."

His comment arrowed straight to her soul, so beautiful and so painful. If it hadn't been for The Inferno, she'd have taken such delight and joy in the words. But she'd never know whether his reaction came from the brand of their Inferno connection or whether it came from the heart of the man.

While desire built, tears filled her eyes, overflowed, leaving hot, wet tracks behind as they slid across her temples and lost their way in her hair. She wanted this man. Wanted to love him and be loved by him. She tugged at him needing the reassurance of his kiss. He gave in to her silent demand and slid upward, the friction of skin on skin whipping up a more powerful storm of raw need. Did it really matter which part of this night was Inferno and which part real? She'd take what he gave her. Rejoice in it. Give herself over to it. And give everything she had in return.

She cupped his face and took his mouth, welcoming him inward. Wrapped him up in arms and legs and endless heat. Fueled a blaze that exploded into a need beyond anything she'd ever imagined. It ran rampant through her veins, filling her very heart and soul. She slid her hands downward to the masculine source of his desire. Cupped him. Slid her fingers over and around him.

"I love you," she told him, squeezing gently. "Please, Constantine. Don't make me wait any longer."

His breath roared from his lungs. "*Cavolo!* Do you have any idea what you're doing to me?" The question escaped through clenched teeth, his Italian so low and desperate she almost didn't understand.

Her mouth tilted upward in a teasing smile. "How could I know since I've never done this before?"

"You learn fast, *piccola*." His gaze warned of retribution. "Allow me to return the favor."

Before she could draw breath enough to respond, he cupped the warm center of her, slipping inward as he had at the lake and teasing her with slow, deliberate strokes. She bowed upward with a soft cry, desperate for his possession but not quite sure how to force the taking. She felt again the telltale flutter, the helpless clenching that would shoot her over the edge. He opened her then, slipping between her legs.

"This was always meant to be," he told her. "Call it fate. Call it The Inferno. You and I were always destined to come together. This couldn't end any other way."

He took her then with a single stroke. Gentle. Powerful. Unyielding. He sheathed himself in the warmth of her body. He moved with her in a primal rhythm as old as mankind. But it wasn't a simple sexual act. It was so much more than that. She could feel the connection in her heart, in her blood and bones, in her very soul. Where once they'd been separate and apart, empty and alone, now they were joined by an unbreakable bond.

Gianna gave herself over to the moment, reveling in it, wishing it would never end. But the rising tide couldn't be turned back. It rose faster and faster, sweeping her along, tumbling her over and over. She felt the odd flutter from before, the flutter becoming a ripple, then a hard, fisting pressure. Unable to help herself, she shattered, safe within Constantine's arms.

He surged home, his hands buried in her hair, his eyes blazing with the strength of his passion and desire. His climax hit, hard on the heels of her own. And as the final rays of the day slipped from the room, he greeted the onslaught of night with a bellow of pure, raw pleasure.

In that timeless transition between night and day, they became one. Forever changed. Forever bonded. Forever mated.

Constantine had no idea how many hours passed before he woke. The darkness was dense and rich, suggesting the blackest, most silent hour of the night. He left the warm nest the two of them had created in the bed and retreated to his room. It only took a moment to feel his way to his overnight bag and find what he needed. Then he returned to Gianna. Returned to where he belonged.

She still slept. He could just make out her sleeping form, the paleness of her skin reflecting the softest of glows from the sickle moon peeking in through the window. Her mass of hair tumbled over the pillow and down her back. And her arm was stretched out across the mattress as though reaching for him, even in deepest sleep.

Gently he took her hand in his and slipped his ring on her finger. Despite the dark, it glittered, tossing off shards of brilliant fire. Then it seemed to quiet, as though content that their final bond was near completion. Satisfied, he returned to the bed and to her arms. And to sleep.

He woke again just before dawn, something alerting him to the emptiness beside him. He was out of the bed in a flash. He didn't need to check the cabin to know she'd gone. A glance outside revealed his Porsche sitting right where he'd left it. That left the woods or the lake. The instant he thought of the lake, understanding hit.

So did fear.

He took off at a dead run, shooting through the cabin, out onto the porch. He didn't waste time with the steps, but vaulted over the railing and raced flat-out for the beach. The splinter of moon was setting, flinging the last of its fitful light at the lake, silvering the mirror-flat surface. A shape broke the liquid smoothness, moving steadily out toward the raft anchored offshore.

He dove into the water and stroked toward her, torpedoing through the water on an intercept course. He caught her just as she reached the raft. She heaved herself upward, every bit as naked as he was, and flopped onto the painted wooden boards, breathing hard. He followed her up, keeping a careful distance so he didn't give in to impulse and strangle her.

When he'd recovered his temper and had himself under complete control, he demanded, "Have you lost your damned mind?"

"Did you know you always speak in Italian whenever you're angry?"

"I'm not angry," he roared. Okay, maybe he didn't have his temper under complete control, but given the circumstances... "What the hell were you thinking, Gianna?"

She sat up. Her breathing hadn't quite returned to normal and her breasts rose and fell, a temptation beyond measure. "I was thinking that I needed to see if I really had gotten over my fear."

"Why didn't you wake me? Why sneak out on your own?"

"If I'd asked you to come with me I wouldn't have known if I wasn't afraid because you were with me, or if I'd really overcome my fear of the water." She spoke gently, as though to a cranky child, which only made him all the more cranky.

"And if you hadn't overcome your fear?" For some reason he was still roaring. "You could have drowned."

"Mmm." She had the nerve to wrinkle her nose at him and smile. "But I would have died happy."

"You think this is a *joke?*"

Her smile faded. "Of course not. I'm sorry I frightened you." She held out her hand. "Look what I found on my finger when I woke."

It was clearly an attempt to change the subject. He fought for patience. "*Piccola,* do you not see that your impulsiveness will one day get you into serious trouble? David. This swim. Please, I beg of you. For the sake of my sanity, would you try to think before acting?"

She shrugged, her breasts bobbing with the movement. "I'll try. Not sure how successful I'll be." Catching the direction of his gaze, she leaned in. "Just so you know, I'm thinking of being impulsive again."

"*Dio,*" he muttered faintly.

"Consider yourself formally notified that I'm about to jump off the raft and swim for shore, where I will impulsively make love to the first man who catches me." She lifted an eyebrow. "Or would you rather I resist the impulse?"

He snatched her into his arms. "Feel free to resist. I, on the other hand, will not."

Together, they tumbled into the water. It took them a long, long time to reach shore. By the time they did, Gianna was no longer the least bit afraid of the water.

Nine

Gianna and Constantine returned to the city in time to join the Dante family for their weekly Sunday-night dinner at Primo's. She was pleased to discover Juice there when they showed off her ring, since it meant she could rub his winning the engagement pool in Rafe's face.

The reaction to their news was loudly celebrated for a solid hour while she and Constantine were inundated by every last family member, all toasting and laughing, offering hugs as freely as marital advice.

When it was Juice's turn, he studied her in concern. "Man, G, I hope you didn't take me seriously when I said you'd have a better shot at my finding Brimstone if you got engaged this weekend."

She glared at him in outrage. *"What?"* she demanded in an infuriated undertone. "You mean I didn't have to agree to marry this guy, after all? You would have found Brimstone for me, anyway? Juice, how *could* you?"

He stared at her, his dark eyes wide with shock. "Aw, hell. Okay, okay. Give me a sec here." He scrubbed his massive hands over his face. "Look. Let me talk to Primo. I'll explain everything, I swear. Maybe he'll just maim me a bit instead of killing me outright."

She let him suffer for a second longer, then grinned. "Man, you are *so* easy. I'm kidding, Juice." She patted his trembling arm and leaned in. "Consider that payback for our last meeting."

His bald head bobbed up and down. "Okay. Payback. I can handle payback." He shot her a look of abashed admiration. "Boy, you Dantes play rough."

Gianna gave a decisive nod. "Don't you forget it."

The next several weeks flew by. She and Constantine both decided on the earliest possible wedding date. Why wait? They'd been apart for so long and wanted each other so desperately that a lengthy engagement seemed not just pointless, but cruel.

After the big announcement, Gianna was instantly swept up in a whirlwind round of shopping and wedding preparation, while Constantine worked day and night at Romano Restoration to clear his calendar for the honeymoon. Between handling proposals for new projects and making the ongoing revisions to the Diamondt account, not to mention the various wedding demands on both their time, she often felt as though they never had a private moment to themselves. Fortunately the Diamondt account and Juice inadvertently came to their rescue.

"Remember when I told you that I might need to fly up to Seattle to meet with Gabe Moretti?" Constantine asked the question over an increasingly rare dinner engagement.

"Sure." She pulled an abbreviated rundown from memory. "Diamondt account. Son-in-law. Deceased wife. Owns her share of the family business."

He saluted her in admiration. "Impressive."

Gianna topped off their glasses of wine. "I don't suppose you're going anytime soon?"

"As a matter of fact, I am." He lifted an eyebrow. "Any chance you can break away from the wedding madness and come with me?"

She offered him a slow smile. "Every chance. As a matter of fact, I was about to ask you a similar question. I just got a lead on Brimstone. Juice contacted me about it today. He's traced the Nancy doll to Seattle."

He eyed her over the rim of his glass. "Don't tell me you're planning to go up there and mug some poor, unsuspecting little girl?"

She chuckled. "That's the general idea. Assuming David hasn't gotten there ahead of me."

She didn't dare tell him the other part of her arrangement with Juice and her brothers. If Constantine found out about that, he'd put a fast stop to a brilliant idea and she flat-out wouldn't allow him to circumvent her plans. Besides, unlike her early morning swim in the lake, she wasn't acting impulsively. She and Juice and her brothers were acting very, very carefully.

Darkness settled over Constantine's expression at the mention of David's name. "I gather you heard d'Angelo's back in town."

She nodded. "Keeping a very low profile from what I understand."

"That might have something to do with the fact that rumors are running rampant around town about some monetary discrepancies."

Gianna smiled without humor. "I guess that means no suite at the Ritz." With luck, the next suite he occupied would be at the nearest penitentiary.

"What is your family planning to do about him?"

"I know what they'd like to do." She also knew what they were *going* to do.

Constantine's gaze turned bitter cold. "They're not the only ones."

"For now, we wait." She stressed the *we*. "Juice is working the problem. Knowing him, he'll find something that'll hang David out to dry."

She could tell Constantine wanted to act, find a way to bring David down himself. Fortunately Juice and Luc were already on top of that aspect of the plan. With luck, it would all be resolved to everyone's satisfaction before much longer. That way she wouldn't have to worry about Constantine taking matters into his own hands. The idea of his getting hold of David sent shivers down her spine. She couldn't risk that happening. Not with Constantine's temper.

He continued to chew on the information. "I heard the International Banking Association has rescinded the award they were going to give the d'Angelos."

"Couldn't happen to a nicer family." She leaned across the table and caught Constantine's hand in her own. Her engagement ring flashed with the same heat and fire that characterized The Inferno. "Forget about David. Let's talk about our trip to Seattle. How long will you be hung up in meetings?"

His gaze sparked. "I'll make sure we have plenty of private time. And speaking of private time…" He shoved aside his half-finished dinner. "I can think of far more important activities than eating. Food can wait. This can't."

A teasing smile played across her mouth. "And what would 'this' be?"

"I see you need a short refresher course." He lifted her out of her chair and carried her in the direction of his bedroom.

"No." Her arms tightened around his neck. "I need a very, very, *very* long one."

Gianna and Constantine flew to Seattle Friday night after work and checked into the Crown, a brand-new hotel within walking distance of the piers, Pike Place Market and the main shopping center. He'd somehow snagged a suite with a stunning western view of the sound and mountains.

After a late dinner, they retreated to the bedroom and silently stripped away their clothes. The room was dark and cool, lit only by the lights of the city and a full moon filtering through a bank of clouds hanging just over the Olympic Mountains. It shimmered across Elliott Bay and slid into the room, gilding the bed in silver.

Unable to resist, she approached and flung herself into his arms for a kiss that expressed all the pent-up desire and frustration that seemed to define their relationship up until now. Her body impacted against the hard, taut lines of his. This kiss proved no different than any of the others. She didn't just surrender, but gave herself up to him. Utterly. It had always been like that between them. She didn't think it could be any other way.

"It's only you. You're the only one it's ever been," she told him.

"Or ever could be?"

The question dropped between them and she closed her eyes against the hard knowledge glimmering within his dark gaze. "I'm sorry. I wish I could answer that question for you," she whispered.

"It doesn't matter." But he'd replied in Italian, giving himself away. "Nor does it change the fact that we're connected, you and I. We have been since the moment we first touched."

It was true, she acknowledged. She came alive whenever

he took her into his arms. When he kissed her. She could practically feel her nerve endings fire, throbbing with excitement, urging her to do things that should have shocked her to the core…and didn't.

He groaned. "Why? Why you and no one else?"

Gianna shook her head, struggling to clear it of the sensual fog with only limited success. She understood his question. It was one she'd asked herself often enough. "I have no idea why," she admitted.

She simply knew that being in Constantine's arms felt right. More, it felt necessary. Necessary to her very existence, whether she wanted it that way or not. Constantine slid his hands into her hair and lifted her closer, deepening the kiss. He was like a man who'd fasted for months, even though it had only been days since they'd last spent the night together. He gazed down at her as though he'd been presented with a delectable banquet, one he couldn't resist. A whispered moan of surrender slipped from her and he breathed it in.

Together they fell back on the bed and she gave herself over to his touch. He stroked her breasts, gently plucking at her painfully sensitive nipples. His calloused fingertips tripped downward, sweeping along her abdomen, then his mouth followed the path his hands took. When he reached the core of her, he scooped his large hands beneath her bottom and lifted her. Took her. Drove her straight over the top. She arched upward and exploded helplessly. Endlessly.

And then he mated his body to hers and took her again.

It was beyond anything she'd experienced before. He called to her in a language that blended English with Italian, sweet words, a tumble of demands, hoarse pleas. She clung to him, moved with him. Drove him as he'd just driven her. Sent him soaring. Up, up, up. And there they teetered before slamming together over the next pinnacle and plummeting into oblivion.

Spent, they curled together, drawing comfort and sustenance, one from the other. And they slept; a sleep of sweet hopes and dreams, wrapped together so tightly two melded into one.

Gianna woke again in the dead of night. The full moon was sinking behind the Olympic Mountains, setting the peaks aglow and silvering the room with its light. At some point Constantine had spooned her against the hard curve of his body. While the moon softened the appearance of the room, it sculpted Constantine's muscles and sinew into granite.

She could tell the instant he woke. The tenor of his breathing changed, deepened, and his hold on her tightened ever so slightly. "What time do you need to get up tomorrow?" she asked.

"Early."

"When are you meeting Moretti?"

He chuckled. "Not so early." He swept her hair to one side and traced a kiss along the back of her neck. "I want time to go through the building and finalize my presentation before we get together. Why don't you join me there around four?"

She shivered beneath his gently insistent touch. "At Diamondt's?"

"Sure." He caught the lobe of her ear between his teeth and tugged, giving a husky laugh at her helpless shudder. "I can introduce you to Moretti. Since this is the first time he and I are meeting face-to-face, maybe it'll help put us on a more friendly footing."

"Okay."

"What about you?" Constantine asked.

"I want to check out the address Juice gave me." She forced her muscles to remain relaxed, difficult enough when he kept touching her. Even so, she couldn't risk communicating any of her tension to him.

"I wish you'd wait until I can go with you," he murmured against her ear.

Oh, Lord. That would be a disaster. "No time," she hastened to say. "We're flying home right after your meeting, aren't we?"

He considered for a minute, his hand stroking her in an absentminded way. Unfortunately there was nothing absentminded about her reaction to his touch. She turned in his arms to face him and slid her leg over top of his. "Okay, fine," he said at last. "But call me right before and right after you speak to this woman."

She nipped at his mouth. "No problem."

She didn't give him the chance to say anything else. The sooner they put the conversation to rest, the better. Of course, the instant he shifted her beneath him, she found she couldn't think, much less speak.

They gave themselves over to one another, gave themselves over to the night. Her soft sigh of pleasure was answered by his hoarse demand. Her cry of completion echoed his roar of satisfaction. Through the night they burned, riding the crest of passion from one wave to the next until the first break of dawn tumbled them back into a deep sleep.

The next morning Gianna woke to discover Constantine long gone. He'd left a single red rose on the pillow beside her and she picked it up, smiling softly. Even better, he'd prepared a pot of coffee for her, using one of Seattle's world-renowned brands. She sipped in appreciation while preparing for the day. After doing a swift run-through with first Luc and then Juice, she pulled out the bold red slacks and jacket she'd chosen specifically for today's mission.

Next, she headed downstairs, speaking at length to the concierge and getting very specific directions to the address she'd been given. She arranged for a cab, requesting it pick her up in half an hour. Then she returned to her room and sat, counting down the minutes, before returning to the lobby. The hope was that the brief delay would give David time to bribe the concierge and obtain the address, or if that failed, follow her to her destination. Once Luc and Juice spotted him, they'd arrange their men in a tidy net around the house, ready to spring the trap when David made his move.

Since it was midday Saturday, the drive to White Center didn't take long. The taxi cruised slowly through a neighborhood overrun with small boxy homes. Though there was an air of shabbiness that encompassed many, for the most part they were tidy with neatly kept lawns and flower beds.

At the last minute she remembered to call Constantine. "I found the house. At least, I think I have."

"Give me the address."

She hesitated. "Why do you need the address?"

"So I know where to send the police if I don't hear from you within the next thirty minutes."

She sighed and did as he requested. "There's no need to worry, Constantine," she reassured. "This will be over before you know it and I'll call you the minute it is."

"What do you mean?" Constantine asked sharply.

"Oh, well, you know," she said, a trifle distracted. "It won't take long to discuss the situation with Mrs. Mereaux. I'm sure Primo will pay her a generous price for Brimstone and that'll be that."

"Gianna—"

"Oh, someone's looking out the window. I have to go. I'll call you as soon as I'm done."

She flipped the cell phone closed before he could say anything further and exited the cab.

Constantine stared down at his cell phone and frowned. Something about his conversation with Gianna felt off, and a sense of wrongness sizzled through him. He glanced at the group hovering over the blueprints spread across a table in the center of the Diamondt building foyer. Getting the account was vital to Romano Restoration's continued growth and expansion. Maybe that explained why he'd been so distracted. So distracted that he hadn't really given his full attention to this Brimstone business.

But now that he did…

It hit him then and he swore, praying he was wrong. He flipped open his phone and dialed Luc's number. No answer.

Juice's number. No answer.

Rafe. Draco. No answer.

He barked an excuse to the men waiting for him and took off at a dead run. Why was it that his future wife always had him running? Even worse, why was it always in terror that something horrible had happened to her?

Gianna knocked on the front door of the Mereaux residence. It opened a moment later and a woman of mixed race, slightly younger than herself, greeted her. She eyed Gianna nervously.

"How long are we supposed to stand here?" she asked, a strong hint of Louisiana Cajun clear in her voice. "I'm sort of new at all this."

Gianna smiled. "Me, too. I think we just need to talk for a minute or two. I'm Gianna, by the way."

"Mia." They shook hands.

"I'm surprised Juice allowed you to do this, Mia. He tends to be very protective about innocents, as he calls us. He was forced to enlist my help or David wouldn't have taken the bait. But you…"

Mia grimaced. "No choice. They had some other woman all set to pretend to be me, but Mr. d'Angelo got the jump on 'em. Nearly caught Mr. Juice standing right over yonder in my front parlor."

"David was here already?" Gianna asked, shocked.

"Surely was." Mia stepped back as planned and allowed Gianna to enter. "Fortunately Mr. Juice had time to hide in the kitchen. And my neighbor was here to take my daughter, Bebelle, for the day. She had her children with her—all five. That d'Angelo man couldn't do much with all them witnesses, now could he? So, he made up some fine excuse about a wrong address and left. Since he'd seen me, I insisted on staying put until they could arrest him."

Gianna closed the door behind her. "I'm so sorry, Mia. We all thought David would follow me. He must have gotten the address from the concierge, instead, and come straight over. So much for careful planning."

"That's what Mr. Juice said." A hint of warmth touched her cheekbones. "He wanted to pull the plug, but I wouldn't let him. Can't risk that man coming back thinking the doll is still here, now can I? That wouldn't be safe for my Bebelle."

"Well, this won't take long. We'll just let David take the doll and our part will be over." Gianna threw an arm around Mia's shoulders and gave her a swift hug. "Are you nervous?"

"A little," Mia admitted. "My main concern is Bebelle. Mr. Juice has assured me any number of times that she's safe with my neighbor."

Gianna grinned, sensing Mia felt more than a passing interest in Mr. Juice. "Well, if Juice said it, you can believe it."

"Would you like something to drink?"

"No, thanks." She wandered over to the couch where the Nancy doll perched and glanced over her shoulder at Mia. "May I?"

"Oh, sure. Help yourself."

"How did you end up with her, anyway?"

Mia shrugged. "It was shortly after my husband died. Bebelle just cried and cried she missed her daddy so bad. One day this strange child came up to her and just put that Nancy doll right in my little girl's arms. Said Bebelle needed it more than she did. Said it was a magical doll and would bring her happiness. And once it did, she should give it away to someone else in need." Mia turned her great, dark eyes on Gianna. "You think she's right? You think it'll bring my Bebelle happiness?"

"Yes, as a matter of fact, I think it will."

Gianna picked up the doll just as a heavy knock sounded on the front door. She stiffened, knowing full well who they'd find there.

Constantine tried Gianna's cell phone for the umpteenth time since flagging down the taxi. The cabbie drove as fast as he dared, the sizable tip thrown his way aiding in breaking a few speeding laws. That didn't change the fact that when he got his hands on his future wife—not to mention his future brothers-in-law—there would be hell to pay. He tried Luc's number again. Juice. Nothing from any of them.

He allowed fury to triumph over panic. It was the only way he could keep from going insane. Hadn't they discussed her impulsiveness at the lake? Hadn't he explained in no uncertain terms that it wasn't a quality he appreciated? Now he understood where it came from. It must be a genetic anomaly that ran down the entire Dante line. Though how that explained Juice, he couldn't say. Maybe it rubbed off with prolonged association.

"This is the street," the cabdriver said, pointing. "But the cops have it blocked. Are we too late, do you think?"

Constantine must have replied in Italian because the driver frowned in confusion. He fought to find the appropriate words in English, couldn't come up with them. Instead he peeled off a number of notes and tossed them in the driver's direction. He was out of the car in a flash.

Please, God, no. Not Gianna. He couldn't survive without Gianna. She was his mate. His heart. His life. He loved her more than he thought it possible to love anyone. If something had happened to her... He picked up his speed.

The police stopped him a few houses before the address Gianna had given him. It took endless minutes to make himself understood, to find the appropriate words in the appropriate language to convince them that he belonged on the other side of their blockade. That his future wife was involved. That she needed him, and only him.

Someone down the line waved him through and he took off at a swift jog. Luc stood talking to a police officer. Gianna was nowhere to be seen. He charged toward her brother and would have taken him down if his bride-to-be hadn't chosen that moment to come flying out of the house and straight into his arms.

"Constantine!" She wrapped her arms tight around his neck. "You'll never believe what happened."

"I'll tell you what's going to happen," he growled, snatching her close and enclosing her in a hold she wouldn't soon escape. "I'm going to knock your brother on his ass."

"I'd really rather you wouldn't. Listen to me." She caught

his face between her hands and forced him to look at her. "I said listen to me, Constantine. They caught David. He's in police custody. I don't think he's going to get out of this one, thanks to Brimstone."

Luc approached, a huge grin on his face. "You should have been here, Romano." He slapped Constantine on his back. "You could have helped us take d'Angelo down."

"Let go of me, Gianna," Constantine demanded.

She clung tighter. "Not if you plan on hitting my brother."

"I said, let go of me."

Luc's attention switched from one to the other, a frown forming between his brows. "I don't understand. What's the problem?"

"What's the…" It took Constantine a moment to recover his breath enough to speak. He seized Gianna around the waist and set her to one side. "How would you like my putting Téa in the sort of danger you've put Gianna in? What would you do to the man who used her in such a fashion and never discussed it with you first?"

Luc froze. For a split second, his gaze landed on Gianna then bounced off again. "You're absolutely right, Constantine. I apologize. I was so anxious to get my hands on d'Angelo that I didn't even think about the risk my sister was taking. I guess I'm so used to the security business it never occurred to me that she'd be in any danger."

Constantine closed his eyes, his fury deflating. "You thought I knew," he said to Luc.

Gianna's brother winced and shot him a look of intense sympathy. "Yeah, sorry. Should have known better. Gia has seven older brothers and cousins, all of whom set a horrible example for her. There's not a trick she hasn't learned."

"I'll keep that in mind from now on."

"Still, I should have spoken directly to you about it."

"Are you very angry?" Gianna had the nerve to ask.

"Furious." Constantine spared her a brief, speaking glance. "We'll discuss it later. Right now I have some very confused businessmen waiting for me."

"I've already given my statement to the police." She checked with Luc, who nodded. "I can leave now, if you'd like."

If he'd like? Words fought for release, none of them fit to be aired. "I don't like," he said gently. "I insist."

She cleared her throat, perhaps becoming aware of the extent of his anger for the first time. "Great." She plastered a cheerful smile on her face and glanced around. "So, how do we get there?"

It was only then that Constantine realized he'd paid off the cab. Luc jumped in and waved Juice over, who waited on the tiny front stoop of the Mereaux house, hovering protectively over the slender woman standing beside him. "You can use our rental while we go to the police station and finalize everything."

Luc had chosen a nondescript sedan and Constantine helped Gianna into the car. He managed to drive a full dozen blocks before he couldn't stand it any longer and pulled over. His hands clenched around the steering wheel. "Okay, let's hear it."

Gianna sighed. "I'm sorry, Constantine. I knew if I told you what we planned, you wouldn't agree."

"Wouldn't agree?" he repeated. He swiveled in his seat to face her. "Have you lost your mind? *Of course* I wouldn't have agreed. I'd never do anything to put you in jeopardy or allowed you anywhere near d'Angelo, especially after what he did to you last time."

A stubborn look settled on her face. "Don't you see? I had to face him the same way I had to face the lake. Luc and Juice wouldn't have let anything happen to me. And the police were alerted in advance. They had officers in the area." She caught her lower lip between her teeth, her jade gaze holding a combination of apology and determination. "I did it, Constantine. I looked him right in the eyes and realized what a contemptible little worm he is."

Constantine fought to temper his anger, to consider the situation from her point of view. "I can't argue with your description. I can and do argue with how you went about it. Did you give a single thought to my take on all this? To how I'd react or my opinion? We're supposed to be a team, Gianna."

She winced. "You're right and I am sorry. I promise I won't keep anything from you in the future. Not that anything like this will ever happen again."

"No, it won't, as I intend to make very clear to each and every one of your relatives." He couldn't help himself. He pulled her close and held her. "Were you very afraid?"

"Not even a little." She tilted her head back and grinned. "Okay, maybe a little, but it was only a very little."

"D'Angelo followed you to the Mereaux residence?"

"More or less. He arrived a few minutes after I did."

"He didn't harm you or the Mereaux woman?"

"No. Mia handled it like a trouper. He came in and demanded the doll. Luc had told us what to say so it would be a clear-cut case of theft." Her brow wrinkled. "Or is it burglary?" She shrugged. "No matter. They taped every last word. Then David ripped open the poor doll and removed Brimstone. Lord, it was huge. And because it's worth so much, taking it makes it a far more serious crime. Somehow I don't think he's going to get out of this one as easily as he's gotten out of so many of his other problems."

"He won't be getting out of those, either. He and his father are under investigation for embezzlement."

"Couldn't happen to a nicer guy," Gianna said cheerfully.

Constantine checked his watch. "Moretti should be arriving shortly. I need to get back to the Diamondt building."

"I gather I'm coming with you?" she asked.

He shot her a hard look. "You, *piccola,* will not be out of my sight for the rest of our stay in Seattle."

She sighed. "Sort of thought you might say that."

Gianna and Constantine arrived at the Diamondt building shortly after four. To her intense surprise, the first person she saw when she entered the foyer was her oldest cousin, Sev. She made a beeline for him.

"Severo Dante, what on earth are you doing here?" she demanded.

He jerked at her question and swept around to confront her. She checked her forward momentum at the last instant, only just preventing herself from giving the man a hug.

He was as tall as Sev—two or three inches over six feet—with hair every bit as black. He also possessed the same intense golden eyes as both her cousin and her grandfather, Primo. His features were equally hard, cut in strong, less-than-handsome lines, but all the more powerful because of it. He'd dressed in a black suit, one that emphasized his broad shoulders and strong, muscular legs, and cloaked him in darkness.

Unable to help herself, she fell back a step, thoroughly intimidated. "I'm sorry. I thought you were my cousin." She glanced over her shoulder, searching for Constantine, before offering her hand with a hesitant smile. "I don't suppose you have any Dante relatives in your background? You could pass for one of my family without any problem at all. The resemblance is really quite amazing."

He didn't speak for a long moment. Then in a voice as

deep and black as his appearance, he asked, "Who are you?"

Her hand dropped slowly to her side. "I'm Gianna Dante. Constantine Romano is my fiancé," she explained stiffly.

His eyes narrowed in open displeasure. To her extreme relief, she felt the reassuring pressure of Constantine's hands on her shoulder. "Is there a problem?"

Moretti hesitated, then shook his head. "I'm satisfied with what I've seen here. Send the contract," he said, his gaze never shifting from Gianna. And with that, he turned and left, flowing from the building like black fog.

"What the hell was that about?" Constantine demanded.

"I think I remember where I heard the name Moretti before," Gianna murmured, stricken. "That's the name of the woman my uncle Dominic had an affair with. The woman he was leaving Aunt Laura for. Oh, Constantine. I think maybe Uncle Dominic did more than have an affair with her. A lot more."

Ten

Constantine stared after Gabe Moretti in disbelief. "You think he's a Dante? Seriously?"

"I don't know." Gianna gnawed on her lower lip. "You saw him. Don't you think he could have passed for Sev's twin brother?"

"Don't jump to any rash conclusions," Constantine warned. "You're far too good at that."

She swiveled to face him, planting her hands on her shapely hips. "Tell me you're not going to rub that in my face for the rest of our lives."

The time had come to deal with her impulsiveness once and for all. He approached and went toe-to-toe with her. "I won't rub it in your face, if you promise not to act rashly."

She smiled sweetly. "I assume that means you want prior approval on every decision I make. How deliciously caveman of you." She swept her hand downward to indicate her pantsuit. "Would you care to approve my clothes, for instance? My shoes? What about my hair?"

"That's not what I mean and you damn well know it," he growled. "Even Luc acknowledged that I should have been informed of what you had planned for today. You admitted that the only reason you didn't was that you knew I would object. So don't act as though I'm coming on like some sort of Neanderthal." He leaned in. "Imagine if the situation had been reversed and I'd been the one in that house. If Juice and your brothers had kept our plan from you. Admit it. You would have been furious."

For an instant, he thought she'd argue the point. Then she blew out a sigh and nodded. "No, you're right. I should have told you, just as I would have expected you to tell me."

A smile built across his face. It was times like this that she blew him away. Her fairness. The frank way she admitted her mistakes. They were just a few of the qualities he adored about her. "I appreciate your honesty."

"Yeah, well. I'm still sort of new at this whole team thing we have going," she admitted.

"As am I." He cupped a hand around the back of her neck and drew her up for a slow kiss. "Look on the bright side. D'Angelo is in jail and unlikely to get out anytime soon. I was just awarded a huge contract. And you may have a new cousin."

She grimaced. "I'm not sure there's a bright side to your last point."

"Time will tell." He released her. "Now that we're a team, how do you suggest we handle the possibility?"

"I don't know," she admitted.

"Should you tell Primo?"

"Tell him that his son may have fathered a child out of wedlock?" She shuddered. "Scary thought."

"Do you want to think about it for a while?"

Her eyebrows shot skyward. "What? Not act impulsively for once? Me?"

He smothered a smile. "I know it'll be a challenge."

"In this case, not so much." She frowned unhappily. "To be honest, I would like to think about it for a while."

Constantine glanced again at the exit Gabe Moretti had taken. "I have a feeling you won't be the only one."

The next several weeks passed with lightning speed. Gianna should have been blissfully happy, but a single shadow continued to hang over her. Not once in all the time she'd been with Constantine had he said those vital three words she'd shared with him the night they'd made love for the first time: *I love you.* He wanted her. No question there. The Inferno burned and connected them in ways that suggested love and a lifelong commitment. But real love? Natural love? Non-Inferno influenced love?

She just couldn't be certain.

How much of his desire and commitment to marry her were based on The Inferno and feeling honor-bound to marry her because they'd made love? And how much of it was based on true feeling? It was definitely a conversation they needed to have before the wedding.

But as the days and weeks passed, Gianna couldn't figure out a way to discuss the problem with him. Or perhaps she couldn't find the right words because, despite facing all of her other fears, she couldn't bring herself to face this one. She couldn't bear the idea of his admitting to her that he didn't love her, that it was all due to The Inferno.

If that's what he believed, she'd be forced to cancel their wedding, something her entire family—not to mention Constantine—would oppose. Oppose? She laughed without humor. She knew her family. And though they were the most loving and generous people she'd ever known, they wouldn't hesitate to drag her to the altar and find a priest who'd marry them regardless of whether or not she said "I do." Considering she and Constantine had experienced The Inferno, they wouldn't give her any other choice. If they knew the two of them had slept together… Well, forget it. The wedding would happen faster than the sizzle of The Inferno.

And still the days passed.

The night before the wedding, Primo threw a party in their honor. "I think it was to keep us from stealing away your fiancé and debauching him," Rafe informed Gianna with a wink.

She laughed. "No bachelor's party?"

"We might try to sneak him off into a corner and debauch him there. Maybe Primo won't notice."

"Doubtful. Primo notices everything and knows everything."

Though there was one thing he didn't know. She hadn't told him about Gabe Moretti, yet. Both she and Constantine had made some subtle inquiries after their return from Seattle. At least, she hoped they'd been subtle. Eventually, they'd discovered that Gabe Moretti was indeed the son of Cara Moretti. And though that fact alone didn't prove Dominic Dante was his father, the family resemblance suggested that possibility. Possibility? Probability. After discussing it with Constantine a final time, she'd decided to turn the entire matter over to her grandfather.

She found him where she often did, in the kitchen. He'd chased off all his helpers and she knew better than to offer her assistance. In this family, the kitchen was her grandfather's domain. "So, *chiacchierona*. Are you nervous about tomorrow?" he asked, his trademark cigar clamped between his teeth.

She hesitated, driven to answer honestly. "A little."

Her grandfather sampled his sauce, eyeing her over the steaming ladle. "And what part makes you a little nervous?"

"Constantine and I haven't known each other very long."

Primo lifted a shoulder in a shrug. "Eh. You have the next sixty years to get to know each other. You have The Inferno, which means your marriage will be passionate, happy and successful. That is all that matters, yes?"

She stared down at the kitchen table and traced one of the gouges her cousin Marco had carved in it years ago. A love scratch, her grandmother had claimed. A nick alongside so many other nicks, all of which helped imbue a piece of furniture with the richness and history of the family who owned it. Gianna smiled sadly. Maybe she wouldn't be as nervous of tomorrow's events if she believed that The Inferno was forever, that someday she and Constantine would have a kitchen table that spoke of generations worth of love and use.

She glanced up, on the verge of telling her grandfather about what she'd learned on her thirteenth birthday. But when she looked into those ancient golden eyes, eyes filled with love and understanding and an absolute certainty in the world as he knew it, she couldn't bring herself to disillusion him.

"Constantine and I met someone in Seattle," she said instead. "I didn't know if I should tell you about it. But I think I better."

Primo turned the flame beneath his sauce to a simmer and snagged a pair of bottles of homemade beer out of the cavernous refrigerator. Popping the tops with practiced ease, he set one in front of her. He took the seat beside her and tapped his bottle against hers. *"Cin cin."*

They both drank. "This man…" She didn't see any easy way to tell him. "He looked just like Sev. And you."

Primo closed his eyes. "His name?"

"Gabe Moretti. He wasn't pleased to meet me." She waited for her grandfather to gather himself before continuing. "Who is he? How is he related to us?"

"I believe he is your Uncle Dominic's son."

It confirmed her suspicions. "With the woman he was leaving Aunt Laura for?"

"This is not an appropriate conversation on the eve of your wedding," Primo said gently. "We will talk of it another time. Thank you for telling me."

She recognized Primo's expression. She wouldn't get any more information out of him. "I'm planning on holding you to that. If Constantine's going to do business with the man, chances are we'll meet again—sooner rather than later. I'd rather not be in the dark when we do."

Primo inclined his head. "You will not mention this to anyone else. *Mi hai capito,* Gianna Marie?"

She made a face. "Yes, I understand. In fact, I had a feeling you were going to say that." She stood. "I'll let Constantine know."

The rest of the night was everything she could have asked, the evening filled with joy, fun, laughter and, most important of all, the warmth of family unity. She wasn't the least surprised when the Dantes gathered in Primo's garden after dinner and began relating old, favorite stories. While her grandparents took turns telling Constantine about their first Inferno meeting—perpetuating the falsehood of The Inferno—Gianna slipped away from the light and crowd and retreated into the shadows.

Tomorrow she'd be a married woman. Would she be one of the lucky ones, like her own parents and grandparents? Or would she and Constantine end up like Uncle Dominic and Aunt Laura?

"Are you okay?" Constantine came up behind her and wrapped his arms around her, pulling her close.

She melted against him with a sigh of happiness. "I'm fine."

"Nervous about tomorrow?"

"You're the tenth person tonight who's asked me that."

"Probably why you're nervous."

She laughed. "That must be it." She turned in his arms and allowed her fingers to drift deep into the thick waves of his hair. "There can't possibly be any other reason."

"No, there can't." His absolute certainty humbled her. "You know I want you more than any other woman I've known."

Not quite a declaration of love. But close. Maybe in time he'd say the words. Maybe in time he'd mean them. Before she could reply, she heard Rafe just behind them, laughing at something Luc said.

He approached, slapping Constantine on the back. "Ready for tomorrow or do you have cold feet? My car's out front. They'd never catch us if you want to make a break for it."

Constantine's brow furrowed briefly as he mulled over "make a break for it." He must have reasoned through the idiom because he laughed. "No breaking necessary. Gianna is the only woman I want. The only woman I'll ever want."

Rafe chuckled. "She'll definitely be the only one. The Inferno will see to that."

Constantine's bleak gaze shifted to Gianna, making her want to weep. "So I understand," he murmured. "Let us hope the reverse is also true."

* * *

The day of Gianna's wedding dawned sunny and temperate. The morning passed in a dreamy haze. Someone came and fixed her hair, then magically vanished. Same with her makeup. While her bridesmaids—a few college friends, along with her sisters and cousins-in-law—hovered and fluttered, laughing and teasing, Nonna and her mother kept her from floating away. Or maybe it was Rafe's words that kept her grounded, slipping into her dream day like a dark, threatening cloud.

She'll definitely be the only one. The Inferno will see to that.

The gown she'd chosen was molded antique lace with a keyhole back and chapel train. The finishing touch was a fabulous Dante fire diamond tiara that kept her lace veil anchored firmly in place. The trip to the wedding chapel took no time at all, or so it seemed to Gianna. One minute she stood in her parents' home, the next she entered the church. The women were all ushered into the bride's room to await the start of the ceremony. She'd been told that Constantine and his groomsmen had already arrived and were relaxing in a nearby room. She could vaguely hear the sound of masculine voices drifting down the hall.

"Are you okay?" Ariana asked in concern. She and Lazz had flown in for the special occasion with their baby, Amata.

Gianna managed a quick smile. "Of course. No worries." Well, except for one.

She'll definitely be the only one. The Inferno will see to that.

It wasn't fair, she realized. As much as she loved Constantine, it wasn't fair to keep him trapped against his will. To force him into a marriage. Not if he didn't really love her. She didn't want an Inferno love. Not one forced on the man she married. She wanted him to love her for herself. Because he had chosen. Because he had made the decision she was the only one for him.

She shot to her feet in a panic. "I need to see Constantine."

For a split second the women all froze, silence gripping the room. Then everyone started talking at once. She couldn't make out a word they said. Nor did it matter. She headed for the door.

Her mother intercepted her, but Gianna shook her head. "Don't, Mamma. I wouldn't ask if it weren't important."

"It is bad luck," Elia protested. "You must wait until after you exchange your vows. Look, your babbo is here. The ceremony is about to begin. It's time for me to take my seat in the church."

Gianna shook her head. "This won't wait. I have to talk to Constantine now. Before the wedding."

Elia turned to her husband. "Alessandro," she called, a hint of desperation slipping into her voice. "Come speak to your daughter."

Before he could, Gianna escaped the bride's room. Her mother followed, the rest of the women on her heels. Gianna found Constantine's room without any difficulty. The door stood open. Masculine laughter erupted from inside, the sound dying the instant they caught sight of her standing in the doorway.

Constantine stood, eyeing her in concern. "*Piccola?* What are you doing here? Is something wrong?"

"I need to talk to you. It's important." She spared her brothers and cousins a swift look. She'd rather they not hear this next part. "Would you excuse us, please?"

They didn't want to leave. But they did it for her. One by one they filed from the room.

"*Dio,* look at you," Constantine murmured. "Words fail me."

Tears misted her eyes and her chin quivered. "You look pretty fine, yourself."

He must have sensed her panic because he stilled. "What's going on?" he asked sharply. "Why are you here?"

"I love you. I just need to tell you that first."

His expression relaxed and he closed the distance between them. He started to reach for her, then paused. "I'm afraid to touch you." Gently he pulled her into his arms and kissed her. "Now tell me what's wrong."

She closed her eyes. He still hadn't said the words, which made her decision so much easier. "I need to do something for you, before we marry."

"I don't understand. Do what?" He glanced briefly at the closed door. "Are you sure this can't wait?" he asked.

Almost. Almost she grabbed the lifeline. But she'd faced all of her other fears. She'd face this one, too. "No, this can't wait." She held out her hands. She could see they trembled, the fire diamond on her engagement ring flashing in agitation. "Give me your hand. Your right hand." The Infernoed hand.

His confusion threatened to break her heart, especially when she knew he didn't suspect what she was about to do. She took his strong, warm hand between her freezing ones. It took every ounce of determination she possessed to say the words that had to be spoken.

"I release you," she told him, her voice trembling. She had a vague recollection of her uncle saying it three times. Third time's the charm? Just in case, she added, "I release you. I release you."

He must have begun to suspect something. "What have you done, Gianna?" he demanded.

The breath shuddered from her lungs. "I've just released you from The Inferno."

"You've *what?*"

Tears spilled over. "I've released you."

"No." He jerked his hand free of hers. "No, you have not done this to us. *Give it back!*"

Her face crumpled. "I don't think I can."

Constantine strode to the door, flinging it open. "Get Primo. Now." He slammed the door closed and turned to confront her. "Why would you do this to us, Gianna? Why try to destroy what we have, today of all days?"

She sank onto a footstool and bowed her head. Her dress pooled around her and she ran shaking fingers over the beautiful antique lace. Such a gorgeous gown meant for such a happy occasion. And look what she'd done to it. To them.

Slowly she lifted her eyes, forcing herself to meet Constantine's infuriated gaze. "I did it because you're not the only one who believes in honor. I refuse to use The Inferno to force you to the altar. I want you to marry me because you love me, not because you have no other choice. You said yourself that you didn't like having the control taken away from you. You've even referred to The Inferno as an infection. All I've done is return your control, cured your infection."

The door burst open and Primo strode into the room. He took one look at Gianna and Constantine, and closed the door behind him. "What is this?" He spoke in Italian, the only indication of his concern. "What has happened?"

Constantine swiveled to confront him, leveling an accusing finger in Gianna's direction. "She took away The Inferno. Make her give it back."

Primo froze for an instant. Then his mouth dropped open and he blinked in astonishment. Tilting back his head, he roared with laughter. "Give it *back?*" Tears filled his eyes, making them glitter like ancient gold and he fumbled for a handkerchief to wipe the dampness from them. "Is this a joke?"

"It's no joke," Constantine said through clenched teeth. "She released me. I want you to make her give me back The Inferno."

Primo patted his pockets until he came up with a cigar. "Give it back," he repeated, still chuckling.

"Primo, you can't smoke that in here," Gianna informed him quietly. "It's against the law."

"Phft. These laws do not apply to me. I am what they call 'grandfathered in.'" But he did refrain from lighting up. He clamped the cigar between his teeth and leveled Gianna with a look. *"Spieghi lei."*

She didn't want to explain. Couldn't explain. Couldn't tell her beloved grandfather the truth about his son and daughter-in-law. Definitely couldn't tell him what she'd learned about The Inferno. "Primo—"

"Subito!"

She shrugged, surrendering to the inevitable. "Constantine's right. I took back The Inferno. I released him."

Primo raised his eyes heavenward. *"Santa Maria, Madre di Dio.* What has gotten into you, Gianna? There are no take backs in The Inferno." He wavered between laughter and outrage. "Where did you hear such nonsense?"

She hesitated. One look at her grandfather's expression warned that he'd have the answer from her, no matter how long it took. "Uncle Dominic and Aunt Laura."

Primo stiffened. "Dominic," he repeated. Spinning around, he crossed to the door and yanked it open. "Get Severo. Now."

Her cousin Sev entered a moment later. He was followed by his wife, Francesca, and Constantine's sister, Ariana.

An instant later her parents slipped into the room, along with her grandmother, Nonna. They settled her in a chair not far from Gianna. That opened the floodgates and the entire family piled in behind them.

"This concerns all of us," Alessandro informed his father. *"La famiglia."*

And that said it all.

Reluctantly Primo nodded. He took a seat beside Gianna and gathered her hands in his. Constantine sat behind her, his solid warmth at her back, a supportive hand on her shoulder. Her family encircled the three of them, love and concern flowing from them in palpable waves.

"You have often been a *chiacchierona* when you should not," Primo said, though kindly. "Perhaps this is one of the times you should have chattered more and chose instead to chatter less. From the beginning, Gianna."

She spared Sev a swift look. Other than her grandparents, his reaction to her story worried her the most. "It was my thirteenth birthday. The day before Uncle Dominic and Aunt Laura died."

Almost in unison, the family crossed themselves. "We were at your uncle's house to celebrate the occasion," Primo prompted. "I remember that day."

Her hands tightened within her grandfather's warm hold. Behind her, Constantine gave her shoulder a reassuring squeeze. "Even at that young age, I was crazy about shoes."

"So was Mamma," Sev murmured.

"Yes. For my gift, she told me to go up to her closet and pick out any pair of shoes I wanted." Gianna sighed at the memory. "I'd never seen so many lovely shoes."

Constantine snorted.

Gianna took instant umbrage. "Believe it or not, she had even more pairs than I do. And her closet…" She sighed. Aware that she was getting a bit offtrack, she forced herself to focus. "I'd probably been up there for a full hour, trying on pair after pair, unable to make up my mind, when Uncle Dominic and Aunt Laura came into the bedroom. I was buried in the closet. They didn't know I was there. Aunt Laura had probably forgotten. Or maybe she assumed I'd already left. They...they were fighting."

Sev's expression darkened. "They did that a lot right before..." He shook off the memory. "Go on, Gianna."

"Uncle Dominic told her he planned to leave and wanted a divorce. Aunt Laura started crying. She said..." Gianna swallowed. "She said 'But what about The Inferno? You told me it would last forever.'"

Sev stiffened. Primo closed his eyes. Nonna lifted a trembling hand to her mouth.

"I'm sorry," Gianna whispered. "I'm so sorry to tell you this."

"Continue," Primo prompted.

"Uncle Dominic said that he'd experienced The Inferno with someone else. If he mentioned her name, I don't recall it. He said it happens sometimes. That it was beyond his control." She felt the ripple of disbelief sweep through her cousins and brothers. She didn't dare look at any of their wives to see how they were taking the news. "Aunt Laura was still crying, but she was also angry. She said that he'd told her when they'd married that he'd felt The Inferno for her. That Primo had told her it only happened once in a lifetime. That she'd never have married him if they hadn't felt The Inferno for each other."

"The Inferno does only happen once in a lifetime," her grandfather said gently.

Gianna shook her head. She looked at him miserably, the pain of disillusioning him worse than anything she'd ever experienced before. "Uncle Dominic said you didn't know because you'd never felt it for anyone else the way he had.

He said that Dantes can feel it for more than one person, but that he could fix things. Take away The Inferno so Aunt Laura wouldn't love him anymore. He took her hand in his and he released her."

"What?" The question came from more than one of her relatives.

"He released her," Gianna repeated. "And it worked."

For the first time in her entire life she heard Primo swear. She was so shocked she could only sit and stare, openmouthed. Her grandfather spared Sev a brief, sorrowful look. "It pains me to say this about my own son, but Dominic lied."

Gianna shook her head. "No. No, he didn't. He left after that and Aunt Laura called a friend. She said that The Inferno was gone. She said she felt it leave when Uncle Dominic released her. And she was glad. Glad The Inferno couldn't force her to love someone against her will any longer. Now she could go sailing with him in the morning while they discussed the divorce and it wouldn't interfere with her decisions." Gianna started to cry. "I'm sorry. I never wanted to tell any of you this because you were all so happy. Now I've ruined it for everyone."

Constantine swept her into his arms and cradled her close. "Shh, *piccola*. You haven't ruined anything."

"Yes, I have. I released you. The Inferno is gone. You won't love me now."

"Is it gone?" he asked tenderly. "All this time I have been sitting here listening to your story and my palm has itched and throbbed just as it always has. Even more important…" He took a deep breath. "I have never in my life told a woman I loved her. I've even resisted saying it to you. Pride, I suppose. A last defense against something beyond my control."

She fought to free herself from his hold, but he wouldn't let her go. "You don't want to love me, do you?"

"I don't want to be controlled by love," he corrected. "So much of my life was spent being controlled by others, by circumstance, by my family's financial difficulties, that I fought what cannot be fought. What I wasn't willing to admit until this moment is that love doesn't mean surrendering control." He looked at her then, his dark eyes filled with an emotion impossible to mistake. "It means surrendering your heart into the safekeeping of someone you love and trust more than anyone else in the world. And that I do freely. *Ti amo, piccola.* I love you."

Helpless tears flowed down her cheeks. "I don't understand. I took away The Inferno."

He laced their hands together. "Stop and feel with your heart. Is it still there, or not?"

Her breath caught. Yes. Yes, it was. She didn't understand it. She stared in wonder at their linked hands. "I still feel it. How is that possible? I released you."

Sev crouched in front of her. "Gianna, you should have told us this long ago. We would have explained the truth." Pain ripped through his gaze. "My parents never felt The Inferno for each other. My father married my mother for her fortune, not because he loved her. He loved another woman, Cara Moretti. *She* was his Inferno soul mate."

"But Aunt Laura said she felt The Inferno."

Sev's mouth compressed. "I'm sure Mamma thought she did. Though Babbo never loved her, not the way she deserved. That didn't change the fact that she adored him. I think she wanted to feel The Inferno. So she convinced herself she did. But it wasn't true."

In all the years since her thirteenth birthday, not once had Gianna ever considered the possibility that her uncle had lied to her aunt. That he could have done such an awful thing to his wife. But he had. Considering how hard the knowledge hit her, it had to be far worse for Sev. Impulsively she threw her arms around his neck and wrapped him up in a fierce hug.

"I'm sorry. I'm so, so sorry."

He patted her back. "I already knew most of it," he reassured her. "I didn't realize he'd used The Inferno to convince my mother to marry him. But it isn't that big of a surprise, considering some of the other things he's done."

The information had also hit Primo and Nonna hard, particularly her grandmother. But there had always been a steely strength buried beneath Nonna's sweetness. "This is a happy occasion, not a sad one," she informed her family. "We are finished here, yes? It is time for the wedding."

"No," Constantine said. His hands slid from Gianna's shoulders and he stood, folding his arms across his chest. "We're not getting married. Not yet."

Gianna rose and spun to face him, panic flaring to life. "Constantine?"

"You released me. That suggests you wanted to be released, too."

Her panic grew, breaking across her in great, messy waves. "No. No, that's not true."

"Then why release me?"

She took a step in his direction. "Don't you understand? I don't want you to marry me because you're honor-bound. I don't want you to marry me because of The Inferno. I want you to love me." Her voice broke and it took her a moment to gather herself sufficiently to speak again. "I want you to love *me*. Just me."

Constantine closed his eyes. He reached for her hand and before she could guess his intentions, slipped her engagement ring from her finger. Her entire family stiffened. Francesca gasped, while Ariana murmured a broken, "Oh, no." He ignored them all.

"Have you never once looked at your ring?"

Gianna stared in horror. "You mean take it off? Before we were married?"

"Of course I mean take it off," he said in exasperation.

"Oh, no. It's bad luck," the women chimed in, practically in unison.

He released a sigh. "Got it. Well, I chose it very, very carefully. Sev can attest to that."

Her cousin nodded. "It took hours. He must have gone through every ring in the entire Eternity line before he settled on this one," he informed her.

Constantine nodded. "That's because all the rings have names. It's part of what makes them so special. I needed one with the perfect name." He tilted it so she could see the tiny script inside the band. "Read what it says."

She needed a moment to blink the tears away. The letters swam into focus, forming words. *Before All Else...Love.* Then she was crying again. "Do you really mean it?"

"I really mean it, *piccola*. Honor means everything to me, you know this. But you... You are my heart and soul." He returned the ring to her finger, this time with an attitude of permanence. "You are not Laura and I am not Dominic. It's our love that makes this marriage honorable. Without it, there would be no honor in the vows we take."

Gianna flung herself into Constantine's embrace. "I was afraid you'd feel trapped. That one day you'd resent me."

His arms closed around her like iron bands. "Do you remember my telling you that I don't like taking off my shoes, not even when I relax?"

"Yes."

"There's a reason for that." He spared her family a brief shamed look before his gaze settled on his sister, Ariana.

Gianna saw compassion in his sister's expression, along with understanding. "Growing up, there was no money. My grandmother Penelope helped out the best she could, but it wasn't nearly enough, not for an estate the size of ours. Do you know how we survived?"

Gianna shook her head.

"My father traded on the Romano name." Considering Constantine's pride, it must have been the most difficult thing he'd ever admitted. "We lived off the charity of others, including the d'Angelos. We sold our illustrious heritage and scintillating company for the bread we ate and the beds we slept in. For loans that were never repaid."

"That's why you wouldn't come to me empty-handed."

He nodded. "And that's why I don't take off my shoes."

She frowned in confusion. "I don't understand."

"Our visits didn't always end well," he explained gently. "When they didn't, we soon learned to be ready to leave at a moment's notice. Fleeing into a cold winter night without shoes is a memorable experience. You learn very quickly not to make the same mistake twice."

"Oh, Constantine," she whispered.

He set her aside and toed off first one shoe, then the other. Crossing to the window, he opened it and tossed his shoes outside. Then he returned to her. "You are all I want. All I'll ever want. Do you understand now, *piccola?*" He cupped her face between his Infernoed hands and kissed her with all the pent-up passion he possessed. "I don't need to keep my shoes close by because I'm finally home. This is where I belong and I'm here to stay. My sense of honor bound me to you. Our love is what will keep us together."

Primo rose to his feet. *"Salute! Alla famiglia!"*

The rest of the family picked up the cheer while Constantine swept his bride into his arms. As one they exited the room in a grand procession to the chapel, laughing

and crying, their happiness spilling out in great joyous
waves over those assembled in the church. Down the aisle
they came.

They were Dantes. *La famiglia*. And that said it all.

One Inferno family.

One Inferno heart.

Soul mates found.

Soul mates bonded—united for all time.

* * * * *

"Ultimately this is about what's best for our son."

To hear Nathan refer to Max as "our son" made Ana's heart twist. For a long time he had been just "her son". She wasn't sure if she was ready to give that up, to share him. But this wasn't about what she wanted. The only thing that mattered was what was best for Max.

"I guess a trial period would make sense," she told him. "Supervised visits of course."

"Of course," he agreed.

It meant having to spend time with Nathan, which she was sure would be heart-wrenching for her. Just having him in her home, remembering all the times they had spent there together, made her feel hollowed out inside. Alone. Since they split, she hadn't so much as looked at another man.

If a year and a half apart hadn't dissolved her feelings for Nathan, maybe she was destined to love him forever.

Dear Reader,

I must confess, I have a really hard time writing these letters. I can't help feeling a bit like a broken record. I find myself, over and over, going on about my characters, and how special they are. How unique and inspiring. But this time I thought I would try something different. I thought it might be fun to tell you about the character writing the characters.

Me.

So here goes. I'm a little shy when I'm in a group of people I don't know. I cannot function without my morning coffee—at least two cups. I hate to blog because I never know what to say. I am married to, hands down, the best husband ever. My children are the most talented and most brilliant in human history and ditto for my grandchildren. I used to love to sew and craft, but now I only have time to crochet. I am also an avid gardener when I can find the time. I am the youngest of three, and when my two older brothers weren't torturing me, they spoiled me rotten. I love animals, spring and poker night. I can not play an instrument, or sing my way out of a paper bag, and my family always, *always* comes first.

So there you have it. Now, forget about me, and enjoy the book!

Best,

Michelle

A CLANDESTINE
CORPORATE AFFAIR

BY
MICHELLE CELMER

Published in Great Britain 2012
by Mills & Boon, an imprint of Harlequin (UK) Limited,
Eton House, 18-24 Paradise Road, Richmond, Surrey TW9 1SR

© Michelle Celmer 2011

ISBN: 978 0 263 89144 7

51-0312

Harlequin (UK) policy is to use papers that are natural, renewable and recyclable products and made from wood grown in sustainable forests. The logging and manufacturing processes conform to the legal environmental regulations of the country of origin.

Printed and bound in Spain
by Blackprint CPI, Barcelona

Bestselling author **Michelle Celmer** lives in southeastern Michigan with her husband, their three children, two dogs and two cats. When she's not writing or busy being a mum, you can find her in the garden or curled up with a romance novel. And if you twist her arm really hard, you can usually persuade her into a day of power shopping.

Michelle loves to hear from readers. Visit her website, www.michellecelmer.com, or write to her at PO Box 300, Clawson, MI 48017, USA.

To Jim, for being the best big brother a pesky younger sister could ask for.

One

Oh, this was not good.

Ana Birch glanced casually over her shoulder to the upper level of the country club deck, hoping to catch a glimpse of the man in the dark leather jacket, praying that she had been mistaken, that her eyes had been playing tricks on her. Maybe it just looked like him. For months after he dumped her she would see his features in every stranger's face. The dark, bedroom eyes and the sensual curve of his lips. She would see his broad shoulders and lean physique in men she passed on the street. Her breath would catch and her heart would beat faster…then sink miserably when she realized it was only someone who looked like him. In the eighteen months since he'd ended their affair, he hadn't so much as called her.

She finally caught sight of him standing by the bar, drink in hand, talking with one of the other guests. Her heart bottomed out, then climbed back up into her throat and lodged there. This was no illusion. It was definitely him.

Oh, God. How could Beth do this to her?

Hitching her nine-month-old son, Max, higher on her hip, she crossed the pristine, rolling green lawn, her heels sinking into the soft, spongy sod. *Note to self: never wear spiked heels to an outdoor kids' party. Or a silk jacket,* she added with annoyance, as Max wiggled and slid south again down her side.

In her skinny jeans and knee-high boots, with her freshly dyed, siren-red hair, she was the antithesis of the society mothers who drank and socialized while harried nannies chased their children. A fact that clearly escaped no one as curious glances followed in her wake. But no one dared insult the heiress to the Birch Energy empire, at least not to her face, which Ana found both a relief and an annoyance.

She spotted her cousin Beth standing by the gigantic, inflatable, plastic-ball-filled, germ-breeding monstrosity, watching her six-year-old daughter, Piper, the birthday girl, screaming and flailing inside with a dozen other children.

She loved Beth like a sister, but this time she had gone too far.

Beth saw them approaching and smiled. She didn't even have the decency to look guilty for what she had done, which didn't surprise Ana in the least. Beth's own life was so abysmally uneventful and boring, she seemed to take pleasure meddling in other people's business. But there was more at stake here than harmless gossip.

"Maxie!" Beth said holding out her arms. Max screeched excitedly and lunged for her, and Ana handed him over. Beth probably figured that Ana couldn't physically assault her while she was holding a baby.

"Why is *he* here?" Ana demanded under her breath.

"Who?" Beth asked, playing the innocent card, when she knew damned well *who*.

"Nathan."

Ana shot a look over her shoulder at Nathan Everette, chief brand officer of Western Oil, standing by the railing, drink in hand, looking as conservatively handsome and casually sophisticated as he had the day Beth had introduced them. He hadn't been Ana's type, as in: he had a successful career, and he didn't have tattoos or a police record. But he was a bigwig at Western Oil, so having a drink with him had been the ultimate "screw you" to her father. Then one drink became two, then three, and when he asked to drive her home she'd thought, what the heck, he's pretty harmless.

So much for that brilliant theory. When he kissed her at the door she'd practically burst into flames. Despite what she led people to believe, she wasn't the precocious sex kitten described in the social pages. She was very selective about who she slept with, and it was never on a first date, but she had practically dragged him inside. And though he might have looked conservative and even came off as a bit stuffy, the man definitely knew how to please a woman. Suddenly sex had taken on an entirely new meaning for her. Then it was no longer about defying her father. She just plain wanted Nathan.

Though it was only supposed to be one night, he kept calling and she found herself helpless to resist him. She was head over heels in love with him by the time he dumped her. Not to mention pregnant.

Nathan glanced her way and their eyes met and locked, and she found herself trapped in their piercing gaze. A cold chill raised the hair on her arms and the back of her neck. One that had nothing to do with the brisk December wind. Then her heart started to beat faster as that familiar awareness crept through her and heat climbed from her throat to the crest of her cheeks.

She tore her eyes away.

"He was Leo's college roommate," Beth said, tickling Max under the chin. "I couldn't not invite him. It would have been rude."

"You could have at least warned me."

"If I had, would you have come?"

"Of course not!" She'd spent the better part of the past eighteen months avoiding him. Having him this close to Max was a risk she simply could not take. Beth *knew* how she felt about this.

Beth's delicate brow pinched, and she lowered her voice to a harsh whisper. "Maybe I thought it was time you stopped hiding from him. The truth is bound to come out. Don't you think it's better now than later? Don't you think he has a right to know?"

As far as Ana was concerned, he could never know the truth. Besides, he'd made his feelings more than clear. Though he cared for her, he wasn't in the market for a committed relationship. He didn't have time. And even if he did, it wouldn't be with the daughter of a direct competitor. That would be the end of his career.

Wasn't that the story of her life. For her father, Walter Birch, owner of Birch Energy, reputation and appearances had always meant far more to him than his daughter's happiness. If he knew she'd had an affair with the CBO of Western Oil, and that man was the father of his grandson, he would see it as the ultimate betrayal. He had considered it a disgrace that she'd had a child out of wedlock, and he'd been so furious when she wouldn't reveal the father's name that he cut off all communication until Max was almost two months old. If it wasn't for the trust her mother had left her, she and Max would have been on the streets.

For years she had played by her father's rules. She'd done everything he asked of her, playing the role of his perfect little princess, hoping she could win his praise. She dressed in clothes he deemed proper and maintained a grade point average that would make most parents glow with pride, but not her father. Nothing she ever did was good enough, so when being a good girl got her nowhere, she became a bad girl instead. The negative reaction was better than no reaction at all. For a while, at least, but she'd grown weary of that game, too. The day she found out she was pregnant she knew for her baby's sake it was time to grow up. And despite his illegitimacy, Max had become the apple of his grandfather's eye. He was already making plans for Max to one day take over Birch Energy. If her father knew Nathan was Max's daddy, out of spite he would disown them both. How could she in good conscience deny her son his legacy?

That was, in part, why it was best for everyone if Nathan never knew the truth.

"I just want you to be happy," Beth said, handing Max, who had begun to fuss, back to her.

"I'm going to take Max home," Ana said, hoisting him up on her hip. She didn't think Nathan would approach her, not after all this time. Since their split he had never once tried to contact her. Not a phone call or an email, or even a lousy text. He'd gone cold turkey on her.

But running into him by accident wasn't a chance she was willing to take. Not that she thought he would want anything to do with his son. "I'll call you later," she told Beth.

She was about to turn when she heard the deep and unmistakeable rumble of Nathan's voice from behind her. "Hello, ladies."

Her pulse stalled then picked up triple time.

Damn it. Ana froze, her back to him, unsure of what to do. Should she run? Turn and face him? What if he looked at Max and just knew? But would running be too suspicious?

"Well, hello, Nathan," Beth said, air-kissing his cheek, giving Ana's arm a not-so-gentle tug. "I'm so glad you could make it. You remember my cousin, Ana Birch?"

Ana swallowed hard as she turned, tugging Max's woolen cap down to cover the small blond patch behind his left ear in his otherwise thick, dark hair. Hair just like his father. He also had the same dent in his left cheek when he smiled, the same soulful, liquid brown eyes.

"Hello, Nathan," she said, swallowing back her fear and guilt. *He didn't want you,* she reminded herself. *And he wouldn't have wanted the baby. You did the right thing.* He had to have heard about her pregnancy. It had been the topic of El Paso high society gossip for months. The fact that he'd never once questioned whether or not he was the father told her everything she'd needed to know.

He didn't *want* to know.

He looked exactly the same, not that she'd expected him to change much in a year and a half. And Nathan's cool assessment of her, the lack of affection and tenderness in his gaze, said she had been nothing more to him than a temporary distraction. A passing phase.

She wished she could say the same, but she missed him as much now, ached to feel that soul-deep connection that she'd never experienced with any other man, the feelings of love that had snuck up on her and dug in deep, and seemed to multiply tenfold every time he showed up at her door. Every fiber of her being screamed that he was the one, and she would have sacrificed anything to be with him. Her inheritance, her father's love—not that she believed for one second that Walter Birch loved anyone other than himself.

There wasn't a day that passed when she looked into her son's sweet face and didn't feel the sting of Nathan's rejection like a dagger through her heart. And now, the compulsion to throw herself in his arms and beg him to love her was nearly overwhelming.

Pathetic, that was what she was.

"How have you been?" he asked in a tone that was, at best, politely conversational, and he did little more than glance at her son. Hadn't he expressed quite emphatically that at this point in his career he didn't have time for a wife and kids? But she hadn't listened. She had been so sure that *she* was different, that he could love her. Right up until the moment he walked out the door.

She adopted the same polite tone, even though her insides were twisting with a grief that after all this time still cut her to the core. "Very well, and yourself?"

"Busy."

She didn't doubt that. The explosion at Western Oil had been big news. There had been pages of negative press and unfavorable television spots—courtesy of her father, of course. As chief brand officer, it was Nathan's responsibility to reinvent Western Oil's image.

"Well, if you'll excuse me," Beth said. "I have to see a man about a cake." Beth shot her a brief, commiserative smile before she scurried off, bailing on Ana when she needed her most.

She hoped Nathan would walk away too. Instead, he chose that moment to acknowledge her son, who was wiggling restlessly, eager for attention.

"This is your son?" he asked.

She nodded. "This is Max."

The hint of a smile softened his expression. "He's cute. He has your eyes."

Attention hound that he was, Max squealed and flailed his arms. Nathan reached out to take his tiny fist in his hand and Ana's knees went weak. Father and son, making contact for the first time…and hopefully the last. Sudden tears burned the corners of her eyes, and a sense of loss so sharp sliced through every one of her defenses. She needed to get out of here before she did something stupid, like blurt out the truth and turn a bad situation into a catastrophe.

She clutched Max closer to her, which he did not appreciate. He shrieked and squirmed, flailing his chubby little arms, knocking his wool cap off his head.

Damn it!

Before she could reach for it, Nathan crouched down and grabbed it from the grass. She cupped her hand around Max's head, hoping to cover his birthmark, but when Nathan handed her the hat, she had no choice but to let go. She angled her body so he wouldn't see the side of Max's head, but as she reached out to take the cap, Max shrieked and lunged for Nathan. He slipped against her silk jacket and she nearly lost her grip on him. Nathan's arms shot out to catch him just as she regained her grip and, heart hammering, she hugged Max to her chest.

"Strong little guy," Nathan said.

"He's high-spirited," she said, realizing too late that Max's left ear was in plain view. *Please don't let him notice.* She swiftly swung Max around and deposited him on the opposite hip. "Well, it was nice to see you again Nathan, but I was just leaving."

Without waiting for a reply she turned to walk away, but before she could take more than a step, Nathan's hand clamped down hard around her forearm. She felt it like a jolt of electricity.

"Ana?"

She cursed silently and turned to face him, and the second she saw his eyes she could tell that he knew. He had figured it out.

Damn, damn, damn.

That didn't mean she couldn't deny it. But not telling him and outright lying were two very different things. Besides, the birthmark was going to be tough to explain.

Oh, well, so what if he knew? He'd been quite firm that he didn't want children. He probably wouldn't even care if the baby was his, as long as she agreed never to tell anyone and never asked for his support. And why would she? Her trust fund kept her and Max living quite comfortably. Nathan could just go on with his life and pretend it never happened.

Nathan reached up and gently cupped her son's face, turning his head so he could see behind his ear. Thinking it was a game, Max batted at his hand and wiggled in her arms.

She'd heard of people going ghostly white but had never actually witnessed it until just then. He definitely knew, and he clearly wasn't expecting this. Hadn't even considered it being a remote possibility.

"A private word?" he asked, jaw tense, teeth gritted.

"Where?" They were at a party with at least two hundred other people, most of whom knew she and Nathan wouldn't have a lot to talk about. Where could they possibly go without drawing attention to themselves? "You wouldn't want to be seen with the daughter of a direct competitor," she snapped in a voice filled with so much pent-up resentment she barely recognized it as her own. "What would people think?"

Nathan's jaw tensed. "Just tell me this," he said under his breath. "Is he mine?"

Oh, boy. How many times had she imagined this moment? What she would say if ever faced with this situation. She had rehearsed the conversation a thousand times, but now that the moment was here her mind was totally blank.

"Answer me," he demanded, sounding far too much like her father.

Did you really sneak a bottle of my good scotch into the school dance? Answer me, Ana Marie Birch!

She had no choice but to tell Nathan the truth, but all she could manage was a stiff nod.

Nathan cursed, anger flashing in his eyes, holding her arm so tight he was cutting off the blood flow to her fingers. In all the time she'd been with him, she'd never seen him so much as raise his voice. His outrage was probably just a knee-jerk reaction. He was upset because she hadn't told him, but would ultimately be relieved when she assured him he had no responsibilities in regard to her son. Financial or parental. He might even thank her for being so reasonable and honoring his wishes. Then he would leave, and hopefully she would never have to see him again.

Of course there was another possibility. One she'd found too disturbing to consider until now. Or maybe she'd just refused to let herself go there. What if he wanted to be a part of Max's life? What if he wanted visitation and a say in the decisions? What if he tried to take Max away from her?

The thought made her clutch her son closer to her chest, which of course made him wiggle in protest. For nine months he had been her entire life. The only person who truly loved and needed her. She refused to let anyone, especially a man like Nathan, who didn't have time for a girlfriend much less a son, take that away from her.

"Should I assume," Nathan asked through gritted teeth, "that you never intended to tell me?"

"To be honest," she said, lifting her chin with a defiance that was meant to hide the fact that inside she was terrified, "I didn't think you would care."

Two

He had a son.

Nathan could hardly wrap his mind around the concept. And Ana was wrong. He did care. Probably too much. The instant he saw her talking to Beth his heart slammed the wall of his chest so hard it stole his breath, and when their eyes met he'd experienced such a bone-deep need to be close to her, he was down the stairs and striding in her direction before he could consider the repercussions of his actions.

After he ended their affair, he must have picked up the phone a dozen times that first week, ready to tell her that he'd made a mistake, that he wanted her back, even though it would have been the end of his career at Western Oil. But he had worked too damned hard to get where he was to throw it all away for a relationship that was doomed from the start to fail. So he had done the only thing he could.

He'd gotten over her…or so he thought. Now he wasn't so sure.

She tried to jerk her arm from his grasp and her grimace said he was hurting her. *Damn it.* He released his grip and clamped a vice down on his temper. He worked damned hard to maintain control at all times. What was it about her that made him abandon all good sense?

"We need to talk," he said in a harsh whisper. *"Now."*

"This is hardly the place," she said.

She was right. If they disappeared together people were bound to notice. And talk.

"Okay, this is what we're going to do," he said. "You're going to say goodbye to Beth, get in your car and drive home. A few minutes after that I'm going to slip out. I'll meet you at your condo."

Her chin rose a notch. "And if I say no?"

She was trying to be tough, trying to play the spoiled heiress card, but he knew better. He knew that deep down the defiant confidence she flaunted like some badge of honor was nothing more than a smokescreen to hide the fact that she was as vulnerable and insecure as the next woman.

"Not advisable," he said. "Besides, you owe me the courtesy of an explanation."

Even she couldn't deny that, and after a brief pause she said, "Fine."

What else could she say? She may have been stubborn and, yes, a little spoiled, but she was an intelligent woman. She walked away, clutching her son—*their* son—unsteady on the grass in her ridiculously high-heeled boots. Hooker boots, his brother Jordan would have called them. Not the typical attire for an heiress, and even less appropriate for a mother, but she never had been one to play by the rules, which was what had drawn Nathan to her in the first place. Her confidence and her spunk had been an incredible turn-on, especially when he was used to dating "proper" women. The kind who would keep him grounded, who wouldn't tempt him from within the safe place he'd carved out for himself and back into the dark side. But she hadn't been nearly as wicked as she wanted people to believe. In fact, she'd coaxed him farther out into the light than any other woman had managed.

Nathan spotted Beth and headed in her direction. He didn't doubt for a second that she knew the baby was his. And the look on her face as he approached said she knew that he knew. "She swore us to secrecy," Beth said before he could get a word out.

"You should have told me."

She snorted. "Like you didn't already know."

"How could I have?"

"Come on, Nathan. You break up with a woman and a month later she turns up pregnant, and you're telling me you didn't even suspect it was yours?"

Of course he had. He kept waiting for a call from Ana. He trusted that if the child was his she would have the decency to tell him. When he didn't hear from her he just assumed the baby was another man's, which he'd taken to mean that she'd wasted no time moving on. Which he couldn't deny stung like hell.

Turned out there really hadn't been anyone else— at least, not that he knew of. That wasn't much of a consolation at this point.

"It was wrong of her to keep it from me," he told Beth.

"Yes, it was. But—and she would kill me if she knew I was telling you this—you broke her heart, Nathan. She was devastated when you ended the relationship. So, please, cut her a little slack."

That was no excuse to keep his child from him. "I have to go. Give the birthday girl a kiss for me."

Beth's brow cinched with worry. "Go easy on her, Nathan. You have no idea what she's been through the past year and a half. The pregnancy, the birth...she did everything on her own."

"That was her *choice*. At least she *had* one." Feeling angry and betrayed by people he trusted, Nathan turned and headed toward the parking lot. Although, honestly, what had he expected? He and Leo had drifted since their college days, and Beth was Ana's cousin. Had he really expected her to break the confidence of a family bond for a casual acquaintance? If that were the case, should Nathan have felt compelled in college to tell Beth how many times he had come back to the frat house to find her husband Leo, then her steady boyfriend, in his room with another girl?

Besides, he thought, as he slipped behind the wheel of his Porsche, maybe he had suspected the baby was his and deep down didn't want to know the truth. Maybe that's why he never called her, never confirmed for his own peace of mind. Maybe the truth scared the hell out of him. What would he do if it was his kid? What would he tell Adam Blair, his boss and CEO of Western Oil? He was having a child who just happened to be the grandson of the owner of the company's leading competitor. That would have been a disaster then, but now, since the explosion at the refinery, and the suspicion that Birch Energy might somehow be involved, it was a whole new ball game. Not only could he kiss goodbye any chance at the soon-to-be-open CEO position, he would probably lose the job he already had.

Besides, what the hell did he know about being a father, other than the fact that he didn't want to be anything like his own father? But the margin for error was still astronomical.

He'd been to Ana's condo in Raven Hill so many times he drove there on autopilot. When he pulled into the driveway, a white luxury SUV was already parked there. She must have traded in her sports car for something more practical. Because that was what responsible parents did. And despite everything, he didn't doubt for a second that Ana would be a good mother. She used to talk about losing her own mother and how her father ignored her. She said that when she had children they would be the center of her universe.

Nathan and his brother Jordan had the opposite problem. Their father had been on their backs, cramming his principles down their throats and bullying them into doing things his way since they were old enough to have free will. Which Nathan hadn't hesitated to exercise in full force, butting heads with the old man on a daily basis. Giving back as good as his father gave, until he'd pushed so far in the opposite direction, was so crippled by rage and indignation, he had lost a part of himself in the process.

He parked beside the SUV, let go of the steering wheel and flexed his fingers. He'd been gripping it so hard his arms ached. He needed to relax. Yes, he was pissed, but going in there half-cocked was only going to make a bad situation worse.

He took a deep, calming breath, got out, and walked to the porch. Ana was standing in the open doorway waiting for him, as she had been countless times before. They couldn't be seen in public together, so they'd spent most of their time together here. Only this time as she let him in and closed the door, she didn't slide her arms around his neck and pull him to her for a long, slow kiss. The kind that made the stress of the day roll off his shoulders, until nothing mattered but being with her. He wondered what she would do if he drew her against him and pressed his lips to hers.

She would probably deck him, and he would deserve it. But it was almost worth the risk. Despite the time that had passed, he wanted her as much now as the first day he met her. As much as the day he walked out the door. Cutting all ties, ending things before they both got in too deep, had been the kindest thing he could do for her. For either of them. And he'd be smart to remember that.

Ana had shed the silk jacket and boots, and in form-fitting jeans, a peasant blouse and bare feet, she looked more like a college student than someone's mother. As always, she was a total contrast to the conservative chinos and button-up shirt that was his standard uniform. His disguise, to hide the real man lurking underneath the spit and polish. He'd never admitted to anyone, not even Ana, how damned hard it could be to keep him contained.

He shrugged out of his jacket and hung it on the coat tree by the door. "Where's the baby?"

"He's in bed."

"I want to see him." He started for the hall that led to the bedrooms, but she stepped in his way.

"Maybe later."

Anger sparked, then ignited, hot and intense, and had his blood pumping through his veins. "Are you saying you refuse to let me see my own son?"

"He's asleep. Besides, I think it's best if we talk first."

He had half a mind to demand to see him, to push his way past her. Hadn't she kept him from the kid long enough? But she was standing there, arms crossed, wearing a mama-bear look that said it would be in his best interest not to screw with her or her child. When it came to their son, she clearly didn't mess around.

He clamped a vice down on his anger and said, "Okay, let's talk."

She gestured across the spacious living room to the couch. "Have a seat."

Her home had always had a relaxed feel, and despite the service that cleaned weekly there had always been clutter. But now, with toys strewn everywhere, it was like walking through a minefield to get to the couch. As he sat he had a vivid memory of the two of them sitting there together naked, her straddling him, head thrown back, eyes closed, riding him until they were both blind with ecstasy. The memory had his blood pumping through his veins again.

"Something to drink?" she asked.

How about a cold shower instead? "No thanks."

She sat cross-legged in the overstuffed chair across from him.

Since he saw no reason not to get right to the point, he asked, "So you thought it was okay to have my child and not tell me?"

"When you heard that I was pregnant, you could have asked," she said.

"I shouldn't have had to."

She shrugged, as if she saw nothing wrong with her actions. "Like I said, I didn't think you would care. In fact, I thought you would probably be happier not knowing. You made it pretty clear that you didn't want a family. If I had told you, what would you have done? Would you have risked your career to claim him?"

He honestly didn't know, which he couldn't argue legitimized her point. But this wasn't just about how it would affect his career. There were other factors to consider, things she didn't know about him. Still, he would have liked the opportunity to make that decision himself. "Either way it was my choice to make, not yours."

"If you didn't have time for me, how could you have time for a child?"

It wasn't just about not having time. She might not have understood it, she probably never would, but he did her a favor when he ended their affair. She made him drop his guard, lose control, and with a man like him that could only spell trouble. He just wasn't relationship material. Not the kind of relationship she needed anyway. The kind she *deserved*. She was too passionate and full of life. Too... sweet. She didn't need him dragging her down.

"What you really mean is," he said, "I hurt you, and this was your way to hurt me back?"

"That isn't what I said."

No, but he could see that he'd hit a nerve.

"This is getting us nowhere," she said. "If you want to talk about Max, fine. But if you came here to point fingers, you might as well leave."

He leaned forward. "You could at least have the decency, the *courage,* to admit you may have made a mistake."

"I did what I thought was best for my baby. For *everyone*." She paused, then added grudgingly, "But I won't deny that I was hurt and confused and maybe not considering everyone's feelings."

Nathan figured that was about as close to an admission of guilt, or an apology, as he was going to get. And she was right: pointing fingers would get them nowhere. Neither would flying off the handle. The only way to discuss this was calmly and rationally. And considering her tendency to leap to the defensive, he was going to have to be the sensible one. In short, he considered how his father would handle the situation, then did the exact opposite.

He swallowed his bitterness, and a fairly large chunk

of his pride, and said, "Let's forget about placing blame, or who wronged who, and why don't you tell me about my son."

"First, why don't you tell *me* what you plan to do now that you know about him," Ana said. There would be no point in him learning about a son he had no intention of seeing. Although he did seem to want to handle this in a civilized manner, and she was grateful. Though she could take whatever he could dish out and then some, it was always more fun not to be verbally drawn and quartered.

"To be honest, I'm not sure what I plan to do," he said. "I'm still trying to process this."

"You're worried about how it will affect your career?"

"Of course that's a concern."

"It shouldn't be. He's your son. You should love and accept him unconditionally. If you can't do that, there's no room in his life for you."

"That's a little harsh, don't you think?"

"No, I don't. He's my responsibility and I know what's best for him. And unless you're willing to claim him as your child, and carve out a permanent place in your life for him—and that includes regular visitation that is convenient for me—you can forget seeing him at all. He needs stability, not a sometimes father who yo-yos in and out of his life on a whim."

An uncharacteristic show of anger hardened his expression. "I imagine you'll be expecting child support as well," he said, jaw tense.

He just didn't get it. He thought she was being obtuse, but this wasn't about the money, or a need to manipulate him. This was all about Max and what *he* needed. "Keep your money. We don't need it."

"He's my child and my financial responsibility."

"You can't buy your way into his life, Nathan. He's not for sale. If you can't be there for him emotionally, for the long haul, you're out of the game. That's nonnegotiable."

She could see he wasn't thrilled with her direct approach, or her list of demands, but that was too damned bad. Parenting was tough, and either he was in or he was out. He couldn't do it halfway.

"I guess I have a lot to think about," Nathan said.

"I imagine you do." She rose from the chair, prompting him to do the same. "When you've made a decision, then you can see Max."

He pulled himself to his feet, looking irritated, and maybe a little shell-shocked. The enormity of what she was asking from him was not lost on her. Being responsible for another human being, knowing she would shape Max into the adult he would one day become, was terrifying and emotionally exhausting…and the most rewarding thing she had ever done or even imagined doing.

Until Nathan understood that and accepted it, he wouldn't get within fifty feet of Max.

"I need some time to think about this," Nathan said.

"I understand. And I want you to know that whatever you decide is okay with me. I would love for Max to know his father, but I don't want you to feel pressured into something you're not ready for. I can do this on my own."

He walked to the door and shrugged into his jacket, glancing down the hall to the bedrooms. For a second she thought he might ask to see him again, but he didn't. "Can I call you?" he asked.

"My number hasn't changed." He would know that if he had bothered to contact her in the past eighteen months.

He paused at the door, hand on the knob, and turned

back to her. "I am sorry for the way things worked out between us."

But not sorry enough to want her back in his life, she thought as he walked to his car.

She didn't doubt it was going to be a very long night for Nathan. Maybe even a long week, depending on how long it took him to make up his mind. He was not the kind of man to act on impulse. He thought things through carefully before making a decision of any kind. He once told her that their affair was the only spontaneous thing he'd done in his adult life. It had been a thrill to know that she'd had that kind of power over someone like him. Too bad she couldn't make him love her, too.

She watched out the front window until Nathan drove away, then she stepped outside and walked across the lawn to the unit next door, rubbing her arms against the cool air seeping through her sheer top. She knocked, and almost immediately Jenny Sorenson, her neighbor and good friend, opened the door, looking worried.

"Hey, is everything okay?" she asked, ushering Ana inside. Max was sitting on the living room floor with Portia, Jenny's fifteen-month-old daughter. Ana hadn't been sure how Nathan would react, so she'd felt it was wisest to keep Max out of the picture.

"Everything is fine. I'm sorry to dump Max on you like that without an explanation, but I didn't have a lot of time."

When Max heard her voice he squealed and crawled in her direction, but then he got distracted by the toy Portia was banging against the coffee table and changed course. Max was an independent kid, and unless he was wet, hungry or hurt, toys took precedence over Mom any day.

"You looked really upset when you dropped him off. I was worried."

"I ran into Max's dad today. He may or may not be back in the picture. He wanted to talk, and I felt it would be best if Max wasn't there." She hadn't told Jenny the details of the situation with Nathan. In fact, up until the time Ana had Max, she and Jenny, a conservative and soft-spoken doctor's wife, had barely said hello. Then one afternoon when Max was a few weeks old and suffering a pretty nasty case of colic, Jenny heard his screams through the open window and stopped by to offer her help. Like Ana, she'd also made the choice to raise her baby without the help of a nanny or an au pair, and she'd been a godsend. She taught Ana a few tricks she'd learned with her own colicky baby, and they had been friends ever since. Still, Ana was selective about what she did and didn't tell her.

"How do you feel about that?" Jenny asked her.

"Conflicted. I'd love for Max to know his father, but at the same time I feel as though I'm setting him up to be let down. If he's even half as bad as my father—"

"It's only fair to give him a chance," Jenny said firmly, glancing at her daughter, who was in a tug-of-war with Max over a stuffed bear. "A baby needs its father."

Even though Portia barely ever saw hers. Brice Sorenson, a busy surgeon, was often out of the house before the baby woke, and home after she was tucked in bed. If they were lucky, they might see him for a few hours Sunday between hospital rounds and golf. Though Jenny hadn't come right out and said it, it sounded as though even when he was home, he wasn't really there. He was older than Jenny, and had grown children from a first marriage. He didn't change diapers or clean up messes, and he'd never once taken a midnight feeding. The scenario struck a familiar and troubling chord for Ana. One she refused to accept for Max.

"The ball is in his court now," Ana told Jenny. And if Nathan wanted any less than what was best for Max, she would cut him out of his son's life without batting an eyelash.

Three

Though Nathan hated that Ana's words made so much sense, after several days of considering his son's well-being, he knew she was right. Either he was in or he was out of Max's life. There was no doing it halfway. But he had to consider how claiming his son could impact his career. He was sure that if the truth came out he could kiss his chances at the CEO spot goodbye. The board would see it as a direct and flagrant conflict of interest. Since they learned that the explosion at the refinery was the result of someone tampering with the equipment, people had been quick to point the finger at Birch Energy—even though as of yet they hadn't been able to prove any sort of connection.

But even more important, how would his being in the kid's life influence Max? Nathan had no idea what it took to be a father—at least, not a good one. The only thing he knew for sure was that he didn't want to be anything like his own father: accepting nothing but perfection, verbally, and sometimes physically, lashing out if anyone dared fall short of his unrealistic expectations.

Nathan was too much like his old man, too filled with suppressed anger to ignore the possibility that he would be a terrible father. Yet he couldn't just forget that there was a child out there whom he'd brought into this world, who shared half of his genetic code. He had to at least try. And if he couldn't be there for Max, even though Ana said they didn't need his money, Nathan would see that Max was taken care of financially for the rest of his life.

He called Ana Wednesday afternoon and asked if he could come by to talk.

"How about eight-thirty tonight? After Max goes to bed."

"You still won't let me see him?"

"Not until I've heard what you have to say."

Fair enough. "I'll see you at eight-thirty then."

"See you then."

He hung up just as Emilio, the company CFO, knocked on his office door.

Nathan gestured him in, thinking that this visit had something to do with the new marketing budget his department had submitted Monday morning. If Western Oil was going to rebuild their reputation with the public, it was going to cost them.

Instead, Emilio said, "Sorry to interrupt," and handed him a small white envelope. "I just wanted to drop this off."

"What is it?"

"An invitation."

"For...?"

"My wedding."

Nathan laughed, thinking that either he'd misheard or it had to be a joke. "Your *what*?"

A grin kicked up the corner of Emilio's mouth. "You heard me."

Nathan knew no one more vehemently against marriage than Emilio. What the hell had happened?

Curiosity getting the best of him, he tore the envelope open and pulled out the invitation, his mouth dropping open when he recognized the bride's name. "This wouldn't be the Isabelle Winthrop who was indicted for financial fraud?"

"Apparently you haven't been watching the news. All charges against her were dropped last Friday."

That explained it. He'd worked late Friday then went to the party Saturday, and since then pretty much all he'd thought about was Ana and his son. He couldn't recall turning on the television or even picking up a newspaper. "And now you're marrying her?"

"Yep."

Nathan shook his head. "Didn't her husband die just a few months ago?"

"It's a long story," Emilio said.

I'll bet it is, he thought. One he was surprised he hadn't heard about before now. But like himself, Emilio was a very private person. And Nathan couldn't be happier that he'd found someone he wanted to be with for the rest of his life. "One I can't wait to hear," he said.

Emilio grinned. "By the way, I looked over your proposal. I'd like to set up a meeting with Adam to go over the numbers. Probably early next week."

"Have your secretary call my secretary."

Nathan spent the rest of the afternoon in meetings, during the last of which they ordered in dinner, which saved him the trouble of having to go out or pick up carryout to eat at home before he changed out of his suit and left for Ana's place. He arrived at eight-thirty on the nose. Sometime since Saturday she had decorated the front of her condo for the coming holiday. Lighted balsam and fir swags framed the door and windows, and she'd hung a wreath decorated with Christmas bulbs and fresh holly on the front door. Nathan hadn't hung a single decoration in his high-rise apartment downtown. He didn't even own any. Why decorate for the holidays when he was never there? If he decorated anywhere, logically it should be his office, since that was where he spent the majority of his time.

Before he could knock on the door it swung open.

"Right on time," Ana said. She was dressed in hot pink sweatpants and a matching hoodie over a faded T-shirt stained with something orange that may or may not have been mashed-up carrots. Her fiery red hair was pulled haphazardly back with a clip, and she didn't have any makeup on. Yet she still managed to look sexy as hell.

Motherhood looked damned good on her.

She stepped aside to let him in. "Excuse the mess, but I just got Max settled, and I haven't had time to straighten up yet."

She wasn't kidding. It looked as if a bomb had gone off in the living room. He had no idea one kid could play with so many toys.

"It looks like there were a dozen kids here," he said, shrugging out of his jacket and hanging it on the coat tree.

"Five, actually. It's playdate day, and it was my week to host."

"Playdate?"

"You know, a bunch of parents get together with their kids and let them play together. Although me and my next-door neighbor, Jenny, are the only actual parents. Two others are nannies, and one is a French au pair. Jenny and I are both pretty sure the au pair is sleeping with the baby's father. And one of the nannies told us that the couple she works for is on the verge of divorce, and he sleeps in the spare bedroom now."

He had no idea playdates could be so scandalous.

"Isn't Max a little young to be playing with other kids?" he asked.

"It's never too early to start socializing children."

Proving that he knew absolutely nothing about parenting. "You don't have a nanny?"

"I love being with Max, and I'm in a position where I don't have to work now. I like being a stay-at-home mom. Not that it's been easy, but well worth it."

His mother had been too busy with her charities and her various groups to take much time for her sons.

Ana gestured into the living room. "Come on in and have a seat. Would you like something to drink?"

He could probably use one. Or five. But no amount of alcohol was going to make this easier. "No thanks."

She waited until he sat on the couch, then took a seat on the edge of the chair. "So, you've made a decision?"

"I have." He propped his elbows on his knees, rubbing his palms together. Ana watched him expectantly. He wasn't sure how she was going to like this. She was probably expecting a definitive answer, but he wasn't ready to give her that. Not yet. "I'd like to have a trial period."

Her brows rose. "A *trial* period? This is not a gym membership we're talking about, Nathan. He's a baby. A human being."

"Which is exactly why I think jumping into this would be a bad idea. I know nothing about being a parent. As you pointed out, I never planned to have a family. For all I know I might be a lousy father. I'd like the opportunity to try it out for a few weeks, spend some time with Max and see how he takes to me."

"Max is nine months old. He loves everyone."

"Okay then, I want to see how *I* take to *him*."

"And if you don't…*take to him?* What then?"

"I'll honor your wishes and remove myself from Max's life completely."

She shook her head. "I don't know…"

"I know you were hoping for a more definitive answer, but I honestly think this is the best way to do this. And it's not a decision I came to lightly. I just…" He sighed, shook his head. "I don't know if I'm ready for this. I've made a lot of mistakes in my life, Ana, and this is too important to screw up."

"I'm assuming there's also the question of how this will go over at work."

"I won't deny that was a factor in my decision. Our current CEO is leaving, and I'm one of the select few who are competing for the position. I don't want to rock the boat."

"So it *is* about work," she said, not bothering to hide the bitterness in her voice.

"I have to consider everything," he said. "But ultimately this is about what's best for our son."

To hear Nathan refer to Max as "our son" made Ana's heart twist. For a long time he was just "her son." She wasn't sure if she was ready to give that up, to share him. But this wasn't about what she wanted. The only thing that mattered was what was best for Max.

Her knee-jerk reaction was to say no way, either he was in or out; but in all fairness, she'd had almost nine months to get used to the idea of being a parent. He'd had a child thrust on him without warning, and now he was expected to make a decision that would impact his and their son's life forever. And hers. Could she honestly blame him for erring on the side of caution? He had clearly given this a lot of thought and seemed to have Max's best interest in mind. Wasn't that what really mattered? Not to mention that Nathan had shown vulnerability, which she knew had to be tough for him. He was a successful and well-respected man. Admitting he might not be able to hack it as a father couldn't have been easy for him. She commended him for his honesty.

"I guess a trial period would make sense," she told him. "Supervised visits, of course."

"Of course," he agreed.

Which meant having to spend time with Nathan, which she was sure would be heart-wrenching for her. Just having him in her home, remembering all the times they had spent there together, made her feel hollowed out inside. Alone. Since they split, she hadn't so much as looked at another man. Not that she'd had a whole lot of time for dating these days, but she had gone out with friends a few times, attended social functions with her father. Men had tried to strike up conversations, asked her to dance, but she just wasn't interested.

If a year and a half apart hadn't dissolved her feelings for Nathan, maybe she was destined to love him forever. Or maybe being around him again would make her realize that he wasn't as wonderful as she used to think. The man was bound to have flaws. Little character traits that annoyed her. Maybe all this time she'd been building him up in her mind, making him into something he really wasn't.

A renewed sense of hope filled her. Maybe this would turn out to be a good thing for her. But they had to be cautious.

"I also think it would be best if no one knew about this," she said.

He looked relieved, probably because he was worried

about his position at Western Oil. But there was more to it than that.

"I think that's a good idea," he said.

"We'll have to be really careful. These things have a way of blowing up, and that could be devastating for Max."

"He's a baby. It's not as if he can pick up a newspaper."

"Not yet. But someday he will. If you decide, for whatever reason, that you can't be a part of his life, I don't want him to know about you. If your identity gets out now, you can bet he'll hear about it eventually. Besides, my father adores Max, but if he were to learn that you're the father, he would know that our affair was just another way of defying him. He would disown me and Max on principle."

"Still trying to win his affection?"

"I don't give a damn what he thinks about me, but Max has a future at Birch Energy, if he should so decide that's what he wants to do. Right now it's his legacy. It doesn't seem fair to deny him that for my own selfish reasons."

"Yet if I decide to be a part of his life you risk that very thing."

"Because knowing his real father is too important. He needs a male influence in his life, and as it stands, my father is the best I can do. And who knows, maybe Max isn't destined to fail him. With me, he never seemed to get over the fact that I wasn't the son he'd always wanted."

"So, is that really all I was to you?" he asked. "Just another way to defy your father?"

At first. Until he wasn't anymore. Until she fell stupidly and hopelessly in love with him. But that would have to remain her little secret. Her pride depended on it. "Does that come as such a shock?"

"Not really, considering we both know it isn't true."

And what about him? Did he get off on making women

fall for him, then breaking their hearts? Was it all just a game to him? And how was she supposed to react to his accusation? If she denied it, she would look as though she were hiding something. If she admitted the truth…well, that wasn't even an option.

She refused to give him the satisfaction of any response.

"So, what days would be best for you to see Max?" she asked him. "His bedtime is eight, so if you want to do weeknights it will have to be before that. Sunday afternoons would work too."

"Weekdays will be tough. I've been swamped at work. I'm lucky if I can get out by nine most nights."

"No one said it was going to be easy. You have to make priorities."

His look said he was poised to jump to the defensive, but instead he took a deep breath and said, "If I go into the office early tomorrow, I could be out of there by six-thirty. That would get me here a little before seven."

"That's a start," she said.

"Tomorrow it is then."

A long, uncomfortable silence followed, where neither seemed to know what to say next. Or maybe they had said all there was to say.

"Well, I guess since that's settled…" He rose from the couch.

"It's been a long day, and I don't know about you, but I could go for a glass of wine." She knew the second the words left her mouth it was a bad idea, but she just wasn't ready for him to leave.

You can't force him to love you, she reminded herself. And she wouldn't want to. She wanted someone without the relationship hang-ups, who loved her unconditionally. If that kind of man even existed.

Nathan studied her, one brow slightly raised. "Are you asking me to stay?"

Yeah, bad idea. "You know what, forget it. I don't think—"

"Red or white?"

His question stopped her. "Huh?"

"The wine. Do you have red or white?" The hint of a smile tugged at his lips. "Because I'm partial to red."

She shouldn't be doing this. She was still vulnerable. She was only setting herself up to be hurt. For all she knew he could be involved with someone else now. Maybe that was part of the reason for the trial period.

Character flaws, she reminded herself. She couldn't find them if she didn't spend at least a little time with the man.

Just this once, and after this, she would see him only if Max was there.

"Then you're in luck," she told him. "Because I have both."

Four

"If you're sure it's no trouble," Nathan said, a part of him hoping she would say it was.

"No trouble."

She walked to the kitchen and he sat back down. He wasn't sure what the hell he thought he was doing. He came here to discuss his son, and now that they had, he had no reason to stay. The problem was, he didn't *want* to leave.

Maybe it was time to admit what deep down he had known all along. He still had unresolved feelings regarding his relationship with Ana. Despite what she probably believed, ending it hadn't been easy for him, either. Ana was the only woman who had ever made him feel like a whole person. Like he didn't have to hide. Almost... normal. But he knew that eventually his demons would get the best of him—they always did—and she would see the kind of man that he really was. Knowing Ana, and the kind of woman she was, she would want to try to fix him.

Well, it wouldn't work. He wasn't fixable. And the less time he spent with her, the better. Especially in situations where Max wasn't there to act as a buffer. So why wasn't he stopping her as she walked to the kitchen and pulled two wineglasses down from the cupboard? Why didn't he get up, grab his coat and get the hell out?

Damned if he knew. Although he was sure good old-fashioned stupidity played a major part.

"So," she said from the kitchen. "You said you're up for the CEO position?"

He turned to face her. She was standing at the counter opening a bottle of red wine. "It's between me, the CFO Emilio Suarez and my brother Jordan."

"Your brother, huh? That must be dicey." The cork popped free and she poured the wine. "If I recall correctly, your relationship has always been...complicated."

"Is that the polite way of saying he's an arrogant jerk?"

"I actually met him at a fundraiser last year," Ana said, carrying the two glasses into the room.

"Did he hit on you?"

"Why? Are you jealous?" She handed him one, their fingertips touching as he took it from her. It was an innocent, meaningless brush of skin, but boy, did he *feel* it. Way more than he should have. If she noticed or felt it, too, she wasn't letting on. She sat back down in the chair, curling her legs beneath her, looking young and hip and sexy as hell. And yes, maybe a little tired.

"I ask," he said, "because Jordan hits on all beautiful women. He can't help himself."

"I believe he was there with a date."

Nathan shrugged. "That's never stopped him before."

"No, he didn't hit on me. Although maybe it had something to do with the fact that I was eight months pregnant and as big as a house."

"Somehow I can't see that stopping him either."

She laughed. "Come on, he's not *that* bad."

He didn't used to be. When they were growing up, Nathan had been his brother's protector. He couldn't begin to count how many times, when they were kids, that he had taken the blame for things his brother had done to shelter him from their father's wrath, or stepped between Jordan and their father's fists. As the older brother he felt it was his responsibility to shelter Jordan, who was quiet and sensitive. A *sissy,* their father used to call him. But instead of the loyalty and gratitude Nathan would have expected, Jordan learned to be a master manipulator, always pointing the finger at Nathan for his own misdeeds. At home, in school. He became the golden child who could do no wrong, and Nathan had been labeled the troublemaker. Not that Nathan hadn't gotten into enough trouble all on his own. But after all these years it still chapped his hide.

"Jordan is Jordan," Nathan said. "He won't ever change."

"When will the new CEO be announced?" Ana asked.

Not until the investigation into the explosion at Western Oil was complete, but he couldn't tell her that. Only a select few even knew there *was* an investigation. The explosion was caused by faulty equipment—equipment that had just been checked and rechecked for safety—and as a result thirteen men were injured. The board was convinced it had been an inside job, and they suspected that Birch Energy—specifically Ana's father—was behind it. The goal was to flush out whoever was responsible. But it had been a slow, arduous and frustrating process.

"We haven't been given a definitive date," he told Ana. "A few more months at least."

"And how will you feel if it goes to Jordan?"

"It won't." Of the three candidates, in his opinion, Jordan was the least qualified, and Nathan was sure that the board would agree. Jordan used charm to get where he was now, but that would only take him so far.

"You sound pretty sure about that."

"That's because I am. And no offense, but I don't want to talk about my brother."

"Okay. What do you want to talk about?"

"Maybe you could tell me a little about my son."

"Actually, I can do better than that." Ana set her wine down, got up from her chair and walked to the bookcase across the room. She pulled a large book down from the shelf and carried it over. He expected her to hand it to him; instead she sat down beside him. So close that their thighs were almost touching.

He liked it better when she was across the room.

"What's this?" he asked.

She set the book in her lap and opened it to the first page. "Max's baby book. It has pictures and notes and every milestone he's reached up until now. I've been working on it since before he was born."

Clearly she had, as the first few pages consisted of photos of her in different stages of her pregnancy, and even a shot of the home pregnancy stick that said "pregnant" in the indicator window. And her earlier self-description that she was "as big as a house" in her eighth month was obviously a gross exaggeration. Other than looking like she had swallowed a basketball, her body appeared largely unchanged.

"You looked good," he said.

"I was pretty sick the first trimester, but after that I felt great."

The next page was sonogram photos—with one that clearly showed the baby was a boy—and notes she'd taken after her doctor visits. The pages that followed were all Max. And damn, maybe Nathan was partial, but he sure

was a cute baby. But as Ana sat beside him slowly turning
the pages, he caught himself looking at her instead. The
familiar line of her jaw and the sensual curve of her lips.
The soft wisps of hair that had escaped the clip and brushed
her cheek. Eighteen months ago he wouldn't have thought
twice about reaching up to tuck it back behind her ear. To
caress her cheek, stroke the column of her neck. Press his
lips to the delicate ridge of her collar bone…

Damn. He would have thought that over time his desire
for her would have faded, but the urge to put his hands on
her was as strong as ever. And for her sake as much as his
own, he couldn't.

"He's a cute kid," he said, as she reached the end of the
book and flipped it closed. "He actually looks a lot like
Jordan did at that age."

She got up and carried the book back to the shelf, sliding
it in place. A part of him hoped she would return to the
couch and sit beside him, and the disappointment he felt
when she didn't was a clear indication that he needed to
get the hell out of there. He should be concentrating on his
son, but all he could think about was her.

He swallowed the last of his wine and pulled himself
to his feet. "It's late," he said, even though it was barely
past nine. "I have an early morning. I should get going."

If his leaving disappointed her, she didn't let on. She
followed him as he walked to the door. "So, we'll see you
tomorrow around seven?" she asked.

"Or sooner if I can manage it." He shrugged into his
jacket and she opened the door. This would normally be the
part where she slid her arms up around his neck and kissed
him goodbye, and usually tried to talk him into staying
the night. God knows he had been tempted, every single
time, but that was always where he drew the line. Sleeping
over insinuated a level of intimacy where he never dared

tread. Otherwise women got the wrong idea. Especially women like Ana.

"I'm glad you came over tonight," she said.

He stopped just shy of the threshold. "Me, too."

"And I meant what I said before, about the choice you make. Even after this, if you decide you can't do this, I won't hold it against you. Being a parent is tough. It takes a *ton* of sacrifice."

"It sounds almost as if you're trying to dissuade me."

"It's also the most rewarding experience I've ever had. It changes you in a way you would never expect. Things I used to think were so important just don't seem that critical anymore. It's all about him now."

He wasn't sure if he was ready to make a child the center of his life. He wouldn't even begin to know how. "Now you're scaring the hell out of me."

She smiled. "I know it sounds daunting, and it is in a way. It's tough to explain. You'll either feel it or you won't, I guess."

Or maybe it was a chick thing, because he'd never heard any of his friends with kids describe it that way.

"I guess we'll just have to wait and see," he said.

"I guess."

He had the distinct feeling she wanted to say something else, so he waited a beat, and when she didn't he turned to walk out. He was one step onto the porch when she grabbed his arm.

"Nathan, wait."

He turned back to her. If she was smart, she wouldn't touch him, but the damage was already done. Now all he could think about was pulling her into his arms and holding her, pressing his lips to hers.

"When we were sitting there looking at Max's baby

book," she said, "it made me realize how much he's changed in the past nine months."

He wasn't sure what she was getting at. "Isn't that what kids are supposed to do?"

"Of course. I just…I guess it made me realize how much of his life you've missed already. I just wanted to say…I wanted you to know that…" She struggled with the words. "I'm…sorry."

Wow. An actual apology. And his surprise must have shown, because she swiftly added, "I still contend that everything I did was in Max's best interest."

"So…you're *not* sorry."

"I did it in Max's best interest, but that doesn't mean it wasn't a mistake."

Maybe there was something wrong with him, but seeing her so humbled was a major turn-on. And the way she was holding his arm, standing too close, was pushing the boundaries of his control.

He leaned in slightly, just to test the waters, to see what her reaction would be. Her eyes widened a fraction and her breath caught. He was sure she would retreat, but instead her pupils dilated and her tongue darted out to wet her lip.

Holy hell.

Not exactly the reaction he'd been hoping for. Or was it? He could be realistic, or he could be smart about this. Realistically, if he leaned in and kissed her, she would kiss him back, and though it might take one night, or five nights, they would wind up back in bed together.

The smart thing to do would be to back off now while he still could, and that was exactly what he planned to do. But it wasn't easy. "I should go."

She nodded, looking slightly dazed. "Okay."

He looked down at her hand and said, "Unless you're coming with me, you're going to have to let go."

"Sorry." She blinked and jerked her hand away, and by the glow of the porch light he could swear he saw her blush. Ana was not the blushing type. She was utterly confident and without shame—on the outside anyway. He couldn't decide who was more arousing, the unflappable vixen or the vulnerable girl.

So he stepped away. "See you tomorrow."

She nodded. "See you tomorrow."

He started down the steps, then stopped just as she was closing the door. "Hey, Ana."

"Yeah?"

"By the way, apology accepted." Then he turned and walked to his car.

Ana closed the door and leaned against it. *Oh my God.* He had almost kissed her. He had leaned in, his eyes on her mouth…

The idea of his lips on hers again made her heart beat faster and her breath quicken. And as wrong as she knew it was, she would have let him. As if she wasn't feeling confused and conflicted enough already.

Sitting there with Nathan, going through Max's baby book, she got to thinking about how precious each and every minute with her son had been. The idea that she had deprived Nathan of that and, even worse deprived Max of the chance to know his daddy, made her feel selfish and thoughtless. What gave her the right? Max's well-being? Well, suppose it hadn't been good for him? What if she had done more harm than good? What if Max grew up with a hole in his life, in his soul?

She hated that Nathan was making her second-guess herself, that she couldn't trust her instincts. Then there was that "apology accepted" remark. What was up with that? Did he mean it, or was he just playing some angle? Did he have ulterior motives? If she were him, she wouldn't be so quick to let her off the hook.

You're giving him too much power, she warned herself.

Not just that, but what in God's name had possessed her to touch him? She hadn't done it consciously. Until he'd asked her to let go, she hadn't even realized her hand was on his arm. She wanted to find his flaws, but not in bed. Besides, she knew for a fact that sexually, he was about as perfect as a man could be. So perfect that it made her blind to everything else. As evidenced by the fact that when he dumped her it seemed to come out of the clear blue with no warning. They hadn't even had so much as a disagreement. As far as she knew, everything was fantastic, them *bam,* it was over. Apparently there had been some problem that she wasn't seeing.

All the more reason not to sleep with him.

Her cell phone rang, and she pulled it out of her pocket to check the display, half-hoping it was Nathan calling to cancel for tomorrow. It was Beth. Ana was supposed to call her when Nathan left, but apparently Beth was impatient.

"Is he gone yet?" she said when Ana answered.

"He left a few minutes ago."

"So, what did he decide? Does he want to be Max's daddy?" Beth had been convinced from the time Ana learned she was pregnant that Nathan would want the baby and would slip easily into the role of being a father. She obviously didn't know Nathan as well as she thought she did.

"He wants a trial period."

"What?" she shrieked. "What the heck for?"

"Lots of reasons. But the gist of it is that he wants what's best for Max."

"Max needs his father. *That's* what's best for him."

"Well, Nathan doesn't see it that way. He's not convinced

he'll be a good father. And he's concerned about the reaction at work."

"So, are you going to let him do it?" she asked.

"What else can I do? I can't force him to want to be Max's daddy."

"But he *is* Max's daddy. He needs to be there for his son."

"I get the feeling there's more to it than he's letting on. He said something about having made mistakes in the past."

"What kind of mistakes?"

"I'm not sure. It was very cryptic. I thought maybe you would know what he was talking about. Maybe something that happened in college?"

"Nothing comes to mind. The only major mistake I've seen him make is leaving you."

She twisted the lock, engaged the deadbolt then switched off the porch light. "I think he almost kissed me."

Beth made a sound of indignation. "Are you serious?"

"Yeah." She walked into the living room and grabbed the two empty wineglasses. "We were at the front door saying goodbye and he was looking at me."

"Looking, or *looking?*"

"Looking." She carried the glasses into the kitchen and set them next to the sink. "Then he *leaned.*"

"He's got a lot of nerve. Does he think having a kid together is an open invitation back into your pants?"

Yeah, about that…she grabbed the bottle of wine and poured herself a second glass. "I sort of…touched him."

"What? Where?"

"His arm. Actually, just the sleeve of his jacket."

"Oh." Beth sounded disappointed, like maybe she thought it would be something more scandalous, like his fly.

Ana took a sip of wine, noticing the lip balm mark on the empty glass. That must be her glass, meaning she was drinking out of Nathan's glass. The idea of putting her lips on the rim where his had been sent a warm shiver down her spine.

Ugh! She was hopeless. She dumped it down the sink and set the glass down.

"I probably shouldn't have invited him to stay for a glass of wine either," she told Beth.

"Maybe this is a stupid question, but did you *want* him to kiss you?"

"No." She paused, then blew out a frustrated breath. "And *yes*. I still have all these feelings for him. But damn it, he already eviscerated my heart once. I would be a moron to go back for seconds."

"You know I'll stand by whatever you decide to do, hon, and this probably goes without saying, but be careful. Don't jump into anything without thinking it through first. Okay?"

"I won't, I promise." At least, she would try. "The problem is, when I'm close to him, it's like my brain ceases to function. Like…animal magnetism or something. It's been that way since the day I met him."

"When are you going to see him again?"

"He's stopping over to see Max tomorrow evening around seven."

"And Max goes to bed at eight-thirty?"

"Yeah, why?"

"Well, if something was going to happen, it would be after that, right?"

"I suppose."

"Then why don't I call you around eight forty-five. That way if you need moral support, I can talk some sense into you."

She hated to think that she would be that weak, but why take chances? "I think that sounds like a pretty good idea."

"You're tough, Ana. You can do this."

Beth was right. She had been through worse things than this, so why, right now, wasn't she feeling so tough?

Five

Any time Ana had spent worrying that Max and Nathan might not bond had been a big fat waste.

Max adored Nathan. He'd been utterly fascinated with him since the second Nathan walked in the door, and spending the last two hours watching them play had flat out been the most heartwarming, confusing and terrifying experience of Ana's life.

For someone who had so little experience with babies, Nathan did everything right. He was gentle and patient, but not afraid to play with Max, who was used to—not to mention lived for—roughhousing with the older kids in the playgroup. "He's all boy, isn't he?" Nathan said, his voice full of pride as he swung Max up over his head, making him squeal. He didn't even seem to mind when Max smashed gluey bits of partially chewed zwieback into his designer shirt, or spilled juice from his sippy cup on Nathan's slacks.

Nathan was a complete natural with Max. So much so that Ana couldn't help feeling a bit like the odd man out. Max was so focussed on Nathan, she had ceased to exist. She was actually a little relieved when it was time to put Max to bed. At least she would get a few quality moments with him when she tucked him in, but then Nathan asked if he could help get Max ready for bed. Since the day he came home from the hospital, Max's bedtime was a ritual that had always been just the two of them. She knew she was completely unjustified in feeling that Nathan was overstepping his bounds. After all, they were *supposed* to be getting to know one another. Still, she couldn't help feeling a little jealous. Especially when she got Max changed and into his pajamas, and it was Nathan he reached for to put him into bed. That was tough.

"What should I do now?" Nathan asked her.

"Just lay him in bed and cover him up." She gave Max a kiss, then watched from across the room as Nathan lay Max, a little awkwardly, into bed, then pulled the blanket up over him.

"Good night, Max," he said, smiling down at him with the same dimpled grin Max was giving him, and though Ana was *dying* to walk over to the crib, if only to make sure he was covered and safely tucked in, to kiss him one more time and tell him she loved him, she knew she had to let father and son have this time together.

She'd just had no idea this would be so damned hard.

"Is that it?" Nathan asked.

She nodded and switched off the lamp on his dresser. "He'll go right to sleep."

Nathan followed her out of the bedroom and into the living room. Things had gone really well tonight, so why was she on the verge of an emotional meltdown? Why the tears brimming in her eyes?

She was being stupid, that was why. Max was still her baby, still depended on her for everything, and no one could take that from her. Having a daddy in his life didn't mean Max would love her any less.

"Well," Nathan said, "he's a great kid."

"He is," she agreed, hoping he didn't hear the hitch in her voice. She walked to the kitchen to load the dinner dishes into the dishwasher, hoping Nathan would take the hint and leave. Instead he followed her.

"That seemed to go well," he said, leaning against the counter beside the stove while she stood at the sink, her back to him.

"Really well," she agreed, blinking back the tears pooling in her eyes. *Stop it, Ana, you're being ridiculous.* Was she PMSing or something? She never got this emotional. She was tougher than this.

He was quiet for a minute then asked, "Ana, is something wrong?"

"Of course not," she said, the squeak in her voice undeniable that time, as was the tear that spilled over onto her cheek. My God, she was acting like a big baby. She had learned a long time ago that crying would get her nowhere. Her father had no tolerance for emotional displays.

Nathan laid a hand on her shoulder, which only made her feel worse. "Did I do something wrong?"

She shook her head. The apprehension in Nathan's voice made her feel like a jerk. He was genuinely concerned, and he deserved an explanation. She just didn't know what to tell him. Not without sounding like a dope.

"Ana, talk to me." He turned her so she was facing him. "Are you crying?"

"No," she said, swiping at the tears with her shirtsleeve. As if denying it would make her tears any less real.

"I'm confused. I thought it went okay tonight."

"It did."

"So…why the tears? Are you having second thoughts about this?"

She shook her head. "It's not that."

"Then what is it? Why are you so upset?"

She bit her lip, looked down at the floor.

He put his hands on her shoulders. "Ana, we can't do this if you don't talk to me."

Please don't touch me, she thought. It only made it worse.

"If I did something wrong—"

"No! You did everything right. Max adored you. It couldn't have gone more perfect."

"And you think that's a *bad* thing?"

"No. Not exactly."

Nathan's brow furrowed with confusion. Of course he was confused. She wasn't making any sense.

"Since the day Max was born it's just been the two of us. He depends on me for everything. But tonight, seeing you two together—" Her voice cracked. *Damn it Ana, hold it together.* "I guess I was jealous. I don't know what I would do if Max didn't need me anymore."

"Of course he needs you."

She shrugged, her shoulders heavy under the weight of his hands, and more of those stupid tears spilled over.

He cursed under his breath, then slid his arms around her and pulled her against him. And, oh God, it was so good. To hell with being strong. She wanted this. She'd wanted it for *so* long. She locked her arms around him and held on, feeling as if she never wanted to let go again. He would have to pry her loose, peel her away from him. She closed her eyes and breathed him in, rubbed her cheek against the solid warmth of his chest. He was so familiar, and perfect.

God, she was pathetic. She wasn't even trying to resist him. And Nathan wasn't making this any easier. Instead of pushing her away, he was holding on just as tightly.

"I think I'm just a novelty," he said. "A new toy to play with."

It took her a second to realize that he was talking about Max. "No, he really loved you, Nathan. It's almost as if he sensed who you were." She gazed up at him. "And that's good. That's the way it should be. It's what I want. I'm just acting stupid."

"I'm sure what you're feeling is totally normal."

He could have the decency to act like a jerk. To tell her she was being irrational and stupid. Instead of being a tool, and making her hate him, he was doing everything right. Where were those flaws she was supposed to be finding?

"You really need to stop being so nice to me," she said.

A grin tipped up the corner of his mouth. "Why?"

"Because you're making it impossible for me to hate you."

"Maybe I don't want you to hate me."

She had to. It was her only defense.

The house phone rang, and she realized that it must be Beth, calling to stop her from doing something stupid.

Too late.

She slid her arms up Nathan's chest and around his neck, pulled his head down to her level and kissed him, and there wasn't even a millisecond of hesitation on his part. Everything in her said, *Yes!* She blocked out the ringing of the phone, and the whisper of her own nagging doubts, and concentrated on the softness of his lips, the taste of his mouth, the burn of his beard stubble against her chin. Good Lord, did the man know how to kiss. He was tender, yet demanding. It was addictive, like a drug, and all she could think was *more*. Her body ached for his touch.

Nathan's big hands tightened around her hips, and suddenly her feet were off the floor. Her butt landed on the hard surface of the countertop, and her legs instinctively wrapped around his waist.

Closer. She wanted to be closer to him. Needed to feel her breasts crushed against the hard wall of his chest. Nathan cupped her behind and tugged her against him, trapping the stiff ridge of his erection against her stomach. He slid his hands upward, under the hem of her shirt, and his warm palms settled against her bare waist.

Naked. They needed to be naked, right now. She wanted to feel his skin, the hard ridges of muscle that used to be as familiar to her as her own body. She clawed at the tails of his shirt, tugging them free from his pants, and Nathan must have had the same thing in mind, because he was sliding her shirt up...

The doorbell rang, followed by frantic pounding. *What the hell?*

Nathan broke the kiss and backed away. "I think someone is here."

No, no, no. This wasn't fair. Maybe if they ignored it, the person would go away. They stood motionless, waiting. Then the bell rang again, followed by more pounding. At this rate, whoever it was, they were going to wake Max.

"I had better go see who it is," she told Nathan. So she could *kill* them.

She straightened her top and darted for the door just as the phone started to ring again. This had better be damned important. She yanked the door open to find Beth standing on her porch, hand poised to knock again, cell phone to her ear. As soon as she snapped her phone closed, the house phone stopped ringing.

"Hi!" she said brightly, muscling her way past Ana into

the foyer. "I was in the neighborhood, so I thought I would stop by."

In the neighborhood? At eight forty-five on a weeknight? Beth lived twenty minutes away. From the frantic knocking she was obviously a woman on a mission, and Ana knew exactly what that mission had to be.

Beth looked past Ana and her eyes widened almost imperceptibly.

Ana turned to see Nathan walking to the door, his tails retucked, clothes neat. To look at him, no one would guess that he'd been about to jump her bones.

"Hello, Beth," he said.

"Hi, Nathan. I didn't realize you were here."

Like hell she didn't, and Ana could see Nathan's bullshit meter zip into the red zone.

"My car in the driveway didn't tip you off?" he asked.

"Oh, is that *your* car?" She cut a look Ana's way. "I hope I haven't come at a bad time."

That was exactly what she was hoping.

"Actually, I was just leaving," Nathan said, grabbing his jacket from the coat tree.

Damn it! "Beth, would you excuse us for just a second?"

"Of course," Beth said, shooting her a look that said, *Don't try anything funny.*

Ana followed Nathan onto the porch, shutting the door behind her. "You don't have to go. I can get rid of her."

"Is that really what you want?"

Her first instinct was a big fat yes, but something made her pause and consider what he was asking. Was it what she wanted? Thirty seconds ago she was one hundred percent sure. But now that she'd had a minute to calm down, to think rationally, she had to wonder if she was making a mistake. She would sleep with him, and then what? Have another brief affair that would end in a month or so with her heart sliced and diced again? Was that worth a few weeks of really fantastic sex? If he decided to keep seeing Max, she would be stuck with him for a very long time. At least until Max was eighteen. And weren't things uncomfortable enough already?

"I think we both know that it would only complicate things," he said, and her heart took a steep dive.

She knew a brush-off when she heard one. What he really meant to say was, *he* didn't want *her*. Hadn't she been the one to start it this time? He had probably only hugged her for comfort, not to seduce her, but she had taken the ball and run with it. He could have stopped her, but after that awful emotional display of hers, maybe he was afraid of hurting her feelings. What could be more embarrassing? Or horrifying?

"You're right," she said, folding her arms against a sudden gust of cool air. Or maybe that chill was her heart turning to ice.

"Are we still okay for Sunday?" he asked.

"Of course. What time is good for you?"

"Why don't I come by around noon? I'll bring lunch."

That had quite the "family" ring to it. The three of them having lunch and spending the afternoon together. But she didn't want to discourage him, not when he and Max had gotten along so well tonight. Because this was about Max, not her. "Um, sure. That would be great."

"Great. I'll see you Sunday." He stepped off the porch into the darkness, and though she was tempted to stand there and watch him go, she had Beth to deal with. She stepped back inside but Beth wasn't waiting by the door.

She found her in the kitchen pouring a glass of wine. "Rough day?"

"It's not for me," Beth said, corking the bottle and

putting it back in the fridge. Then she held the glass out for Ana. "It's for you. You look like you need it."

She did. She took the glass from Beth. "I take it you weren't just *in the neighborhood*."

"Let's just say I had a hunch that a phone call wasn't going to cut it. Too easy to ignore if you're otherwise occupied. Besides, I've always preferred the direct approach."

Ana took a swallow of wine then set the glass on the counter. "Good idea."

"If I hadn't shown up, you would have slept with him, wouldn't you?"

She had been two seconds from dragging him to her bedroom. Or hell, they may have done it right there on the kitchen counter. It wouldn't have been the first time.

Her look must have said it all, because Beth folded her arms, cocked one hip and said, "Forget Max. *You're* the one who needs supervised visits."

"No, because it's not going to happen again. We just decided that it would complicate things too much."

"He says that now—"

"No, he means it. I think that was just his polite way of saying he's not interested."

Beth's brow furrowed. "Then why put the moves on you?"

"He didn't."

Beth looked confused, then her eyes went wide. "*You* seduced *him?*"

"I tried." Ana shrugged. "I guess that lean the other day wasn't a *lean* after all."

And the hug had been nothing more than a friendly gesture. He didn't want her eighteen months ago, and he didn't want her now.

"Oh, sweetie," Beth said, pulling her into her arms for a hug. She was getting that a lot today.

"I'm so stupid."

"No you're not." She held Ana at arm's length. "He's the stupid one for letting you go in the first place. He doesn't deserve you."

"Yet I still love him." She wished she could turn her feelings off like a spigot, the way her father did. She wished that she were stronger. And she wished this wouldn't hurt so much. "I'm pathetic."

"You just want to be happy, and you want your son to have what you missed out on. A complete, cohesive family. There's nothing pathetic about that."

Max might never have a mommy and daddy who loved each other, but it was possible that he would at least have two parents who loved him. If that was the best she could do for her son, she could live with that.

Six

Nathan sat in his office Tuesday afternoon, browsing on his phone the photos Ana had emailed him of his visit Sunday. Though he had spent a couple hours with Max Thursday, and nearly the entire day at Ana's on Sunday, it didn't really hit home the bond that had begun to form between him and Max until he saw pictures of the two of them together. He hadn't realized how alike they looked. Not just features, but expressions and mannerisms. And he hadn't noticed the adoration in Max's eyes when he gazed up at him. The kid was really taking to him, and Nathan couldn't deny the tug of parental affection.

Ana, on the other hand, seemed as though she could take Nathan or leave him. He had hoped they might get a chance to talk about what had happened Thursday night, but she'd made herself pretty scarce. Other than snapping a few pictures, she'd spent most of her time in the spare bedroom with her scrapbooking paraphernalia, updating

Max's baby book. A few times when he did try to start a conversation she'd given him the brush-off. Apparently she'd had no trouble whatsoever forgetting that kiss.

He had known that hugging her was probably a bad idea, that he was tempting fate, but she had looked so confused and miserable that he hadn't been able to stop himself. He knew the instant her body was pressed to his, and her arms wrapped around him, that he had to kiss her, but then she'd slipped her arms around his neck and kissed him first. If Beth hadn't shown up, he didn't doubt for a second that they would have wound up in bed together. And it would have been a huge mistake, because as he suspected at the time, Ana was only reacting to the highly emotional situation. When he gave her an out, she gladly took it.

Oh, well, easy come, easy go.

He wasn't sure what kind of game she was playing with him. He just wished he could shut his feelings off so easily.

Nathan tried to get himself invited to stay for dinner Sunday, but Ana wasn't biting. She said they had plans for the evening, although she didn't say what they were. He had hoped they could have a quiet family dinner, he could tuck Max into bed again, then he and Ana could relax with a glass of wine and talk. He had forgotten until recently how much he enjoyed spending time with her. He left her condo at four-thirty wondering what was more disappointing: not being with Max, or not being with her.

Since the instant Beth had introduced Nathan and Ana he had been drawn to her. And while it was true that their relationship had begun based on little more than sex—and really fantastic sex at that—he found what he missed most about her were the times they just talked. She had a very unique and quirky way of looking at the world. Despite her station in Texas society, there were no pretensions, no ego. She was who she was, and when he was with her, he almost felt he could be who he was, too. That she was the kind of woman who would accept him. But accepting him, and deserving him, were two very different things. But damn, had he missed her when it was over.

It would never work for them, so why was he sitting here devising plans to spend more time with her? Things like leaving work early and showing up at her door unannounced with dinner tonight.

There was a knock at his office door, and he looked up to see his brother let himself in. "Hey, what's up?"

"Did Mom call you?"

"When I was in a meeting. I haven't had a chance to call her back. Why, is something wrong?"

"No. She wants you to bring the wine this year."

"The wine?"

Jordan laughed. "For Christmas dinner. It's a week from this Saturday."

"Seriously?" Nathan looked at his desk calendar. It seemed as though just a week ago it was Thanksgiving. And frankly, dinner with his mother once a year was more than adequate. "Maybe I'll have the flu this year."

"If I have to go, so do you."

"I have an idea. How about neither of us goes?"

"She's our mother."

"She gave birth to us. The nanny was our mother. Maybe we should go have dinner with her."

"It's *Christmas,*" Jordan said. "The time for forgiveness."

He sighed and leaned back in his chair. "Fine. I'll call her and let her know."

"Should we get her a gift?"

Nathan folded his arms. "How about a plaque that says *Mother of the Year?*"

"Funny."

He might consider it if he thought for a second that she would appreciate the gesture. But when a twelve-year-old kid spent a month's worth of allowances to get his mother a necklace for her birthday, only to find it crammed down into the garbage the next day, it left a lasting impression.

"Isn't it enough that I'm spending an entire evening with her?"

"It's not going to bother you if I get her something?"

"Not in the least."

"So," Jordan said offhandedly. "Anything new with the investigation?"

Nothing Nathan could tell him. Though Adam and the board had promised to keep Jordan in the loop in regard to the investigation, he needed plausible deniability. Jordan was operations officer and worked closely with the men in the refinery. They respected and trusted Jordan. If they knew there were agency operatives working undercover among them and thought that Jordan was a part of it, that respect and trust would be lost. That was too important to sacrifice, especially now.

Besides, as of the last report that had landed on Nathan's desk, the agency hadn't made any progress in the investigation and was no closer to learning who tampered with the equipment. And Jordan had seemed particularly antsy to get results lately. He valued each and every man at the refinery, and he didn't want to believe that someone he trusted could be responsible for the explosion.

"Nothing new," he told his brother.

"If there were, would you tell me?"

He didn't answer.

Jordan shook his head. "That's what I figured."

If he thought for a second that he could trust his brother, he would tell him the truth, but Jordan would only take the information and use it to benefit himself. Everything was a competition to him. He was convinced that was why Jordan fought for the CEO position at Western Oil. It was some sort of twisted sibling rivalry.

"Anything else?" Nathan asked him.

"Nope, that's it," Jordan said, then added on his way out the door, "Don't forget to call Mom."

He should probably do that now before he forgot. Hopefully he could make it quick. He picked up the phone and dialed his mother's place and the housekeeper answered. "Your mother is with her bridge club, Mr. Everette. You can try her cell."

"Could you just let her know that I got her message and I'll bring the wine for Christmas dinner?"

"Of course, sir."

After he hung up, he sat back in his chair and considered all the work he should get done this afternoon, and weighed it against spending time with Max and Ana. They won, hands down.

He shut down his computer, got up and grabbed his overcoat. His secretary, Lynn, looked up as he walked past, clearly surprised to see him in his coat.

"I'm taking off early today. Would you please cancel my appointments for the rest of the day?"

Her brow furrowed with worry. "Is everything okay?"

It was pretty sad to know that he was so chained to his job, he couldn't leave work early without his secretary thinking something was wrong. "Fine. I just have a few personal things I need to take care of. I'll be in early tomorrow. Call me if anything urgent comes up."

He ran into Adam, the CEO, on the way to the elevator.

Adam looked at his watch. "Did I fall asleep at my desk? Is it after eight already?"

Nathan grinned. "I'm leaving early. Personal time."

"Everything okay?"

"Just a few things I need to take care of. By the way, how is Katie?" Adam's wife, Katie, lived two hours away in Peckins, Texas, a small farming community, where she and Adam were currently building a house and awaiting the birth of their first baby.

"She's great. Getting huge already."

Nathan was sure the long-distance relationship had to be tough, but Adam's beaming grin said they were making it work. Nathan wondered what it would be like to be that happy, that content as a family man. Unfortunately, he would never know.

"She's actually in town this week," Adam said. "She was thinking of having a small holiday gathering this Saturday. Just a few people from work and a couple of friends. I don't suppose you could make it."

He had been hoping to spend Saturday evening with Ana and Max, but with the CEO position in the balance, now wasn't a good time to be turning down invitations from the boss. "I'll check my schedule and let you know."

"It's last-minute, I know. Try to make it if you can."

"I will."

Nathan was stopped two more times on his way to the elevator, then he was corralled into the coffee shop in the building lobby briefly before he finally made it out the door and to his car. He stopped at home to change, noting as he stepped in the door the absolute lack of anything even remotely festive. He didn't even bother to display the Christmas cards that had been arriving in a steady stream the past couple of weeks. He never decorated for the holidays. He didn't have the time or, truthfully, the inclination. Most of his Christmas memories were the kind better off forgotten.

When he bought this place five years ago he'd had it professionally decorated, mainly because he didn't have time to do it himself. It was aesthetically pleasing, but it had no heart. He'd never put his own stamp on it. He spent so little time there, he might as well be living in a hotel. In contrast, Ana's condo, despite being a mess most of the time, was a home. When they were dating he'd spent most of his free time there instead of bringing her back to his place. The truth was, he never brought women home.

Recalling the stains on his slacks the last two times he visited Max, this time Nathan opted for jeans and a polo shirt. He was out the door by four, and pulled in Ana's driveway beside her SUV at four-ten. A gust of cold northern wind whipped around him as he walked to the porch. He knocked on her door, hoping she wouldn't be angry with him for stopping by unannounced.

She pulled the door open, Max on her hip, clearly surprised to see him. "Nathan, what are you…" She trailed off, looking him up and down, taking in his windblown hair, his casual clothes. "Whoa. That *is* you, right?"

Ana may have been confused, but Max wasn't. He squealed with delight and lunged for Nathan. Ana had no choice but to hand him over.

"Hey, buddy," Nathan said, kissing his cheek, and he told Ana, "I got out early today, so I thought I would come by and see what you're doing."

She stepped back so he could bring Max out of the brisk wind and shut the door behind them. She was dressed in a pair of skinny jeans and a sweatshirt, her feet were bare and her hair was pulled back into a ponytail. Damn, she was pretty. The desire to pull her into his arms and kiss her hello was as strong now as it had been a year and a half ago.

"You got out *early?*" she said. "I thought you were swamped."

He shrugged. "So I'll go in early tomorrow."

"But we don't have a visit scheduled."

"I wanted to see Max. I guess I missed him. I thought I would take a chance and see if you weren't busy."

"Oh." She looked as though she wasn't quite sure what to make of that. "We sort of have plans. We were going to have an early dinner then go get a Christmas tree."

"Sounds like fun," he said, more or less inviting himself.

"You hate the holidays," she said.

"Who told you that?"

"*You* did."

Had he? "Well, then, maybe it's time someone changed my mind." He paused, then said, "Is that Thai place you used to love so much still around?"

She folded her arms, eyeing him skeptically. "Maybe."

"We could order in. My treat."

The hint of a grin pulling at the corner of her mouth said she was close to caving. "Well, I suppose if I'm going to get a free meal out of it…"

He grinned and handed Max over to her so he could take off his coat.

Ana sat on the couch, listening to the all-holiday music channel on the satellite radio, watching as Nathan set up the Christmas tree in the stand.

This was probably a really bad idea. She probably shouldn't have invited Nathan to come tree hunting with them. The more she saw of him, the harder it was to keep her feelings in check, but Max had been so happy to see him, and Nathan had seemed pretty darned happy to see him, too. She just hadn't had the heart to turn him away. Besides, getting a Christmas tree was supposed to be a family activity. Not that she and Max and Nathan were a family. Not in the conventional sense, anyway. And Max was so little it wasn't as if he would remember it.

So, was she doing this for Max, or for herself?

Good question.

Max had fallen asleep in the car on the way home and had gone straight to bed, so there was really no reason for Nathan to be here. She was perfectly capable of setting the tree up by herself. So why, when he offered to do it, had she said yes? Why wasn't she telling him to go?

Because she was pathetic, that's why. Because spending the afternoon with him, and going to pick out a tree together, had been everything she could have imagined it would be. Because she wanted them to be a family, wanted it so badly she was no longer thinking rationally.

She'd been doing her best to avoid Nathan, to give him and Max time to get to know one another, but it seemed as though the less she talked to him, the more he tried to talk to her. She was all for them being friends, but her feelings were still a bit raw. They were going to have to set some rules about his popping in unannounced. Especially if he decided to be a permanent part of Max's life, which certainly seemed to be the way he was leaning. She hadn't brought it up yet. She figured he would broach the subject when he was ready.

"So, what do you think?" Nathan asked, stepping back to admire his work. "Is it straight?"

"It's perfect." The tree was larger than she usually got, but she'd figured what the heck, it was only for a few weeks, and she knew Max would be so excited when he woke up and saw it in the morning. Tomorrow night, after the branches had time to settle, they would decorate it. Everything about this holiday season would be special because it was Max's first.

Nathan grabbed his hot chocolate from the credenza where he'd set it and sat down on the couch beside her, resting his arm across the cushion behind her head. And he was sitting so that their thighs were nearly touching. What was this? A first date? Did he have to sit so close? There was a perfectly good chair across the room. Why didn't he sit there? Or even better, why didn't he leave? Would it be rude to ask him to go?

With the fireplace lit, and only the lamp by the couch on, there was an undeniable "date" vibe in the air. Or maybe she was mistaking intimate for cozy. Cozy and *platonic*.

"I had fun tonight," he said, sounding surprised by the realization.

"Does that mean you're changing your opinion about the holidays?"

"Maybe. It's a start at least."

"Well then, maybe I should let you help us decorate the tree tomorrow."

Ugh! Did she really just say that? What was *wrong* with her? It was as if her brain was working independently from her mouth. Or maybe it was the other way around.

Nathan grinned. "I may just take you up on that."

Of course he would. She was supposed to be avoiding him, not manufacturing family activities that Max would be too young to remember anyway. She was only making this harder on herself.

"What was it you disliked so much about Christmas anyway?" she asked him.

"Let's just say it was never what you would call a heartwarming family experience."

"You know, in all the time I've known you, you never once talked about your mom and dad," she said. "I take it there's a reason for that. I mean, if they were awesome parents I probably would have heard about it, right?"

"Probably," he agreed. Then nothing.

If she wanted to know more, obviously she would have to drag it out of him. "So, are they still together?"

"Divorced." Nathan leaned forward to set his cup down on the coffee table. "Why the sudden interest in my parents?"

She shrugged. "I don't know, I guess it would be nice to know about the family of the father of my baby. Especially if he's going to be spending time with them."

"He won't be."

"Why not?"

"My mother is an elitist snob and my father is an overbearing bully. I see her two or three times a year, and I haven't talked to my father in almost a decade."

Her father would never be parent of the year, but she couldn't imagine him not being a part of her and Max's life.

"Besides," Nathan added, "they're not 'kid' people. Jordan and I were raised by the nanny."

"I think if my mom had lived, my parents would still be together," she said. "I remember them being really happy together."

Her father had loved her mother so much, in fact, that he never got over losing her.

"I don't think mine were ever happy," Nathan said.

"So why get married?"

"My mom was looking for a rich husband and my dad was old money. I was born seven months after the wedding."

"You think she got pregnant on purpose."

"According to my grandmother she did. As a kid you overhear things."

She didn't even know how to respond to that. What a horrible way for Nathan to have to grow up, knowing he was conceived as a marriage trap.

Ana would make it a point to assure Max that even though his parents didn't stay together, he was wanted and loved dearly from the minute he was conceived. Which was exactly what Nathan's mother should have done, whether it was true or not.

Then she had a thought, one that actually turned her stomach. "This is why you thought you wouldn't be a good parent, isn't it?"

"I haven't had the best role models."

He sure hadn't. And why was she was just hearing about this now? Talk about being self-absorbed. Why hadn't she asked about his family when they were dating? Why hadn't she tried to get to know him better?

She thought she loved Nathan, but the truth was, she hardly knew anything about him. Had she been so self-centered, so busy having "fun" that she hadn't even thought to ask? Or was she just too busy talking about herself?

No wonder Nathan had dumped her. If she were Nathan, *she* would have dumped her!

"I'm a terrible person," she said.

He looked genuinely taken aback. "What are you talking about?"

"Why didn't I ever ask you about your family before? Why didn't I know any of this?"

He laughed. "Ana, it's not a big deal. Honestly."

"Yes, it is," she said, swallowing back the lump that was filling her throat. "I feel awful. I remember talking about me all the time. You know practically everything about me. My life is a freaking open book! And here you had all this…baggage, and I was totally clueless. We could have talked about it."

"Maybe I didn't want to talk about it."

"Well of course you didn't. You're a *guy*. It was my responsibility to drag it out of you by force. I never even asked. I didn't even try to get to know you better. I was a lousy girlfriend."

"You were not a lousy girlfriend."

"Technically I wasn't even your girlfriend." She got up from the couch and grabbed their empty cocoa cups. "I was just some woman you had sex with who talked about herself constantly."

She carried the cups to the kitchen and set them in the sink.

Nathan followed her. "You didn't talk about yourself *that* much. And besides," he added, "it was really *great* sex."

Seven

Ana swiveled to face Nathan, not sure if he was joking or serious, if she should laugh or punch him. And whatever his intention, it hurt.

"That's really all it was to you?" she asked. "Just great sex?"

Only after the words were out did she realize how small and vulnerable she sounded. *Way to go, Ana. Why not just blurt out how much you loved him, and that he broke your heart? Why not throw it all out on the line so you can look like an even bigger fool?*

"What difference does it make?" he asked, his eyes dark. "You were only using me to defy your father."

Ouch. She should have known that remark would come back to bite her.

"And for the record," he said, stepping closer, trapping her against the edge of the counter, "it was not just about the sex. I cared about you."

Yeah, right. "Dumping me was certainly an interesting way to show it."

"I ended it *because* of how I felt for you."

What? "That makes *no* sense. If you care about someone, you don't break up with them. You don't treat them like they're the best thing in your life one day, then tell them it's over the next!"

"I know it doesn't make sense to you, but I did what I had to do. What was best for *you.*"

For *her*? Was he joking? "How in the hell do you know what's best for me?"

"There are things about me, things you wouldn't understand."

Just when she thought this couldn't get much worse, he had to lay the *it's not you it's me* speech on her. As if she hadn't heard that one a dozen times before. Well, if it wasn't her fault, why did she keep getting dumped? Why was she always the one with the broken heart?

"This is stupid. We covered all of this eighteen months ago. It's done."

She shoved past him but he grabbed her arm.

"It's obviously not done."

"It is for me," she lied, and tried to tug her arm free.

"You weren't the only one hurt, you know."

She made an indignant noise. "I'm sure you were devastated."

His eyes flashed with anger. "Don't do that. You'll never know how hard it was leaving you. How many times I almost picked up the phone and called you." He leaned closer, so his lips were just inches away. "How tough it is now, seeing you, *wanting* you so damned much and knowing I can't have you."

Her heart skipped a beat. He wasn't just telling her what she wanted to hear. He meant every word he'd said.

He still wanted her. And despite everything else that had happened between them, as much as she'd tried to fight it, to be smart about this, she wanted him, too. But she didn't tell him that. Instead she did something even worse. Something monumentally more stupid.

She pushed up on her toes and kissed him.

For one tense and terrifying instant she wasn't sure how he would react, if she was making a huge mistake. But Nathan's arms went around her, his hands tangling through her hair, and his tongue swept across her own in that lulling, bone-melting way of his.

Her knees went soft and her pulse skipped and everything in her screamed *yes!*

He should be telling her that this would only complicate things, and the important thing right now was to keep it civilized, for Max's sake. He should be, but he wasn't.

He broke the kiss and pulled back to look at her, cradling her face in his hands, searching her eyes.

Her heart sank. "Having second thoughts already?"

He smiled and shook his head. "No. Just savoring the moment."

Because it would be their last. She knew it, and she could see it in his eyes. They would get this one night together, then things would have to go back to the way they were. They would have to go back to just being Max's parents. There was no other way. Not for him, anyway. It sucked, and it hurt—boy, did it hurt—but not enough to make her tell him no. She wanted this, probably more than she'd ever wanted anything.

"You're sure this is what you want?" he said, always the gentleman, always worried about her feelings, and her heart, even when he was breaking it. But this one was worth a little pain.

She stepped away from him, grabbed a quilt from the

back of the couch and spread it out on the rug in front of the fire. Nathan watched, his eyes dark, as she stripped down to her bra and panties then laid down on the blanket. He had this look, as though he wanted to devour her, and every part of her hummed in anticipation. Her skin heated and her pulse jumped.

He tugged his polo shirt up over his head, then shoved his jeans off and kicked them aside. He was perfect. Lean and strong and beautiful. The glow of the fire licked and danced across his skin as he got down and stretched out beside her. He propped himself up on one elbow, gazing at her.

"My body is a little different than the last time you saw it," she said.

He touched her stomach, stroking it with the backs of his fingers, and the skin quivered under his touch. "Does that bother you?" he asked.

She shrugged. "It's just a fact."

"Well," he said, leaning over and pressing a kiss to the crest of her breast, just above the lace edge of her bra, "I think you're even sexier than you were before."

As long as he kept touching her, she didn't care how she looked. He eased the cup of her bra aside, exposing her breast to the cool air, and her nipple pulled into a tight point. He teased it lightly with his tongue, then took it in his mouth and sucked. Ana moaned softly and closed her eyes. Nathan reached around to unfasten her bra, working the clasp with a quick flick of his fingers. The low growl of satisfaction as he pulled it off said he either didn't notice that her breasts weren't quite as firm as they had been before, or he simply didn't care.

For a while he seemed content to just touch and kiss and explore her, and oh, could the man do amazing things with his mouth. The problem was, he was only doing them above the waist. And though God knows she loved kissing him, and putting her hands on him was like pure heaven, she was crawling out of her skin, she was so hot for him. But every time she tried to move things along, he would cut her off at the pass.

She enjoyed foreplay as much as the next woman, but even she had limits. But hadn't that always been his M.O.? For him, foreplay wasn't a means to an end. It was an art form. And sex had always been not only satisfying, but fun.

"You know you're driving me crazy," she said.

His grin said that he knew exactly what he was doing. "There's no rush, right?"

"I wouldn't exactly call this *rushing,* Nathan."

"Because I know the second I touch you, you're going to come." As if to prove his point, he slid his hand down her stomach, dipping his fingers an inch or so under the waist of her panties. She bit her lip to keep from moaning, digging her nails into his shoulders, but his smug smile said she wasn't fooling him.

"Well what do you expect after *three hours* of foreplay?" she said.

He laughed. "It hasn't been three hours."

It sure felt like it. He didn't seem to understand that most men pretty much grew bored with the foreplay after five minutes. Nathan, on the other hand, seemed to be going for some sort of world record.

"I'd just like to make this last," he said.

"Did I mention that it's been *eighteen* months? Honestly, I think I've waited long enough."

His eyes locked on hers, and he slid his hand inside her panties again. The second his fingers dipped into her slippery heat she was out on the ledge and ready to fall over. She just needed one little push….

"Not yet," Nathan whispered, pulling his hand away. She groaned in protest. He sat up and tugged her panties off, and she nearly sobbed, she was so ready. Pushing her thighs apart, he knelt between them. He wrapped his hands around her ankles and slowly slid them upward, dipping in to caress the backs of her knees, then higher still, easing her thighs wider. With the pads of his thumbs he grazed the crease where her thigh met her body, then he dipped inward…

She was so close…falling over…

He pressed her legs apart, lowered his head…she felt his warm breath…the wet heat of his tongue…

Her body locked in a pleasure so intense, so beautiful and perfect that a sob bubbled up from her throat. Only when she saw Nathan gazing down at her, brow furrowed with worry, did she realize that tears were leaking from her eyes.

"Are you okay?" he asked. "Did I hurt you?"

She shook her head. "No, it was *perfect*."

"Then what's wrong?"

She sniffled and wiped at her eyes. "Nothing. I think it was just really intense. Maybe because it's been so long. Like a huge emotional release, or something."

He didn't look as though he believed her. "Maybe we should stop."

He was going to back out now? *Seriously?* "I don't *want* to stop. I'm fine."

He sat back on his heels. "You don't look fine."

She pushed herself up, leveled her eyes on him, so he would know she was serious. "Let's put it this way. If you don't make love to me right now, I'll have to hurt you."

Nathan would have had to be a total moron not to realize that Ana was feeling emotional and vulnerable. She was crying, for God's sake. They'd had some pretty intense sex in the past and she'd never burst into tears. And maybe it meant he was a heartless bastard, but he was having a tough time telling her no. Or maybe it was just really hard to think straight with Ana sliding her hand inside his boxers.

"I want you, Nathan," Ana whispered, rising up on her knees beside him, and when she kissed him, she tasted salty, like tears. Despite that, he didn't try to stop her when she pushed him back onto the blanket. Maybe it was wrong, but for the first time in a long time, he didn't feel like he had to be the good guy. The responsible, respectable, never-let-your-emotions-get-away-from-you guy. Being with Ana made him want to *feel*.

It always had.

Which gave this the potential not only to become very complicated, but dangerous, too. Because lately, the self-imposed numbness just wasn't cutting it. And when Ana grasped his erection, slowly stroking him, he sure as hell didn't feel numb. Words could not adequately describe how damned fantastic it felt.

"So, what's it going to be?" she said, looking anything but vulnerable. "Sex, or potential physical trauma?"

Concise and to the point. He'd always liked that about her. When it came to feeling things, Ana had never been one to hold back. She hadn't been afraid to put herself out there. He wouldn't deny that at times it had scared the hell out of him. But at least with her he always knew where he stood. She didn't manipulate or play games. And only because she seemed to know exactly what she wanted now would he let this happen.

He reached over and tugged his wallet from the back pocket of his jeans, fishing out a condom. She snatched it away from him and tore it open.

"You in a hurry?" he asked.

"What part of 'I haven't had sex in eighteen months' didn't you get?"

She might have been surprised to learn that since her, there had been only one other woman for him. And that was over a year ago. A rebound relationship that had been brief and, quite frankly, not very exciting. Of course, compared to Ana, not many women were. That used to be the kind of woman he preferred. Someone who wouldn't excite him or challenge him. But being with Ana had changed him. She'd more or less ruined him for other women. In and out of the bedroom.

"That doesn't mean we can't take our time," he said.

She threw a leg over his thighs and straddled him, and he knew that there was no use in arguing. He could see things hadn't changed. He had a short window of time in which she let him have control—which was nowhere *near* three hours—and then she angled for the dominant position. He knew that when she reached that point, there was no reasoning with her.

She pulled the condom from the wrapper and he braced himself because he knew exactly what was coming next. She'd done it dozens of times before.

With a saucy smile she said, "Goes on better damp," then she leaned down and took him in her mouth. He groaned and fisted the blanket as she used her tongue to wet him from tip to base.

If she kept that up, this would be over in ten seconds.

She sat back on her heels, wearing a smile that said she knew exactly what she was doing to him, and it was payback time. She rolled the condom on like a pro, then centered herself over him, flush with anticipation. Her body was a little rounder than before, her breasts fuller and her hips softer, and he didn't think he'd ever seen anything so beautiful.

"Ready?" she asked.

As if he had a choice.

She braced her hands on his chest and sank down slowly, inch by excruciating inch. He hissed out a breath as her hot, slippery walls closed in around him. Though he would have considered the opposite to be true, he could swear she was even tighter than she'd been before having Max. Maintaining even a shred of control was going to be close to impossible. Ironic, considering the way he'd just been teasing her.

"Oh, Nathan," she moaned, eyes closed, slowly riding him. "You wouldn't believe how amazing this feels."

He wanted to tell her that actually yes, he would, but he was barely hanging on. If he so much as uttered a sound he was going to lose it. And he'd be damned if he was going to let himself climax first. That just wasn't the way he did things. He needed to take the upper hand before he completely lost control.

Nathan flipped Ana over. She let out a gasp of surprise as her back hit the floor. She opened her mouth to protest, but as he plunged himself deep inside of her, a moan of pleasure emerged instead. Arching into his thrust, her legs wrapped around his waist, nails digging into his shoulder. He barely had a chance to establish a rhythm before her body started to quake, clamping around him like a vise, and he couldn't have held back if his life depended on it. In that instant time ground to a screeching halt and there was nothing but pleasure.

When time started moving again, he looked down at Ana lying beneath him, eyes closed, breathing hard, her hair fanned like crimson flames against the blanket. The woman was pure sex.

"You okay?" he asked.

Her eyes slowly opened, filled not with tears this time, but a satisfaction he was pretty damn sure she could see mirrored back in his own gaze. She nodded and said breathlessly, "I know we probably shouldn't have done that, and it's going to complicate the hell out of things, but...damn...it was *so* worth it."

Sex with Nathan had always been out-of-this-world fantastic. But tonight he shot her clear to a different *galaxy*.

She wasn't sure if it was so good because it had been so long, or because it was the first time after having Max. Or if Nathan was just really, really good at making her crazy. Whatever the reason, it was a shame that they could never do it again.

Nathan must have been thinking the same thing. He rolled onto his back, sighed slow and deep, and said, "I guess we should have the talk now."

She threw an arm over her eyes and groaned. "Do we have to? Can't we just enjoy the afterglow for a while?" She looked over at him. "In fact, could we just not talk at all?"

He rolled onto his side and propped himself up on his elbow. She wondered if he had the slightest clue how sexy he looked like that. How difficult it would be to keep her hands to herself now. "You want to wait till later?"

"No, I mean *never*. I have no expectations of this being anything but one time, and I'm assuming you don't either. So, it happened, it's over, end of story. Let's not ruin it by having a conversation."

His this-is-too-good-to-be-real look made her smile. "You're sure about this?"

"It is what it is. Analyzing it to death isn't going to change anything. In fact, it would probably just make things even more complicated. At this point my only concern is Max."

"If that's how you feel."

She really did, for the most part anyway. Did she want more? Of course. Sentiments of love would be nice, and she certainly wouldn't balk at a marriage proposal. Hell, at this point she'd be happy with a semipermanent, exclusive sexual relationship. But she knew that wasn't smart, because ultimately it was going to end, and she refused to put herself in a position to get her heart stomped on again.

There was someone else out there for her. He probably wouldn't be as wonderful as Nathan, or as good in bed. And she would probably never love him the way she loved Nathan, but loving someone too much wasn't such a great thing, either.

"It is," she told him. "I mean, it was probably just something we needed to get out of our systems. You know?"

"Well then, there's a problem."

She frowned. "What problem?"

He lowered his eyes and she followed his gaze down to his crotch.

Oh boy. He clearly hadn't gotten it out of his system yet.

Okay. This was not a big deal. They were already lying here naked, so she couldn't really see the harm in doing it one more time. Or heck, two more times if that's what it took. And since Nathan used to have the libido of an eighteen-year-old, and that probably hadn't changed, it was a distinct possibility.

But after tonight, it was definitely over.

Eight

Nathan sat in his office the next morning, feeling more relaxed and all around happier than he had in a very long time. Eighteen months, to be exact.

Only problem was, that happiness never lasted.

His life would be going really well, and he would start to think that things were different, that her love had changed him, then something would happen to flare his temper and he would realize that nothing had changed. Wasn't it better to get out while it was still good? Because the last thing he wanted to do was hurt Ana. This situation, their relationship, was supposed to be about Max and what was best for him, yet lately it seemed to be more about Ana and Nathan. Letting this go any further would be a mistake. So, the next time she tried to put the moves on him—and knowing Ana, there would probably be a next time—he would nip it in the bud. He would be the rational one.

Whether she wanted to believe it or not, he knew what was best for her.

His secretary buzzed him. "Mr. Blair needs to see you in his office."

He shoved himself up from his chair and headed down the hall to Adam's office.

"They're waiting for you," Adam's secretary said, gesturing him through the open office door.

They? Had he forgotten a meeting? His mind hadn't exactly been in the game the last few days, but that was what his secretary was for, and she hadn't said anything.

Adam sat behind his desk, and Nathan was surprised to see Emilio standing by the window. If it was a scheduled meeting, Jordan wasn't there yet.

"Shut the door." Adam said.

"What about Jordan?"

"I sent him to the refinery."

There was only one reason why Jordan would be excluded from a meeting. There had been some sort of news about the explosion.

He shut the door and took a seat across from Adam's desk. "So I take it there's been a development."

Adam and Emilio exchanged a look, and Emilio said, "Something like that."

He wasn't sure he appreciated the fact that Adam would discuss it with Emilio before him. Until the CEO position was filled, they were supposed to be on a level playing ground.

Nathan sat straighter in the chair, looking from one to the other. "Whatever it is, I see you've already discussed it without me."

"We have a few questions for you," Adam said, looking so solemn that Nathan had to wonder if he'd done something wrong. They couldn't possibly know about Max and Ana.

"So ask," Nathan said.

"I know you and Jordan aren't very close," Emilio said. "But do you know anything about his personal finances?"

"We don't exactly share stock tips. Why?"

"Are you aware of any reason he would have to deposit or withdraw any large sums of cash?"

They were looking into Jordan's personal finances? Had they been checking Nathan out, too? Despite all the animosity he had toward Jordan, that ages-old instinct to defend his brother worked its way to the surface. "Are you accusing my brother of something?"

"A week before the accident someone deposited two hundred thousand dollars into Jordan's account, and a few days later he wired thirty thousand dollars out."

"To whom?"

"I'm afraid we don't have access to that information," Emilio said.

"But what you're saying is, you think he's responsible for the sabotage?"

"You can't deny it looks suspicious."

He looked from Adam to Emilio. "You think that someone paid him, and he paid someone else to tamper with the equipment?"

"That's one possibility," Adam said.

"Why?"

"Jordan is ambitious," Emilio said. "It happened before everyone learned the CEO position was opening up. Maybe he felt he'd hit a ceiling."

"His commitment to this company and his dedication to the men at the refinery has been exemplary," Nathan reminded them. In fact, it was truly remarkable, despite the social and economic differences, how deeply the workers at the refinery respected and trusted Jordan. Not only was he the man in charge, but when he was among the workers, he was one of them.

"Maybe someone made him an offer he couldn't refuse," Emilio said. "But expected something in return first."

"Ambitious or not, I can't see him putting anyone's life in danger to further his career."

"Maybe no one was meant to get hurt, but something went wrong," Adam suggested. "You have to admit, he was the one hit hardest by this. Maybe he feels guilty."

"If he got a better offer, why is he still here?"

"To avoid suspicion? Or maybe now that the CEO position is opening up, he has a reason to stay."

"Or maybe," Emilio offered, "since there were injuries, it killed the deal."

"Look, you know that my brother and I don't have the best relationship, but I'm having a hard time wrapping my head around this." Or maybe he just didn't want to believe that his own brother could be responsible, that he could be that self-serving. Maybe he didn't like that what they were suggesting had credibility.

"Believe me, we don't like it either," Adam said. "But we can't ignore the possibility. If he were involved somehow, and it came out later that we had proof and did nothing about it—"

"You could confront him," Nathan said.

Emilio laughed. "This is Jordan we're talking about. If he's guilty, do you honestly think he'll admit it?"

Good point. Jordan would just as soon slice off a limb than admit he'd made a mistake.

"His secretary will be starting her maternity leave in a few weeks and the investigation firm has suggested we place an undercover operative directly into Jordan's office," Adam said. "He'll just think she's a temp."

"If he finds out, he's going to be *pissed*."

"So we have to make sure he doesn't find out," Adam said. "And we have until then to find another way. Maybe you could try talking to him. Maybe he'll let something slip."

"Honestly, I'm the last person he would confide in. We don't talk. Ever. If nothing else, that would only raise his suspicions."

"If not for Jordan, this company wouldn't be where it is today," Adam said. "If he's innocent, I don't want to risk losing him."

"We took a chance trusting you with this," Emilio said. "I have brothers, so I know it's a lot to ask. But we can only do this if you're behind it one hundred percent."

He knew they were right, and he hated that underneath the need to defend his brother, there was a nagging suspicion that maybe it was true. Either way, they needed to know.

"I'm in," he said.

He knew he was doing the right thing. Still, it felt like a betrayal. But with Jordan's career on the line, maybe this was the best thing he could do for his brother.

Although it got him wondering, as he headed back to his office, if they were investigating Jordan, did that mean he was under investigation as well? But why would he be? He could count on one hand how many times he had actually been in the refinery, and the men who worked there were strangers to him. But if his relationship to Ana and Max were to get out, it could not only hurt his chances at the CEO position but cast doubt over him as well.

He was leaning toward the idea of making Max a permanent part of his life, but at this point it would undoubtedly complicate things. Ana hadn't been pushing him to make any decisions, but he knew it was only a matter of time before she would expect an answer from him. They couldn't go on living in limbo this way. Especially after what happened last night. Which, the more he thought about it, the more he realized what a mistake it probably was. It was clouding his judgement. Making him forget that there were other issues to think about, like whether or not he even deserved to be someone's parent. What if he was destined to repeat his own parents' mistakes? What if he turned out to be like his father, harsh and judgmental? Or, even worse, like his mother? Too absorbed in his own life to care that he had a vulnerable and confused kid desperate for his attention. And if he did lose the CEO position over this, or even his job, would he end up resentful and bitter?

If he could hold Ana off just another few months, until he'd had time to really consider what he was doing, at least until the CEO decision was made...

He'd left his cell phone on his desk, and when he got back to his office there were two missed calls. One from a number he didn't recognize, and one from Ana. Neither left a message. Maybe Ana had decided that they needed to have that talk after all. He was half-tempted to wait and call her back later, until he considered the possibility that her call may have had something to do with their son. What if he was sick or injured? His pulse skipped at the thought.

He dialed her number and she answered on the second ring. In the background he could hear Max babbling happily, and the sudden gush of relief he experienced nearly knocked him back in his chair. In barely over a week, the little runt had managed to weasel his way into Nathan's heart.

The question was, did he deserve Max's love?

"You called?" he asked Ana.

"Yeah. Sorry to bother you while you're working, but

I had something I wanted to ask you. Have you got a minute?"

"Sure."

"I sort of need a favor, but I want to say right up front that you are under absolutely no obligation to do this. I can ask Jenny. I just thought maybe you would want to do it instead."

"Do what?"

"Babysit Max Saturday night. I was invited for a girls' night out with Beth and some of our friends."

"Babysit as in just him and me?"

"Yeah. I thought you might like to get some quality time together. I wouldn't be leaving till seven-thirty, and he goes to bed at eight-thirty, so he'll be asleep most of the time."

The fact that she trusted him to be alone with Max rendered him speechless for several seconds.

"If you don't want to—"

"It's not that I don't want to. I just…I'm a little surprised that you would ask me, considering my vast lack of experience with kids."

"Well, Max adores you, and you know his bedtime routine. Besides, he's pretty easygoing. I can't imagine that he'll give you any trouble. And if you do decide to be a permanent part of his life, you can't keep coming over here and just visiting him forever. You'll have to get used to being alone with him. Sometimes overnight."

The idea both intrigued and made him nervous as hell. He would have to baby-proof his apartment, buy toys and baby furniture. With two extra bedrooms he definitely had the space. These just weren't things he'd taken into consideration before.

"But like I said, if you're not comfortable watching him,

it's okay. I don't want you to think that I'm trying to push you into something you're not ready for."

"No, I'd like to do it," he said, and realized, for all his doubts, he really did.

"Great! Can you be over at my place around seven-fifteen? That will give me time to show you where everything is before Beth picks me up."

"I can do that."

"I don't know what you're doing tonight, but Max and I were going to decorate the tree around seven."

With a dinner meeting scheduled for six-thirty with his team, there was no way he was getting out of work before eight tonight. So he might see him for ten minutes before he went to bed. Meaning he would be going over there to see *her*, not Max, which he didn't think was a good idea after last night.

"I just can't swing it tonight, but maybe I can stop by around lunchtime tomorrow."

"Sure. That would be great." She paused, then asked, "By the way, did you get anything in the mail from Beth and Leo yet?"

"I don't know." He'd brought a pile of mail with him to work this morning but hadn't had time to go through it yet. "Hold on, let me look."

He grabbed the pile and rifled through it until he saw the greeting-card-sized envelope with Beth and Leo's return address. He tore it open, but it wasn't a card. It was an invitation to their annual New Years Eve party. Nathan went every year, except last year, and only because he figured he would run into Ana there. He'd known she was expecting, and the idea of seeing her, pregnant with another man's baby...hell, for all he knew she would bring the father with her. Had he known it was his kid, he might have felt differently.

"I take it you got an invitation too?" Nathan said.

"Yeah. I wondered if you were planning to go. I wanted to, but with us both there…well, it might be a little weird having to pretend we don't like each other."

"We can't stop socializing just because we'll run into each other. That's not fair to either of us."

"I guess not. So you're going to go?"

If only to prove that this thing between them didn't have to be a big deal. "Yeah, I'm going."

"Then I am too," she said.

They talked for a few more minutes about Max, and though Ana never once mentioned what had happened last night, it hung between them unspoken. He could hardly believe he was thinking this, but maybe not talking about it hadn't been such a hot idea after all. Not if it was going to make things awkward. He would probably feel worse if he had been the one to make the first move. Not that he couldn't have told her no. But that would have left her feeling dejected and hurt.

In other words, he slept with her to spare her feelings? How philanthropic of him. Why couldn't he just be honest with himself and admit that he slept with Ana because he wanted to? He *still* wanted to. It would take a hell of a lot more than one night to get her out of his system. Maybe a lifetime of nights. And if she came on to him again, good idea or not, he wouldn't be pushing her away.

He would just have to hope that she didn't.

Only after he'd hung up with Ana, and checked his schedule for his next meeting, did Nathan realize the mistake he'd just made. He was supposed to go to Adam and Katy's holiday get-together Saturday evening. That was what he got for not checking his schedule before committing himself. He'd been so enticed by the idea of spending some real quality time with his son, he hadn't even considered he might have another obligation.

Damn it. Emilio and his fiancée would be there, and he knew his brother would never miss an opportunity to score a few brownie points. Leaving him the odd man out. He could call Ana back and tell her he couldn't make it, but something told him that wouldn't go over really well.

He knew going into this that being a parent would require sacrifice. Besides, Adam had assured him it was okay if he didn't come, that he knew it was last-minute.

Nathan just hoped he meant it. He'd come too far, was too close to getting everything he wanted to throw it all away.

Everything was going to be fine.

Ana sat on the couch, one eye on Max in his exersaucer and one on the clock. Nathan was due there any minute to babysit. And though she was maybe a tiny bit nervous about leaving him and Max alone for the first time, she was crazy nervous about Nathan being here. Their lunch date Thursday—using the word *date* in the loosest of senses— had fallen through, so she hadn't actually seen him since they slept together Tuesday night. They had talked on the phone a couple of times, but that wasn't the same as seeing someone face-to-face.

So much for her brilliant theory about sleeping with Nathan to get him out of her system. All that did was make her want him more, make her fall just a little more in love with him. But what was the point of being in love with someone who didn't love her back?

Easy. There wasn't one.

What had she expected? That sleeping with her was going to make Nathan suddenly realize that he loved her and couldn't live without her? Clearly that wasn't going to happen. She didn't doubt that he cared about her, and desired her. Just not enough to want to spend the rest of his life with her. She was fun in the short term, just not marriage material.

Wasn't that the story of her life?

He may have been *her* one true love, but obviously she wasn't his. And even if he were willing to settle for a life with her and Max, she wanted more than that. She had no illusions about who she was and what she needed from a relationship to be happy. With all her insecurities, she needed someone who adored her. Someone who put his love for her above all else.

Nathan would never be that man. Not for her, and probably not for anyone else. He was too independent, too focused on his own life to devote himself completely to someone else.

The only exception to that rule seemed to be Max.

The bell sounded and she shot up off the couch like a spring. *Jeez, Ana, relax.* She forced herself to walk slowly to the door, glancing at her reflection in the foyer mirror. She didn't get out much these days, so she'd really taken her time getting ready. Usually by this point in the evening she was a disheveled mess, but even she had to admit that she looked pretty hot. Who knows, maybe she would meet someone at the bar tonight. She had wanted to devote her life 24/7 to Max when he was an infant, but he was practically a toddler now, and old enough that she could start thinking about dating again.

If she could just get her mind off of Nathan. She only hoped when she saw him, there wasn't any of that morning-after awkwardness. Even though technically it was more than four mornings after.

Heart in her throat, she pulled the door open. Nathan stood on the porch, looking windblown and sexy as hell.

He usually dressed casually when he came to see Max, but this time he was still wearing his suit.

He looked her up and down, taking in her clingy black cashmere sweater, leggings and knee-high, spike-heeled boots. His eyes widened and he said, "Wow, you look great."

She both loved and hated the warm glow of satisfaction that poured through her veins.

"Thanks," she said, stepping back so he could come in out of the cold. Only when he was inside did she realize how tired he looked, as though he'd been up for several days straight.

"Sorry I'm a few minutes late," he said. "A meeting ran long. I didn't even have time to go home and change."

"You look exhausted."

He shrugged out of his overcoat. "It's been a long week. We're about to go into production with a new ad campaign. Everything that could go wrong has. Thankfully we'll be shutting down for the holidays. I need a break."

From across the room Max let out a squeal and jumped excitedly as he spotted Nathan.

"Hey buddy." Nathan crossed the room to greet him, lifting him out of the exersaucer and hugging him. "I missed you."

Ana's heart melted. "He had an extra long nap today so he might stay up a little bit later for you. Just make sure he's in bed by nine. We have to be up early to get ready for breakfast at my father's house."

"You do that often?"

"A couple of times a month. My father is pretty busy most of the time, but he likes to see his grandson."

"And you, I'm sure."

"No, it's pretty much all about Max. My father and I barely say two words to each other. Unless he's lecturing me on how to raise Max, then he has plenty to say. But it's a one-sided conversation."

"Sounds a bit like my mother," Nathan said. "She loves to hear herself talk. Is your dad single? Maybe we should set them up."

"So you could be my stepbrother? It would be fun explaining that one to Max."

Nathan laughed. "Good point." He gestured to the Christmas tree. "It looks nice."

"We decorated it Wednesday night."

"We?"

"Me and Max, although admittedly I did most of the work."

This wasn't so bad. They were both being incredibly polite, but that beat having nothing to say at all.

Ana glanced at the clock. "Beth is going to be here soon. Why don't I show you where everything is, so I don't have to make her wait." Although the idea of staying home with Nathan and Max was far more seductive right now. But as Beth had implored on the phone the other day, Ana needed to get out and have fun. And she would. She would force herself.

Nathan had already been through the bedtime routine several times, but she showed him where the clean diapers and wipes were, and the pajamas in case Max dirtied the ones he was wearing.

"I left instructions in the kitchen on how to make a bottle, but you've seen me do it before," she told Nathan. "You have my cell number, so don't hesitate to call if you need anything."

"I'm sure I can manage," he said. "Although lately I've developed a healthy respect for parents with young children. People don't realize what a daunting responsibility it is. And you're doing ninety-nine percent of the work."

"It's twice as hard for single moms," she said as they walked back into the living room. "I'm fortunate that I have the financial means to raise my son however I choose. There are so many women who struggle on a daily basis, working two or three jobs to keep up. I've seriously been considering starting a local foundation for single mothers."

"To help financially?"

"Financially, emotionally, whatever they need. We could offer job-training programs and legal help to get support from the deadbeat dads who refuse to own up to their responsibility."

"It sounds like quite an undertaking."

"Which is why I've only *talked* about starting it. For now at least, Max comes first."

"I think you should do it," he said.

It was definitely part of her long-term plans. And she couldn't deny that the idea of being responsible for something so big and important was a bit intimidating. She didn't even know for sure if it would be well received. Especially from someone like her. Despite having changed her ways, the press still liked to perpetuate the "party girl" persona. What if no one took her seriously?

She wouldn't know until she tried.

Outside, Beth laid on the horn.

"That's my ride," she said. She pulled on her coat and grabbed her purse from the foyer table. She considered giving Max a kiss goodbye, but with Nathan holding him it might be a little weird. She blew him a kiss instead and said, "Bye, baby, I love you."

"Have fun," Nathan said.

"You too." She forced herself to walk out the door and down to Beth's car.

"So," Beth said a she climbed in. "First time leaving Nathan and Max alone?"

Ana fastened her seat belt. "Yep."

"Are you nervous?"

"A little, maybe. But I'm sure they'll have fun."

"How about you?" Beth asked with a mischievous smile. "Are you ready for some fun?"

Not just ready, she was long past due.

Nine

Despite the music and the dancing, and the delicious margaritas, not to mention the men who had asked her to dance, Ana just couldn't seem to relax. All she could think about was Nathan and Max, and how she would much rather be at home with them than in this flashy, overrated meat market. But the flack she would get from Beth if she caught a cab home early wasn't worth the trouble.

What had happened to the carefree party girl? The one who would crawl out of her skin at the thought of a night at home? The one who had always been in motion, always in high gear and looking forward to the next adventure. Had motherhood really changed her so much? Or had it been Nathan? Back when they had first begun dating, she suddenly became not so opposed to the idea of settling down.

"So I guess tonight wasn't such a hot idea," Beth said on the way home.

Was she really that transparent? Beth sounded so disappointed, Ana was overwhelmed with guilt. "I'm sorry. I guess I just miss Max."

"We've been out lots of times since you had Max and missing him never stopped you from having a good time." She glanced over at Ana. "When a drop-dead gorgeous man asks you to dance and you barely give him a passing glance, I'm guessing it has more to do with Max's babysitter."

"I slept with Nathan." She hadn't even meant to tell her. She just sort of blurted it out.

Beth winced. "Okay. I guess I saw this coming."

"It's not going to happen again."

Beth shot her a look. "Of course it isn't."

"I mean it. We both agreed that it was just something we needed to get out of our systems, and now it's over."

"That is the dumbest thing I've ever heard. Get him out of your system? With *sex*? You *love* the guy. Sleeping with him is just going to make you want him more."

"Unfortunately I didn't figure that out until *after* I slept with him. It wouldn't be half as humiliating if I hadn't been the one doing the seducing. Why do I keep doing this to myself?"

Beth reached over and squeezed her hand. "I'm sorry, sweetie. Guys are scum."

"He's actually not. That's the really awful part. He's a great guy. A good man. He's just not the man for me."

Beth pulled up in front of her condo. "But you definitely aren't going to sleep with him again. Right?"

"Definitely not." Especially if that meant making the first move again. She had degraded herself enough.

"You want me to come in with you and stay until he leaves? Just in case?"

"It's after midnight. You should get home." She grabbed

her purse from the floor where it had dropped. "Besides, I think I learned my lesson."

Beth kissed her cheek. "Love you. I'll talk to you tomorrow."

Ana got out of the car, waving as Beth drove away, then she made her way, a bit unsteadily, to the front door. What a lightweight she'd turned out to be. In her party days she could single-handedly drain an entire pitcher of drinks and still ace a sobriety test. Tonight she'd had three margaritas and she could barely walk a straight line.

She unlocked the door and stepped inside, surprised that all the lights were off. So was the television. From the glow of the fire she could make out Nathan's form lying on the couch. He had looked beat when he got there. He must have fallen asleep.

She wobbled on her spike heels, so she tugged off her boots and crossed the room to wake him. But as she got closer she realized it wasn't just Nathan there. Max lay curled up on his chest, head tucked under Nathan's chin, sound asleep. One of Nathan's arms was flung over his head, and the other was wrapped protectively around his son. Sudden tears welled in her eyes, and a lump the size of the entire state of Texas plugged up her throat.

It was, hands down, the sweetest thing she had ever seen in her life.

She sat on the edge of the couch and stroked her son's soft little cheek. He was out cold, and so was Nathan. She rubbed Nathan's arm to wake him.

His eyes fluttered open and he gazed drowsily up at her. "Hey, what time is it?"

"A little after midnight. I take it Max couldn't sleep."

Nathan rubbed Max's back. "He woke up around ten," he said softly. "I think he was upset that you weren't here.

He wouldn't go back to sleep, so I brought him out here with me. I guess we both fell asleep."

"I hope he wasn't too much trouble."

"Not at all. Did you have a good time?"

"Yeah, it was great," she lied. "It's always nice spending an evening with the girls."

"I guess I should get him into bed."

Ana rose from the couch. "You want me to take him?"

"I've got it." He pushed himself gently up from the couch, cradling Max against his chest.

Ana followed them into Max's bedroom and watched as he laid Max in bed and covered him. Max was so dead to the world he didn't even stir. She tucked the blankets around him and smoothed his hair back from his forehead. "Good night, sweetheart. Pleasant dreams."

They stepped out of his room and she shut the door, then they walked to the living room. "Thanks for watching him."

"It was no problem at all."

"So, everything went okay? Besides him waking up, that is."

"Yeah. We had fun." He looked at his watch. "I should get home. You have an early morning."

She wanted to invite him to stay. Offer him a drink, maybe throw herself in his arms and beg him to make love to her.

All the more reason to let him leave.

"I really do need to get to bed," she said, and to herself added, *alone*.

They walked to the foyer. "Maybe I could come by tomorrow afternoon to see Max," Nathan said. "We could get dinner."

Seeing him two days in a row was a bad idea, but she

heard herself say, "Sure. We should be back from my dad's place around one."

"I'll call you then." He pulled on his coat, turned, and with his hand on the doorknob, he just stopped.

She considered saying something snarky, like *the door isn't going to open itself,* but only to hide the fact that her heart was suddenly beating out of her chest. She wasn't even sure why. She just…had a feeling. A feeling that something big was about to happen.

He let his hand fall from the knob and he turned to her. "I don't want to leave."

Her heart rose up and lodged in her throat. *Tell him he has to. Tell him you have to get to sleep. Don't tempt fate.*

"I was going to make myself a cup of tea," she told him instead. "Would you like one?"

"I'd love one."

Nathan stood in the kitchen, watching as Ana put the kettle on to boil, got two mugs down from the cupboard and dropped a tea bag in each one. The truth was, he hated tea. But if choking down a cup meant spending a little while longer with her, it was a sacrifice he was willing to make.

He knew she had to be up early, and if she had told him to leave he would have without question. He had half-expected her to come on to him again. She'd had opportunity. And when she hadn't, he'd felt almost… slighted. He knew they were supposed to be keeping their relationship platonic, for Max's sake, but what if that wasn't enough for him? What if he wanted more?

Which was exactly why he shouldn't be here. It wasn't fair to Ana to lead her on this way. The fact that she looked so damned sexy wasn't helping matters. There wasn't a single thing about her that he didn't find arousing and irresistible. He wanted to believe that she'd dressed that way for him, and not some random stranger she had been hoping she might meet. After all, that was how he had met her. They happened to be at the same bar and Beth had introduced them.

That was assuming she had been at a bar tonight. She hadn't actually said where she was going, just that it was a ladies' night out. Considering the way she'd been dressed, that seemed the logical conclusion. But this was a woman who had worn spike-heeled boots to a six-year-old's birthday party. For all he knew she'd been at a Tupperware party tonight.

"So, what did you and Beth do tonight?" he asked, keeping his voice casually conversational.

"We went with a couple of friends to a new hot spot downtown."

Aka a bar. "How was it?"

She shrugged. "A typical meat market. But the DJ was decent and the drinks weren't watered down."

"But you had a good time?"

"It was…fun."

How fun? he wanted to ask, even though it really wasn't any of his business. But what if she had met someone else? Could that be the reason she was giving him the cold shoulder? If that was the case, it sure hadn't taken her long to move on, had it?

The kettle started to boil, so she poured water into the cups. "What do you take in your tea?"

"Sugar." Or for all he knew she could have been seeing someone else this entire time. The fact that she hadn't slept with the guy didn't mean she wasn't planning on it. Maybe she was just taking it slow because of Max.

Or maybe he was letting his imagination get away from

him. He'd seen no hint of any man in her life—no one besides Max, that is.

"So, you go out to bars often?" he asked.

She set his cup, as well as the sugar bowl and a spoon, on the counter for him. "Not lately, but I'm thinking it's about time I get back into the game."

"Which game is that?"

"Dating."

Was she telling him this to piss him off, or make him jealous? Or was she really that clueless to the feelings he had for her? Was she taking this *friendship* thing a step too far? Confiding things he really didn't want to hear?

"You think going to bars is a good place to meet men?" he asked. If she heard the snip in his tone, she chose to ignore it.

She shrugged and said, "I suppose not. I met you at a place like that, and look where it got me."

She sure knew how to hit below the belt. *Way* below the belt.

"Not that I would go back and change things even if I could," she added. "Max is the best thing that ever happened to me."

"It's just me you wish you could remove from the equation," he said.

"That's not what I meant. My point is, men don't go to bars looking for long-lasting monogamous relationships. All I have to do is mention I have a son and they practically run screaming in the opposite direction." She palmed her cup. "Then of course there are the men who would pretend to be Max's best buddy if it meant getting their hands on my trust fund. For a woman in my position, it's hard to know who to trust."

"Maybe until Max gets a little older, it would be better if you just concentrated on taking care of him."

She laughed, but it came out cold and bitter. "That's really easy for you to say."

"How do you figure? Why would you assume it's any easier for me?"

Clearly he'd hit a nerve. She glared up at him. "You can do whatever you want, when you want, and be with whomever you please. With a baby to care for 24/7, I don't have that luxury."

He took a step closer. "For the record, there's only one woman I want to *be with*. But *she* thinks it would be too complicated."

Her eyes widened slightly and she turned toward the window, gazing out into the darkness. "Please don't say things like that."

He stepped up behind her, could feel her shoulders tense as he laid his hands on them. "Why not?"

"Because you know I can't."

And he couldn't stand the idea of her being with anyone but him. He slid his hands down her arms, then back up again. "You don't want me anymore?"

He knew she did, and maybe it was selfish of him, but he wanted to hear her say it. And maybe…maybe this time things could be different. He couldn't even recall the last time he'd let his temper get the best of him. Maybe he'd really changed.

"I do want you," she said softly. "Too much. But I know you'll just hurt me again."

"So, you're finally willing to admit that I actually did hurt you. That's a start."

"I think you should leave."

"I don't want to." He eased her hair aside, pressed his lips to the side of her neck. She moaned softly and leaned back, her body molding against his.

"I can't sleep with you, Nathan."

He eased her sweater aside and kissed her shoulder. He could feel her melting, giving in. "Who said anything about sleeping?"

"Please don't do this," she said, but he could tell she was losing her will to fight him.

"What if things could be different this time? What if *I'm* different?"

She went very still in his arms, and he knew he'd gotten her attention. "What are you saying, Nathan?"

He turned her so that she was facing him. "I want to be with you, Ana. With you and Max."

She looked confused, and terrified. And hopeful. "You're not just saying that to get me into bed, are you?"

"Does that really sound like something I would do?"

She shook her head. "No. But what about work? Your career."

Good question. "We would have to keep our relationship secret for a while. At least until I'm offered the CEO position. Once I'm under contract, they'll have a tough time getting rid of me. Besides, it won't take them long to realize that when it comes to work, my loyalty is to them."

"How long?"

"Adam is resigning in early spring at the latest. He plans to be gone before their baby is born. I'm assuming the new CEO will be announced at least a month prior."

"So, we're talking another three or four months of sneaking around?"

"Worst case, yes. But it could be sooner." He touched her cheek, smoothed back the fiery strands resting there. "After that, I don't care who knows."

She still looked wary, so he pulled out the big guns. "I think we owe it to Max to at least give it a try, Ana. Don't you?"

Whatever fight she'd had left in her, whatever doubts

she still harbored, dissolved in front of his eyes. "I guess if we're doing it for Max…," she said, sliding her arms up around his neck. "As long as you promise not to hurt me again."

"I promise," he said. As he kissed her, lifted her off her feet and carried her to her bedroom, it was a promise he intended on keeping.

Ten

Ana woke the next morning to the shrill of her cell phone ringing on the bedside table. That was her father's ring tone. She pried her eyes open to check the time on the digital clock—9:05 a.m.

Oh hell. She was supposed to be at his house five minutes ago for breakfast. She had completely forgotten to set her alarm.

She grabbed her phone and flipped it open. "Hey, Dad."

"Where are you?" he snapped. "Did you forget that we had plans this morning?"

"I'm sorry. I forgot to set my alarm and I overslept."

"In other words, you were out clubbing last night, and you couldn't be bothered to drag yourself out of bed at a decent hour so I could see my grandson."

He made it sound as if she'd slept half the day away. It was 9:00 freaking a.m. To this day he refused to ever entertain the possibility that she wasn't the irresponsible party girl she'd been before she had Max. And how did he know that she'd gone out last night? She'd tried to keep a low profile, and she hadn't seen anyone who looked like the media following her. Or was he just assuming that because it was the weekend, she would be out?

Defending herself was a waste of time. He wouldn't believe her anyway. "If I get up now and get ready, we can be there in an hour."

"Don't bother. It's clear where your priorities lie. And here I was beginning to believe that you'd finally grown up. Thank God your mother isn't here to see this."

She didn't bother to point out that if her mother were still alive, her life would have been completely different. *Both* their lives.

Instead, she was going to apologize again, and do a little groveling—for Max's sake—but he hung up on her before she got the chance.

Talk about needing to grow up. She mumbled a derogatory term she wished she had the guts to say to his face, then dropped the phone back on the bedside table.

"I take it your dad is pissed off."

Ana nearly jumped out of her skin at the rumble of Nathan's voice beside her. She had just assumed she was alone.

She rolled to face him. He lay on his back, eyes still closed, bare-chested and beautiful. Excitement, and joy, and *hope* bubbled up from somewhere deep inside of her. In all the time they had been seeing each other, he had never once spent the night. Even if they stayed up making love until 4:00 a.m., he always went home. So this could only mean one thing. He actually meant what he'd said last night. He wanted to make this work.

Until that very instant she hadn't been one hundred percent sure. It wouldn't be the first time a man lied to her to get what he wanted. Even though, as far as she knew, Nathan had never lied to her about anything. And though he hadn't told her he loved her, or said anything even remotely resembling a marriage proposal, maybe it was just a matter of time now.

"He was pissed enough to hang up on me," she told him. "And he accuses *me* of needing to grow up. If I did something like that to him, he would freeze me out for months. Maybe even years."

"So let him."

"The only reason I try to keep things civilized is for Max. And maybe I feel a little sorry for my dad. It's pathetic, really, the way he shuts people out. He's been that way ever since my mom died."

Nathan opened his eyes and looked over at her. "That's no excuse."

No, but he was still her father. Although now, with Nathan planning to claim Max as his son, they didn't need her father to be the man in Max's life. Maybe it would be best if she cut all ties, at least for a while. Maybe it would be the wake-up call he needed to see that it was no longer acceptable to treat her this way. "You're right. It isn't. Maybe it's time he learns that."

But not yet. Not until after the holidays. It just seemed cruel to deny him his grandson's first Christmas.

Nathan lifted his arm to make room for her, and she curled up against his side, laid her head on his warm chest, feeling the *thump-thump* of his heart against her cheek. He wrapped his arm around her and kissed the top of her head. "Since you're not going to your father's, why don't you and Max and I go out for breakfast."

"Do you really think that's a good idea? What if someone sees us together?"

"There's a diner I go to by the university. Odds are pretty slim we'll run into someone we know there."

"Okay. That sounds like fun."

"When does Max usually wake up?"

"He should be up anytime now."

Under the covers she felt the warmth of his hand settle on her hip, then slip down to stroke her right cheek. "Do you think we might have time for a quick shower?"

She slid her hand under the covers and down his stomach. He groaned as she wrapped it around his erection and squeezed. "I think it can't hurt to try."

Though he should have put a few hours in at the office yesterday, Nathan ended up spending the entire day and the whole evening with Ana and Max. First they went to breakfast—where no one seemed to recognize them or care who they might be—then they did some last-minute shopping for Max. Because the temperature was mild, they took Max to the park for a while, pushing him on the baby swings and walking him in the stroller down the nature trails. They picked up Thai food on the way back to her place and had dinner, and though he could tell Ana wanted him to spend the night again, he had to be into work early the next morning.

He left after Max went to bed, and when he walked into his apartment, it felt even less like home than usual. If things with Ana and Max worked out the way he was hoping—and he was hoping they would—they would have to think about getting a place together. Preferably a house with a huge yard for Max to play in, in a family-friendly neighborhood with parks. In the current market, he was sure they could get a great deal. But he didn't want to get ahead of himself. He couldn't make a move until he had the CEO position in place.

He spent the rest of his evening online, on the F.A.O. Schwartz website, buying more gifts than Max would probably ever have time to play with, and paying exorbitant shipping prices to guarantee his purchases would be delivered by Christmas Eve. He had already committed himself to dinner with his mother and Jordan Christmas night, but he planned to be at Ana's Christmas Eve after the office party, and Christmas morning when Max opened his presents. It was hard to believe that it was only six days away. And he had a slight problem. He had no idea what to get Ana. She wasn't really into fine jewelry, and besides, that just seemed so…impersonal. What did a man get a woman who had the means to buy herself anything she could ever need or desire?

He wanted to get her something he knew she would really appreciate, something she would never think to get herself. He was in his office Monday morning combing the internet for ideas, waiting for inspiration to strike, when his mother called.

"I've been invited to take a holiday cruise with a friend, so I won't be available to spend Christmas with you and your brother," she told him, without having the decency to sound even the least bit regretful. He was sure wherever she was going would be warm and exotic, and her "friend" was probably significantly older and very rich.

"Well, have a good time," he said, wondering if she heard the relief in his voice.

She didn't suggest they try to reschedule, or even bother to apologize. She just wished him a happy holiday then hung up. His mom, the ice queen. But if nothing else, her call gave him one hell of a gift idea.

He did a quick internet search, finding exactly what he wanted on the first hit. It was perfect!

He considered contacting a travel agent for the finer

details, but with Ana's name on one of the tickets, he decided it was best he did this himself over the internet. He made the arrangements, printed off his confirmation email and cleared the history on his browser five minutes before he was due to meet several members of his team downstairs in the lobby coffee shop.

The meeting lasted through lunch, and just as they were gathering their things to head back upstairs his secretary called. "Your brother is here wondering when you'll be back to your office," she said. "Should he wait or come back later?"

"I'm on my way up now," he said, punching the button for the elevator.

"I'll tell him to wait."

He rode up to the top floor, feeling pretty damned proud of himself for choosing what he considered the ideal gift for Ana. Something she would never expect in a million years. He was out of the elevator and halfway down the hall to his office when he realized that he'd left the confirmation email on his desk. It didn't have passenger names on it, just the itinerary, but that alone would be suspicious. Maybe he would get lucky and Jordan wouldn't look at anything on his desk, though he knew the possibility was slim.

He nodded at his secretary as he passed and stepped into his office to find Jordan standing by the window, looking out. He turned when he heard Nathan walk in.

"What's up?" Nathan asked, walking to his desk. The email was right where he'd left it, on the blotter next to his laptop. He dropped the folder he was carrying on top of it and sat down.

"I suppose she called you," Jordan said.

"I guess there is a Santa, and he gave me exactly what I wanted this year."

"Did she tell you who her new 'friend' is?"

"Nope, and I didn't ask."

"He's a baron. She met him on her last trip to Europe. He's twenty years older than her. Old money."

"There's a shocker."

"I don't suppose you've talked to Dad."

He shot his brother a look. Hell no he hadn't, and for the life of him, he had no idea why Jordan still did.

"He's getting married again."

"How many times does that make?"

"Five. She's a twenty-eight-year-old flight attendant. He met her when he was on a business trip to New York. She's relocating here from Seattle to move in with him."

"I give it six months."

"I know you don't want to believe this, but he's mellowed a lot since we were kids. He asks about you every time we talk. I know he'd like to hear from you."

"That's not going to happen."

"Jesus, Nathan, sometimes I think you're even more stubborn than he is." He started to walk out, then stopped and turned back. "By the way, I just have to ask, what's a single guy doing buying a trip for three on a Disney cruise?"

Inwardly Nathan cursed, but on the outside he didn't even flinch. "Not that it's any of your business, but I didn't book the trip for me. I did it for a friend. He was worried his wife would find out and he wanted it to be a surprise for Christmas."

He couldn't tell if Jordan believed him or not, and maybe it wasn't the best excuse, but it was the best he could do on such short notice.

After several seconds Jordan shrugged and said, "I'd better get back to work."

Phew. Tragedy avoided. He hoped.

A few minutes after Jordan left Ana called him on his cell.

"Do you think you can make it over before Max goes to bed tonight?"

"I'll definitely try." Although, having spent most of the morning on the internet, he hadn't gotten nearly as much accomplished as he'd hoped. Which was why, while most of his team were off Christmas Day through New Year's, he would be putting in a few hours in the office.

"Let me know when you think you can get here. I can keep Max up a little late if I have to."

"I will. And by the way, I got your Christmas present today."

He could hear the smile in her voice. "What a coincidence, because I got yours too."

"What are the odds we got each other the same thing?"

She laughed. "Slim to none, and if you did get me what I got you, I'm afraid I would have to seriously rethink our relationship."

"In that case, you don't have to worry. And I should also mention that I picked out a few things for Max, too. They should be delivered on Christmas Eve."

"I almost forgot to ask, what time do you think you'll be finished at your mother's Christmas Day? I was thinking we could meet back at my place afterward."

"I'm not seeing my mother on Christmas."

"Why not? I thought you and your brother were having dinner with her."

"Change of plans. She decided to go on a cruise with a friend' instead."

"Seriously?"

"She met him in Europe last month. He's a baron."

"Are you telling me that she ditched her sons for some guy she *barely* knows? That's terrible!"

"That's my mother."

"So, what are your plans?"

"I haven't actually made any yet. Jordan didn't ask what I was doing, so I'm assuming he's got something else planned. I'll probably just hang around my apartment until you get back from your dad's place. When do you typically leave?"

"As early as humanly possible. It's usually just the two of us and it's very…awkward. Although, this being Max's first Christmas, he'll probably expect us to stay longer. I'm still not even sure when we're having dinner. I tried calling him twice today. Once on his cell, then again at his office. His secretary said he was in a meeting, but that usually just means he doesn't want to talk to me. He's probably still pissed about yesterday morning. I think he's convinced that I was out all night partying. There was a blurb in the society pages Sunday morning about me being out clubbing, and someone snapped a photo of me coming out of the bar. The paparazzi is getting really sneaky. I didn't even see them this time."

"And being the devoted father that he is, he of course believes the *press* over his own daughter," Nathan said.

"The ramifications of my rebellious phase. The gift that just keeps on giving."

"He seriously doesn't see that you're not that woman anymore? That you're mature and responsible, and an incredible mother."

"If he's noticed, he's never acknowledged it."

"How is he going to feel when he finds out about us?"

"Truthfully, I don't care anymore. I'm getting tired of the game. If it weren't for Max, I would probably spend Christmas Day at home with you. Preferably next to the fire in my flannel pajamas."

"We'll plan that for next year," Nathan said, realizin

that he was anticipating that there would be a next year for them. And a next, and a next.

"I guess this year we'll just have to settle for Christmas dinner apart. I left my dad a message, but I haven't heard back yet. I'll let you know as soon as I do."

Adam stuck his head in Nathan's office. "Sorry to interrupt. Have you got a second?"

For the boss, always. He gestured Adam inside, noting that he shut the door behind him. "Miss Maxwell, can I call you back?"

He knew Ana would understand that was code for *Someone who can't know who I'm really talking to just walked in.* "Sure. I'll talk to you later," she said.

He shut his cell phone and asked Adam, "What's up?"

"I just wondered if you'd had a chance to talk to your brother."

"About?"

Adam looked a little taken aback. "The suspicious financial discoveries."

Could he make himself look like more of an idiot?

"Sorry, but no, I haven't." Lately he'd been too wrapped up in his own life to give it much consideration. "Like I said the other day, Jordan and I just don't talk. I was supposed to have dinner with him Christmas Day, and I thought I might be able to get something out of him then, but the plans fell through. But even that was a long shot. If I start prying into his personal finances, he's going to get suspicious."

"I understand. I wanted to ask anyway, just in case. It looks as though we'll have to go through with replacing his secretary with an agency operative. He'll be told that she was sent by our temp company."

"I really think that's going to be the best way to get the

information we need. Although for the record I still believe he's innocent."

"I hope that's the case." Adam turned to leave, then stopped with his hand on the doorknob and turned back to Nathan. "Is everything okay with you?"

"Of course. Why do you ask?"

"Lately you've seemed a bit...distracted. That, and you've been taking more time off than usual."

"Do you have an issue with my performance?"

"No, not at all. And in case you're worried, it isn't something that will have a negative impact when it comes to your bid for the CEO position. I consider you a friend, and I was concerned."

Though Adam didn't come right out and say it, Nathan could tell that he wanted some sort of explanation. Considering the circumstances, and put in his position, Nathan would feel the same way. "The truth is, I've been seeing someone," he told Adam. "It's still pretty casual at this point, but it has definite possibilities."

"I'd like to meet her. Will you be bringing her to Emilio's wedding?"

"Unfortunately I don't think she's available." Available or not, there was no way he could bring her. Which wasn't fair to either of them, but it was the way it had to be.

"First I got married, now Emilio is tying the knot." Adam grinned. "Maybe you'll be next."

"Yeah, let's not get ahead of ourselves."

"Settling down, having a family, it's not such a bad thing, Nathan," he said, as he walked out.

He wished he could tell Adam that he already had the "having a family" part nailed down. He wanted to be able to brag about his son, show photos around the office and to his friends.

Just a few more months, then and he and Ana would be home free.

Eleven

This was ridiculous.

It was four on Christmas Eve night, and Ana still hadn't heard one word from her father about Christmas dinner the next day. She had called him half a dozen times this week, leaving messages, asking him to please call her back. She had even resorted to apologizing yet again about Sunday morning, and telling him how wrong she was.

That was yesterday, and he still hadn't acknowledged her.

She looked at the clock, knowing Nathan would be there any minute, then she glanced at the phone, wondering if she had time to give him one more quick call.

Why? Why should she call him again? She already apologized and practically begged his forgiveness. Maybe he thought that making her spend Christmas alone was the ultimate punishment. Although she couldn't see him passing on an opportunity to shower Max with gifts.

Knowing him, he would wait until the absolute last second to pick up the phone and expect her to be at his beck and call. It was astounding that a man responsible for running a multi-billion-dollar corporation could exhibit such childish behavior. Well, she was sick of playing his games, and it was time he realized that. Nathan didn't have any plans for dinner tomorrow and she would much rather spend the evening with him anyhow.

If her father didn't call by the time Nathan got here and she made other plans, he would miss Max's first Christmas.

Feeling only slightly guilty, she dropped her phone on the kitchen counter. She turned toward the open bottle of wine breathing on the table to pour herself a glass, but the doorbell chimed.

Four o'clock, right on time. Maybe she should think about giving Nathan a key, so he could let himself in from now on. She dashed for the door, and pulled it open.

"Merry Christmas!" Nathan said, grinning as he stepped inside.

Before he could even get his coat off, she threw her arms around his neck and kissed him. It wasn't until she backed away that she noticed the ornately wrapped box in his hand. It was around the size of a shirt box, only thinner.

He handed it to her. "Do you have room for this under the tree?"

"Barely," she said, nodding to the Christmas tree and the dozens of wrapped packages that had arrived earlier that day. "Did you buy out the entire store?"

"Close to it, I think." He shrugged out of his coat and followed her into the living room, where she set the gift under the tree near the front. "Where's Max?"

"Taking his afternoon nap. He should be up any minute. Would you like a glass of wine?"

"I'd love one."

"So, you're technically on holiday break?" she asked as they walked to the kitchen.

"I may stop into the office for a few hours between now and New Year's to catch up on a few things, but my entire team is gone. My only other plans are to spend as much time as possible with you and Max."

She poured two glasses of wine and handed him one. "I have a proposition for you."

"Okay," he said.

"How would you like to have Christmas dinner with your son this year?"

His brow wrinkled. "What's wrong? Did something happen with your dad?"

"No. In fact, absolutely *nothing* has happened. He still hasn't called me back. For all I know he isn't going to. I'm tired of these silly little mind games. So I decided I would just make other plans."

"And if he calls at the last minute, expecting you to come?"

"I'll regretfully decline."

"You're sure about this?"

"Absolutely." She rose up on her toes to kiss him. "There's no one else in the world Max and I would rather spend the holiday with."

He grinned and wrapped an arm around her waist, pulled her against him. "In that case, I accept."

"We'll have to run to the grocery store after dinner. For a turkey and all the trimmings. I've never actually made one, but I'm sure I can find a recipe on the internet."

"If we can even find a turkey. I imagine the stores will be pretty cleaned out by now."

"Then we may have to settle for grilled cheese and tomato soup. That's about all I have right now. My dad always sends me home with so many leftovers, I didn't stop at the market this week."

Nathan grinned down at her, smoothed her hair back and kissed her softly. "As long as I'm with you and Max, I really don't care what we eat."

That just might be the sweetest thing anyone had ever said to her. Even though it was last-minute, and she hadn't had time to plan, she wanted to make their first Christmas together a special one.

From the baby monitor she heard Max beginning to wake up. "You want to get him while I look for recipes?"

He gave her one more sweet, bone-melting kiss, then went to get their son.

Ana spent the next hour online, discovering that not only was there *a* turkey recipe, there were about ten thousand! She chose one for turkey and stuffing that sounded tasty and looked fairly easy to pull off, then she assembled a shopping list of everything she would need, hoping that the stores wouldn't be as cleaned out as Nathan had predicted. When she was finished they packed Max up and went to the diner for dinner, then stopped at the market on the way home. The small, privately owned organic place she usually went to was out of everything. They tried the larger commercially owned organic store a few miles away, but they too were cleaned out of all the holiday fixings.

They packed Max back up into the car and tried the national grocery chain store next. Though it was packed to the gills with last-minute shoppers, they hit pay dirt in the meat department. Not only did they have turkeys, but they were already thawed, which she had learned online often took days. The only problem was the smallest they had was twenty-six pounds.

"We're going to be eating turkey for a month," Nathan said, dropping it in their cart.

Probably, but she didn't care. She probably wouldn't have even cared if they never found a turkey. Spending the evening with him and Max, shopping together as a family, was more than she ever could have hoped for.

They hit the produce department next, and she was relieved to find that they carried organic versions of most of the items she needed. They picked up three different varieties of pies in the bakery department, plus the bread they would need for the stuffing. By the time they got in the checkout line—which had to be twenty carts long— their shopping cart was practically overflowing. They stood in line discussing their plans for the next day, and by the time their things were rung up and bagged, it was way past Max's bedtime. He fell asleep in the car on the way home, and Ana got him into bed while Nathan brought in the groceries and got his overnight bag from the trunk of his car.

He offered to help her put everything away, but she shooed him out of the kitchen and insisted he go watch TV. When he snuck back into the kitchen half an hour later for a beer, he was dressed in flannel pajama bottoms. And nothing else.

Arms folded, she looked him up and down. "Are you trying to lure me out of here?"

He grinned. "Is it working?"

She licked her lips. "If I didn't have about a million things to do…"

He gave her a quick kiss. "Actually, it was too warm with the fire going. But if you're not finished in here soon, I may have to take you against your will."

After he was back to watching TV, Ana put the rest of the groceries away and prepared things for the following morning, thinking how absolutely perfect the evening had been. Almost too perfect, just like the last time.

Everything seemed to be going really well then, too, and out of the blue he'd dumped her. Maybe if she knew for sure why he had done it then, she wouldn't worry now. Or maybe she should stop being paranoid and be thankful for this second chance.

It was past eleven when she shut off the kitchen light and headed out into the living room. The television was still on, but Nathan was lying on the couch asleep. She grabbed the remote from the coffee table and switched it off. Though they should probably get to bed so she could get up early to start the preparations for dinner, she had this sudden, soul-deep need to be close to him.

She undressed and dropped her clothes in a pile on the floor then climbed on the couch, straddling Nathan's thighs. He must have really been out cold because he didn't even budge. She considered gently shaking him awake, but wondered how far she could go, what it would take to wake him in other, more fun ways.

She leaned over, pressed her lips to his hard stomach, trailing kisses down until she reached the waist of his pajamas. She stopped to check his face, but his eyes were still closed. Other parts of him, however, were waking up. She hooked her fingers under his waistband and eased it down, and he didn't even stir. Leaning over him, she first teased the tip of his erection with her tongue, and when that got her no response, she took him in her mouth.

She heard a moan, then felt his hands on her head, his fingers tunneling through her hair. That was more like it, she thought, taking him in even deeper.

She sat back, and Nathan smiled up at her with heavy-lidded eyes. "At first I thought I was dreaming," he said. "It's not often a man wakes up to find a gorgeous naked woman on top of him."

She grinned. "Well then, maybe I should do it more often."

"I could get used to that." He cupped her face, pulled her down for a slow, deep kiss. He stroked her bare shoulders and her back, sliding his hands down to cup her behind, then he tugged her forward, bucking upward, so that his erection rubbed her just right. She dug her nails into his shoulders, moaned against his lips. With one slow, deep thrust he was inside her.

It felt so damned good, but she couldn't shake the feeling that something was missing. Then it hit her. No condom.

Damn it, damn it, damn it.

He was moving inside of her as she slowly rode him, no barriers, nothing to come between them, feeling so close to him, so connected. She didn't want to stop. But intercourse without a condom, even if they stopped and put one on now, was like playing Russian roulette. And she had the proof of that sleeping down the hallway. But her period was due in two days, so the chances that she would conceive were pretty slim.

But that wasn't a decision she had any right to make alone.

She pushed herself up, bracing her hands on Nathan's chest. "We have to stop."

He groaned an objection, thrusting upward. "No we don't."

"We forgot to use a condom."

"I know."

"You *do*?"

He laughed lightly, stroking his hands up her sides, cupping her breasts as he thrust upward once, then twice, making her crazy with need. "Did you honestly think I wouldn't notice?"

"You don't care?"

"I was going suggest we grab one, but I thought I would be polite and satisfy you first."

"I'm pretty sure that's how I conceived Max."

"So are you saying it's too late? The damage is already done?" He said it so casually, as if they were talking about the weather. She figured he would be at least marginally concerned at this point, but he kept up those slow, deep thrusts.

"My period is due soon, so odds are pretty good that I'm not even fertile, but there's always that million-to-one chance."

"Are you opposed to the idea of having another baby?"

"Well, no, but—"

"Then let's not worry about it."

Well, if he wasn't going to worry, if he was comfortable with the consequences…

Nathan tugged her back down to him, kissed away the last of her doubts, his hands, his mouth making her crazy, until she was so close…

He caught her face in his hands and looked in her eyes. "I love you, Ana."

Those four, simple words drove her over the edge, and Nathan was right behind her. After, she tucked her head under his chin, limp and relaxed, and Nathan held her.

It was hard to believe how much had changed in only a few weeks. It felt too good to be true. In a way she almost wished she *would* conceive, then he would have to stay with her.

As quickly as the thought formed, she knew how wrong it was. And dangerous. Not to mention untrue. Besides, why would she even think that she needed a way to trap him? He said he loved her, that he didn't care if she got pregnant again. Everything was perfect.

And if it was so perfect, why this feeling of unease? And if she loved him, why hadn't she said so?

Nathan woke to the aroma of fresh coffee.

It was barely 8:00 a.m., but Ana's side of the bed was empty. He rolled onto his back and rubbed the sleep from his eyes. Last night on the couch had been pretty incredible. He used to believe that she was too passionate to be good for him, that she would make him lose control. What he hadn't understood, but what was becoming clear now, was that she was exactly what he needed. The passion he felt for her was like a vent for all the pent-up negative energy. She kept him centered.

She was the one who would save him, the one he could depend on to keep him in line. She would teach him to be a good father. To Max, and maybe to another baby. Right now, the possibilities seemed endless. And all he knew for sure was that he needed to move forward.

He rolled out of bed wondering if Max was up yet. He couldn't wait to see his face as he opened all of his gifts.

He tugged on his pajama bottoms and a sweatshirt, then went looking for Ana. The Christmas tree lights were on, and holiday music was playing softly in the living room. She was in the kitchen, wearing pink flannel pajamas, an apron tied around her waist, washing dishes by hand. The turkey was already stuffed and resting in a pan on the stove.

When she saw him she smiled. "Merry Christmas."

"Good morning. I smell coffee."

She gestured to the coffeemaker with her elbow. "I just made a fresh pot."

He walked behind her, looping his arms around her waist, and kissed her cheek. "How long have you been up?"

"Since six. I wanted to get the turkey ready to go in the oven before Max woke up."

He watched over her shoulder. "Is there anything I can do to help?"

"You could pour us some coffee while I finish these dishes. I heard Max stirring, so he should be up any minute now."

As if on cue, they heard a screech from the baby monitor.

"On second thought," Ana said, "why don't you get him and I'll pour the coffee?"

When he got to Max's room, he was standing in his crib, clutching the railing. He squealed happily when he saw Nathan.

"Merry Christmas, Max. Are you ready to open presents?" He lifted him out of his crib, quickly changed his diaper—which even he had to admit he was getting pretty good at—and carried him out to the living room. Ana was waiting with their coffee and milk for Max. Nathan sat on the couch, and Max curled up in his lap to drink his bottle.

Just as they got settled Ana's cell phone started to ring. She rolled her eyes and said, "Ugh. It's my dad."

"You don't have to answer it," Nathan said.

"No. I refuse to play that game with him." She snatched it up off the table and flipped it open. "Hello, Dad."

She listened for several seconds, then said, "I've been calling all week. When I didn't hear back I assumed you weren't having dinner this year and I made other plans." Another pause, then she said, "No, I will not change my plans. I have a stuffed turkey waiting to go in the oven."

Nathan could hear her father in full rant clear through the phone.

"I regret that the food will go to waste. If you had called

me back and let me know—" More yelling from his end.
"No I am not trying to be difficult. I just can't—" She
lifted the phone away from her ear, snapped it shut and
shook her head. "He hung up on me. Apparently dinner
was at three."

"Are you okay?" he asked.

She shrugged and tossed her phone onto the table. "It's
his loss. He needs us more than we need him."

She was right. They were a family now. Her father had
become the odd man out. And Nathan couldn't help feeling
a twisted sense of satisfaction over that. Professionally,
Ana's father was at the top of his game, respected and
feared. Personally, he was a miserable excuse for a human
being.

"So," Ana said, smiling at Nathan and Max, "Who
wants to open presents?"

Twelve

Ana sat curled up on the couch in front of the fire, sipping coffee and watching Max play with his presents, although he seemed to be having as much fun with the boxes as the actual toys. Nathan sat on the floor by the tree, assembling all of the "some assembly required" items. He had loved the "World's Greatest Dad" beer mug from Max, and the San Antonio Spurs season tickets from her. And she still couldn't believe he had booked them a week on a Disney cruise! Honestly, she had expected something less original, like fine jewelry, for which she'd never really formed an affinity. She inherited all of her mother's jewelry and wore that when the event necessitated it. But a trip, just the three of them, where no one would know or care who they were, sounded like heaven on earth.

Overall, she would have to say this had been a pretty awesome Christmas so far. Despite her father's call. She couldn't even work up the will to be angry about it. She just felt sorry for him. He didn't know her at all anymore. Maybe he never had. And the really sad part was that he didn't even want to try.

Oh well, his loss. Maybe if she held her ground, and refused to let him manipulate her any longer, it would force him to take a good hard look at himself.

Although somehow she doubted it. She'd always just assumed he started acting this way after her mother passed away, but what if he'd always been so self-centered and stubborn? Ana was only six when her mom died. Maybe her memories of them as a happy family were nothing but childish fantasies.

"Finished!" Nathan said, holding up the assembled toy triumphantly.

"And it only took you an hour," she teased.

He got up from the floor and sat beside her on the couch. "I have to admit, I have a new appreciation for all the toy assembly my father did over the years. Although I could have done without the shouting and cussing."

"In our house the butler assembled the toys."

He slipped an arm around her shoulder and pulled her close. "Things will be different for Max."

She leaned her head against his shoulder and smiled. "I know."

For a long time they sat there together, listening to Christmas music, watching Max play. Eventually Ana had to get up and put the turkey in the oven, then she got all the side dishes prepared, and the potatoes peeled and ready to boil. When Max went down for his afternoon nap, Ana and Nathan crawled into bed and made love. Afterward, Nathan fell asleep, so Ana showered, dressed and checked the turkey's progress. It still had another hour to cook, but it was already a deep golden brown and smelled delicious. So far so good.

She'd left her phone on the kitchen counter with the ringer off, and when she checked the display she saw that there was a missed call from her father at 3:05 p.m. Maybe he thought she'd been bluffing, and was probably calling to find out why she wasn't there. She hoped he learned a lesson from this, but knowing him, he would only accuse her of being selfish.

Well, that didn't matter anymore. She couldn't make him see something that he didn't want to see.

Ana straightened up the living room, stacking all of Max's new toys back under the tree until she could decide on a permanent home for them. At four she heard Max begin to stir and was about to go in and get him when the doorbell rang. She wasn't expecting anyone, and most people didn't just stop by on Christmas Day.

She walked to the door and pulled it open, her jaw dropping in surprise when she saw who was standing on her porch. "Dad, what are you doing here?"

"Since you insist on being stubborn, I had no choice but to bring Max's gifts to him."

She was stubborn? Was he kidding? "Now isn't a good time."

"Who is it, Ana?" Nathan asked from behind her, holding Max, both still wearing their pajamas, hair mussed from sleep. Her father shouldered his way past her through the door. When he saw Nathan he blinked in surprise.

"Who the hell is this?" he asked, looking from Ana to Nathan, then his eyes narrowed, and she could tell the instant recognition set in. He turned to her, jaw tense, teeth gritted. "Why am I not the least bit surprised?"

"It isn't what you think," she said.

"Is this how you punish me? By consorting with the competition?"

That stung, but she tried not to let it show. Besides, hadn't it started out that way?

He turned to Nathan. "If you'd kindly hand over my grandson, then you can get dressed and get the hell out of my daughter's house."

Nathan didn't even flinch. He met her father's eye, wrapped an arm protectively around Max and said, "There's no way in hell I'm handing my son over to you."

"Max is *this man's* son?" Ana's father growled, and Nathan had the feeling he'd just opened one big fat can of worms, but he hadn't been able to keep his mouth shut. He'd be damned if he was going to let that arrogant bastard boss him around. Nathan's role as Max's father trumped the position of grandfather any day of the week.

"Yes, Nathan is Max's father," she said, with no apology, no regret.

"Ana what in *God's* name were you thinking?"

"This is none of your business, Dad."

"The hell it isn't. Where was he when you were pregnant? For the first nine months of Maxwell's life? Or have you been seeing him all this time? *Lying* to me."

"Nathan didn't even know about Max until a few weeks ago. But he's here now."

"Not if I have anything to do with it." He turned to Nathan. "I understand you're in line for the CEO position at Western Oil. I can only imagine how your connection to my family will go over with the board."

Nathan tensed. He should have seen this one coming. "I suppose I'm about to find out."

"No you won't," Ana said. "Because my father isn't going to tell anyone. Because if he does, he'll never see his grandson again."

Her father scoffed. "Maxwell adores his grandfather. You would never keep him from me."

"If you ruin the career of the man I love, you're damned right I would."

He blinked. "You're not serious."

"You don't think so? *Try me.*"

"In that case, I want a paternity test. I want proof that he's Maxwell's biological father."

Nathan opened his mouth to tell him to go to hell, but Ana spoke first. "*You* want? Because I don't see that's it's any of your business. That's between me and Nathan. Who, for the record, never even asked for one. He trusts me, unlike my own father, who apparently thinks I was slutty enough to be sleeping with multiple partners."

He leveled his eyes on her. "Well, it wouldn't be the first time, would it?"

Ana sucked in a breath, and Nathan's temper shot from simmer to boil in a heartbeat. If it wasn't for the fact that he was holding Max, he might have actually taken a swing. But for his son's sake, he clamped a vise down on his anger. He stepped in front of Ana, saying in a very calm and even tone, "You're talking about the woman that I love. And that is the *last* time you will ever speak to her that way. Understand?"

Maybe her father realized he'd gone too far, because he actually backed down. "You're absolutely right, that was uncalled for. I'm sorry, I didn't mean it."

"I'm going to get Max dressed," Ana said softly, taking him from Nathan, leaving Nathan alone to deal with her father.

That wasn't the sort of thing Ana was just going to forget, and he had the feeling her father realized that. Though Nathan thought he was getting exactly what he deserved, a part of him was sympathetic. He knew what it was like to lose his temper and say or do things he later regretted. The difference was, he'd been man enough to learn how to control it. Maybe this would be the wake-up call her father needed. Maybe he and Ana could begin to repair their fractured relationship.

After an awkward silence, her father said, "I have gifts for Max. Should I bring them in?"

He was actually asking Nathan's permission? Maybe he figured he had better odds with Nathan than with Ana. And unless her father was doing something to hurt Max, Nathan didn't feel it was his place to stand between him and his grandfather.

"Sure, bring them in."

He opened the door and gestured to the man standing on the front walk. He'd been stuck in the cold waiting, his arms filled with packages. His driver, Nathan was assuming, when he saw the Rolls Royce parked at the curb.

It took the man three trips back and forth to bring it all in, while Nathan and Ana's father stood not speaking. This was definitely not the way Nathan had expected to spend his Christmas. Families had a funny way of screwing up plans.

"So," Ana's father said, when his driver had brought in the last of the gifts and gone back to the car. "Do you have plans to marry my daughter?"

He should have expected this. Still, the question caught him a bit off guard. "The thought had occurred to me."

"I supposed it's too much to expect you to ask my permission."

Was he kidding? At this point he would be lucky to get an invitation to the wedding. "I can't see that happening."

"I suppose you'll be expecting a job with my company, and a corner office."

Could the guy be more arrogant? Did he think the

entire world revolved around him? "I already have a job," Nathan said.

His brow furrowed. "I'm not sure I like the idea of my son-in-law working for a competing company."

Nathan didn't give a damn what he liked or didn't like. And he would have a serious problem working for someone like Ana's father, especially if he turned out to be the one responsible for the sabotage. Besides, he hadn't even proposed yet. Nor did he have any plans to in the immediate future.

Ana appeared in the foyer, holding Max. She'd dressed him in his Christmas outfit. "Have you eaten yet?" she asked her father.

"No."

"Would you like to stay for dinner?"

He glanced over at Nathan. "If it's not an imposition."

Did he suddenly see Nathan as the man of the house, or was he just afraid of making the wrong move?

"Why don't you take Max while I finish dinner and Nathan showers," Ana said. He removed his coat and took Max from her, carrying him into the living room. Ana gestured Nathan down the hall, and he followed her into her bedroom. She closed the door and leaned into him, wrapping her arms around his waist, burying her face against his chest.

"You okay?" he asked, rubbing her back.

"After what he said to me, am I crazy for inviting him to stay?"

"If he meant it, maybe, but I don't think he did. I think he probably felt threatened and was lashing out without thinking. Men like him are used to being in control. Take that control away and they say and do stupid things."

"I guess that makes sense." She lifted her head and gazed up at him. "Thanks for defending me."

"You defended me first. Did you really mean what you said?"

"What part?"

He touched her cheek. "When you said that I'm the man you love."

"I did mean it." She rose up on her toes to kiss him, whispered against his lips, "I love you, Nathan."

Those four words made his whole holiday. The ultimate Christmas gift. Women had said it before, but it hadn't meant half as much coming from anyone else. No one knew him, or understood him, the way Ana did. "I love you, Ana."

Her lips curved into a smile. "I better get back into the kitchen before I burn dinner."

"I'll be in to help you in a minute."

She gave him another quick kiss, then left him alone. While he was in the shower he could swear he heard the doorbell, but he couldn't imagine who else could possibly stop by. Maybe it was the driver, or he could have been hearing one of Max's new toys.

He shaved, and dressed in a polo and slacks, then headed out to help Ana. The second he stepped into the living room he saw that there was in fact someone else there and was incredulous when he realized the man sitting on the floor playing with Max was his brother, Jordan.

In that instant this went from one of the best Christmases of his life, to the holiday from hell.

Jordan saw Nathan standing there and rose to his feet. "Hey, big brother. Merry Christmas."

"What the hell are you doing here?" Nathan asked.

"He came by when you were in the shower," Ana said, walking into the living room, wiping her hands on her apron. That part was pretty obvious. Unless Ana had been hiding him in a closet all morning.

Ana's father was sitting on the couch, looking amused by the entire situation.

"Is there something wrong with wanting to spend Christmas with my brother? And my *nephew*?" Jordan asked.

Nathan shot a look Ana's way.

"I didn't say a word," she said. "He already knew."

Nathan looked at Jordan questioningly.

"You've been acting weird for weeks," Jordan said. "Then you give me that lame excuse about the cruise. You insult my intelligence, Nathan."

They needed to have a word. Several, in fact. But he wasn't going to do this in front of Ana and her father. And especially not Max.

"Why don't we step outside," Nathan said.

Jordan scoffed. "It's cold and raining."

"Don't be a sissy," Nathan shot back, realizing, when the false cheer slipped from Jordan's face, that he sounded just like their father. Somehow his family always managed to bring out the worst in him.

Jordan walked to the door and grabbed his coat. Nathan pulled his own coat on and followed him out onto the porch. It was cold and damp and the sky was spitting down icy rain.

"Isn't this cozy," Jordan said, dropping all pretense of holiday cheer. "You spending the holiday with Ana Birch and her daddy. I guess now we know who to blame for the sabotage."

"Jordan, do you really think I could do that?"

"You can't deny this looks pretty damned suspicious."

"Not that it's any of your business, or I feel I need to justify my actions in any way, but her father wasn't supposed to be here. He just showed up, which I'm sure you can understand. Besides, I wasn't even seeing Ana when it happened. I didn't even know I had a son until a few weeks ago. I broke up with her before she knew she was pregnant."

"Did she think it was someone else's?"

He gritted his teeth and glared at Jordan.

Jordan shrugged. "Just a thought."

"She planned to raise the baby alone."

"What if *she's* responsible for the sabotage?"

"Ana?" That was the most ridiculous thing Nathan had ever heard. "Not a chance."

"Why not? What if she was bitter and wanted to get back at you for dumping her? Or maybe she did it for her father."

"She wasn't exactly lusting for revenge. If anyone had the right to be pissed, it was me. And as for her father, they aren't exactly on the best of terms."

"He's her meal ticket."

"She lives off a trust left by her mother. She doesn't get a penny from Birch Energy. And even if she did, she doesn't have a malicious bone in her body." Nathan had to wonder, if Jordan really was responsible for the sabotage, would he so vehemently try to blame someone else? Or was that just his way of deflecting suspicion off himself? Had he caught on that he was being investigated?

Nathan had been quick to defend Jordan, but he honestly didn't know anymore.

"How did you find out that it was Ana I was seeing?" Nathan asked.

"I followed you, genius. You're not exactly 007, you know."

Apparently he wasn't, not that he'd expected someone to be tailing him. "How did you know Max is my son?"

"I didn't. Not until I saw him up close. He looks just like you, and the birthmark was a dead giveaway." He blew hot air into his hands, then stuck them into his coat pockets. "Are you going to marry her?"

That was the second time he'd been asked that question today. "I'd say there's a good possibility."

"You know that's going to mean a job offer from old man Birch."

That's the second time that had come up, too. "Why would I want to work for him when I'm CEO of Western?"

Jordan grinned. "You've got to get through me first."

"I plan on it."

Jordan shivered and stamped his feet. "It's cold as hell out here. Can we maybe go back inside now?"

Nathan folded his arms. "Who said you're invited?"

"You would make your baby brother spend Christmas alone?"

"My baby brother who just accused me of sabotage."

Jordan shrugged. "Okay, so maybe I overreacted."

"And how do I know you're not going to run to Adam and the board with this?"

"I'm ambitious, but that would just be too easy. I prefer a fair fight. Besides, I guess I owe you one."

It was the first time Jordan had ever acknowledged what Nathan had done for him. *Who knows,* Nathan thought, *maybe there is hope for us yet.*

The front door opened and Ana stuck her head out. "Sorry to bother you, but everything is ready. I just need someone to carve the turkey."

Jordan shot him a questioning look.

"Do you mind if my brother stays for dinner?" Nathan asked her.

"We've got plenty of food," she said, then added sternly, "But I *do not* want my son's first Christmas to turn into World War Three. As long as everyone plays nice, it's fine with me."

Jordan flashed her a charming, borderline flirtatious smile. "I always play nice."

He did, Nathan thought wryly, *right up until the second I turned my back and the knife came out.* But it was Christmas, the season for forgiveness, and for his son's sake, Nathan would put aside the bitterness and be a family.

Thirteen

As they sat down to dinner, Ana warned everyone that she wasn't much of a cook, and to eat at their own risk. And maybe it was beginner's luck, or she had hidden talents, because the meal was hands down the best Christmas dinner Nathan had ever had. Even her father, who Nathan had the feeling was not typically liberal with the compliments, raved about the food. Nathan hoped that now he would see how talented and resourceful Ana really was. In many ways she was still the woman he'd met a year and a half ago, only so much more, and he was proud of the person she had become.

Jordan, who in contrast was very liberal with the compliments, whether he meant them or not, seemed genuinely impressed. Nathan was surprised that despite the mixed company, the evening wasn't nearly as awkward as he would have expected. It probably helped that everyone deliberately avoided the subject of the oil business. Even her father seemed to realize that he was on shaky ground. He seemed humbled. Maybe his making that comment, hurtful as it was, was a blessing in disguise.

Ana's father left at seven-thirty, and Jordan hung around playing with Max until it was time for him to go to bed. If nothing else, it looked as though he would be a good uncle.

"He's a great kid," he said, after Ana took Max into his room to get him ready for bed, and Nathan walked Jordan to the door. "What is it with all the kids lately? It must be something in the air. First you, then Adam, now Emilio."

"What about Emilio?"

He pulled on his coat. "That's right—you left the party yesterday before he made his announcement. His fiancée is pregnant. They just found out. I didn't think *anything* could shake that guy. He's like granite, but I think he may have actually been a little misty-eyed. He looks really happy."

"There's definitely something to be said for finding the right woman," Nathan told him. "Maybe you'll be next."

"The problem I find is that there are so *many* right women, I'm not sure which one to choose."

Nathan grinned and shook his head. "It'll happen. Probably when you least expect it. You'll meet someone and you'll just know."

"Was it like that with Ana? Because I recall you saying that you broke it off."

"And it might have been the worst mistake of my life. I'm just lucky that she was willing to give me a second chance."

"You're getting sentimental, which can only mean you've had way too much to drink."

Actually he was stone-cold sober, but he didn't argue.

Jordan slugged his arm. "Go sleep it off. And Merry Christmas."

"Merry Christmas. And drive safe." He watched his brother disappear into the night, then he shut and locked the door and set the alarm.

He found Ana in the kitchen washing dishes by hand. "Is the dishwasher broken?"

"It's already full and running. This is what's left."

He stepped up behind her, slipped his arms around her waist, nibbled her ear. "Are you sure you don't want to leave these for tomorrow?"

"It's tempting, but I really hate waking up to a dirty kitchen." She smiled up at him hopefully. "If we do it together it'll take half the time."

Half the time ended up being an hour. When they were finished, they heated mugs of spiced cider in the microwave then cuddled up on the couch in front of the fire. Ana had barely spoken since everyone left, and Nathan was beginning to wonder if something was wrong.

"Is everything okay?" he asked her. "You've been awfully quiet."

She sighed and rested her head against his chest. "Just tired. It's been a really long day."

"That it has."

"It didn't work out exactly as we planned, but I think it went okay."

"Better than I anticipated, considering the guest list."

"It was really strange opening the door and seeing my dad there. And even stranger when your brother showed up."

"Yeah, that was definitely unexpected."

"He was really good with Max. I wouldn't have pictured him as a kid person."

"As long as it's someone else's, I guess. He doesn't seem to have any desire to settle down and have a family of his own. Of course, neither did I."

"This is probably a terrible thing to have to ask, since he is your brother, but he's not going to say anything to the board at Western Oil about us, is he? I know that you were concerned about him finding out."

"He said he wouldn't. He said he wants a fair fight."

"And you trust him?"

"You don't?"

She shrugged. "Maybe it's because of the things you've told me, or just a gut feeling, but it seems as though he really resents you."

"He has no reason to resent me. I saved his hide more times than I can count. He *owes* me."

She lifted her head and looked up at him. "Saved it from what?"

"Our father. He was a hard-ass, and he liked making his point with a belt, or the back of his hand, or sometimes even his fists."

Her eyes went wide. "Your father *hit* you?"

"I told you before, he was a bully."

"I just figured that you meant he bossed you around. I didn't think he was physically abusive. And you protected Jordan from him?"

"Jordan is younger than me, and up until college he was small for his age. Real quiet and shy. I was tougher, and a lot bigger, so I took the knocks for him."

She was staring at him, mouth open in awe. "You let your father hit you instead?"

He wasn't sure why that came as such a surprise to her. Maybe because she was an only child. "I was the oldest. It was my responsibility to watch out for Jordan."

"It seems like it should have been your father's responsibility to find a more constructive way to discipline his children. Or your mother's responsibility to protect you both. Why didn't she stop him?"

"She probably didn't want to risk losing her meal ticket."

"So she let her husband abuse her children? That's just *wrong*. They put people in jail for that sort of thing. I believe it's called depraved indifference." She wasn't just mildly disturbed, she was furious. Maybe because she was looking at it from the point of view of a parent.

"It's not worth getting this upset, Ana. It was a long time ago."

"It's just not fair," she said, reaching up to touch his cheek. "You should have had a better childhood. It's not right that your parents failed you so badly."

"Maybe, but the world doesn't always work the way it should."

"And look at all you've done with your life, despite it. You're the CBO of a billion-dollar company. That's a huge accomplishment."

"You want to hear something weird? Your dad sort of offered me a job."

She laughed. "Seriously?"

"He said he didn't like the idea of his son-in-law working for a competing company."

"Did you remind him that you're not his son-in-law?"

"Well, not yet. He was talking about the not-so-distant future."

Her brow crinkled. "Are we planning to get married in the not-so-distant future? Because I think I missed the memo."

"Unless you don't want to marry me," he said.

She sat up and set her cup on the coffee table. "I didn't say that. I just didn't know that *you* wanted to. We've never actually talked about it."

Of course they had. "I told you I wanted to make this work, that I wanted to be with you. Eventual marriage seemed like a foregone conclusion."

"A single woman never takes that for granted. And when she does, she tends to get her heart filleted and handed back to her in little pieces."

It took him several seconds to connect the dots, and when he did, he understood why she wouldn't take anything he said for granted. "You're talking about me, right? When we were seeing each other before Max."

She shrugged. "I thought everything was going great, that we had a future. You kept telling me how happy you were. Then pow, out of the blue you dumped me."

"I guess I did, didn't I?" He pulled her into his arms and held her. She snuggled up against him, soft and warm. She was so tough all the time, so direct and resolute, he sometimes forgot that she had a sensitive and vulnerable side. She'd gone through life probably feeling abandoned by her mother then rejected by her father. Then Nathan came along and made her feel wanted, and he let her down, too. He wasn't going to let that happen again. Besides, he needed her as much as she needed him. He needed to show her that he meant what he said. That this time it was different.

"I have an idea that I wanted to run past you," he said.

She tilted her head back and looked up at him. "I'm listening."

"I've been thinking that eventually we're going to need a bigger place. Something single-family, with a big yard for Max. Because of work, I thought it would be best to wait, but it is a buyer's market. It couldn't hurt to start searching now."

She sat up a little straighter, looking as though she wanted to let herself be excited, but she was still wary. "Are you sure? What if we find something right away?"

"Worst case, we could move in and I can keep my apartment as my formal mailing address. Although I doubt anyone would question me buying a house. Emilio, our CFO, owns investment properties all over."

She still looked unsure.

"If you don't want to, we can wait," he said.

"It's not that at all. I want this. I really do. It's just… everything is happening so fast."

"And it seems to me that it's about a year and a half past due."

"I just don't want us to rush into anything. I want *you* to be sure."

"I am sure." It was the most sure he had been about anything in a very long time. Ana grounded him. He would be a fool to let her go again.

She smiled. "Okay then. Let's look for a house."

"I'll call an agent after the first of the year." They would have to work out the logistics of actually viewing the properties, since they couldn't be seen together house hunting, but they would figure something out.

She leaned back against his chest and sighed. "I'm exhausted."

"Why don't you go crawl into bed. I'll get the lights and check on Max."

She yawned and shoved herself up from the couch. "I'll see you in there."

As she shuffled off, yawning and rubbing her eyes, Nathan shut off the lights and unplugged the Christmas tree. On his way to bed he slipped into Max's room. He was asleep on his stomach, and as usual he'd kicked the covers off.

Nathan tucked the blanket up around his shoulders, then he pressed a kiss to his fingers and touched them to Max's cheek. When the three of them were living together, he could do this all the time, since odds were pretty good that he wouldn't be home every night in time to tuck Max into bed. A lot of women would have a problem with their husbands or significant others working such insane hours, but Ana grew up around the oil business, so it was second nature to her. Even back when they were dating the first time she'd never made an issue out of his work schedule.

Nathan closed Max's door behind him and walked to the bedroom, pulling his shirt over his head, wondering if Ana was too tired to make love. He got his answer when he stepped into the room and heard her slow, even breaths from under the covers.

She was out cold.

He put on his pajamas and crawled into bed, curling up behind her. She murmured something incoherent and cuddled against him. And as the digits on the clock neared midnight, he couldn't imagine a better way to end his Christmas than lying in bed, holding the woman he loved.

So why did he have a nagging voice in his head saying that things were so good, so perfect, something was bound to go wrong?

Fourteen

"Are you sure that you and Nathan are okay?" Beth whispered, taking Ana's empty champagne glass and handing her a fresh one. "You've barely even looked at each other all night."

"That's the point," Ana said, sipping the champagne, knowing that if she was going to make it to midnight she was going to have to pace herself. She and Nathan had already arranged to meet upstairs in the guest bedroom right before the clock struck twelve so they could share a New Year kiss. And maybe share a little more than that. From the minute she poured herself into the crimson party dress, he'd been gunning to get her back out of it again. And though he looked utterly delicious in his tux, she much preferred what he was hiding underneath it.

Since Christmas Eve, Nathan had spent every night at her place. Every day he brought more of his things, and he'd arranged for the service that picked up and delivered his dry cleaning to start coming to her condo instead of his apartment.

If someone had told her a month ago that she and Nathan and Max would be more or less living together now, she would have called them crazy.

Beth handed the empty glass to a passing waiter and asked Ana, "So you two are bitter rivals tonight?"

"No." She glanced over at Nathan, who was standing across the room with a group of elegantly dressed couples. He seemed to sense her watching and glanced her way. Other than the slight tilt of his lips, he did nothing to acknowledge her. "Just indifferent," she told Beth. "Sometimes acting as though you hate someone is even more suspicious than not acknowledging them at all."

"Ma'am?" One of the servers approached Beth. "We're running short on cocktail napkins."

"There's another box in the pantry," Beth told her, and she stared at Beth blankly. Beth sighed and said, "I'll show you."

They walked off in the direction of the kitchen, and Ana crossed the great room to the Christmas tree beside the stone fireplace. It put hers to shame. It was so tall it nearly kissed the peak of the vaulted ceiling. There was another equally grand tree in the foyer at the base of the staircase. Beth always went all out on the holidays, enlisting a professional to decorate the estate inside and out. In fact there were so many white lights adorning the house and the trees and shrubbery throughout the grounds Ana was sure that it was visible from space.

"That's quite a tree," Nathan said, stepping up beside her, as though he was just making polite conversation with a fellow party guest.

"Yes it is," she agreed.

He leaned in and said softly, "Sort of puts ours to shame."

She smiled and whispered back, "Funny, but I was just thinking the same thing."

"Next year," he said.

"If we want one this big we'll need a great room with a vaulted ceiling."

"Should we put that on the list?"

In preparation for house hunting, they had begun making a list of the features they both wanted in a home. Nathan had even been looking at available properties online and already found several possibilities. Ana just wished she could shake the feeling that things were moving too fast.

Was it that she'd been hurt so many times that she was afraid to trust it, or was it her instincts telling her something was wrong? She just wasn't sure.

"Ana Birch?" someone said from behind her.

She turned to find a short, plump, vaguely familiar woman. She had blond, poofy hair that accentuated her round face, and wore a dress that was just a smidge too clingy for someone her size. "Yes?"

"It's me, Wendy Morris!" she bubbled excitedly. "From St. Mary's School for Girls!"

It took a second, then Ana was hit with the memory of a young, bubbly cheerleader wannabe who was always so desperate to be accepted by the popular girls she made an annoyance of herself. "Oh my gosh, Wendy, how are you? I haven't seen you in ages."

"Well, it's Wendy Morris-Brickman now," she gushed proudly, flashing a ring in Ana's face. She turned and shouted across the room, "Sweetie, come here!"

A man who looked to be about Nathan's age, with thinning hair and round glasses, in a tux that didn't quite accommodate his stocky build, crossed the room. Wendy hooked an arm through his in what looked like a death grip. He couldn't have been more than two inches taller than his wife, and though Ana wouldn't have considered him unattractive, he was very…nondescript. Bordering on mousy.

"This is David Brickman, my husband. David, this is Ana Birch, my good friend from high school."

More like casual acquaintances, but Ana didn't correct her. She accepted David's outstretched hand. It was warm and clammy.

"Nice to meet you," he said, but she realized he wasn't even looking at her. His eyes were on Nathan, who was still standing beside her.

Wendy looked up at Nathan and asked Ana, "And this is your…?"

"Nathan Everette," he said, shaking her hand, then extending his hand to David.

David looked at his hand, then glared up at Nathan, red-faced with anger.

What the heck?

"You have no idea who I am, do you?" David asked.

Nathan blinked, and she could see him wracking his memory.

"We attended Trinity Prep together," David said, with a venom that took Ana aback.

Who was this guy? And why would he be so openly rude?

Nathan must have recognized him, because suddenly all the color drained from his face. "David, of course," he said, but he looked as though he might be sick.

"Let's go, honey," David said, dragging his confused wife in the opposite direction.

"What the hell was that about?" Ana whispered.

"Later," Nathan said, before he walked away, too.

She couldn't exactly go after him, not without rousing suspicions, but she wanted to know what was going on. Maybe Beth would have an idea.

Sipping her champagne, she walked to the kitchen, but Beth wasn't there. In fact, she didn't see her anywhere. Beth was the consummate hostess. She would never just disappear in the middle of her own party.

Ana found Leo in the study showing off his college football trophies.

"Have you seen Beth?" she asked him.

"She's probably upstairs freshening her lipstick," he said.

Ana headed up the stairs to the master suite. The door was closed so she knocked gently.

"I'll be down in a minute!" Beth called.

"It's Ana. Are you okay?" she said.

There was silence, then the door opened. And Beth clearly was not okay. Her eye makeup was smudged and tears streaked her cheeks.

"Beth, what's wrong?"

She pulled Ana into the room and shut the door. "I'm just having a minor meltdown. I'll be okay in a minute."

"Did something happen?"

Beth sat on the edge of the bed. "It's nothing."

"It's obviously not *nothing* or you wouldn't be crying."

"It's Leo," she said with a shrug. "You know how men are."

"What did he do?"

"I went in the pantry to get the napkins and he was in here." At Ana's questioning look she added in a shaky voice, "With a paralegal from his firm."

Oh hell. "I take it they weren't in there getting napkins."

Beth laughed through her tears. "Not unless they were crammed down her bra."

"That rat bastard," Ana said, furious on Beth's behalf. She'd seen him two minutes ago and he hadn't looked the least bit remorseful. She always thought that Leo was the perfect father and husband, and that he and Beth had the ideal marriage. So much for that delusion. "Do you think it was a minor indiscretion, or is he having an affair?"

"There have been a lot of late nights at the office the past month or so, and calls on his cell phone that he has to take in his study. And our sex life has ceased to exist, so I'm guessing she's the new flavor of the month."

"The *month?* Are you saying that he's done this before?"

"Usually he's much more discreet. He's never brought one home. At least, not that I've known about. He always says that he's sorry, and it won't happen again, but it always does. I thought that when we got married he would settle down, that I would be enough."

He was screwing around on her in *college,* too? And she *still* married him? "Beth, why do you let him treat you this way?"

"I love him. Besides, what choice do I have? I don't want to be a divorced single mom. My parents adore Leo. He's from a good family and he has the perfect career. They would be *horrified.*"

Ana loved her aunt and uncle, but they always had been too hung up on appearances. "Screw your parents. You have to do what's right for you."

Beth dabbed at her eyes. "I'm not like you, Ana. I'm not strong. I don't like to be alone."

"You think I'm strong? Beth, I'm the most insecure person on the planet. But I'd rather be alone and miserable than with someone who had so little respect for me that h would cheat. You deserve so much better than that. And think about the message you're sending your daughter."

"There's no way she could know. She's too little."

"She is now, but unless you put a stop to this, eventually she's going to figure it out. Do you want her to think it's okay to let her husband cheat on her? Do you want her to go through what you're going through right now?"

She bit her lip and shook her head. "Are you terribly disappointed in me?"

"Of course not! I love you and I'm always going to be on your side. I just want you to be happy."

"He looked really sorry, and he said he would end it, and it wouldn't happen again. Maybe he means it this time."

And why would he stop when he knew he could get away with it? When the only repercussion of his actions was making his devoted wife miserable.

"Beth, you need to do something. If you don't want to leave him, then tell him you want to go to marriage counseling."

"But my parents—"

"Forget your parents. Do what's best for you and Piper." She took Beth's hand and gave it a squeeze. "I'll stand right by you, and help you in any way that I can."

"I'll think about it," she said, then she dabbed her eyes and squared her shoulders. "I need to fix my face and get back downstairs to my guests. It's going to be a new year soon."

And for Beth, Ana feared it was going to be an unhappy one. No matter what she decided.

Ana left her alone to pull herself together and headed back downstairs, wishing there was something she could do or say to help Beth, to make her see that she didn't have to put up with that kind of treatment. Especially from a man who supposedly loved her.

She nearly ran into Nathan as he climbed the stairs.

"Where did you go?" he whispered, even though there was no one in the immediate vicinity to hear him.

She jerked her chin up toward the second floor. "Bedroom. We need to talk. You would not believe what just happened."

"Actually, I was just leaving."

"*Leaving?* As in going home? But…Jenny has Max all night. We can stay out late."

"I'm not much in the mood for celebrating."

What the hell? How could a night that had started out so well suddenly crash and burn?

"Is it because of David Brickman? Why was he so rude to you?"

"It's a long story."

"One I'd love to hear," she said, grabbing his sleeve and leading him back upstairs to the guest bedroom where they had planned to rendezvous.

When they were inside with the door closed, he asked "So, what happened with you?"

"Not me. Beth. She caught Leo in the pantry in a compromising position with a woman from work. She said he's been cheating on her for years. Even back in college before they were married."

"I know."

He mouth fell open. "You do?"

"I lived in the same house with him for two years. He didn't exactly try to hide it."

"Why didn't you ever say anything?"

"What was I supposed to say? Who am I to pass judgment on anyone?"

"So you think that sort of behavior is acceptable?"

He sighed. "Of course not."

"How can you even be friends with someone like that?"

"He didn't cheat on me. What Leo does or doesn't do, and who he does it with, is none of my business."

Ana took a deep breath and blew it out. "You're right. I didn't mean to snap at you. I'm just so *angry* right now. At Leo for hurting Beth, and at Beth for putting up with it."

"I know." He reached for her, pulled her into his arms and just held her. It was exactly what she needed.

She rested her head against the lapel of his jacket, breathed in the scent of his aftershave. The guy sure had a knack for making her feel better. And she knew that he would *never* be unfaithful to her.

"So what's the deal with that David Brickman guy? Why was he so rude to you? Oh, and for the record, I was not 'good friends' with Wendy in school. I barely knew her. And she obviously has pretty lousy taste in husbands."

"Actually, he was completely justified."

"What?" She looked up at him. "How? What did you ever do to him?"

"There are things about me, things I haven't told you. Things I would rather forget."

"Like what?"

"You know how there's always that kid in school, the one who preys on the smaller, weaker kids? The kid who's always getting into trouble, getting into fights?"

"Of course. Is that who that guy was?" If so, he was probably the shortest, least threatening bully in history.

"No, that was *me*."

Her mouth dropped open and she actually laughed, the notion was so completely ridiculous. "Nathan, you are the nicest, most patient and caring man I have ever met."

"That wasn't always the case. My dad bullied me, so went to school and bullied kids who were smaller and weaker than me. The therapist I was seeing said it made me feel empowered."

"You saw a therapist?"

"In high school. It was court mandated as a part of my probation."

"Probation?"

"After I put my father in the hospital."

She sucked in a breath. "What happened?"

He sat down on the edge of the bed and she sat beside him. "I had gotten suspended again for fighting, and as usual that meant a beat-down from my father. But I don't know, something inside of me just snapped, and for the first time I fought back. I laid him out in one punch, and as he fell he cracked his head open on the credenza. I was arrested for assault."

"It sounds more like self-defense to me."

"The police didn't think so. Of course, they didn't get the whole story. My mother sided with my father, of course."

That was just sick.

"On the bright side, that was the last time he ever laid a hand on me, so it wasn't a total loss. And the therapy did me a world of good. It helped me learn to deal with my anger. Although to this day it can still be a struggle."

She was having some anger issues of her own right now. Between Beth's husband and Nathan's parents, she was beginning to get the feeling that there was no justice in the world. The worst part was that she had the distinct impression that despite everything he'd overcome and accomplished, Nathan still believed he was damaged somehow.

And she feared there wasn't a damned thing she could do about it.

Fifteen

Nathan was in the conference room with his team going over the final schedule for the television spot that would begin shooting the next day, when a call came in from Adam.

"I need to speak with you," he told Nathan, and something in his tone said it wasn't going to be great news. Maybe there had been a development in the investigation.

"Can it wait?" he asked. "We're almost finished in here."

"No, it can't."

Okay. "I'll be right in."

He told his team to finish up without him then took the elevator up to the top floor and walked to Adam's office, a knot in his gut. He hoped this didn't have anything to do with Jordan, and that they hadn't discovered more evidence to incriminate him. Seeing Jordan on Christmas Day, watching him play with Max, had given Nathan hope that he and his brother might repair their damaged relationship. Of course, he still wasn't sure what had damaged it in the first place. But things didn't seem as tense now as they used to be.

"Go right on in," Adam's secretary said.

Adam sat behind his desk, his chair turned so he was facing the window. He must have heard Nathan come in because without turning he said, "Close the door." When Nathan did, he said, "Have a seat."

Nathan did as he was asked. He was a little surprised that Emilio wasn't there, too. And why wasn't Adam saying anything? After a minute of silence, Nathan asked, "Am I supposed to guess why I'm here?"

Finally Adam turned to him, face stony. "I've had some disturbing news today."

"From the investigation firm?"

Adam shook his head. "From another source. But it relates to the investigation."

"Is it about Jordan?"

"No, it's about you."

Nathan's pulse skipped. "Me?"

"I've been told that you have ties to Birch Energy. That you have a connection to the owner's daughter and recently had a meeting with Walter Birch himself. Tell me that they're wrong."

Son of a bitch.

It was Jordan. It had to be. This was his idea of a *fair fight*?

Nathan clenched his fists, digging his nails into his palms. If he was going to explode, he couldn't do it here. And he had no choice but to tell Adam everything. "I did not have a *meeting* with Walter Birch. We both spent Christmas Day at his daughter's place."

Adam's brows rose. "Why?"

"I'm in a relationship with Ana Birch," he said. "And we have a son."

Adam looked truly stunned. "Since when?"

"I only recently found out he's mine," Nathan said. "About a month ago. Before that I hadn't actually seen or talked to Ana in a year and a half."

"So you weren't in contact with her at the time of the accident," Adam said.

"No, I wasn't."

Adam looked relieved. "This source didn't outright say that you were the saboteur, but it was heavily insinuated."

Thanks Jordan. So much for brotherly devotion. "Don't think for a second that I don't know who this 'source' is. Besides Walter Birch, my brother is the only other person who knows about my relationship with Ana. He was there on Christmas during this so-called meeting."

"This person seemed genuinely concerned, Nathan."

"He's not. He just wants to win. And apparently he'll do anything to make it happen. Including making false accusations against his own brother." And after Nathan had *defended* him. Well, never again. They were finished. As soon as Nathan was done with Adam, he and his baby brother were going to have a talk. Probably their last.

"How serious is the relationship?" Adam asked.

"We're planning to get married. But that will in no way diminish my loyalty to Western Oil."

"I believe that, but convincing the rest of the board won't be so easy. You can't deny that there is a clear conflict of interest."

"Are you telling me that my job is at stake?"

"As long as I'm president, your job is secure. But if the rest of the board finds out it could take you out of the running for the CEO position. In fact, I can almost guarantee it."

"So what you're saying is, I'm screwed."

"I said *if* the board finds out. I'm not going to tell them, but I also can't stop anyone from leaking the information."

"You don't think the board will see through his attempts to discredit me?"

"In light of the sabotage, I think the board will see it as a legitimate concern. Our first board meeting of the year is next Wednesday. If it comes up, I will do whatever I can to defuse the situation. But I can't promise anything. All I can tell you is that unless there is proof of a direct violation to the terms of your contract, your current position is safe. And as far as I'm concerned, there's no basis whatsoever for termination."

But his chances at the CEO position were basically in the toilet—and even if they weren't now, Jordan wouldn't rest until they were.

Nathan left Adam and walked straight to Jordan's office, his anger mounting every step he took.

"Is my brother in?" he asked Jordan's very pregnant secretary.

"Yes, but he asked not to be disturbed."

I'll bet he did, Nathan thought, walking right past her desk, ignoring her protests, and shoving through the door. Jordan was sitting behind his desk, feet up, talking on the phone. Startled, he jumped to his feet when Nathan barged in.

"Can I call you back?" he said to whoever was on the line, and after he hung up said, "Geez, Nathan, you ever hear of knocking?"

Nathan slammed the door. "You sleazy, back-stabbing son of a bitch."

Jordan's brow rose. "Is there a problem?"

"Do not insult my intelligence. Did you honestly think

wouldn't know it was you who ratted me out? That I'm too stupid to figure it out? This is your idea of a fair fight?"

Jordan shrugged. "The way I look at it, there's nothing unfair about what I did."

"And it doesn't bother you in the least that you just betrayed your own brother?"

He walked casually around his desk, as if he didn't have a care in the world. "This has nothing to do with the fact that we happen to be related. This is business. I'd think you would know the difference."

Nathan crossed to where his brother stood. "You looked me in the eye and lied to me, Jordan. After all the years I watched out for you, and protected you—"

"Who asked you to?" Jordan growled, so fiercely Nathan actually flinched. "I never needed or *wanted* your help."

"You don't give a damn about anyone but yourself, do you?"

"I'm going to beat you, Nathan. And it has nothing to do with experience, or education, or who's stronger. The fact of the matter is, I'm not screwing the daughter of our direct competitor, and you are." He stepped closer, getting in Nathan's face. "Although from what I've read, you're probably not the only one."

Before he even knew he'd swung, Nathan's fist connected solidly with Jordan's jaw, knocking him back several feet. That was how it was with his temper. It came out of nowhere, blindsiding him. And after he'd spent the better part of his childhood protecting his baby brother, never did he imagine being the one doing the hitting.

Jordan dug a handkerchief out of his suit jacket and pressed it to the corner of his bleeding mouth, but he was smiling. "All that therapy, and you still turned out just like him."

Jordan's words sliced through Nathan, cutting to the core. He was right. After all these years, hadn't he learned that using his fists was never the answer?

Suppose someday Ana really pissed him off? Or Max? Would he lose control and hit them, too? He thought being with Ana had changed him, made him a better man, but he had obviously been wrong. He stormed out of Jordan's office and walked blindly to the elevator. What kind of man would he be if he put his own child and that child's mother in danger?

A monster. And that was exactly what he was.

He took the elevator down to the lobby and headed out to the parking lot to his car, so rattled that he barely recalled the trip there as he pulled into Ana's driveway. He used his key to get inside, but she and Max weren't there.

Good, it was better that way.

He went to the bedroom, grabbed a duffel bag out of the closet and started stuffing his clothes inside, marveling at just how many of his things he'd managed to bring over in a week's time.

What the hell had he been thinking?

He was in the bathroom grabbing his toothbrush and razor when Ana appeared in the doorway.

"Hey, what's with the duffel—" She actually jerked back when she saw his face. "Oh my gosh, you're white as a sheet. What happened?"

Ana thought for sure that Nathan was going to tell her someone had died.

"I have to leave," he said.

"Why? Where are you going?"

"Back to my apartment," he said, and at her confused look added, "Permanently."

She felt the color drain from her face and her heart plummeted to her toes. "You're dumping me?"

"Trust me when I say you're better off without me. You both are." He pushed past her and walked back into the bedroom, tossing his things into the duffel bag sitting on the bed.

No, this could not be happening. Not again. "Nathan, please, tell me what happened. Did I do something wrong?"

"You didn't do anything." He zipped the bag shut. "Jordan ratted me out."

Damn it. She *knew* it. She knew they couldn't trust him. "So you're leaving me so you can still be CEO?"

"It has nothing to do with work. It's me. I confronted Jordan, words were exchanged, then I hit him."

If her brother had betrayed her that way, she would have hit him, too. "It sounds like he deserved it."

"Violence is never the answer. It's not safe for you to be around me. Not you and especially not Max."

"Nathan, that's ridiculous. It's one thing to get in a fight that's unprovoked, to bully someone, but Jordan betrayed you and you lost your temper. You would never do anything to hurt me and Max."

"Are you sure about that? And is it a chance worth taking?"

"I'm one hundred percent sure."

"Well, I'm not." He grabbed the bag and headed out of the room.

She followed him. "No! You are not going to do this to me again, damn it!"

He pulled the front door open and she hurled herself at it, slamming it shut again.

"We need to talk about this, Nathan."

He gazed down at her, looking tired. Tired and resigned. Just the way he'd looked the last time, and she knew in that instant that he wouldn't be changing his mind. "There's nothing to say."

The ache in her heart was so intense she winced. "You said you wouldn't hurt me."

"I thought I'd changed. I was wrong."

"What about Max? He needs you."

He shook his head. "He's better off without me."

He put his hand on the doorknob, but he wouldn't look at her. She could stand there blocking the door until hell froze over, but he was still going to leave. He was already long gone. Walking out the door was just a formality now.

She moved away from the door and he pulled it open. He had one foot on the porch when she blurted out, "If you leave, this is it. I'm not giving you another chance. Not with me or Max. Walk out that door and you're out of his life forever."

He paused, half in, half out of her life, and a kernel of hope bloomed in her chest. Maybe faced with the reality of losing them permanently would shake some sense into him.

He turned, looked her in the eye, and her heart started to beat wildly.

Please, please don't do this.

"I'm sorry, Ana," he said, then he stepped out the door and was gone.

After he left Ana's condo that night, Nathan drove around for hours. He knew he should go home, but his apartment just wasn't home any longer. He finally rented a hotel room and slept there, and that was where he'd been staying for the past week. And as for work, he'd been functioning on autopilot.

He missed Ana and Max. He hadn't even known it was possible to miss someone as much as he missed them.

There was a gaping hole in his heart, in his soul, and the essence of who he was, and the desire to live the life he'd worked so hard building, was slowly leaking out. Before long, there would be nothing left but an empty shell. Without them in his life, he felt, what was the point?

He hadn't talked to his brother since the day of their confrontation, but Wednesday morning Jordan knocked on Nathan's office door. Nathan should have told him to get lost, but as Jordan had pointed out, this was business. Nothing personal. When they were at the office he had no choice but to talk to him.

"Have you got a minute?" Jordan asked.

Nathan gestured him inside.

"So, the board meeting is this afternoon," Jordan said, as if Nathan wasn't already well aware of that fact.

"So it is," he said.

"You should know that I had planned to go to the board and tell them about you and Ana."

"I figured as much."

"Well, I changed my mind. I'm not going to do it."

"Am I supposed to thank you?"

"No. I just thought you would want to know."

"It wouldn't matter now anyway. We split up a week ago."

He looked truly taken aback. "You split up? Why?"

"What difference does it make?"

"Nathan, if it's because of what I said—"

"When you insinuated the woman I love is a slut?"

Jordan actually looked remorseful. "I was just trying to ruffle your feathers. I didn't think you would take me seriously."

"Then you'll be relieved to know that it has nothing to do with that."

"Damn, I'm sorry it didn't work out. What about Max?"

"I'm not seeing Max either."

"*What?* Is she keeping him from you?"

"It was my own choice."

"Are you crazy? You love that kid. And he adores you. I've never seen you so happy."

"It's the only way I can keep them safe."

"From what?"

"Me. Like you said, I'm just like *him*."

He rolled his eyes. "Nathan, those were just words said in the heat of the moment. I was trying to piss you off, *trying* to make you hit me."

Huh? "You wanted me to hit you?"

"Because I knew it would make you feel lousy when you did. Because…" He drew in a deep breath and blew it out. "Hell, I don't know. Maybe it's the enormous chip I've been carrying around on my shoulder for the past twenty or so years."

"You *resent* me. Jordan, I took—"

"You took care of me, I know. You defended me against the whole damned world. Did it ever occur to you to let me defend myself or, instead of fighting my battles for me, teaching *me* how to fight them? Maybe I didn't need you to be my damned savior."

His words stunned Nathan. All these years he assumed he was doing his brother a favor by protecting him. Had he actually done more harm than good? "I guess, since I was older, I considered it my responsibility to take care of you."

"Do you have any idea how guilty I used to feel when Dad would whale on you for something I did? After a while I started to resent you for it, for thinking I was too weak to take care of myself. Then it got to the point when I actually enjoyed getting you in trouble, watching you take the knocks for things I did. I wanted you to feel as weak and as small as I did."

"Jordan, I was only trying to help. I had no idea I was making you feel that way."

Jordan shrugged. "So, now you know. And this thing with Ana and Max, you don't want to screw the pooch on this one. You'll regret it for the rest of your life."

"I would regret it a lot more if I hurt them."

"You're not going to hurt them. Not physically anyway. Over the years I've given you a hundred reasons to clean my clock, and look how long it took for you to actually take a swing at me. And the expression on your face afterward..." Jordan laughed and shook his head. "You looked like you backed over a puppy with your car. That alone was worth the sore jaw."

Nathan grinned for the first time in a week. "I really looked that bad?"

"It was freaking awesome. And it astounds me that after all the years, and all the bullshit, you don't hate my guts. No matter how hard I push you, how big of a jerk I am, you're still there for me. If I called you at 3:00 a.m. from some bar, too wasted to drive, and said I needed a ride, you would drop everything and pick me up." He paused, then said, "Which I guess in a way makes *you* the weak one, not me."

"Because if I called you for a ride in the middle of the night...?"

"I'd tell you to call a damn cab, then I'd roll over and go back to sleep."

No, he wouldn't. Nathan didn't know how he knew. He just did. If Jordan didn't care about him, they wouldn't be having this conversation. Maybe there was hope for them yet.

"Don't think this changes anything," Jordan said.

"When it comes to the CEO position I'm going to leave you in the dust. Then I'll be your boss. Think how much fun that will be."

"You have to get through me first."

Jordan grinned, turned and walked out of Nathan's office.

Nathan sat there for a minute, a little stunned, trying to process what had just happened, what had been resolved, and trying to figure out what it meant, but it felt as if the walls were closing in on him. He needed to get out of here. He needed fresh air, a chance to clear his head and really think.

He grabbed his coat and headed out of his office, telling his secretary to cancel all his appointments and that he would be back later that day.

Maybe. The truth was, he didn't know where he was going or how long he would be there. The way he was feeling, he could get in the car, pick a direction and never look back.

Instead, after driving in circles for a while, he found himself in the last place he'd ever expected to be. His father's house.

Sixteen

The Everette family estate looked exactly as it had the last time Nathan was there ten years ago, and ten years before that. In his entire life he didn't think it had changed much.

Maybe that should have been a comfort, but it wasn't.

He had no idea why he was here or what he planned to do, but suddenly he was out of the car and walking up to the porch. It was as if he was following some predetermined flight plan he had absolutely no control over.

He climbed the front steps and stopped at the door, raising his hand to knock. Then he dropped it back down to his side.

What the hell was he doing? There was a damned good reason he'd spent the last ten years avoiding this place. Avoiding his father. This wouldn't solve anything.

He turned to leave, stopping as his foot hit the first step, unable to go any farther. Damn it. Somehow he knew that until he did this, until he faced his father, he wouldn't be able to move on with his life. He would be caught in a perpetual cycle of self-doubt from which he might never break free. He needed to do this for himself, and for Max.

Before he could change his mind, he walked back to the door and rapped hard. Besides, what were the odds that he would be home at two in the afternoon anyway?

The housekeeper opened the door. When she saw who was standing there, she slapped a hand to her bosom, which along with her middle seemed to have expanded over the years, and her hair was more silver than the pale blond it used to be. "Nathan! My goodness, it's been years!"

"Hi, Sylvia. Is my father by any chance home?"

"As a matter of fact he is. He's just getting over a cold, so he's working from home today."

Dumb fricking luck. "Can you tell him I'm here?"

"Of course! Come on inside. Can I take your coat?"

"I can't stay long."

"Well, I'll go get him then."

She hurried off in the direction of the study while Nathan looked around. Unlike the outside, someone had given the interior a major overhaul. The gaudy and nauseating pastels his mother had been so fond of had been replaced with a more Southwestern feel. Probably one of his father's multiple wives made the change.

"Nathan! What a surprise!"

He turned to see his father walking toward him, and blinked with surprise. For some reason he expected him to look exactly as he had the last time he'd seen him. And though only ten years had passed it looked as though he had aged double that. His hair was more salt than pepper and his face was a roadmap of lines and wrinkles. He was the same height he'd always been, but he seemed smaller somehow, a scaled-down version of his former self. In slacks, a button-down plaid shirt and a pullover sweater, he looked more like Mister Rogers than the monster Nathan remembered.

"Hi, Dad."

"I would shake your hand but I'm just getting over a terrible cold. I wouldn't want to risk passing my germs along to you."

"I appreciate that." Besides, he wasn't here to exchange pleasantries.

"Why don't we sit in my study? Can I get you a drink?"

"I can't stay long."

"Your brother tells me you're both competing for the CEO position at Western Oil."

That shouldn't have raised his hackles, but it did. "I didn't come here to talk about Jordan," he snapped.

His father shrank back visibly. He nodded and stuck his hands in his pants pockets. "Okay, what did you come here for?"

He honestly had no clue. "This was a bad idea," he said. "I'm sorry to have bothered you."

He turned to leave, and got to the door before he realized that he couldn't go, not until he had some answers. He turned back to his father. "I have a son."

His father blinked with surprise. "I—I didn't know. How old is he?"

"Nine months. His name is Max."

"Congratulations."

"He's a great kid. He looks a lot like me, but he has his mother's eyes. And he has the Everette birthmark." A ball of emotion rolled up into his throat. "He's beautiful and smart and I love him more than life itself, and I'm probably never going to see him again."

"Why?"

"Because I'm so damned afraid that I'm going to do to him what you did to me." He hadn't expected to blurt that out, and clearly his father hadn't, either. There was nothing like getting right to the point.

"Why don't you come in and sit down?" his father said.

"I don't want to sit down. I just want to know why. Why did you do it? Tell me why so I can figure out how to be different."

"Not a day goes by that I don't regret the way I treated you and your brother. I know I wasn't a great father."

"That does not help me."

His father shrugged. "I guess…it was the way I was raised. It's all I knew."

Great. So, it was some twisted family tradition. That was just swell. "So in other words, I'm screwed."

He sighed and shook his head. "*No*. You have a choice. Just like I did. I chose not to change. I spent twenty miserable years with a woman I loved more than life itself, and all she wanted from me was my name and as much of my money as she could get her greedy hands on. I was bitter and heartbroken, and instead of taking it out on the person who deserved it, I took it out on my kids."

"You actually *loved* her?" Somehow he found that hard to believe. She was just so…unlovable. Stunningly beautiful, yes, but cold and selfish.

"Of course I loved her. Why did you think I married her?"

"Because she was pregnant."

"She didn't find out she was pregnant until after we were engaged. Almost two months, if memory serves."

Nathan shook his head. "That can't be right. I heard grandmother and Aunt Caroline talking when I was a kid. They said you *had* to get married."

"Your grandmother never liked your mom. She thought she was beneath the Everette name. She was furious when she found out that I proposed. I think she had herself convinced that I would come to my senses and break the engagement, so when your mom got pregnant, I guess in her own twisted way, your grandmother probably thought we *had* to get married."

Nathan was beginning to think that everything he knew about his life was wrong. Or at the very least grossly misinterpreted. There was only one thing that didn't make sense...

"You said it's the way you were raised, but didn't your father die when you were four years old?"

"I don't really remember him, but as far as I know, my father never laid a hand on me."

It took a second for the meaning of his words to sink in. "Are you saying Grandmother..."

"She looked harmless, but that woman was mean as a snake."

Damn. It was bad enough for a boy to be bullied by his father, but coming from his mother it had to be even more humiliating and degrading. Then to be married to a woman he loved who didn't love him back. Picking on his sons, who were too young to defend themselves, must have made him feel empowered.

"Son, the bottom line is that your grandmother was a very unhappy person, and so was I. I was a miserable excuse for a father. And nowhere does it say that you're destined to be just like me. You can be whatever kind of father you want to be. *You* make the choice."

If it was his choice, then he *chose* to be different. And if he made mistakes, they would be his own, and hopefully he would learn from them along the way.

"I have to go," he told his father.

He nodded, but he looked...sad. And for a second Nathan actually felt sorry for him. Which beat the hell out of hating him.

"Maybe you could stop by again sometime," he said. "I don't know if your brother told you, but I'm getting married. *Again*."

"He mentioned it."

He shrugged. "Who knows, maybe this one will stick."

"Maybe I could bring Max by to see you some time."

"Does that mean you will be seeing him again?"

If Ana would let him. And even if she didn't, being in his son's life was something he considered worth fighting for.

But before he fought that battle, he had a board meeting to crash.

"Okay," Beth said, pressing the End button on her cell phone and jotting down a date and time in her daily planner. She set the book on the coffee table and sank back into the couch. "I have an appointment with the marriage counselor next Monday at 7:00 p.m. I made it later just in case Leo decides to come with me."

But they both knew he wouldn't. At least not yet. After finding a hotel room charge on Leo's credit card bill, from two days *after* New Year's, Beth finally took a stand. She insisted they go into counseling, and when he refused, she decided to go alone.

It was definitely a start.

Ana put her hand on Beth's arm and gave it a squeeze. "I'm very proud of you. This is a huge step."

"One that I wish my husband was making with me. But if he doesn't love me enough to try to save our marriage, maybe it isn't worth saving." Tears welled in her eyes, but she took a deep breath and blinked them back. "But I'm going to get through it." She put her hand over Ana's. "We both are."

Yeah, except Nathan did love her, and he loved Max

and he wanted to be with them, but he was just being a big idiot. And she was an idiot for believing him when he said he wouldn't hurt her. But never again. He'd had his chance and he blew it. A few days ago she might have taken him back. She had still been in the mourning stage, crying every time she thought about him, but now she was angry—and boy, was she *angry*—and if he dared show up at her door, she was going to be the one gunning to "hurt" someone.

"I should probably pick Piper up from the babysitter's and get home to make dinner," Beth said. "Or better yet, maybe I'll just grab something on the way home. Maybe Thai or sushi, Leo's least favorites."

The doorbell rang and Ana's heart dropped into her knees. The way it had every time the doorbell rang this past week. But it wasn't going to be Nathan. It never was. She didn't want to see him even if it was, but it was just an automatic reaction, like Pavlov's dog.

"I better get that," she said, pushing herself up from the couch, deliberately not looking out the window before she pulled the door open.

She sucked in a surprised breath when she saw Nathan standing on her porch. *Way to play it cool, Ana. Great job.*

"Hi," he said, and her heart dropped from her knees and landed in the balls of her feet. He looked *good*. So good that for a second she forgot to be angry. She very nearly launched herself at him.

"I'm very mad at you," she said, more to remind herself than to warn him.

"I just want to talk," he said, and the deep rumble of his voice danced across her nerve endings, making her shiver.

Whatever you do, just stay mad. Do not throw yourself into his arms.

"I have company over right now," she said.

"And I was just leaving," Beth said from behind her.

She turned to Beth and glared at her. Traitor.

Beth pulled her coat on and kissed Ana's cheek. "I'll call you tomorrow." As she stepped down to the porch beside Nathan she looked up at him and said, "Hurt her again and I will take you out."

Nathan's brows rose a fraction, and she could swear she saw the hint of a smile. What did he have to smile about? She hoped he wasn't here thinking he was going to get her back. Because that was not going to happen.

He stepped inside and took off his coat. He was still dressed for work. "Is Max here?"

She shook her head. "He's at Jenny's for a play date."

"That's good. We can talk without any distractions."

"Who says I want to talk?"

"Well, you let me in, didn't you?"

Not a smart move on her part. Because maybe she wasn't quite as mad as she'd thought.

"Can we go sit down?" he asked.

That would be a bad idea. She wanted him close to the door so she could shove him out on a moment's notice if she got any funny ideas. Or if he did. "I'm comfortable right here."

He shrugged and said, "Okay."

"So, what did you want to talk about?"

"I have had an interesting day."

"Oh yeah? And why should I care?"

"My brother and I had a heart-to-heart talk today. I think we may have resolved a few things."

"That's good, I guess. Although I still wouldn't trust him."

"And I went to see my dad."

Whoa. She definitely hadn't expected him to say that "Why?"

"I'm not sure. I went out for a drive, and I just ended up there. Maybe subconsciously I figured that when you have a problem to solve, it's best to go to the source. He was my source."

She folded her arms and against her better judgement asked, "How did that go?"

"It was…enlightening. It would seem that my dad actually loved my mom, and when he proposed to her, she was in fact not pregnant."

"Oh."

"He loved her so much that he stayed married to her, even though he knew she only wanted his money. And he was miserably unhappy."

"That's kinda sad."

"That's the difference between him and me, I guess. I wasn't unhappy. At least, not until I screwed everything up. Before that, I was really, really happy."

Yeah, so was she. But it was *over.*

She inched closer to the door. If he kept this up, he was out of here. Or maybe she should just run.

"I think I wanted you to fix me," he said. "I just needed to figure out that the only person who can fix me is *me.*"

If she yanked the door open, grabbed his sleeve and tugged she could probably muscle him onto the porch. "Are you saying you're *fixed* now?"

"I'm saying that I've isolated the problem, and though I'm not one hundred percent there, I'm definitely a work in progress. But there is a problem."

Well that was good, because she needed a problem or two to firm up her resolve. "What problem?"

"I'm in love with you, and I miss my son, and without the two of you in my life permanently, I don't think I can be happy."

Don't even think about it. You are not giving him another chance. She was inches from the doorknob...

"I went before the board today."

"What for?"

"To tell them about you and Max. I assured them that being married to a Birch was not going to diminish my loyalty to Western Oil. I don't know if they believed me, but they didn't take me out of the running. I guess time will tell."

"Nathan, why did you do that?"

"Because it was wrong of me to try to hide you. Max is my son. Keeping his existence a secret is tantamount to saying that I'm ashamed of him. And I'm not. I love him and I'm proud of him and I want everyone to know that. And I want them to know that I love his mother, and I want to spend the rest of my life loving her." He reached up and touched her cheek. "And *she* is the most important thing to me. Not the job."

She had waited an awfully long time for someone to feel that way about her. To put her first. "You know, you're making it really hard for me to stay mad at you."

He grinned. "That's sort of the point, since I could really use one more chance."

Like she had any hope of resisting him now. She threw her arms around him and hugged him hard. "One more. But if you screw up this time, I swear I'm siccing Beth on you."

"This time you're definitely stuck with me." He wrapped his arms around her, held her close. "I missed you. And Max. This has been the most miserable week of my life."

"Mine too." But she was good now. Really, really good.

"I love you, Ana."

"I love you, too. Why don't I go get Max? He's going to be so happy to see you."

"Wait. Before you do, there's one more thing we have to talk about."

His face was so serious, her heart plunged. "What?"

He reached into his jacket pocket and pulled something out. It took her a second to realize that it was a small velvet box. A *ring* box. Then he actually dropped down on one knee.

Oh my God. Her heart was beating so hard she thought for sure it would break right through her chest.

He opened the box, and inside was a diamond solitaire ring. It was so beautiful it took her breath away. "Ana, would you do me the honor of being my wife?"

She had fantasized about this day since she was a little girl but could never have imagined how truly special it would be. She was getting everything she ever wanted. That and so much more.

"Yes I will, Nathan," she said, through a sheen of tears—happy ones this time—and with a grin, he slipped the ring on her finger.

* * * * *

A sneaky peek at next month...

Desire

PASSIONATE AND DRAMATIC LOVE STORIES

2 stories in each book - or £5.49

My wish list for next month's titles...

In stores from 16th March 2012:

- ❏ Enticed by His Forgotten Lover – Maya Banks
- & The Billionaire's Borrowed Baby – Janice Maynard
- ❏ Reclaiming His Pregnant Widow – Tessa Radley
- & To Touch a Sheikh – Olivia Gates
- ❏ An After-Hours Affair – Barbara Dunlop
- & Millionaire Playboy, Maverick Heiress – Robyn Grady
- ❏ Much More Than a Mistress – Michelle Celmer
- & Bachelor Untamed – Brenda Jackson

Available at WHSmith, Tesco, Asda, Eason, Amazon and Apple

Just can't wait?

Visit us Online

You can buy our books online a month before they hit the shops! **www.millsandboon.co.uk**

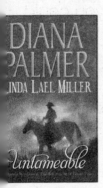

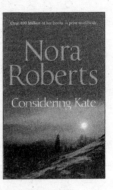

The World of Mills & Boon®

There's a Mills & Boon® series that's perfect for you. We publish ten series and with new titles every month, you never have to wait long for your favourite to come along.

Blaze.
Scorching hot, sexy reads

By Request
Relive the romance with the best of the best

Cherish™
Romance to melt the heart every time

Desire™
Passionate and dramatic love stories

Browse our books before you buy online at
www.millsandboon.co.uk

M&B/WO

Have Your Say

You've just finished your book. So what did you think?

We'd love to hear your thoughts on our 'Have your say' online panel
www.millsandboon.co.uk/haveyoursa

- 🌹 Easy to use
- 🌹 Short questionnaire
- 🌹 Chance to win Mills & Boon® goodies